Praise for Hired Guns

"Tempered with a wry grin and the wink of an expert Western wordslinger, Steve Hockensmith delivers the action fast and hard as iron."

— Richard Prosch, author of *Hellbenders*

"Steve Hockensmith has jumped to the front of the line to establish himself as a top-shelf creator of westerns... [He] isn't a writer to watch, he's a genre wordsmith with his own voice whose already here and giving us fortunate readers his very best."

— C. Courtney Joyner, author of the *Shotgun* series

HIRED GUNS

ALSO BY STEVE HOCKENSMITH

Holmes on the Range Mystery Series

HIRED GUNS

DOUBLE-A WESTERN DETECTIVE AGENCY ADVENTURE

BOOK ONE

STEVE HOCKENSMITH

**ROUGH
EDGES
PRESS**

Rough Edges Press
An Imprint of Wolfpack Publishing
1707 E. Diana Street
Tampa, FL 33609

roughedgespress.com

Paperback ISBN 978-1-68549-507-7
eBook ISBN 978-1-68549-506-0
LCCN : 2024942621

HIRED GUNS

PART ONE

SCHUCK, FORTENBERRY, AND CLAYPOLE

CHAPTER 1

Diehl glanced to the right, up the rocky incline that came to a jagged peak high against the blinding, bright afternoon sky. It was a brief look, no more than three seconds. But it was all Diehl needed. When he looked away, focusing again on the narrow trail and the switchback just ahead that veered sharply up the mountain, he was gritting his teeth.

"Son of a bitch," he muttered. "You've done it to me again."

"What did you say?" Newburgh snapped.

"I wasn't talking to you," Diehl said.

He stopped his dust-covered pinto, forcing the men riding behind him—Newburgh on his big Morgan and Romo bringing up the rear with the swayback nag and the sluggish, balky pack mule—to rein up as well.

"Have *I* done something wrong?" Romo asked.

"I wasn't talking to you either," Diehl said.

Newburgh tried to look back at Romo, but he was a hefty man perched precariously on his oversized horse, and he could only turn so far.

"Perhaps he's talking to the mule," he said. "He may as well. I stopped listening to him hours ago."

"I don't think the mule *can* listen," Romo said with a wobbly smile. "I think she's deaf."

"So's the person I was talking to," said Diehl. He looked up at a puffy white cloud. "What did I ever do to You, anyway?"

The cloud didn't reply.

Diehl dropped his gaze and swiveled to look out over the vast yellow-gray vista of the desert. He lifted an arm and pointed at a distant mesa. Newburgh and Romo peered at it.

"Umm…what are we looking at?" Romo asked.

"Nothing," Diehl said. He waved his hand as if making a point about the bluffs stretched across the horizon. "I'm just pretending to admire the view."

"A lunatic," Newburgh said, shaking his head. "The man's a lunatic."

For a moment, Diehl — tall, slim, brown-haired, with a touch of gray at his temples and weariness in his pale blue eyes — said and did nothing. Then with one swift, smooth motion, he pulled his Winchester from its scabbard and dropped from his saddle. He walked to an outcropping of large rocks beside the trail, turned his back to the biggest, and started tugging at the top of his trousers with his free hand.

"Now what are you doing?" Newburgh asked.

Diehl dropped to a crouch beside the boulder. "What does it look like I'm doing?"

"It looks like you're about to…you know." Newburgh cleared his throat. "Relieve yourself."

"Exactly. And I'm hoping the men watching from the bluffs aren't wondering why I took my rifle along."

Romo stiffened. Newburgh harrumphed.

"Look the other way," Diehl said. "I'm supposed to be doing something disgusting here."

"Oh, you *are*," said Newburgh, averting his eyes. Unlike Diehl, who was wearing a battered Stetson and a sheepskin coat and plain, faded work clothes, Newburgh was dressed like Stanley setting off to find Dr. Livingston—puttees, jodhpurs, khaki jacket, pith helmet.

He pulled out a handkerchief to pat his sweaty, fleshy face. "Does the Mexican sun bake some men's brains, Alfonse? He seemed sane in Tucson."

Romo eyed the barren slopes above them and said nothing.

Diehl levered a round into the chamber of his Winchester. The hard, mechanical sound of it seemed to stir up unhappy memories. He looked down at the rifle and frowned.

"I'm telling you somebody's up there," he said. "More than one somebody."

"Really? Just like somebody's been following us?" Newburgh said.

"Somebody *has* been following us."

"So you keep insisting. Only tell me this." Newburgh jabbed a chubby finger up at the summit. "How did they get ahead of us without being seen? By anyone other than you, I mean."

"I didn't say the somebody following us and the somebody ahead of us were the same somebody."

Newburgh rolled his eyes. "Pathetic."

"You two ought to take cover too," Diehl said. "Whoever's up there is sure to have noticed all the *pointing*, Newburgh."

Romo dismounted, pulled out his own rifle—a battered carbine that looked older than him—and hustled over to join Diehl by the rocks.

Newburgh just leaned back in his saddle, the leather creaking as he jutted out his round belly.

"Lovely. Now he's got you doing it," he said to Romo. "You, who should know better."

Romo squatted beside Diehl, then pivoted to squint up at Newburgh. His small frame and boyish, earnest face and simple, well-tailored clothes—black suit and white shirt—made him look like a college student confused by a professor's disapproval.

"Why should I 'know better'?" he asked.

"Because you're Mexican, Alfonse," Newburgh said.

"Alfonso," Romo corrected.

Newburgh went on as if he hadn't heard him. "Just because

we're in Sonora you're not going to see bandits behind every cactus. Or so I would have hoped."

"There *are* bandits in Sonora, Mr. Newburgh," Romo said.

"Have you seen any today?" Newburgh asked.

Romo's eyes darted toward Diehl. "Well…no."

"And these bandits you haven't seen," said Newburgh, "they'd be so stupid they'd waylay prospectors who haven't begun prospecting yet? With nothing to steal but pickaxes and pans and slats for a sluice box?"

"And food," said Diehl. "And guns. And ammunition."

Newburgh harrumphed again. "You shouldn't believe the blood and thunder you read in the newspapers. It's fiddle-faddle to be ignored." He gave Diehl a haughty glare. "Like the unfounded fears of fainthearted shop clerks."

Diehl sighed and looked away.

"I've been more than a shop clerk," he mumbled.

"So…what are we going to do?" Romo asked.

"*You* are going to get back on your horse before it wanders off with our mule," Newburgh told him. "*I* am going to carry on and find that abandoned mine you were supposed to lead us to. And *Mr. Diehl*…he can keep cowering here until he regains his manhood."

Romo's eyes widened. He made no move to get up and return to his horse. Without a word, he turned to look at Diehl.

Diehl nodded down at the young man's carbine. "You any good with that old thing?"

"I can't say. I just bought it yesterday in Nogales."

Diehl's head dropped.

"I'm a fair shot though," Romo went on. "I bagged a lot of quail when I was a boy."

"Quail. When you were a boy," Diehl said, staring down at his boots. "Well, *Alfonso*, your targets are about to get bigger."

He leaned to look up and down the trail winding along the mountainside. He pointed to his left, back the way they'd come.

"I'm going to head that way then work my way up for a better look. You cover me."

"Cover you?" Romo said.

"You know…if someone tries to shoot me, you shoot them?"

"Oh. Right."

"Tommyrot! I'm not going to sit here broiling while you hunt for imaginary *banditos*," Newburgh said. He turned to the mountaintop and cupped a hand to his mouth. "Hola! Amigos! We have-o mucho oro! Gold! Come-o and-o get it-o!"

"Newburgh, you damn fool!" Diehl spat.

Newburgh held his hand out toward the peaks and gave Diehl a "told you so" look.

"See?" he said. "Nothing."

There was a *pop* from the bluffs above, followed by a thud and a puff of dust from the front of Newburgh's jacket.

The horses flinched and whinnied. The mule didn't.

"Dios mío!" Romo gasped.

"Oh," said Newburgh.

There was another *pop*, another thud, another puff of dust from Newburgh's chest.

The horses nickered nervously. Again, the mule didn't react at all.

Newburgh slowly, slowly, slowly slid sideways from his saddle.

When the big man's bulk came crashing to the ground, the horses trotted forward a few steps, shaking their heads. The mule, tethered to Romo's saddle, brayed as it was dragged along.

Newburgh rolled onto his back and groaned.

"*Stay still,*" Diehl hissed at him.

Newburgh began struggling to push himself up.

"Don't move," Diehl said.

Newburgh sat up.

Romo started toward him. Diehl thrust out an arm to hold the younger man back.

"I do believe…I have been…shot," Newburgh said, staring down in shock at the two bloody holes in his jacket. He looked over at Diehl and smiled. "Is there a…doctor in the house?"

More shots rang out, louder than the first—from a bigger, closer gun.

Newburgh flopped back, arms splayed wide.

The horses bolted. The mule, tied loosely with a bowline hitch so it wouldn't drag Romo along if it went over a cliff, dug in its hooves and jerked its lead rope free. It came to a stop beside Diehl and Romo as the galloping horses disappeared around the curve in the trail.

The sound of pounding hooves died away slowly, then there was silence. It was broken by a burst of harsh, rapid Spanish. One man was shouting, then another, then yet another.

Diehl could only catch the curses. He'd heard those often enough. The rest was coming too fast from too many men.

"What are they saying?" he asked Romo, who was staring in horror at Newburgh's body on the other side of the mule.

The younger man blinked, then cocked his head and listened. "They're yelling at whoever finished off Mr. Newburgh. They're mad at him for spooking the horses." Romo frowned. "He says it doesn't matter because there was bound to be more shooting anyway."

"Cállate! Cállate! Cállate!" one of the men bellowed.

Diehl didn't need a translation for that. "Shut up! Shut up! Shut up!" he was saying.

The other men obeyed.

So there was a leader.

"Hola, Americanos!" the man called out. "Bienvenido a Mexico! Hablas Español?"

Romo looked at Diehl.

"Don't answer," Diehl said.

"Sí? No?" the bandit yelled. "Huh?"

He paused, waiting for a response, before going on.

"He says he's sorry about our friend, but it shows that they're serious," Romo translated. "They'd rather not fight though. They'll spare us if—"

Diehl barked out a bitter laugh. He knew what "déjanos del oro" meant.

"If we leave them the gold," he said.

He glowered at Newburgh. Not that Newburgh noticed. He was on his back, motionless, unblinking eyes pointed up at the sun.

A shaft of gold appeared between Diehl and the body.

The mule, oblivious to everything, was unleashing a stream of urine.

"Come-o and-o get it-o," Diehl sighed.

The bandit chief began shouting down to them again. Diehl caught the words for "gold" and "mountains" and "friends" and "peace." And something more.

He heard the clatter of rocks and pebbles sliding down toward the trail to the left. Then he heard it to the right.

The leader kept jabbering at them about *misericordia*—mercy—even as his men were creeping down the incline.

It was too late to outflank the bandits. They were doing the flanking first. The only question now was when the shooting would begin again.

It didn't stay a question long. There was a blast from the right, and a bullet ricocheted off the top of the boulder, showering Diehl and Romo with a spray of gray chips.

Diehl and Romo instinctively shrank down further. The mule just stopped pissing and stared off placidly at nothing.

Another shot from the same direction thudded into the ground near Diehl's boots.

"Damn," Diehl growled.

He took one quick, crouching step away from the rocks, pivoted toward where the shots had come from, and started firing. He didn't even spot who he was shooting at until he pulled the trigger the third time and a man in a white shirt and a wide-brimmed hat arched his back, dropped his rifle, and started rolling down the slope fifty yards away.

There was a loud *crack* behind Diehl, and when he dived back behind the boulder, he saw that Romo had popped up to fire in the opposite direction.

"Get down!" Diehl barked as the young man laboriously cocked the hammer and worked the lever in preparation for another shot.

There was a ragged volley of return fire, and bullets slammed into the rocks and dirt all around Romo. He yelped and ducked down beside Diehl.

The mule swished its tail as if shooing off a fly but otherwise took no notice of the battle. There could be no question now as to whether or not it was deaf.

"We won't get away with that again," Diehl said. "Our only chance—and it's not a good one—is to hunker down here and hope we can fight 'em off when they…what?"

Romo was gaping in dismay at the mule.

Diehl peered beneath the animal, thinking some of the bandits might be slipping over the ridge beyond it. He saw nothing but rocks and sky.

"What?" Diehl said again.

Romo lifted a trembling hand and pointed at the biggest box on the mule's back.

The one marked DYNAMITE.

"Son of a *bitch*," Diehl said.

If just one stray shot hit that box, every stick of dynamite inside would go off.

Diehl was about to be killed by an exploding mule.

He shook his head. Then he started to laugh. Then he stopped and shook his head again.

He picked up a rock the size of a teacup and threw it at the mule's haunch. It bounced off and clattered down onto the trail.

The mule kicked back with its right leg and craned its neck to throw a glare at Diehl.

And that was all. It didn't leave.

A bullet smashed into the boulder behind Diehl and Romo. Then another plowed into the ground between them and the mule.

Romo clasped his hands and closed his eyes and began murmuring softly. Praying.

"Don't give Him the satisfaction," Diehl said.

Romo opened one eye. "What?"

Diehl nodded at the other man's carbine. "Your hands'll do more good on your gun."

Another shot spat up dust and pebbles not far from their feet. The bandits were getting a better angle now. It was only a matter of time. One way or another—caught in a crossfire or blown to bits by a mule-bomb—their time was almost up.

There was a soft, slow, steady crunching noise to the right. Then the same sound came from the left.

The bandits were close enough now for Diehl to hear their footsteps.

"Get ready," he whispered.

Romo nodded, both eyes open again, and clutched his carbine tightly.

Darkness fell over a big rock about thirty feet off.

A shadow.

Diehl brought up his rifle.

The boom came before he squeezed the trigger. A distant blast that echoed longer than any previous shot.

There was a grunt, then a thud and a clatter. The shadow Diehl had been watching disappeared.

"Qué?" a man said.

"Quién?" said another.

"Dónde?" said a third.

What?

Who?

Where?

Another shot rang out, and this time the grunt-thud-clatter that followed was accompanied by the sight of a limp body rolling down onto the trail.

"Vamonos! Vamonos!" a man cried, and there was nothing soft or slow about the sound of footsteps now. The bandits were fleeing.

"This is our chance!" Diehl said.

He stood and looked for a target. He saw one immediately—a man wearing bandoliers scrambling up the slope. Diehl drew a bead on the point where the bandoliers crossed—X marked the spot—and put a bullet in his back. Romo rose up beside him as he did the same to another man, then another.

Romo brought up his carbine...then lowered it again.

"They're running away," he said.

"Right," said Diehl, hunting for a fresh target. "And we don't want them coming back."

He trained his Winchester on a bandit rushing toward a crest sixty yards up the incline.

There was another far-off bang, and the man threw out his arms, dropped his rifle and toppled backward.

Three of his fellow bandits scrambled past him and disappeared over the ridge.

"Damn," said Diehl.

Three bandits—four if you counted the chief, who'd probably stayed safe at the top of the grade to begin with—was more than enough to ambush them again down the trail.

Diehl slowly moved his gunsight along the ridgeline, hoping to spot the rounded dome of a sombrero rising up as one of the men dared a peek back at him. A surprising sound echoed down instead.

A short, piercing shriek. Followed by another scream that lasted longer but ended just as abruptly.

Two shots rang out from the ridge, but there were no bullet strikes around Diehl or Romo. Whoever was doing the shooting and whoever was getting shot—both were up the hill.

A man in a blue tunic and moccasin boots stepped out onto one of the jutting bluffs. His long, dark hair and breechcloth fluttered in the breeze. He lifted the rifle he was carrying over his head with one hand.

Romo raised his own rifle to take aim.

Diehl reached over and shoved the barrel down.

"Don't you see?" Romo said. "It's an Apache!"

Diehl nodded. "I see."

He let go of Romo's rifle, then cupped his hands around his mouth.

"Hola, Eskaminzim!" he called.

"Hello, you dumb son of a bitch!" the Apache called back.

Diehl dropped his hands and sighed.

"You *know* him?" Romo asked.

"He called me a dumb son of a bitch, didn't he?" Diehl said. "We know each other."

He cupped his hands to his mouth again.

"Where's Hoop?" he shouted.

Eskaminzim pointed down at Diehl with his rifle. Even from sixty yards off the big grin on his face was easy to see.

"Where do you think, you blind pendejo?" the Apache laughed.

Diehl looked over his shoulder. Romo turned too, and his jaw dropped.

A tall, brawny, bearded Black man was climbing up onto the trail about thirty feet away. He was wearing a green shirt, a brown Stetson, and gray trousers held up with suspenders. In his hands was a long, heavy-looking rifle.

Diehl gave the man a nod and a smile.

"Hoop," he said.

The man returned the nod. Not the smile.

"Diehl," he said.

He had a Southern accent that stretched the name out till it broke in two. *Deee-ul.*

Diehl stepped out to glare around the mule at Newburgh's body. Flies were already finding the holes in it.

"Told you we were being followed," Diehl said to the corpse.

"Who are these men?" Romo asked.

"Old…colleagues of mine," Diehl said. "Looking for me, I assume?"

"That's right," the man called Hoop said. He gave Newburgh a brief, dismissive glance as he walked toward Diehl.

The mule noted that someone was joining them on the trail with nothing but a twitch of the ears and a swish of the tail.

"Got a message for you," Hoop said. He pulled a folded piece of paper from a trouser pocket and held it out to Diehl. "From the old man."

Diehl took the letter but didn't open it. "Job?"

Hoop nodded. "Job."

"Same old shit?" Diehl asked.

Hoop nodded again. "Same ol' shit. Only the pay's not as good and the odds are worse."

Diehl looked down at the letter in his hand and took a deep

breath. He'd thought he was done working for the old man—
thought he was done killing—but what the hell. It was better than
getting shot or starving.

He'd squandered his chance to start over. Maybe this was a
new one.

Maybe God wasn't out to get him after all.

The mule finally noticed that Diehl was standing behind it.

It kicked him.

CHAPTER 2

Diehl didn't get much sympathy from his "old colleagues."

The big Black man, Hoop, looked down at Diehl on the ground rubbing his upper thigh—the part of him that had taken the worst of the mule's kick—and shook his head.

"I suppose now you expect us to catch your horses for you," he said.

The Apache, Eskaminzim, came trotting down the slope nearby. He pointed at the mule and grinned.

"I'm glad she didn't get shot," he said. "I like her."

"Are you all right?" Romo asked Diehl.

Diehl pushed himself to his feet. "That mule didn't kick me any harder than I should be kicking myself. Riding into an ambush like that…"

"Good thing the little badger wasn't here to see it," Eskaminzim said. He nodded at the letter Diehl still clutched in his left hand. "He might tell Hoop to tear that up."

"'The little badger'?" Romo asked.

Diehl opened his mouth to answer him, then sighed and turned to Hoop instead. "Yes. Go catch the horses. Romo and I will stay here and take care of him."

He jerked his thumb at Newburgh's body.

Hoop cocked his head but said nothing.

"Please," Diehl added.

Hoop grunted, then turned and started up the trail.

"Come on," he said to the Apache.

Eskaminzim paused to stare at Newburgh. "A man like this takes a lot of burying. You should let the vultures do the work."

"We'll do it," Diehl said, limping toward the body.

"He was stupid," Eskaminzim said.

Diehl shrugged. "He was my partner."

"I understand," Eskaminzim said. "Hoop and I know what's it like to have a stupid partner."

He burst out laughing and trotted off.

Diehl stuffed the letter Hoop had given him into his back pocket, then slowly, groaning, kneeled beside Newburgh. He'd been careful to keep the body between himself and the mule, yet he still looked up to give the animal a wary glare.

"Don't get any ideas," he said.

The mule kept staring straight ahead.

Diehl waved away the nearest flies, then began patting Newburgh's body. He lifted a watch from the big man's jacket by its long gold chain.

"What are you doing?" Romo asked. His look of disgust made it plain he thought he knew the answer.

Diehl put the watch down on the ground, then pulled a wad of folded papers from one of Newburgh's pockets. "Looking for an address. So I can send his things to his family."

"Oh," said Romo.

Diehl flipped through the papers—receipts, maps, and finally a letter—then looked up.

"You're not sure what kind of men you've fallen in with," he said.

"No," said Romo. "I'm not."

"Well, say what you will about us, we're not thieves. Not me and Hoop, anyway. Eskaminzim...it depends on what kind of horses you've got."

Diehl went back to his search, pulling out a compass and a flask and a handful of coins. He stuffed everything into his own pockets, then stood.

"Help me drag him over there," he said, jerking his chin at the spot where he and Romo had taken cover fifteen minutes before. "We'll bury him under rocks. Eskaminzim's right. He's too much for a grave."

When they were done covering Newburgh with loose slabs of shale, Diehl leaned against a boulder and patted the sweat from his face with a red neckerchief. Romo walked to the other body on the trail, one of the bandits Hoop had killed with his big buffalo rifle. He'd landed on his side, face covered by a limp arm. One foot still wore a tattered sandal. The other was bare.

"What about him?" Romo said. He gestured at the other corpses scattered up the hillside. "And them?"

"Amateurs," Diehl sighed.

"What?"

"Amateurs," Diehl said again, louder. "There aren't many rebels running around anymore, right? And all that bickering between them? They haven't done this that often. Just some hard-up locals, probably."

"I meant what should we do with the bodies?"

"They've got their own friends to take care of 'em. In fact..."

Diehl snatched up his Winchester and spun to face the zigzagging trail above them. Two men were riding down leading a string of three horses.

Hoop and Eskaminzim. Diehl relaxed...a little.

"We need to go," he said.

A minute later, four mounted men were headed down the mountain leading one riderless Morgan horse and one peevish, hoof-dragging mule.

———

The letter Hoop had brought remained in Diehl's pocket, unread, as the men rode down the winding trail. When he wasn't keeping his eyes on the steep drops on one side, Diehl was scanning the rocky bluffs above them on the other, hunting for the glint of sun on steel that had given the bandits away the first time. Eskaminzim thought at least one of the bandits had gotten away, and Diehl knew not to doubt him.

When they finally rode out onto the cactus-pocked desert flats, speed—as much as they could get with the truculent mule slowing them—was the important thing. Hoop said the job was north, in Arizona Territory. So north they went with the letter still tucked away unopened.

Hours later they stopped to rest the horses at a thin trickle of a stream.

"Next water's miles off," Hoop said as his mustang lowered its head for a drink. "And ain't long till dusk."

Diehl nodded. "We'll make camp here."

"Oh, will we?" Eskaminzim said.

He turned to Hoop.

Hoop kept his gaze on Diehl.

"Yes," Hoop said gravely. "We will make camp here."

Eskaminzim grinned. "Good idea, Hoop!"

He hopped down from his horse, stretched out by the stream, and plunged his face into the water.

Romo looked back and forth between the three men with obvious confusion.

"They're just reminding me I'm not in charge," Diehl explained. "Yet."

Hoop slid from his saddle and kneeled at the stream beside Eskaminzim.

"Read the letter, Diehl," he said. "Then we'll see."

———

Once they had the animals on the picket line for the night, the men gathered in a circle nearby, each leaning back against his saddle. There would be no fire.

"No need to send an engraved invitation to anyone looking for us," Diehl told Romo.

"What's an 'engraved invitation'?" Eskaminzim asked.

"A card. Like a letter," Hoop said. "It's how fancy White people invite each other to tea parties."

The Apache laughed and jerked his head at Diehl. "Like the little badger's letter to him!"

"Kinda," said Hoop.

He took a slurp of juice from the can of peaches he'd opened for his dinner.

Still chuckling, Eskaminzim pulled out a knife with a six-inch blade and began stropping it methodically against a rock in his other hand. He stared at Romo as he ran the edge back and forth over the stone.

Romo kept his head down and pretended to clean his rifle.

There was still just enough light to read by.

Diehl finally unfolded the letter.

Diehl —

Three times you've told me that you're done with guns, and twice you've changed your mind. I'm sending this message in case you've encountered cause to change it again.

I am one of the principal partners in a new enterprise: the A.A. Western Detective Agency, based in Ogden. The past few months I have spent in communication with many old acquaintances from our days with the Army and the railroad, informing them of this new venture and its services. Until recently, this netted me only Christmas greetings and wishes for a happy new year. But now we have a client—one with a problem requiring the kind of special attention that you and our other former comrades can provide.

The operators of the Gruffud-Cadwaladr Mine of Pima County, Arizona Territory find themselves in conflict with a larger and more powerful concern: the Consolidated American Mining Corporation. Consolidated American has made multiple attempts to buy the mine and, finding its offers rebuffed, has resorted to more vigorous forms of persuasion. Consolidated's representative has acquired the services of local toughs—the usual

*trash swept up off the streets, I'm told—and a campaign of harassment
and outright violence has begun.*

*The A.A. Western Detective Agency has been engaged to protect the
mine and persuade Consolidated American to direct its energies elsewhere.
Being a fledgling operation, we have few resources to bring to bear. None, in
fact, beyond the unique talents of our agents. I am confident, however, that
your flair for novel strategies, combined with Sergeant Hoop and Eskaminzim's unmatched tactical skills, would carry the day.*

*I can offer you five dollars a day, with a bonus of three hundred if the
situation is resolved in some permanent fashion. I require no reports from
you beyond word that you are headed to Pima County and, later, have met
with success there. It is not necessary or indeed desirable for me to be
apprised of whatever you choose to do in between.*

*If you accept this proposition, report posthaste to the Gruffud-
Cadwaladr Mine. If you do not accept this proposition, I wish you luck
with whatever new endeavor you have set yourself to. It is not easy for a
man of peace to make his way in this world. Men of force, I need hardly
remind you, can always find employment.*

Col. C. Kermit Crowe, Director
The A.A. Western Detective Agency
Chamber of Commerce Building, Room 303
Ogden, Utah
February 3, 1894

*PS Diana tells me this letter lacks warmth and should not be sent without
the addition of some personal touch given our long association. So, Diana
and I are fine. I hope you are as well.*

Diehl finished reading the letter just as the final orange rays of
sunlight were swallowed by the now-black mountains. He looked
around at the other men.

Romo and Eskaminzim were watching him, the Apache with a
little self-amused smile it would soon be too dark to see.

Hoop was tilting the can of peaches over his gaping mouth to
pour the last trickle of juice down his throat.

"You read this?" Diehl asked him.

Hoop tossed the empty can over his shoulder. "Of course."

"Well…what do you think?"

Hoop shrugged. "I don't think you're worth a dollar a day more than me."

"He doesn't think you're worth a *penny* more than him!" Eskaminzim laughed. "That's what he said when he read it!"

The Apache watched Diehl eagerly. He seemed to be hoping Diehl would take offense.

Diehl stifled a sigh.

"What do you think about *the job*?" he asked Hoop.

"Sounds like an excellent opportunity," Hoop drawled, "for a man to get himself killed."

"And yet you're going."

"But are *you*?" Eskaminzim asked. "We need you, Diehl."

Diehl knew better than to accept the compliment. He cocked an eyebrow at the Apache and waited.

Eskaminzim's smile broadened. "Without a White man playing boss no one would listen to us. Even a maricón like you is better than nothing!"

Diehl glanced over at Romo. "You see the respect I get."

Romo just kept watching warily.

"So," said Hoop, "*are* you coming?"

Diehl took a deep breath and slumped back against his saddle.

"Somehow prospecting has its allure," he said. "Yeah. I'm coming."

Eskaminzim nodded, looking excited.

Hoop didn't react at all.

Romo spoke up for the first time in half an hour.

"What is this job you're accepting?"

"Mine security. In Arizona Territory," said Diehl. "Want to come?"

"Me?" said Romo.

"Him?" said Hoop and Eskaminzim a second apart.

"Sure," said Diehl. "Romo's an engineer. Thrown out of work when the silver mines started shutting down last year. He handled himself all right in that fight. He might come in handy. Plus, we need bodies."

Romo's eyes widened.

"Men, I mean. To fill out the ranks," Diehl said. "Dollar a day, guaranteed. Better than listening to your stomach growl while you wait for crazy gringos to guide into the mountains."

"How do you know this little cabrón didn't lead you into that trap today?" Eskaminzim asked, jabbing the blade he'd been sharpening Romo's way.

"Because I'm a good judge of character...*cabrón*," Diehl replied.

Eskaminzim laughed. "You're right about me. But him? No. All Mexicans are liars, cheats, and back-shooters."

"I resent that remark," Romo said quietly but firmly.

"Good!" Eskaminzim blurted out with glee. He hopped to his feet. "You wanna fight?"

"Umm..." said Romo, staring at the knife in Eskaminzim's hand.

"Don't worry. We'll make it fair," the Apache said. "Hoop, give him your knife."

"No," said Hoop. He was barely watching what was happening, choosing instead to wrap himself in a huge buffalo-hide campaign coat he'd unpacked earlier. Once he had it buttoned, he slapped on a flap-eared beaver hat. It looked like an upright grizzly had wandered into camp.

Eskaminzim turned to Diehl.

"No," Diehl said.

"Fine," the Apache spat.

With a flick of the wrist, he whipped the knife into the ground at his feet. The blade buried itself in the sandy soil all the way up to the handle.

"No weapons but these." Eskaminzim held up his hands and wriggled his fingers, then gestured for Romo to get up. "Come on, little pollito. Show me how brave Mexicans are."

"Umm..." Romo said again.

"Just say no," Diehl told him.

"Uhh...no," Romo said.

Eskaminzim bent down and jerked his knife from the earth.

"You're no fun," he said. He turned and stalked off into the thickening gloom. "I'm going looking for wolves. They'll fight."

He stepped behind a tall saguaro cactus, its thick branches bent upward like a man raising his arms in surrender, and disappeared.

"Is he crazy?" Romo whispered to Diehl.

Diehl shook his head. "Bored."

Somewhere in the dark distance, Eskaminzim yipped like a coyote.

Hoop stretched out flat on the ground and crossed his arms over his chest.

"Long as you're wandering around, you may as well take first watch!" he called out.

Eskaminzim howled like a wolf.

Diehl turned to Romo. "No hard feelings if you don't want to stick with us, Alfonso. We'll just go our separate ways in Nogales."

Eskaminzim chirped like a cricket, then imitated—or perhaps not—a fart.

"Um…I'll think about it," Romo said.

"Fair enough," said Diehl. He eased himself down, curled up under his blanket, and closed his eyes. "Well, sweet dreams."

Hoop was already snoring. Within a minute, Diehl was doing the same.

Romo lay back, head resting on his saddle, and watched the stars grow steadily brighter as he waited for sleep to come.

He waited for a long, long time.

CHAPTER 3

Romo dreamed of his father measuring a customer for a new suit. Only his father hadn't been a tailor. He'd been a banker. The customer was President Diaz. Romo's father smiled.

Then the customer was a snorting, drooling hog, upright in the same black morning coat, and Romo's father still smiled—even though he now had a bullet hole in the side of his head.

The hog reached out a hoofed foot, broke off Romo's father's nose, and popped it into its mouth. And *still* Romo's father smiled.

The sound of the hog's chewing was monstrously moist at first, punctuated by happy snorts and grunts. But as the chomping went on, the sound turned hard, sharp, grating. Familiar.

Romo opened his eyes to a desert dawn, orange crowning the yellow hills and feathery clouds tinged purple and pink. His father and the hog were instantly gone, not even a memory. The scraping sound remained. Romo turned toward it.

Eskaminzim was crouched nearby, knife in one hand, flat-topped rock in another. He went on stropping the blade without looking down at it. His eyes were on Romo.

There was no sign of Diehl or Hoop.

The Apache grinned.

"Buenos días," he said.

"Bueno—" Romo croaked.

He cleared his throat and tried again.

"Buenos días."

Eskaminzim brought his knife up to eye level and turned it this way and that, examining the blade. The silver was streaked with red.

"I don't know what else you might be good at, but I'll give you this," he said. "You sure are good at sleeping."

He wiped the blade on the sand by his feet, then began running it over the rock again.

Romo tried to remember where he'd left his rifle. Was it to his left or to his right?

Slowly, never taking his gaze off the Apache, he stretched his hands out beneath his blanket, feeling for the old carbine's battered stock.

"Relax, lechuza," Eskaminzim said. He raised the knife and inspected the blade again. "You should be glad I keep this so sharp."

He stood and looked off to his right.

"Done?" he said.

Romo sat up and saw Hoop and Diehl approaching. Each carried a shovel.

"Done," Hoop said.

"Time to go," Diehl told Romo.

He walked up and dropped his shovel by the younger man's feet. Hoop did the same.

"Get those on the mule and saddle your mount," Diehl said. "Rápido."

"Right," said Romo. But he didn't move until Eskaminzim walked off with Hoop and Diehl.

As he headed for the picket line with the shovels, he watched the three men head up a rise nearby and stare off to the south toward the mountains they'd left the day before.

When he rounded the clump of brittlebush and stubby palo verde trees that hid their animals, he saw that all the horses but his were saddled. The mule had already been loaded with gear too. He secured the shovels as best he could—mule packing was new to him—then hurried back for his saddle and blanket and rifle.

A few minutes later Romo was ready to ride—and so were Diehl, Hoop, and Eskaminzim, who joined him without a word as he slid his carbine into its scabbard. Hoop took down the picket line, and the others swung up onto their saddles.

"What did you need the shovels for, Mr. Diehl?" Romo asked.

Diehl nodded to the left. "Taking care of our visitors."

Romo turned but saw nothing other than a tight knot of blossom-topped yucca and, beyond it, the blank Sonoran expanse. Then he noticed how the soil by the yucca was just the slightest bit darker than the ground around it, and there were none of the usual tufts of tough, scrubby grass.

The patch of disturbed earth was about six feet by four. Just the right size for a grave.

"Friends of our friends from the mountain," Diehl said. He jerked a thumb up at the sky. "We don't need buzzards leading the next bunch straight to us."

Romo gaped at Diehl in disbelief. "You killed men here last night?"

"You didn't miss much," Eskaminzim said. "There were only eight of them."

The Apache smirked, then sent his black-and-white pinto trotting off.

"He's exaggerating," said Diehl. He rubbed his chin and looked thoughtful. "Or maybe I lost count..."

He gave his paint his heels and led Newburgh's big Morgan off after Eskaminzim.

Hoop was in the saddle now too, but he didn't follow the others right away. He'd taken off his buffalo coat and beaver hat, so he didn't look like a towering wall of fur anymore. He was just a towering man again—one who stared at Romo, then the mule behind him.

"I hear that mule is deaf," he said.

Romo nodded. "That's right."

Hoop grunted. "So what's your excuse?"

Romo didn't know what to say to that. Not that it mattered.

Hoop pointed his horse to the north and rode off.

———

They kept to a steady trot as they headed toward the border. Eskaminzim led the way, still followed by Diehl, then Hoop, then bringing up the rear with the balky mule, Romo. Romo could see the other men swiveling to scan the horizon behind them from time to time, but whenever he looked back, he saw nothing but the usual hard-baked sand, scrub, and rocks. Still, it made him nervous to lag alone behind the others, and after a few hours he took his old mare up to a gallop—or as close to a gallop as the mule would allow—and caught up to Hoop.

"Don't do that again," Hoop said when Romo slowed down beside him. "We still have a lot of country to cross."

"They can take it," Romo said, nodding first down at his horse, then back at the mule.

Hoop glowered at him. "It's not the animals I'm thinking of. It's *that*."

He pointed back at the yellow swirls of dust Romo had kicked up. Most of it was settling already, but some had puffed up into a hazy cloud that kept on rising.

"Oh. Sorry," Romo said. "I'm new to all this. I'll try to do better."

"Hard to do worse," Hoop said. But he looked over at Romo with an expression that seemed, for once, almost tolerant. "Why would you care about doing better anyway, boy? Unless you're taking Diehl's offer seriously. Thinking of risking your life for a dollar a day."

Romo shrugged. "A dollar a day sounds good when you've been earning nothing a day for eight months. I was down to my last centavos when Mr. Diehl and Mr. Newburgh hired me."

Hoop's look turned skeptical. "You were supposed to be their guide to a lost mine, huh?"

"It wasn't like that," Romo said. "It's not a lost mine. Just abandoned. Mr. Newburgh and Mr. Diehl thought they could still make something of the vein if they could find the right place to get at it. I know where the mine is, and I'm an engineer, and not a half-bad surveyor. So yes. I was their guide. And their mining consultant." The young man's expression soured. "And their servant, Mr. Newburgh seemed to think..."

"How'd him and Diehl come to be partners?"

"They met when Mr. Newburgh was outfitting for his expedition in Tucson. Mr. Newburgh's original partner backed out, and Mr. Diehl—"

"Was tired of being a counter clerk in a two-bit general store," Hoop cut in with a weary nod, as if he'd heard the story ten times.

"Well, tired of being assistant assistant manager," Romo said.

Hoop cocked an eyebrow. "Assistant assistant manager?"

"That's what Mr. Diehl told me his title was." Romo suddenly realized how stupid that sounded. "I guess he might have been making a little joke."

"All of Diehl's jokes are little," Hoop said.

"How is it you know him?"

Hoop swiped off his Stetson and ran a sleeve over his sweat-dappled forehead. The night chill had completely burned off, and the sun had risen high over the distant peaks to the east.

"Son, I'll answer you," Hoop said, plopping his hat back on. "But I never speak more than fifty words before noon, and I've only got three left before I'm over my quota. So..."

Hoop held up the index finger of his right hand.

"Army," he said.

He put up his middle and ring fingers too.

"Railroad police."

He put his hand back on his saddle horn.

"Umm...no more words till noon?" Romo said.

Hoop took a deep breath. "You seem like a decent enough kid, so I'll give you some on credit. I don't know what's waiting for us in

Pima County, but you should ask yourself if that dollar a day is worth killing for. Or dying for."

He turned his gaze away from Romo and said no more.

Romo rode along in silence after that. He seemed to have run out of words too.

———

None of the men spoke again until Eskaminzim reined up on a rise overlooking two dark clusters running from south to north on a row of rolling hills. The first was Nogales, Sonora. The second was Nogales, Arizona Territory. Twin towns huddled close—but not too close—against the Mexican-slash-American border.

The other men lined up beside Eskaminzim.

"You can make it alone from here, Alfonso," Diehl said. "Tell you what—you can have that mule and everything on her back. That should more than cover whatever I owe you." He gave Romo a sidelong look. "Or you can carry on with us, and we'll square up later."

Hoop and Eskaminzim turned to watch Romo.

For a moment, the young man kept his gaze on the buildings below, uncertainty on his face, shoulders slumped. Then he straightened up and tried to look resolute.

"Let's get going," he said. "Pima County is still a hundred miles away."

He pointed his horse toward the northwest and dug in his heels.

The horse stepped forward. The mule didn't. It just stretched out its neck and brayed angrily. For a few seconds it looked like the dead weight of it was going to jerk it free of its hitch. But Romo gave his old horse a "Yeehaw!" and it strained forward again, and this time the mule slowly, reluctantly, complaining all the way, started toward the United States.

Diehl smiled as he watched them trot off.

"So…another new recruit, huh?" Hoop said.

"We've seen plenty come and go," said Diehl.

"And we've buried plenty."

Diehl stopped smiling. "Well, who knows, Hoop? Maybe he's the recruit who's going to finally bury *us*. We keep doing this, and someone's gotta."

He started after Romo. Eskaminzim and Hoop looked at each other, then did the same.

CHAPTER 4

They rode northwest. They sold Newburgh's Morgan. They *didn't* sell the mule though Romo desperately wanted them to. They sent a telegram to Col. C. Kermit Crowe in Ogden, Utah.

OFFER ACCEPTED STOP EXPECT BILLING INFORMATION
OR FUNERAL ARRANGEMENTS SHORTLY STOP DIEHL

They got directions to the Gruffud-Cadwaladr Mine once they figured out to just ask for "the G-C." They followed the road toward the rocky bluffs the mine bore into. They stopped.

Nine men stood in their way.

The road was wide and deeply grooved with ruts from ore-laden wagons that were nowhere in sight. The men stretched across it like a picket fence, glaring at Diehl and the others. All wore gun belts. Three held Winchesters. One had a shotgun.

"Who do you think they are?" Romo said.

They were less than a hundred yards from the men. Close enough to see their shabby clothes and unshaven faces and all-around seediness.

They weren't miners pressed into service as guards. They looked more like they'd been swept up off the floor of a bar that morning.

"They're colleagues," Diehl said. "Of a sort."

"The worst sort," said Hoop.

Eskaminzim smiled. "No. The best sort. If you're us."

"Um…what does any of that mean?" Romo asked.

No one answered. Diehl just trotted out to take the lead.

The men up ahead were white. They'd expect him to do the talking. He'd decided to oblige.

One of the men lined up across the road—the one with the biggest belly and the grayest stubble and the most battered Stetson —and held up a hand, signaling for Diehl to stop.

Diehl slowed his horse to a walk, then came to a halt ten yards from the man. Hoop and Eskaminzim and Romo stopped behind him.

The flabby man lowered his arm.

"Where do you think you're going?" he asked.

"We've got business at the G-C," Diehl replied loudly. "Who the hell are you?"

And he winked.

The flabby man blinked at him, as if he wasn't sure he'd just seen what he'd seen. Because he didn't understand the wink, after a moment he decided to ignore it.

"We're concerned local citizens is what we are," he said. "We've heard more agitators are headed this way, and we want to make sure they get the welcome they deserve."

His grubby friends chuckled.

"That's perfect," Diehl whispered to them. "Keep it up."

The chuckles petered out, replaced by confused looks.

"Are any of them close enough to hear?" Diehl asked the men, voice still low. "Spying from the rocks, maybe?"

"Any of who?" the flabby one said.

"The miners, of course," Diehl said under his breath. "We've got to make this look good."

He scowled and jabbed a finger at the man.

"Look, you—I don't know anything about any 'agitators,'" he said, booming again. He jerked his thumb back at Romo and the mule. "I'm just here to deliver dynamite and nitro to the G-C Mine."

He gave the men in the road another wink.

"Why do you keep doing that?" the flabby man asked.

Diehl shushed him.

"Because we were sent by you-know-who to get a look at conditions up at the you-know-what," he said through gritted teeth. "Now call me a son of a bitch."

"What?" said the flabby man.

"Call me a son of a bitch and tell me you won't let us through and we'll pull on you and you'll be 'caught by surprise'—" Diehl winked yet again. "Then we'll head up to the mine and get the lay of the land."

The flabby man scratched his jowls.

"Schuck didn't say anything about letting through spies," he said. But he spoke quietly, his eyes darting back and forth.

"Go on. Call him a son of a bitch, Bill," one of the other men said.

"Don't be a chowderhead, Bill," said another. "Claypole sent him. Call him a son of a bitch."

"Come on, Bill, hurry it up," Diehl whispered. He stiffened in his saddle and raised his voice again. "You have no right to stop us on a public road!"

"We'll stop who we please, you son of a bitch!" Bill replied stiffly.

Diehl gave him a nod and a smile.

"Nice," he said.

He drew his Colt from its holster. Behind him, Hoop did the same, while Eskaminzim whipped out his Winchester.

"Reach for the sky, varmints!" Diehl barked.

The men in the road did as they were told. The ones holding the rifles and shotgun looked unsure but lifted their heavy weapons over their heads.

"And put down the artillery!" Diehl shouted at them.

"Sorry. I should've had you do that first," he added in a whisper as they bent toward the ground. "Now let us ride past, then once we've topped that rise up ahead everyone shake your fists at us. Got it?"

Bill and some of the men started to nod.

"*Don't nod,*" Diehl snapped.

"Oh. Right," said Bill. "We got it."

"Good," said Diehl. "Hopefully, we'll be in and out of here in an hour. First round in town tonight's on me."

He started his horse forward, and the line of men swung back like a gate opening.

"Thank you, gentlemen," Hoop said, swiveling to keep his Colt trained on Bill as he rode past.

Romo swiveled to watch the men too, but for a different reason. He couldn't believe one of them wasn't about to shoot him in the back.

Eskaminzim went last. As he passed the men, he spun all the way around on his pinto to cover them with his Winchester.

"Don't forget to look really mad," he said as he rode his horse backward up the incline. "Like you can't believe you had to let an Apache and a Black hold guns on you."

"We know what to do," Bill growled.

Diehl, then Hoop, then Romo disappeared over the rise. As Eskaminzim joined them, Bill and the other men began silently shaking their fists at him.

"This seems kinda dumb," one of them said.

"We should say something," suggested the man beside him.

"Leave it to me," said Bill. He cleared his throat.

Diehl looked back and smiled as "Son of a biiiiiiiiiitch!" echoed after them up the road.

"I can't believe that worked," said Romo.

"More amateurs," said Diehl.

"And a lot of luck," Hoop added. "Which ain't gonna count for much when the professionals show up."

Diehl shrugged. "Maybe they never will."

"When's the last time our luck held that long?" Hoop said.

Diehl had no answer for that, at least not one he cared to say out loud.

CHAPTER 5

As they carried on up the hill—Diehl in the lead and Eskaminzim, still riding backward, last—they passed two black holes blasted into the rock. One would've looked like a plain cave entrance if it weren't for the big shards of scorched, shattered shale scattered around it. The other was covered with metal grating and seemed to drop straight down into the bowels of the earth.

"What do you make of those holes, Alfonso?" Diehl said.

"Test excavations," said Romo. "They were looking for other approaches to the vein."

Diehl cocked an eyebrow at Hoop. "Might come in handy."

Hoop nodded. "Be nice not to worry about shoveling next time."

"What do you mean?" Romo asked.

"Just thinking ahead," said Diehl, turning away again. "In case."

He didn't say in case what.

A minute later they rode out onto a plateau bordered by a curling *C* of steep bluffs. The mine works—just a black spiderweb across the rocks when seen from the valley below—came into view up close. Straight ahead was a mill building bristling with smoke-stacks and a long trestle up to the main shaft head and, scattered between them, heaps of pulverized waste rock. Large, empty wagons were lined up on the left by corrals and barns for horses and mules.

It looked like everything you'd need for a small mine operation. Except miners. Those were nowhere in sight.

"Where is everybody?" Romo said. "The place looks abandoned."

"Not entirely," said Hoop.

His eyes were locked on one of the big, boxy ore bins at the bottom of the tramway from the shaft. Eskaminzim finally faced forward to follow his gaze.

"I see him," said Diehl.

"See who?" said Romo.

A shot rang out, and a puff of dust kicked up six feet ahead of Diehl's paint. All the animals whinnied and danced nervously except for the mule, which just brayed in irritation as Romo's nag skittered back toward it.

"*Him*," Eskaminzim said to Romo.

"Aim to the side next time!" Diehl shouted as he got his horse settled. "There's a thing called a ricochet, you know!"

"Who are you?" a man called back. He was leaning out around the bin fifty yards ahead, a rifle in his hands. It was pointed squarely at Diehl.

"We're from the A.A. Western Detective Agency! And if anyone's going to be shooting at intruders from here on, it's us!"

"You're from the Double-A?" the man asked.

"Yes!" Diehl replied. He added a muttered "I guess" to himself, then looked back at Hoop. "Is that what people call us?"

Hoop shrugged.

"Throw down your weapons!" the man said.

Diehl turned to face him again.

"Nah," he said.

"'Nah'?" said the man.

"'Nah'?" said Romo, freezing. He'd already been reaching for his rifle.

"What do you mean, 'nah'?" the man asked.

"It means 'nah'!" Eskaminzim yelled at him. "Who doesn't understand 'nah'? It's a very simple word, even in your ugly language!"

"We don't throw down our weapons," Hoop added. "Gets 'em all dusty."

"Now look here!" the man said, voice quivering with frustration. "My next shot's not going to ricochet and not going to the side! If you don't do what I say, it's going straight through your leader's head!"

Hoop snorted. It wasn't clear if he was dubious about the man's seriousness, his accuracy with a rifle, his description of Diehl as their "leader," or his assumption that shooting Diehl would be a deterrent.

"Nah," Diehl said again.

The man made a sound that was half growl and half exasperated curse.

Diehl opened his mouth to say something other than "nah," but someone else spoke first.

"What is going on here?"

A woman stepped around the far side of the mill building. She was dressed like a respectable lady in a high-necked maroon dress with skirts that swept a fraction of an inch over the dirt. An older, bearded man—perhaps sixty-five to her forty—came toddling up beside her. He was dressed respectably as well, in a bowtie, vest, and coat above yellow breeches stuffed into shiny brown boots.

Diehl tugged on his hat brim. "Ma'am. Sir," he said, acknowledging the new arrivals. "Colonel C. Kermit Crowe sends his regards from Ogden."

"You're from the detective agency?" the woman asked. She was slender and tall, with fair hair pulled back in a bun. If she'd been younger, men would have called her "pretty." Now though, she was old enough to have made the transition to "handsome."

Diehl gave her a nod. "That's what I've been trying to tell your associate…" He gestured at the man by the ore bin. "When he's not threatening to shoot us."

"They wouldn't disarm themselves, Catrin!" the man protested.

"You never told us who you are!" Diehl snapped back. He turned again to the lady and softened his tone. "Now what kind of detective agency operatives would we be if we tossed down our guns for every man in the shadows making demands? We wouldn't be alive to extend our services to you today, would we?"

The woman just stared at him in suspicious silence.

"I think it's them, Catrin," the old man said. There was a lilt to his words not unlike an Irish accent, and he gave a quick roll to the "r" in "Catrin." He scratched unhappily at his thick gray mutton-chops. "Only I assumed there would be more."

"'Brave hearts bend not so soon to care,'" said Diehl.

"Oh, god," Hoop muttered. "Here we go."

"'Firm minds uplift the load of fate,'" Diehl went on. "'They bear what others shrink to bear...and boldly any war await.'"

The old man popped his eyes at him.

"What's that now?" he said.

"'Brave Hearts,' Charles Swain, 1857," said Diehl. He turned his attention back to the lady. "There aren't many of us, but I assure you we're the best money can buy."

The woman smiled almost imperceptibly. "All right, I'm convinced. That you are who you say are, anyway. As for the rest...I suppose we'll see." She turned to the man with the rifle. "Richard, show them where they can take care of their horses and tidy themselves, then bring the gentleman to my house. We'll get acquainted in the parlor."

She gave Diehl a parting nod, then left.

The old man lingered, glowering at Diehl skeptically, before scurrying after her.

"All right," Richard said sullenly. He finally stepped out into the open, revealing himself to be a handsome if doughy man in the dark trousers and white, gartered sleeves of an office worker. He jabbed the end of his rifle at the corrals nearby. "Over there."

Diehl dismounted and led his horse toward the corrals. The others did the same, though it took some tugging for Romo and his horse to get the mule moving again.

"I remember that poem you quoted. 'Brave Hearts,'" Hoop said to Diehl. "You changed the words."

"Just one," Diehl said. "Didn't seem like good salesmanship."

He recited the passage again.

"'Brave hearts bend not so soon to care, firm minds uplift the load of fate. They bear what others shrink to bear, and boldly any *doom* await.'"

Richard, it turned out, was the mine manager. Full name, Mr. Richard Utley. Diehl got him to introduce himself as they watered their horses and "tidied themselves" by wiping the trail dust from their faces.

"Mine manager, huh?" Diehl said. He flapped his handkerchief up at the tall—and empty—trestles looming above them. "Doesn't seem to be much to manage at the moment."

"I'll let Miss Gruffud explain that," Utley said stiffly.

Diehl gave his forehead one last pat, then slapped his hat back on and stuffed his kerchief away. "I must say, Mr. Utley, you don't seem very happy to see us."

Utley glared at Eskaminzim as the Apache plunged his head into the same trough the horses had been guzzling from.

"Why should I be?" Utley said. "When I first saw you, I thought Claypole had finally sent some of his hired guns to kill us. Now that I know you four are *our* hired guns...the only ones we've got..."

Eskaminzim's head was still underwater. He started blowing bubbles.

Utley looked on with obvious disgust.

"Your arrival strikes me as cold comfort, Mr. Diehl," he said.

The bubbles stopped, and Eskaminzim went limp.

"Is he all right?" Romo asked Hoop.

Hoop looked philosophical. "Depends on what you mean by 'all right.'"

Diehl was ignoring them.

"I won't argue with the logic of that, Mr. Utley. It's best not to get comfortable when men like us are needed," he said. "So this Claypole…he's the one trying to horn in here?"

Utley was watching Eskaminzim with alarm now. The Apache was still slumped face-first in the trough, not moving at all.

"I'll let Miss Gruffud explain that too," Utley managed to whisper.

Eskaminzim finally jerked his head up and gave his sopping hair a shake that sent water spraying over the other men. A horrified Utley jumped back like he'd been splashed with blood.

"I miss anything?" Eskaminzim said.

"Nope," Hoop told him.

Eskaminzim stuck his face back in the water.

"Miss Gruffud's house is that way," said Utley, jerking his head to the left. "I'll meet you outside."

He turned and marched quickly away.

Diehl walked over and tapped Eskaminzim on the shoulder.

Eskaminzim held up a finger, blew some more bubbles, then lifted his face.

"When you're done drowning yourself, keep an eye on the road," Diehl said. "The rest of us are going to meet with the lady."

"I'm not invited to the tea party?" Eskaminzim asked.

Diehl shrugged. "Someone's got to watch our backsides." He nodded at Romo. "Maybe you'd like me to ask Alfonso to do it instead?"

Eskaminzim hopped up and went to fetch his Winchester.

"Nah," he said. "I hate tea anyway."

CHAPTER 6

The Gruffud house was a gable-pocked Gothic jutting up beside an identically incongruous home on the edge of the plateau, as far as possible from the mine entrance and mill. It was clear which home was Miss Gruffud's because Utley was waiting by the front steps as they walked up. The other house—Cadwaladr's, presumably—flew the stars and stripes from a pole atop the widow walk.

"Miss Gruffud asked to speak with *you*, Diehl," Utley said. He flapped a hand at Hoop and Romo without looking at them. "Surely we don't need every member of your little gang at this meeting."

"You're absolutely right, Utley. We don't," Diehl said without stopping. "As I'm sure you've noticed, I left my associate Eskaminzim on guard duty."

And he breezed past Utley and started up the steps to the veranda. Hoop and Romo went with him.

Utley spun and leaped up the steps to get in front of them before they reached the front door. He cleared his throat, straightened his jacket and tie—put on since leaving the others at the corral—and knocked. It was a soft knock. One that spoke loudly of deference.

The sound of quick, light footsteps grew steadily louder, and the front door swung open to reveal a tall, gangly, fortyish woman dressed in the black-and-white of a maid. Her dark hair was pulled back so tight it seemed to stretch the skin of her pinched face across her skull like drying leather.

"Good afternoon, Juana," Utley said. "I've brought these... gentlemen to see Miss Gruffud and Mr. Cadwaladr."

It came out sounding like a request rather than a report, as if Utley half-expected the maid to slam the door in his face or tell him to use the servants' entrance.

Instead she stepped back.

"You may come in," she said.

The men headed inside.

"Gracias," Romo said to the maid.

Juana gave him an icy stare, then turned her attention back to Utley. "This way."

She led them across the shadowy foyer, passing a brown-bannistered staircase and a portrait of a burly, steely-eyed man standing beside a tripod-mounted sextant. Next to the picture was a dark oak door, and the maid went through to a parlor room aglow with bright sunlight. Miss Gruffud and Mr. Cadwaladr were waiting for them there, the lady standing at one of the windows, the old man slumped in a plush armchair.

"The guests you've been expecting," Juana said.

Only they weren't expected. Not Hoop and Romo, anyway. Cadwaladr sat up straight and stared at them baldly as they walked in, and Miss Gruffud froze for a moment, haloed by the sun outside. But the lady, at least, recovered quickly.

"Welcome, gentlemen," she said smoothly. "I wish I could offer you something refreshing to drink—lemonade or agua fresca—but all we have at the moment is water."

"Because of that little blockade down the road?" Diehl asked.

Cadwaladr gave the arm of his chair an angry thump. "That's right! We haven't been able to get up and down the road in six days. The mine's been idle. Nothing but a hole in the ground doing no good to anyone!"

The man's accent grew stronger as he went on, the words becoming ever more trilled and guttural. By the time he was done, it barely sounded like he was speaking English.

"Clearing the road will be our first priority," Diehl said. "Those men...they work for your competitor, I assume? Consolidated American?"

"They deny it, but of course they do," Utley spluttered, face reddening. "Filth, that's what they are. Hired thugs!"

"Richard," Miss Gruffud said, her tone half indulgent, half impatient, as if she'd heard the same little tirade too many times.

Utley took a deep breath.

"Sorry," he grumbled. "But it is an outrage."

Miss Gruffud turned to her maid, who was still standing stiffly beside the door.

"That will be all for now. Thank you, Juana."

The woman nodded once silently and went gliding from the room. Once the door was shut behind her, Miss Gruffud focused on Diehl again.

"The ruffians on the road claim to be concerned citizens trying to keep out unwanted elements. Labor organizers and foreigners and the like," she explained. "But yes, we assume they're being paid by Henry Claypole. He used to run a Consolidated American mine near Tucson. The Python. Which, strictly speaking, was never competition for us, except for labor. They mined silver, we mine copper. Aside from the occasional threat to us not to recognize unions or hire non-whites—that last threat we've ignored, by the way—Claypole left us alone. Then the bottom dropped out of silver and Consolidated shut down the Python and decided to switch to copper. Quickly. And by any means required."

"They've been harassing our workers, as well," Utley added. "Not just on the road, but in town. All they have to do is *start* for the mine, and they're threatened, beaten, even shot at. One of my millmen is laid up with broken ribs. A mucker had his teeth knocked out. It's got to stop!"

Diehl nodded silently, looking at the man in a way that suggested he'd adjusted his assessment of him. Utley actually seemed to care about his men—which was more than could be said of many mine managers.

"The message is clear," Miss Gruffud said, looking pained. She cared too. "We won't be allowed to operate, so we may as well sell out."

"Well, then...we need to send a message of our own," Diehl said.

Cadwaladr cocked his head skeptically. "With only four men?"

Diehl grinned smugly and opened his mouth to answer.

"We can make ourselves heard," Hoop cut in. He glowered at Diehl in a way that seemed to say *no more poetry!*

Miss Gruffud noted the look with a quizzical smile. "And how do you propose to do that, Mr....you must pardon me. We seem to have bypassed proper introductions in favor of business. My name is Catrin Gruffud. My father was Noah Gruffud." She gestured toward Cadwaladr. "Mr. Cadwaladr's partner in this mine. And you gentlemen are?"

Diehl gave the lady a shallow bow. "Oswin Diehl, ma'am. And this is Ira Hoop and Alfonso Romo. Our colleague Eskaminzim is keeping watch for more visitors."

Miss Gruffud acknowledged the introductions with a nod. "And how long have you worked for the A.A. Western Detective Agency?"

"Not long, but only because the agency is a new endeavor for an old comrade. Col. Crowe," Diehl said. "Sergeant Hoop and Eskaminzim and I have worked under him in one capacity or another for...my goodness, Sergeant. It's coming up on twenty years, isn't it?"

"My goodness," Hoop said, deadpan.

Utley gave him a dubious look. "'Sergeant ' Hoop?"

Diehl glared at him, obviously dialing his estimate of the man back down.

"Tenth Cavalry, Utley," he said. He looked at the lady, and his expression turned pleasant again. "After leaving the service, Col. Crowe employed us as operatives of the Southern Pacific Railroad Police. When he retired from the S.P., we went our separate ways.

So you can imagine our excitement when the opportunity arose to work together again."

Hoop regarded Diehl with a heavy-lidded, stony-faced gaze of the *you are so full of shit* variety.

Diehl pretended not to notice.

"And why are *you* here?" Cadwaladr asked Romo.

"Oh. Um. You see. W-well," Romo stammered.

He didn't seem to know why he was there either.

"Mr. Romo is our mining and demolitions expert," Diehl said. "We thought it best to bring him along in case the Consolidated people attempt any sabotage."

"Your mining and demolitions expert?" Utley scoffed. "I've got boots older than him."

Romo stiffened. "I have a degree in engineering from Cornell University and experience working for Compañía Minera de Peñoles in Sonora, Mr. Utley. And if you care to discuss why you still seem to be using stamp milling rather than tube mills and cyanide, I would be happy to accommodate you. You might find the conversation illuminating."

Cadwaladr bursting out laughing. "The lad got you there, Richard! If you're not careful, he'll end up with your job!"

Utley gave Miss Gruffud a sheepish glance and generally looked like he wanted to crawl under the carpet. "We'll convert to cyanide milling when we can afford it," Utley grumbled.

"Well…now that we're all acquainted, we should get to work," Diehl said. "Just three quick questions first. Speaking of what you can afford, how much cash would be available to us to cover expenses?"

Cadwaladr's grin instantly evaporated. "We're already sent your Col. Crowe a considerable retainer. What sort of 'expenses' would we be expected to pay now?"

Diehl shrugged. "That depends on what's required. Some options are costly. Some require less money…and more risk."

"We can make eight hundred dollars available to you to use as you see fit," Miss Gruffud announced.

"Catrin—eight hundred?" Cadwaladr protested. "When you've told me we don't have a dime for other expenses?"

"That's all the cash we still have on hand!" said Utley.

Miss Gruffud didn't look away from Diehl.

"I'll need half of it now," he said. "In small bills."

Cadwaladr harrumphed. The lady nodded.

"Mr. Utley can accommodate you when we're done here," she said.

"Excellent. Thank you," said Diehl. "My second question relates to the first. You have an attorney in town?"

"Of course," Miss Gruffud said.

"Then we'll expect ad hoc access to his services, billable to the mine," Diehl said.

For some reason that got a small smile from Miss Gruffud.

"That is acceptable," she said.

"*Catrin!*" Cadwaladr howled. "Who knows how much that could be?"

The lady spoke over him.

"And your third question?" she asked Diehl.

"Relates to the second," he said. "How would you assess law enforcement around here—good, bad, or indifferent?"

Miss Gruffud wrinkled her nose as if the very topic fouled the air. "The county sheriff is bad. Very bad. Consolidated American property, bought and paid for. But he's also very far away. The constable down in town isn't exactly indifferent. He's simply ineffectual."

"A coward is what he is," Cadwaladr declared, giving the arm of his chair another thump. "As long as those brutes harass us outside city limits, he insists on staying out of it."

Diehl and Hoop exchanged a look.

"That's worked out well for Claypole up to now," Diehl said.

"But from here it works well for us," Hoop finished for him.

Utley scowled at them. "What are you talking about?"

"Operational autonomy, Utley," Diehl said. "I suggest you don't ask to know more than that." He looked at Cadwaladr, then Miss

Gruffud. "That's my advice to all of you, actually. And now we'll get to it…unless there's more you think *we* should know first?"

Miss Gruffud shook her head. "No. You seem more than ready. I must tell you, I'm encouraged by your zeal, Mr. Diehl. 'Brave Hearts' indeed. I can only hope your results are as impressive as your oratory."

"You'll soon see, ma'am."

Diehl and the lady looked into each other's eyes.

Hoop seemed on the verge of rolling his.

"Open the road to town, man! Get the miners back to work!" Cadwaladr demanded, oblivious.

Utley just glared.

"Good day then, Miss Gruffud. Next time we'll have lemonade," Diehl said. "If you could bring that money out to the corral, Utley?"

With that, he turned and headed for the door. Hoop and Romo followed after each gave the lady a parting "ma'am."

Juana was hovering by the portrait in the foyer. She escorted the men to the front door as if worried they'd detour to the kitchen and help themselves to the silverware.

"I didn't know you were a Cornell man, Alfonso," Diehl said.

"My parents wanted me to go to university in the United States," Romo said. "Work on my English. Make connections."

Diehl chuckled. "And now here you are…"

They stepped outside, and Juana closed the door firmly behind them.

Diehl put on his hat and started down the steps from the veranda.

"You're too good for us, Alfonso," he said.

Hoop put his hat back on as well.

"We're all too good for us," he said.

Romo blinked at Hoop, confused, but didn't ask what he meant. He had the feeling he was about to learn for himself anyway.

CHAPTER 7

The nine sour, seedy men blocking the road to the Gruffud-Cadwaladr Mine scratched their stubble and kicked at rocks and eyed each other unhappily until one of them finally put their unease into words.

"You think those fellas we let past are really spies?" said a thin, red-haired man they called Rusty.

"Sure, they are," said pot-bellied Bill. He was the closest thing they had to a leader, being the biggest and loudest man there.

He didn't offer any further counterargument than that "Sure, they are" and he farted to indicate that the debate was over.

"Where'd they come from, then?" asked a man called Bull who was just big and loud enough to challenge Bill for control of the group. "I ain't never seen 'em around."

"Well, of course, you haven't," said Bill. "Claypole must've had 'em brought in from somewhere else. What good are spies if everybody knows 'em?"

"Yeah, but how come *we* don't know 'em?" Bull persisted. "We work for Claypole too. By way of Schuck, anyway."

Schuck had been "chief of security" at the Python, the mine Claypole managed. Which meant he was in charge of running off union men and Mexicans and ensuring that other troublemakers and screwups met with unfortunate mishaps. He was also in charge of recruiting barroom goons to rough up miners.

"Because sending in spies ain't something you tell every loud-mouth about," said Bill. "You gotta be subtle."

He pronounced it "sub-tile."

"Dumb-ass," he added, sneering at Bull.

"You gotta be what now?" said Rusty.

"Who's a dumb-ass?" said Bull.

"You're a dumb-ass," said Bill.

"I don't think it's pronounced that way, Bill," said Rusty.

Bill ignored him. Bull was stepping up so close to him the two were practically bumping bellies.

"*You're* a dumb-ass," said Bull.

"Nobody calls me a dumb-ass," said Bill.

"Nobody calls *me* a dumb-ass," said Bull.

"I just did," said Bill.

"Well, *I* just did," said Bull.

"I think we're losing sight of the real question here, boys," said a man called Goat. He was neither big nor loud but compensated with a well-practiced talent for sidling up to more powerful men. "Why don't I run down to town and just *ask* Mr. Claypole if he sent up spies? I bet he'd appreciate our checking."

"Good idea," said Bull, still staring straight ahead at Bill.

"Horseshit idea," said Bill, glaring back at Bull. "Claypole don't want any 'checking' from the likes of us. He don't want anything to do with us at all."

Goat stroked the long, salt-and-pepper chin whiskers that had given him his name. "You know, you might just be right there, Bill. He's too sub-tile for that."

"I really don't think that's how you say it," said Rusty.

"I'll go ask Schuck instead," Goat went on.

"No need," said a man they called Whisper.

No one heard him.

"No. Don't go running to Schuck either," Bill told Goat.

"Here they come now," said Whisper, pointing.

"You just don't want Schuck and Claypole knowing what a fool you are," Bull said to Bill.

"What a fool *I* am?" sputtered Bill.

"Well, I'll be," said Rusty, looking up the road and pointing just as Whisper had done. "Here they come now."

The rest of the men spun around to face the same direction.

Whisper sighed.

Three of the strangers—the white one, the black one, and the little Mexican who dressed like a bank teller—were riding slowly down the road from the G-C Mine.

"Spread out," Bill commanded.

"Yeah, spread out," said Bull.

The men spread out.

Bill raised his arm, signaling the strangers to stop. They rode closer, then spread out too, so that two lines faced each other on the road—three men on horseback, nine men on foot.

"Where's your Indian?" Bill asked.

"Occupied elsewhere," the White man said. He looked amused in a way that had no warmth to it—as if the joke, whatever it might be, was for him and him alone.

"Don't make any sense for 'spies' to go up to the G-C and come back down without their own mule," said Bull.

The black man looked over at the white one.

"Someone's payin' attention," he said.

The White one smiled. His eyes though, remained cold.

"Indeed," he said. "Makes me feel all the more confident we're doing the right thing."

The Black one didn't look confident at all. Not that he looked nervous. He didn't. He just looked skeptical.

He grunted, then moved his gaze back to the men lined up before him. His head—his whole body—stayed still after that. But his eyes never stopped moving steadily up and down the row, lingering only when one of the men fidgeted or shifted his hands.

"And what is this 'right thing' you're doing?" asked Bill.

"Scouting for talent," the White man said.

Bill and Bull both scowled.

"What's that supposed to mean?" said Bill.

"You don't work for Claypole at all, do you?" said Bull.

The White man's smile grew a little broader and a little colder. He answered Bull first.

"No. We don't. That was a lie."

The admission was so blunt—and so easily obtained—it caught Bull and Bill and the rest by surprise. None of them reacted even as the man admitted to even more.

"We work for the G-C," he said. "And I think you should too."

Bill managed to speak on behalf of the group a split second before Bull could.

"Wait," he said. "What?"

"That's the 'right thing' you asked about," the man told him. "Making you a job offer. You've been standing here guarding the road, and clearly you've been doing it pretty well. So I think you should stick to it. Only instead of keeping the road free of mine workers, I propose that you keep it free *for* mine workers. It'll actually be easier—and it'll pay better too. Just tell us your names, and Alfonso here'll put you on the payroll."

The young Mexican was ready for the signal. Moving with painstaking slowness, his eyes on the men in the road, he dipped his right hand into his coat pocket and pulled out a notepad and pencil.

"Who wants to go first?" he said.

He brought up his notepad and licked the tip of his pencil.

"What are you? Crazy?" Bull said to Diehl.

"Oh. You're right. How silly of me," Diehl replied. "We haven't discussed terms. What's Claypole paying you?"

"His man Schuck's been giving us a dollar a day," said Rusty.

"Shut up, Rusty," Bill growled at him. He turned to face Diehl again. "No one's paying us to be here, mister. Like I told you on your way up—we're a volunteer committee keeping out dangerous elements as a public service."

"I understand. Concerned citizens acting for the common good." Diehl put his left hand to his chest. "It warms the heart. And here's where your civic-mindedness pays off. Perhaps this Mr. Schuck has been making contributions to show his support for your committee and its fine work? A dollar a day per man, more or less? Well, I want to be a pillar of the community too."

He slipped his hand inside his sheepskin coat. When it came sliding back out again, it was holding a stack of cash.

"I'm ready to donate *three* dollars a day per man," he said. "First week payable in advance."

"Sixteen dollars apiece for each of us?" Bull asked. "Right now?"

Diehl blinked at him, then smiled. "Twenty-one dollars apiece, friend. The G-C will need you here every day, you see. To keep its workers safe from dangerous elements. Shall Alfonso sign you up? It's not a payroll now, of course. It's...a list of volunteers being compensated for their time by members of a grateful public."

"Huh?" said Bull.

Diehl shrugged. "Or we can just go back to calling it a payroll. The bottom line is...who wants some money?"

"I'm in," said Whisper.

"I'm in," said Rusty.

"Full name, please," Alfonso said to Rusty.

Whisper cursed, but no one heard that either.

"Hold it," Bill snapped. He cocked his head and planted his fists on his hips—the right hand just inches above his gun. "What's to keep us from taking that whole wad and leaving your bloody carcasses out here for the coyotes?"

Alfonso froze over his notepad. Diehl froze too, a breeze rippling across the bills he was holding up.

Of the three men on horseback, only the Black one now had both hands free.

"Another excellent question," Diehl said. "Sergeant Hoop...at your discretion."

The Black man remained utterly still. His eyes though, slid across Bill and Bull and the rest one more time. Then he spoke again, loudly—but not in any language the men in the road understood.

There was a gunshot, and Rusty's big, round-domed Boss of the Plains went whipping off his head.

Rusty and the men around him cringed and cried out and started to scatter or reach for their guns.

"Don't move!" Diehl barked.

The cash was still in his left hand. His Colt was now in his right.

Hoop had drawn his gun too.

The men in the road stopped. Some of them started to put up their hands.

"Oh, don't bother with that. No cause for alarm," Diehl told them mildly, smiling again. He jabbed his gun at Bill. "We were just answering the man's question."

"No cause for alarm?" Rusty whimpered, putting a shaking hand to his uncovered head.

"Sorry about that," Hoop said. "Safest to choose a big target. I decided on the biggest hat…this time."

He looked down at Bill's bulging gut, then stared hard into the man's eyes.

Bill's gaze darted along the horizon to the left, then the right. There was no sign of the man who'd fired at them. Just rocks and scrub and sky.

"Back to the business at hand," said Diehl, giving his stack of bills a little waggle. "Who's ready to get paid?"

———

They were *all* ready by then. Bill, Bull, Rusty, Whisper, Goat, and the rest—each gave Romo his full name and pocketed his twenty-one dollars. They answered Diehl's questions too.

What did Schuck look like? Where could he be found? What was Claypole like? Where did the G-C's miners live? And did they have a leader?

"Thanks, men," Diehl said when they were done. "We'll be back before nightfall. In the meantime, you keep guarding the road."

Rusty pushed back his perforated hat—retrieved from the sage it had landed in—and scratched his red hair.

"I don't mean to ask a stupid question," he said, "but could you remind me who we're guarding the road *from*?"

"Anyone who'd interfere with travel to or from the Gruffud-Cadwaladr Mine," Diehl said.

"Oh." Rusty scratched his head again. "So...like...*us*."

Diehl nodded approvingly. "Exactly. Keep the road safe from yourselves. Or anyone like you."

"Leave it to us," said Bull.

Diehl gave him a salute, then steered his horse through the men and trotted off down the hill. Hoop and Romo went with him, the latter looking nervously over his shoulder every few seconds.

"Don't worry," said Hoop. "They won't shoot us in the back with Eskaminzim out there with my Sharps on 'em."

Romo glanced back again. "Yes, well...maybe not now. But what about later? The first time they realize Eskaminzim *isn't* watching them? Those men can't be trusted. If they turned once, they might do it again."

"Oh, some of them will. Maybe most. Maybe all," said Diehl. "But what matters is that Schuck and Claypole will have to shell out even more money to buy back each one they can get. This isn't a war, Alfonso. It's business. For everybody. So what we're going to do is make this particular acquisition prohibitively expensive for the Consolidated American Mining Corporation. Surely a Cornell man can understand that."

"I understand," said Romo. And he looked back yet again. "It doesn't change the fact that those men are scum...and now they're making more than me."

Hoop snorted out a bitter chuckle. "Yeah, they're scum, all right. Selling their loyalty to the highest bidder. What kind of a man does that?"

He glanced down at the gun on Romo's hip, then looked him in the eye again.

Diehl sat up straight in his saddle and began reciting with full-throated grandiloquence.

"'Take the world as it is! There are good and bad in it...and good and bad will be from now to the end. And they, who expect to make saints in a minute, are in danger of marring more hearts than they'll mend.'"

He slumped down again, a thin smile on his face.

"'Take the World as It Is.' Swain. 1860."

"Well, don't look at me," said Hoop. "I take the world as it is, and I don't believe in saints."

"I do," Romo said quietly.

Diehl looked over at him, his smile growing a little brighter.

"I do too, Alfonso. They're out there," he said. "There just aren't any here."

He turned away to face the road. The town of Hope Springs—a jumble of sun-bleached wood and adobe with a stream running along its eastern side—stretched out before them at the bottom of the hill. Somewhere amid its false-front businesses and ramshackle dives were Consolidated American's Claypole and Schuck and the dozen other men whose guns they'd hired.

Diehl, Hoop, and Romo kept riding toward them in silence.

CHAPTER 8

About a half mile from town, the three men swung east, putting themselves on the other side of a strip of mesquite trees that ran along the shallow, rocky creek there. After that they headed south, passing the eastern outskirts of Hope Springs from cover. When they turned west again, recrossing the brook, a gaggle of children playing in the water spotted them. The kids—some brown-skinned, some white—went sprinting off toward a cluster of small, simple houses that covered a meadow and hill nearby.

"Pa! Pa!" shouted one little girl as Diehl, Hoop, and Romo rode slowly across the stream.

"Papá!" cried another.

A man emerged from one of the nearest homes, then ducked inside again only to return a moment later with an axe. Another stepped from a different shack holding a rusty hog-leg. A woman peeped fearfully around him.

"You kids get inside!" she said.

Most of the children scattered like a brood of frightened chickens, but a few of the more curious ones lingered to stare at the strangers.

"You should mind the lady," Hoop told one of them—a barefoot boy who looked to be five or six.

The boy raced off.

"Who the hell are you?" said the man with the axe. He was holding it in both hands, ready to start chopping.

Diehl, Hoop, and Romo reined up. More men and women were emerging from the little houses before them. Some looked frightened, some angry.

"We're operatives of the A.A. Western Detective Agency out of Ogden, Utah and we're here to help," Diehl said. "We've been hired by Miss Gruffud and Mr. Cadwaladr to protect their mine."

Diehl looked around at his audience. He was being watched by about two dozen men and women now, and more were approaching

"And their mine workers," he said.

There were murmurs all around.

"Finally," one woman said.

Another scoffed in disbelief.

"Is Jory Skewes here?" Diehl asked. "We'd like to talk to him in private."

"Why?" snapped the man with the pistol. Its long, mottled barrel was pointed at the ground, and it looked as likely to explode as fire. But Diehl didn't want to put it to the test.

"Because we were told Skewes speaks for the miners," he said. He nodded at the man's gun. "And I assume the other side has those too. Ones that'll do their work at a distance."

"We're pretty sure Claypole and Schuck's men ain't around at the moment," Hoop added, scanning the trees and hills. "All the same—no need to keep offering easy targets."

There were more murmurs, and a few of the men and women shrank back into their doorways.

"They're right," said a squat, barrel-chested man with a bruised and blood-crusted face. He waved the men on horseback forward. "Come with me. I'm Skewes."

The man turned and led them toward another little house, no bigger or fancier than the rest, a short distance off. A plump woman in a gingham dress watched from the porch as they approached. She had the features and light-brown complexion of a Louisiana Creole. She also had the scowl of a woman not to trifle with.

"Did I hear right?" she asked Skewes. "They work for the G-C?"

"That's what they say," Skewes said.

The woman glared at the three newcomers.

"Well, if they're lying, I've got a butcher knife right where I can get at it," she said.

Skewes glanced back over his shoulder.

"The wife," he explained.

"I figured," said Diehl.

"Ma'am," said Hoop, tugging at the brim of his hat.

Mrs. Skewes just grunted and went inside. Her husband followed her.

Diehl, Hoop, and Romo swung down off their horses and tied them to the rickety fence around the Skewes's house. When they went in, they found Skewes waiting for them at the dining table while his wife put a coffeepot on the stove.

She hadn't been lying about the knife. It was on a table beside the coffee grinder.

"Leave the door open," Mrs. Skewes told Romo, who was coming in last.

"Yes, ma'am," he said.

The miner with the axe was out by the fence, watching. The man with the rusty gun joined him, as did another with what looked like a baseball bat.

Skewes gestured at the empty chairs around the table. "Gentlemen."

Diehl looked around the room—noting its bright new wallpaper and well-swept floorboards and simple but sturdy furnishings—as he and Hoop and Romo sat.

"Nice place," he said.

"It's small, but Lisette's made the most of it," Skewes said. "We thought we'd be here a long time."

"You still can be," said Hoop. "You just need to go back to work."

Skewes opened his mouth to answer.

His wife stomped over to the table before he could get the first word out.

"You see what happened the last time he tried to go back to work?" she said, pointing at her husband's battered face. "Show them your mouth, Jory."

Skewes grimaced. "They don't need to see that."

"Show them your mouth, Jory."

Skewes sighed, then opened his mouth wide. He turned his head and pointed to scabbed toothless gums on the left side.

"Schuck himself did that," Mrs. Skewes said. "Had his thugs hold him while he knocked out half his teeth. The dirty son of a bitch."

Skewes looked pained. "Lisette…"

"Said next time he'd take his *eyes*," Mrs. Skewes went on. "What kind of man says something like that?"

"One who wants to scare you," Diehl said. "And he's succeeded."

"Damn right, we're scared!" Mrs. Skewes snapped back. "We'd be crazy not to be! Do you want coffee!"

She was so worked up she'd shouted her question.

She took a breath and cleared her throat.

"I mean," she said demurely, "would you gentlemen care for a cup of coffee?"

"Thank you, ma'am, but no. I don't think we're going to be here long," said Diehl.

Hoop looked at the men watching the conversation from outside. "Your friends seem ready for a fight, Skewes. If *all* the miners were—"

"But they're not," Skewes cut in. "Not ready to fight the way Schuck and his men would. Mean. With guns."

"That's why we're here," Diehl said smoothly. "Now you've got your own mean men with guns to back you up."

"How many?" Skewes shot back. "All I see is you three. Who else did that detective agency of yours send here to help us?"

Diehl fidgeted in his seat.

"There's one more of us up in the hills," he said.

"So the answer is *four*?" Mrs. Skewes scoffed.

"It's a matter of quality, not quantity," said Diehl.

Mrs. Skewes jerked a thumb at Romo. "Oh, yeah? When this one looks like he should be behind a counter taking pennies for peppermint sticks? No offense."

"None taken," Romo said, though it looked like he was lying.

"We've started recruiting more men. Evening the odds," Diehl said. "But we can't beat Consolidated American if the miners aren't with us."

Mrs. Skewes took an angry step toward the table. Romo and Skewes flinched. Diehl and Hoop didn't.

"So that's why you've come here?" the woman snapped at Diehl. "To convince my husband he should get himself killed for old Cadwaladr and Miss Priss up there on the hill?"

"No, ma'am," Diehl replied calmly. He looked across the table at Skewes. "To see if your husband would fight for his livelihood."

Mrs. Skewes pointed at her husband's face again. "He *did* fight! And look what it got him!"

"*Lisette*," Skewes said. "That's enough."

His wife spun around and stomped back to the stove muttering something indecipherable but, from the sound of it, not particularly ladylike.

"Look...I understand," Diehl said. "You don't know if you can trust us. And you *do* know what to expect from Schuck." He looked over at Hoop. "We need to address both those problems. Today."

Hoop gave him a single silent nod.

Diehl turned back to Skewes. "We've been told Schuck's spending his time at a cantina. El Leon Rojo."

"That's right," Skewes said. "It's on the south side, right on the edge of town, so he can keep an eye on who's coming and going."

"And get outside town limits quick when he's got dirty work to do," Mrs. Skewes added bitterly.

"And he's got about a dozen men with him?" Diehl asked. "Local riffraff? Not anyone he brought in from out of town?"

Skewes cocked his head in confusion but nodded. "Who told you all this?"

"More riffraff," said Romo.

"First things first," Diehl said. He threw a quick warning glare at Romo before continuing. "Be outside El Leon Rojo in twenty minutes, Mr. Skewes. I want you to see something."

Skewes looked skeptical.

Mrs. Skewes looked like she was thinking of reaching for her butcher knife.

Diehl jerked his head at the three men outside. "Bring your friends. I want them to see it too."

He stood, gave Mrs. Skewes a parting "ma'am," and walked out. Hoop and Romo followed him. The men standing guard by their horses stepped back as they approached. They didn't step back far though. They stood nearby, one cradling his axe, the other his gun, the other his baseball bat, as Diehl, Hoop, and Romo untied their horses and swung up onto their saddles.

Miners and their wives and children watched them silently, suspiciously as they slowly loped off through the other houses.

"Think they'll fight?" Diehl asked Hoop when the little community was behind them and a livery on the outskirts of Hope Springs just ahead.

Hoop shrugged. "Depends on what happens next."

"What *does* happen next?" Romo asked.

Diehl heaved a sigh. "The part of the job I hate."

"Too bad Eskaminzim's not here," said Hoop. "This is the part of the job he loves."

When Romo heard that, he blurted out a sound before he could stop himself.

"Uh oh."

CHAPTER 9

Diehl stopped walking where the sidewalk ended. Hoop stopped on his left, Romo on his right.

Their horses were tied to a post in front of a printer's shop five doors down, where the respectable businesses started. Beyond that, heading south toward the edge of town, was a seedy saloon, an even seedier saloon, an alley lined with ramshackle cribhouses, and yet another seedy saloon. Last of all, set off a little from the others, sat a saloon so seedy it could have been mistaken for an abandoned barn if not for the words painted over the doorway—there was no door —in haphazard whitewash.

El Leon Rojo.

"I wonder," Diehl said to Hoop, "if there's any way *you* could be the one to…"

Hoop started shaking his head.

"But, Hoop," said Diehl, "you know you're better at…"

Hoop kept shaking his head.

"I mean," said Diehl, "we can't be sure that I'd even manage to…"

Hoop went on shaking his head.

"Shit," Diehl said.

Hoop started nodding.

"But why does Mr. Diehl have to do it?" Romo asked.

"Because it would probably get a Black man hung," Diehl said.

Hoop kept nodding.

"But it might get *you* killed right now," Romo said to Diehl.

"That's a chance I'm willing to take," said Hoop.

This time Diehl did the nodding.

They started toward El Leon Rojo again. The smell of the place, raw alcohol and sour beer and sweat and tobacco and urine, hit them when they were still well beyond the doorway. But it didn't keep them from going inside.

On the left was a "bar" consisting of planks atop busted barrels. On the right were more barrels, what passed for tables in the place, scattered amid a hodgepodge of chairs and stools that looked like they'd been salvaged from the local dump. There were a few posters and prints tacked to the unpainted wooden walls, but they were so faded and the light so dim it was impossible to say what they'd once depicted. The floor was sawdust strewn over dirt.

The customers were as promising as the decor. Despite the name of the place and the fact that the mousy, mustachioed barman looked Mexican, they were almost all white. With one exception, they were also all slovenly and scruffy. Most sported battered Stetsons, a couple aggressively tilted bowlers. Their clothes were a mix of shabby work duds fit for a derelict cowhand and—beneath the bowlers—scuffed, ill-tailored suits. They all wore guns and expressions of casual, bored contempt.

The one man who stood out, sat in a place of honor—at the only actual table, placed directly in front of the doorway to give him an unobstructed view of the road out of town. Unlike the others, he was dressed neatly, in a black suit with a paisley vest and matching purple necktie. He also wore a brown leather gun belt that clashed with the rest but looked glossy-bright and well saddle-soaped. His broad, flat face was cleanly shaven, his expression alert. On the table before him, just to the left of the huge, raw-knuckled hands that bulged beyond his starched cuffs, was a kettle and a dainty teacup.

There could be no mistake. This was Schuck.

"A professional. Doesn't drink on the job," Diehl said to Hoop, voice low. "Admirable."

Hoop gave the copper kettle a significant look. "Useful too."

Diehl nodded. He glanced up at Schuck's face as he, Hoop, and Romo walked toward the bar. He looked away for a few steps, then glanced at the man again. Then he stopped and stared.

"By god, that's him!" he said.

Hoop and Romo stopped too.

The roughs around them perked up, some looking grim, some excited, some merely bleary eyed.

Schuck looked amused. Whatever he was about to be accused of —beating some friend or family member or arranging to have an agitator go into a mine and never come out—he not only wouldn't deny it, he was proud of it.

"That's the man who defiled my Helen," Diehl said.

Schuck's smug smile froze, then melted away. Now it was his men who looked amused.

"You sure?" Hoop asked Diehl.

"Sure I'm sure! How could I ever forget the son of a bitch who'd do that to her?"

The grins on the men around them widened. This was the perfect antidote for their boredom.

"You're mistaking me for someone else, mister," Schuck told Diehl. "I've never messed with any woman." He threw a halfhearted leer at his men along the bar. "Named Helen."

The men chuckled.

"That might be true—and you know why," Diehl snarled. "Helen's my mule."

The chuckling stopped. All movement stopped. Time seemed to stop.

Diehl scowled at Schuck with what looked like rage.

Schuck gaped at Diehl in utter confusion.

Schuck's men gawked at the two with a mixture of uncertainty and delight.

Hoop and Romo watched Schuck's men in tense, coiled silence.

None of it changed for a long moment. Then the little barman set everything in motion again.

"Oye. Psst," he whispered to Romo. "Dijo que 'Helen' es una mula?"

Did he say Helen is a mule?

"Sí," Romo said.

"Mierda," said the barman.

Crap.

"Want us to throw this asshole out?" one of the sweaty, doughy-faced men in cocked bowlers asked Schuck.

In the time it takes to blink, Hoop had his gun on the man and the others near him on the far side of the cantina.

Romo followed suit more slowly, but in time to cover the men lined up at the bar.

"This is between him…" Hoop said. He nodded first at Diehl, then at Schuck. "And the animal lover."

Diehl took a step toward Schuck's table.

"Helen's never been the same, you sick bastard," Diehl said.

He took another step toward Schuck. Then another.

Schuck clenched his fists—obviously regretting that they were resting on the table, by his teacup and kettle. Not at his side by his gun.

"Well?" Diehl said, stepping so close now he could've spat in Schuck's face. "Aren't you even going to say you're sorry?"

Schuck whipped his right hand off the table. But before he could get it underneath on his gun, Diehl lunged forward and shoved the table hard into his stomach. Schuck cried in pain and surprise as he was pushed back off balance and pinned to the rough wall behind him. He still managed to flail for his gun though.

Diehl grabbed the kettle by the handle and whipped the metal body once, twice, three times into Schuck's face. With the fourth blow he changed to a wide-arced smash that brought the now blood-covered kettle down squarely on the top of Schuck's head.

There was a *thunk*. Perhaps also a *crack*.

Schuck slumped forward, groaning, his arms falling slack at his sides.

"Jesus," one of his men said.

But Diehl wasn't done. He reached down, yanked Schuck's gun from its holster and dropped it to the sawdust. Then with his left hand he jerked Schuck up straight by his hair while with his right he flipped aside the table.

Schuck tried to say something, but his lips and nose were smashed, and all that came out were gurgles and bloody bubbles. He lifted his arms to swat feebly at Diehl.

Diehl pulled him forward by the hair and threw him to the floor. The big man landed face down, arms splayed out.

Diehl walked around to Schuck's right hand and lifted up a foot.

"Mules have…" he said.

He stomped on Schuck's hand. There was a crunching sound, and Schuck screamed.

Diehl ground his heel in for a moment before walking around to the man's left hand.

"Feelings too," he said.

He stamped on the other hand.

There was more crunching, more screaming.

Romo turned his head to watch in wide-eyed horror.

"*Kid*," Hoop snapped at him. "Eyes left."

Romo turned his attention back to the men at the bar. None of them had seized the opportunity to go for a gun though. They were as mesmerized by Diehl's viciousness as Romo had been.

Schuck stopped screaming. He remained face down though, whimpering and wheezing and bleeding into the dirt and sawdust.

"Let that be a lesson to you, Derringer," Diehl said. "If I ever catch you back in Idaho, you'll get worse."

"Derringer?" the man in the cocked bowler said.

"That's right. Sean Derringer," Diehl said. "He left Pocatello two years ago. After what he did to Helen."

One of the men at the bar shook his head. "You're wrong, mister. That there's Frank Schuck, and he's worked for the Python Mine over on the Gila River for four or five years now."

"What?" Diehl gasped. "Are you sure about that?"

The man at the bar nodded. So did a half dozen other men.

Diehl looked over at Hoop. "Oh, goodness."

"Oops," said Hoop.

Diehl kneeled next to Schuck.

"Golly, Frank," he said, "I can't tell you how sorry I am about this little misunderstanding."

A noise came out of Schuck that might have been "What?"

Diehl looked up, scanning the room for a few specific faces.

The barman. Two men in a dark corner in sombreros. A terrified-looking geezer hunched over a barrel.

The men in the cantina who *didn't* work for Schuck.

Diehl turned toward the doorway to look for more witnesses. And he found them.

Skewes and his three miner friends were there, gazing inside in utter wonderment.

Diehl looked down at Schuck again.

"But remember, Frank, I never threatened you," he said. "And you did go for your gun, didn't you? A fellow has a right to defend himself, even if he's accused a man of something he didn't do. I'm sure you understand."

He reached down and patted Schuck on the back.

Schuck yelped.

"Well," Diehl said, standing and turning to Hoop, "I guess we ought to go somewhere else for that drink. They've got a bit of a mess to clean up here, and we wouldn't want to get in the way."

He pulled out his money, peeled off a ten note, and slid it onto the plank before the barman.

"For your trouble," he said.

Then he walked out.

Hoop and Romo followed him slowly, moving backward, guns still drawn.

"I'd ask if you want to join us," Diehl said to Skewes as he stepped outside, "but I believe you have work to do too."

He spread out his arms toward the road—and the Gruffud-Cadwaladr Mine in the jagged, desolate hills it wound away into.

CHAPTER 10

The mine was alive with flickering lights and the clatter of machinery and men's voices as Diehl headed toward the two imposing homes perched on the lip of the plateau. Diehl knew the master of the house on the left wasn't there. Old Cadwaladr had hurried down to town the second he heard the road was safe. "Supplies!" he said.

"Poker," Skewes whispered. "Or faro or blackjack or whist…"

Diehl walked up to the house on the right and knocked on the front door.

There was a long moment of silence, then the sound of slow, light steps.

The door swung open, and Juana, Miss Gruffud's gaunt maid, glared out at Diehl.

"Yes?" she said.

Diehl lifted the brown paper sack in his left hand.

"I brought something for Miss Gruffud from the greengrocer in town," he said. "In case Mr. Cadwaladr doesn't have it on his shopping list."

Juana stared at the bag as if she were being offered a handful of dung. But eventually she took it in her bony fingers and peered inside. She saw six yellow lumps the size of a child's fist.

Lemons.

Juana looked up at Diehl again. Her expression didn't change. It still seemed like she was looking at dung.

"Is that all?" she said.

"That was all they had," said Diehl.

"I meant is that your only business here?"

"Oh. Yes, I suppose so. Except to offer my compliments to the lady along with the lemons."

Juana grunted. "Next time you can bring deliveries around to the back."

She closed the door firmly in his face. Diehl stared at it for a few seconds, chuckled—he was accustomed to being distrusted and disliked—then turned to go.

He was a dozen strides from the house when the door opened again.

Diehl swung around to find Juana glowering out at him.

"Miss Gruffud would like to invite you inside," she said. "For lemonade."

The look on her face had finally shifted a bit. Now it looked like she'd taken a bite out of one of the lemons.

Diehl gave her a smile.

"What a lovely notion," he said. "I do believe I'll take her up on that."

He walked back up the steps and headed inside. Juana managed not to slam the door behind him, but it was a near miss.

———

Romo looked back wistfully at the mine entrance and mill as he and Hoop started down the hill to relieve Eskaminzim…wherever he was. Diehl had sent the G-C Mine's newly hired "guards"—Bill and Bull and the rest—home for the day once the miners were safely past them. But Eskaminzim had remained somewhere out in the rocks to keep an eye on the road. Now night was falling, and it was time to give the Apache a break from picket duty.

It was clear though, where Romo wanted to be. With the miners, not the mercenaries.

Hoop followed his gaze.

"You can poke around the mine works tomorrow, if you want," Hoop said. "There should be some time when you're not needed to stand around with a gun."

Romo grinned, chagrinned to find himself so transparent. "Thanks. I'd like that…though I'm not sure Mr. Utley would."

"Tell him you're checking for sabotage. Official A.A. Detective Agency business. Hell…you probably actually *should* check for sabotage now that I think of it. It'd make sense for Schuck's boss, Claypole, to try to gum up the works now that the miners are on the job again."

"You think he'd try something more than that tonight? Something more…direct?"

"Like sending someone up to take potshots at us?" Hoop said with a shrug. It was hard to see the gesture, for he was draped in his huge, woolly buffalo coat. He had his beaver hat on again too. "Born and raised in Georgia," he'd explained to Romo as he put them on. "Never could get used to the chill of a desert night."

"We'll see," he told Romo now. "Diehl's banking on Schuck being in charge of what troops they've got on hand. Claypole might not even know the names of the men working for him. Could take him days to organize a response to that beatdown and the G-C reopening." Hoop shrugged again. "Could take him hours."

Romo took another look back. This time he was looking over his left shoulder, not his right toward the mine owners' homes. The last they'd seen of Diehl, he was headed that way with the lemons he'd bought in town.

"And in the meantime," Romo said, "Mr. Diehl gets to visit with Miss Gruffud while we shiver in the dark by the side of the road?"

"Rank has its privileges. White skin too," Hoop said. "He'll take his turn on watch tonight though. Maybe a bit late, maybe smelling of lilacs, but he'll show."

"He's a strange mixture, isn't he? Spouting poetry one minute, beating a man's face to a pulp the next. Then paying a call on a lady with a sack of lemons." Romo shook his head. "I can't understand a man like that."

"Maybe you'll learn to understand," Hoop said. "And maybe you won't."

"Talk talk talk," someone said from the gloom to their right. "Who are these old women out gossiping when men know to be quiet?"

Eskaminzim leaped off a boulder and landed in front of Hoop and Romo.

"Oh! I should have known!" he said. "It's you!"

"All quiet out here?" Hoop asked him.

"It was till you two came along."

Eskaminzim trotted past them up the road.

"You taking good care of that?" Hoop said, pointing at the Sharps rifle the Apache was carrying away with him. Its deadly long-range accuracy wouldn't do them any good in the dark of night.

"Like it was my very own," Eskaminzim said. "Who knows? One day maybe it will be. I get to keep it when you die, right?"

"I ain't saying. Don't want to put ideas in your head."

Eskaminzim glanced back, and even in the dim light of the moon his broad grin was easy to see.

"I always have ideas in my head." He stopped, smile fading, and jerked his head at the plateau up the road. "Hey…no one up there's going to shoot me, right? They know who I am?"

"Don't worry," Hoop said. "We warned the G-C folks we work with a crazy Apache."

Eskaminzim nodded, grinning again. "Good." He started jogging up the road again. "Don't die tonight, Hoop. I might like to go home with your rifle, but if I go home without *you*, Onawa will kill me."

He disappeared into the darkness, his footsteps fading away a second later.

"Who's Onawa?" Romo asked.

"His sister," Hoop said. "My wife."

"Are you saying Eskaminzim is your brother-in-law?"

"That's what they call your wife's brother, ain't it?" Hoop said. "You know, I think he was onto something about all this talk talk talk. I've been getting too damn chatty lately."

"Must be my irresistible charm overcoming your natural terseness."

Hoop grunted through clamped lips and went back to trudging down the hill.

"Did you just run out of words for the day?" Romo asked.

This time Hoop didn't even grunt.

———

Juana brought lemonade to Diehl and Miss Gruffud in the drawing room. Not a full pitcher—six lemons wouldn't get you that. She only had two crystal goblets, half-full, on a silver tray.

She served the lady first, of course, offering her the tray in such a way that one of the glasses was directly before her. Miss Gruffud took it.

Juana brought the tray to the armchair Diehl was in and bent down—though not too far—to offer him the remaining glass. Diehl stretched out an arm to take it. He thanked Juana, then tried not to look too obvious as he took a quick sniff of the dandelion yellow drink it held.

He didn't smell bitter almonds or, god forbid, saltpeter or anything else blended in with the lemonade. So he raised his glass and made a toast.

"To the Gruffud-Cadwaladr Mine...and her rightful owners."

Miss Gruffud returned the gesture. "To the A.A. Western Detective Agency...and its skillful operatives."

They each took a sip.

"Perfect," Miss Gruffud told the maid, who was standing at attention nearby.

Juana gave her a nod and a tight smile.

Diehl took a moment to savor the lemonade—and the fact that

Juana hadn't poisoned him. At least not with something that killed quickly.

"Yes...delightful, Juana," he said.

The maid stared at him, her expression going dead.

"That will be all for now," Miss Gruffud told her. "Thank you."

Juana nodded once, favored Diehl with another glower, then left.

"Your maid makes good lemonade. Conversation not so much," Diehl said once the door was closed behind her. He didn't say it loudly though, remembering how the maid had been hovering outside the door that morning.

"One doesn't hire maids for their conversation."

"Or gunmen...yet here we are."

Diehl raised his glass to the lady.

She returned the salute. She hadn't changed out of the austere, high-necked, long-sleeved dress she'd been wearing earlier, but she seemed softer, warmer, more approachable now. She sank back into the divan across from Diehl and smiled.

"Is that what you consider yourself, Mr. Diehl? A gunman?"

Diehl looked down at his hands. The knuckles were free of scrapes, the fingers unbruised. But only because a teapot had been handy that afternoon.

"No, not really. Not usually," he said. "When I worked for the Southern Pacific Railroad Police, I wasn't exactly a policeman and wasn't exactly a detective and wasn't exactly a guard. Mostly, I guess, I was still a soldier. I suppose I still am." Diehl shrugged and met the lady's gaze again. "I just change flags a little more often than most."

"And at the moment you're fighting under the Gruffud-Cadwaladr flag?"

Diehl smiled. "It's better than many a man could choose."

The lady shifted on the divan, sitting up straighter. Her expression turned serious.

"And what's your soldier's assessment of our current situation?"

"Well, we've won the day. But the night...and the next day... and the next? Who knows? By eliminating the pressure that Mr. Schuck had been applying up to now, we might have broken

Consolidated's offensive. Or we might have simply turned back a feint." Diehl grinned again. "We'll have to watch our flanks."

Miss Gruffud nodded gravely. "Spoken like a true soldier. You were an officer."

It was a statement, not a question.

Diehl understood the assumption. Enlisted men might talk about offensives and feints. But would they quote poetry?

A few he'd known might have, actually. But most people would assume otherwise.

"Yes," Diehl said.

"West Point?"

"Yes."

"Impressive."

"Not particularly." Diehl pointed at himself. "Second to last in the Class of '76. Thank God for Dick Carey. Rich as Croesus, dumb as a rock." Diehl sighed. "He's a senator now."

"Oh," Miss Gruffud said, looking dubious.

"If you're worried about my grades, don't be. I could just never bring myself to care about the disposition of the tsar's artillery at Austerlitz. That's no reflection on the quality of service you'll be receiving from me, I assure you. When it comes to soldiering, I acquired my real education post-graduation."

Miss Gruffud nodded in a reserved way that didn't quite seem to accept Diehl's assurances.

"Let me guess," she said. "In your youth you were more interested in poetry than warfare."

Diehl raised his glass to her again. "You are an astute judge of character. Yes. Actually, that's why I ended up at West Point. My father didn't approve of poetry. He did approve of war."

Miss Gruffud nodded again, a little of her warmth returning. "I understand. Fathers and their expectations. They can be difficult to manage, can't they?"

Diehl gave the lady a "Do tell" look—downturned mouth, cocked head, raised eyebrows.

She laughed it off. It was the first time Diehl had heard her laugh, he realized. He liked it.

"But let's stick to poetry," she said. "I have a feeling you won't object?"

"Miss Gruffud, it would be my preference to *always* stick to poetry."

"Well, then…"

She stretched out her free hand, palm up, and waited expectantly.

"You'd like to hear some?" Diehl said.

"Cultured individuals are few and far between in Arizona Territory. Whatever you'd care to share would be a rare treat."

"All right. It's been a long while since I had such a refined audience, but I'll do my best. Perhaps we'll start with a little more Swain…?"

Diehl put his glass on a side table, then stared off at a corner of the room. After a moment, he began.

> *Tapping at the window,*
> *Peeping o'er the blind.*
> *It is really most surprising.*
> *He never learns to mind!*
> *It was only yester evening*
> *As in the dark we sat*
> *My mother asked me sharply,*
> *"Pray, Mary, who is that?"*
> *Who's that? Indeed! You're certain*
> *How much she made me start.*
> *Men seem to lose their wisdom*
> *Whene'er they lose their heart…*

"Is he doing what I think he's doing?" Utley muttered. "*Really?*"

The mine manager turned his head and moved his ear closer to the window. He couldn't make out the words clearly through the glass. But the monotonous drone of the mercenary's voice and the few nonsensical snippets Utley could catch—"Men seem to lose their wisdom whene'er they lose their heart," etc.—made it clear what the son of a bitch was up to.

"Reciting poetry to her," Utley growled. "Pitiful."

He listened a while longer before adding, "It better not work, damn it."

He moved back to focus on Miss Gruffud again, trying to gauge her response. She looked interested, perhaps even impressed, but not rapt. Not worshipful. Not inflamed with barely checked passion.

The way he wanted her to look at *him*.

He glared at Diehl again. The man didn't look special. Slimmer than Utley, yes, but older and more weathered too. And the expression on his face as he babbled his pompous nonsense—chin raised, eyes half-lidded, smug curl to his thin lips—made him look like a fool.

"Pretentious asshole," he grumbled.

"You're at least half right," someone said behind him. "What's 'pretentious'?"

Utley yelped and whirled around and yelped again.

A figure with long, dark hair and a red cloth wrapped around his forehead and a rifle in his hands stared back at him.

The Apache.

"Just…just…just…" Utley stammered. "Just checking on the lady's safety."

"Oh, that's nice of you," the Apache said. "But that's what I'm here for. To make you feel safe." He stepped closer and gestured at Utley with his rifle. "You don't feel safe?"

"No! Yes! Well…" Utley raised a trembling hand and pointed up at the window. "The lady…just checking…for extra…extra safety."

There was a clattering behind him, then a whoosh.

Someone was putting up the window. Utley didn't want to see who.

"Back to the mine! Work to do! Thank you! Good night!" he cried.

He scurried off into the night.

———

"What was that all about?" Diehl asked Eskaminzim.

"I was coming up to get some sleep in the stable and I saw someone over here," Eskaminzim said. "So I came to see who."

"He was watching us?"

"Just checking on his boss woman, he said. You know. For extra-extra safety."

Eskaminzim grinned. Both he and Diehl knew what Utley really wanted to protect Miss Gruffud from.

"Was that Mr. Utley?" the lady asked from inside.

"Yes," said Diehl. "He was…patrolling the perimeter."

"Surely he doesn't need to do that now that you're here."

"That's what I told him!" Eskaminzim called out.

Diehl reached up to close the window.

"Wait!" Eskaminzim said.

Diehl paused, looking profoundly irritated.

"What does 'pretentious' mean?" Eskaminzim asked.

Diehl looked even more irritated.

"Puffed up. Fake. Trying to be something more than you are," he said.

Eskaminzim nodded thoughtfully, then turned toward Utley, who could still be seen hurrying away toward the mine entrance.

"Hey! Utley!" the Apache yelled. "You were *completely* right about Diehl!"

Utley didn't look back.

Diehl slammed down the window.

Eskaminzim chuckled to himself, then headed for the stable.

CHAPTER 11

Fortenberry started to knock on the hotel room door, then stopped himself. He swept off his bowler hat, slicked down his thinning hair, straightened his collar, and cleared his throat. *Then* he knocked.

After a moment, he heard footsteps. When the door opened just wide enough for someone to peep out, he found himself face to face with a trim, mustachioed man in shirt and black trousers. The man stiffened and widened his eyes, and for a second Fortenberry thought he was going to slam the door on him.

"Who are you?" the man said.

"My name's Fortenberry, Mr. Claypole. I work for you."

"No, you don't," Henry Claypole announced loudly. He leaned out and did a quick left-right scan of the hallway. When he was sure they were alone, he stepped back and dropped his voice to a whisper. "What do you want?"

Fortenberry lowered his voice too. "Mr. Schuck sent me. At least I think he did..."

"What do you mean you *think* he sent you?"

"It's pretty hard to understand him, sir. His face is...well, there was a fight, sir. More of a beating, really. And Mr. Schuck can't really talk much at the moment. Or walk. Or sit up. Or breathe. He wants you to get him home to Tucson, sir. That's why he sent me to see you. I think. It's not really clear, to be honest, sir." Fortenberry fiddled nervously with his derby. "He's not thinking very well either, sir."

"I can see that," Claypole said, looking Fortenberry up and down with a frown. "Before we go on, please assure me that you were discreet."

"Discreet, sir?"

"In coming here. To my room. No one saw you?"

Fortenberry shook his head. "Mr. Schuck was able to tell me the room number, so I didn't have to ask at the desk. I could just leave him in his room and come up here."

"And *you saw no one?*"

Fortenberry furrowed his heavy brow. He thought he'd just answered that question.

"No. Like I said, I just walked out of Mr. Schuck's room and—"

"All right, fine, fine," Claypole cut in. "So who administered this beating to poor Frank? Miners?"

Fortenberry shrugged, looking pained. "I don't know, sir. I don't think so, sir. It was a stranger, sir. Said something about a man trifling with his mule."

Claypole scowled skeptically. His right hand was still on the door, and it looked like he was thinking again about slamming it shut.

"But some of the miners did go up to the G-C afterward," Fortenberry added quickly, "and your men on the road didn't turn them back, and a while ago your men came back down to town, and they said they don't work for you anymore—although a few said they might if they got paid four dollars a day, with two weeks' advance—and it's all pretty confusing, sir. Mr. Schuck's not much help, and those of us who still work for you don't know what to do."

"You. Don't. Work. For me," Claypole said. "None of you work for me. Remember?"

"Oh. Right, sir. Of course, sir. Sorry, sir."

Claypole waved the apology away. "How bad off is Frank?"

"Pretty bad. His face looks like a horse stepped on it. And I didn't even mention his hands. Both smashed." Fortenberry shook his head sadly and dropped his voice even lower, to a whisper so quiet Claypole had to cock his head to hear it. "Can't even hold his own doodle when he makes water."

Claypole grimaced, then glowered silently at Fortenberry as if unsure more talk with the man could be worth it.

Fortenberry found it odd that a man so concerned about discretion would want to hold this conversation in a hallway, but he lacked the courage to say they should continue it on the other side of a closed door. All he could do was suggest it by peering hopefully past Claypole's shoulder.

Claypole leaned to the side to block his view.

"How many men are left?" Claypole asked.

"Of the ones who *don't* work for you, you mean?"

Fortenberry winked to show how discreet he was being.

Claypole kept glowering.

"Eleven you can still rely on," said Fortenberry. He rubbed his stubble-covered chin. "Make that ten. Well, nine I can guarantee. Maybe eight."

Claypole held up a hand. "Stop. Please. While there are still some left."

He gave Fortenberry a weak blink-and-you'd-miss-it smile, then lowered his arm.

"This is very upsetting about Frank," he said. "I usually leave such matters entirely to him. And our directive here...the stakes this time..." He paused to gnaw on the nail of his left thumb. "Certain people not known for their patience are going to be extremely displeased if certain people here can't apply the economic and personal pressure that another certain person..." Claypole put the freshly chewed thumbnail to his chest. "Must have in order to make other certain people bow to the wishes of the aforementioned impatient certain people of the first part."

Fortenberry nodded.

"I understand," he lied.

Claypole looked mildly surprised but gave him a "Bully for you" and another here-and-gone smile.

"I find I must ask—being intentionally ignorant of the usual particulars—what you think Frank might do next," he went on. "You know. Were he capable of doing…well, anything."

"Oh, I didn't know Mr. Schuck long, but I'm pretty darned sure I know *exactly* what he'd do," Fortenberry said.

Claypole cocked an eyebrow. "Oh?"

"Sure. He'd beat the shit out of certain people. Or worse."

Fortenberry pressed a finger to the side of his nose and winked again.

"Ah. Very good," Claypole said. "I admire how you've entered into the spirit of the thing. Why don't you just…carry on with that, hmm?"

"You mean me and some of the boys should…"

"I'm not *telling* you to do anything," Claypole snapped. "Just *do* it."

"Yes, sir."

"Immediately."

"Of course, sir."

"With the fullest vigor…whatever that might look like."

"I understand, sir."

"All right, then."

The two men stared at each other for a moment. Then Claypole stepped back and swung the door closed.

Fortenberry listened to the man walk away, angry at himself. He should've brought up money. Schuck had been paying him and the others a "retainer," he called it. Ten dollars a week plus drinks at El Leon Rojo and assorted bonuses for thrashings well-delivered. But if Fortenberry was going to take on more responsibility, he should be getting more cash too.

He raised a first to knock again, then thought better of it. He slapped on his bowler and headed for the back stairs.

There'd be more money for him, he was sure. But first he should prove he could earn it.

CHAPTER 12

Eskaminzim's eyes popped open. He was lying on his back looking up at knotty gray wood. He sat up and listened for a moment, then smiled when he heard heavy breathing from the next stall over.

Diehl hadn't stayed much longer in the boss woman's house. Not as long as Diehl would have liked, certainly. He'd come to the stable ten minutes after Eskaminzim got there.

Eskaminzim stood and started brushing straw from his hair and shoulders.

Diehl gasped, kicked his feet, and jerked himself upright.

"I'm up, I'm up, I'm up!" he said.

Eskaminzim was known to find creative ways to awaken a man who slept too long.

"Surprised you're not waking up in a feather bed?" he asked Diehl.

A horse snorted nearby, its way of saying "Hey, I'm trying to sleep over here!"

"With better company?" Eskaminzim added.

"For your information, Miss Gruffud offered me the use of a guest room," Diehl said. "I declined."

"Because you'd miss me?"

"Because if I fell asleep in a feather bed, I'd never want to leave it."

Eskaminzim shook his head. "I'll never understand why you people like those things. I tried one once. It was like lying in corn mush."

Diehl slowly pushed himself to his feet. It took him several seconds to straighten his back.

"Oh, sure," he groaned. "Nothing beats sleeping on straw that smells like horse piss."

"Well, we're not here to sleep, are we?" Eskaminzim said. "Or do *anything* in feather beds."

"Nothing like that was gonna happen," Diehl said. "Miss Gruffud is a lady."

A lady whose interest in entertaining had faded fast after the interruption from Eskaminzim and Utley.

"Oh. I see. A lady," Eskaminzim said. "Like Miss Abel in Bisbee. Or whatever-her-name-was in Yuma. Or Mrs. Rexroad at Fort Concho."

"Poetry lovers," Diehl sighed.

"That's not what Major Rexroad said."

Diehl rubbed his temples.

"I've known you too long," he muttered.

He bent down again—very, very slowly—to retrieve his hat from a hay bale.

Eskaminzim walked from the stall he'd been sleeping in, passing the two rifles—his Winchester and Hoop's Sharps—leaned against the wall nearby. When he looked outside and saw that it was still a dark night with heavy clouds hiding a crescent moon, he didn't bother going back for one of the long guns. He had his knife. He didn't care for pistols, useless for fighting at a distance and great for shooting yourself in the leg, but if he needed one he could acquire it quickly enough. That had always been the case in the past, anyway.

"I'll send Hoop and your puppy up for some sleep," he said. "Unless the Mexican's asleep already."

"Romo's got a lot to prove, and he's probably scared shitless," said Diehl. He strapped on his gun belt and began knotting the leg tie. "He's awake. I bet he won't sleep till this over."

"Oh? You *really* want to bet?"

"Just an expression," Diehl said.

Eskaminzim never made bets for money. He'd bet for the chance to punch you in the stomach or shave off one of your eyebrows.

"If you trust the Mexican, you should show it," he said.

"I showed it by asking him to come here."

"But why? If you really think he's good enough, let's put it to the test. With stakes…before the stakes are our lives."

"Not taking the bait," said Diehl.

Eskaminzim cursed in Spanish—according to him, Mescalero-Chiricahua was too civilized a language for profanity—and kicked at a horse turd.

"I'll see you down on the road," he said.

Meaning he'd see Diehl. There was no guarantee Diehl would see him.

He headed off into the darkness.

Diehl snatched up his own Winchester—possibly useless, certainly comforting—and stepped outside. He paused for a long look at the lights still burning by the mine and the two black-spired silhouettes—the Gruffud and Cadwaladr homes—farther off to the right.

This was what the G-C Mine should look like. Active, but peaceful.

Diehl wondered how long it would last.

With his free hand, he popped his jacket's wool collar to keep the night chill off his neck. Then he started toward the road.

Romo was snoring. Not loudly. But clearly enough to leave no doubt that he was sound asleep even though he was sprawled belly-down across a boulder to supposedly keep an eye on the road below.

He began twitching and muttering, and Hoop leaned a little closer to catch his words.

"Por favor…por favor…no me coma, Señor Presidente."

Please don't eat me, Mr. President?

Hoop shook his head. Either he hadn't heard right or Romo was having one hell of a dream.

"Baja el arma, Papá," Romo groaned. "Baja el arma…"

Put down the gun, Father.

At least that made a little more sense. Maybe Romo's dad was about to save him from Señor Presidente.

Hoop let him keep dreaming. Eskaminzim could wake him when he showed up to relieve them. That would be something to see. The experience might help the young man stay awake on watch next time.

Hoop turned his attention back to the road. His eyes weren't as sharp as they used to be—not back when he could pick a Comanche off his horse from a quarter mile away. But despite the clouds obscuring the night's slim slice of moon, he could make out the serpentine strip of packed dirt that wound down to town and the rocky slopes and bluffs around it. Not with any detail. Just lines and shapes in a dozen different shades of murky gray.

And movement—Hoop saw that too, now. To the east of the road, in the rocks. Little patches of black two hundred yards off. Coming closer.

Five? Six? Seven? More? And Hoop here alone with the Mexican.

"Pero no tengo buen sabor, Señor Presidente," Romo moaned.

But I don't taste good, Mr. President!

"Shit," Hoop said.

A coyote yowled in the distance. A coyote that wasn't a coyote.

Hoop didn't smile. It wasn't the time for that. There might never be another time for that. You never knew. But the glowering frown on his face relaxed a little, unbent itself, straightening into something that looked more like grim determination.

He put a gentle hand on Romo's shoulder and gave the younger man a preemptive, "Shhhh!"

Romo awoke with a start and wide, panicked eyes, but managed to stay quiet.

Hoop leaned in close.

"Work to do," he whispered.

———

"You hear that?" said Bill.

"Hear what?" said Bull. "The coyote?"

"Might be a coyote," said Bill. "Might not."

"Shut up," said Fortenberry.

Bill and Bull couldn't see him, but they knew he was crouched behind a rock to their right, near three of the other men Schuck had hired when he'd come to town. Three more men were strung out in the darkness to their left. They were all hiding on the same side of the road even though Bill had suggested they split into two groups. That way they could create a crossfire when the miners headed down to town. Fortenberry was afraid they'd shoot each other.

Bill and Bull thought Fortenberry was a fool. But they couldn't resist getting paid to protect the miners during the day *and* ambushing them at night.

"Might be the Apache," whispered Bill.

"Naw. Indians don't really go around imitating animals," said Bull, not lowering his voice at all.

"Yes, they do."

"No, they don't. That's a bunch of bunk—like how good they are at tracking and hunting and sneaking around without being seen. It's all applesauce."

An owl hooted.

Bill sat up straight and stared wide-eyed into the darkness.

Bull kept talking.

"I should know. I grew up right next to the Crow Reservation, near Billings. Clumsiest, loudest people you ever come across. At least the ones I saw."

"That's cuz the ones who were good at sneaking saw you first!" one of the men to the right said.

"Shut up!" said Fortenberry.

A crow cawed.

Bill pulled out his gun.

"You ever hear a crow at night?" he said.

"A crow crow? Like the bird?" said Bull.

"Yes, like the bird! Like that just now!"

Bull shrugged. "Not that I recall. That doesn't mean anything though. Cuz if it's the Apache you're worried about, let me tell you something. Indians don't fight at night."

"Where'd you hear that?" said a man off to the left somewhere.

"Aw, everyone knows it," said Bull.

"I don't," said Bill.

"Me neither," said the man to the left.

There was a clatter and a thump from the same direction, as if someone had fallen among the rocks.

"Stop making so much damn noise!" Fortenberry snapped.

"Sorry," said the men to the left. "I'll try to be more quiet."

There was another thump, followed by a low groan that came and went quickly.

"Sorry, sorry," the man to the left said. "Sure is dark tonight, isn't it?"

Bill peered into the blackness.

"Who is that, anyway?" he said.

"It's me," said the man to the left.

"Who's 'me'?" said Bill.

"I don't know," said the man. "Who are you?"

"If you dumb sons of bitches don't shut up," Fortenberry growled, "I'm not going to wait for the damn miners. I'm gonna start shooting. You understand me?"

"Sure, boss," said one of the men hunkered down with him.

"Yeah, yeah," said Bull.

"I understand," said the man to the left.

"Absolutely," said a voice from the rocks behind them.

"Completely," said another—one with a Southern accent.

For a moment there was silence.

"Uhh...who is that back there?" Fortenberry said.

"We're—" one of the men behind them began.

Bill cut off whatever he was about to say. First with a shot in the man's general direction. Then with a yell.

"We're being bushwhacked, boys!"

After that Bill went back to shooting. Bull swung around with his gun and joined in, as did the men with Fortenberry.

"Wait!" Fortenberry shouted. "Hold on!"

There was a blast and a flash of light in the darkness about twenty yards away, and Bill dropped his gun and slumped to the ground. More blasts and flashes followed from a little farther off, and the men by Fortenberry went down.

Bull drew a bead on the nearest burst of light. But before he could pull the trigger, a figure sprang from the shadows and plunged a knife into his side. With a quick slash, the blade sliced open his stomach, and Bull's scream quickly turned to shocked gurgles as he fell forward onto his face.

The roar of gunfire stopped, and the sounds that replaced it were quieter. Bill moaning. Bull gasping and shuddering. Footsteps —some coming closer, some moving quickly away.

The man with the knife—Eskaminzim—looked down at Bull stretched out by his feet.

"How's that for fighting at night?" he said.

Bull shook one last time, then was still.

Eskaminzim stepped over to Bill and moved the man's dropped pistol out of reach with his toe. Bill was on his knees, arms wrapped around himself, head down.

"I'm dead," he whimpered. "I'm dead."

"But still you keep talking," said Eskaminzim. "Typical white eye."

One man, then another, then another—Diehl and Hoop and Romo—moved out of the rocks to check the other bodies. Hoop pointed at the road.

A single survivor was running frantically down the hill. A burly, breathless man in a tatty suit and a bowler hat. Fortenberry.

"We gonna allow that?" Hoop asked.

Diehl thought it over. Romo watched him with a troubled look on his face. Diehl pretended not to notice.

"Yes. I believe we will," Diehl said. "He can't go to the law about an ambush that went wrong. The only ones he can tell are his employers. And we *want* them to know about this."

"I'm dead," Bill said again.

Diehl moved closer to peer at him.

"Bill, isn't it?" he said. He shook his head. "You take our money, then you do this? I'm disappointed in you. Not surprised, but disappointed. And it was you who started the shooting, wasn't it? Bill, that's what got you killed."

Bill lifted his head to look at Diehl, then noticed Bull's lifeless body lying nearby.

"Oh, Bull...Bull...Bull," he said. He began to weep. "What an asshole."

There were distant shouts and the sounds of more footsteps on the road.

Romo turned toward the top of the hill.

"Must be some of the miners coming to see what's going on," he said.

"Don't let them down here," said Diehl. "And don't tell them about all this."

He waved a hand at the bodies scattered around them.

"What am I supposed to say?" Romo asked.

"We shot a puma," said Diehl.

Romo frowned. "That was a lot of shooting for a puma."

Diehl shrugged. "We shot an extremely well-armed puma."

"Tell them whatever you want," Hoop told Romo. "Just get up there and tell it *now*."

"All right," Romo said.

He turned to go.

"Alfonso," Diehl said. "One question."

Romo turned around again.

"Yes?"

"That test excavation you spotted on our way up to the mine yesterday. How deep do you think that would be?"

"I don't know. But most test shafts go down hundreds of feet."

Diehl and Hoop looked at each other.

"Let's just hope we don't fill it up by the time this is over," said Hoop.

Romo turned and hurried off up the hill, grateful for an excuse to miss what was coming next.

Eskaminzim nodded down at Bull. "We're gonna have to be careful when we move the ones I killed. They're pretty messy."

"That's nothing new," said Hoop.

Diehl squatted down beside Bill, who was still crying softly and clutching his stomach.

"How's it going there, partner?" Diehl asked.

"How do you think?" Bill said.

"I ask because we need to tidy up the unpleasantness here. And, well…that includes you. But I'm not sure you're going to stick to our schedule, if you know what I mean."

Bill looked up, a scowl on his tear-streaked face. "I'm dying as fast as I can, you bastard."

"Thanks, Bill. I appreciate it."

Diehl straightened up and turned to Eskaminzim. He met Eskaminzim's steady gaze, glanced down at the knife in the Apache's hand, then looked him in the eye again.

Eskaminzim started toward Bill, who'd gone back to crying into his chest.

Diehl walked off toward the men who'd been with Fortenberry —the ones who were killed by nice, comparatively clean bullet wounds.

"What's your preference tonight, Sergeant?" he said. "Shoulders or feet?"

"I'll get 'em by the feet," said Hoop.

Behind them, Bill's weeping stopped.

CHAPTER 13

In the morning, Skewes led a dirty, disheveled, exhausted crew of twenty men out of the mine. He paused to talk with Utley, who'd stepped out of his office in the mill when he saw the miners leaving. Then he headed for the road again.

Diehl and Romo were there at the top of the hill with their rifles. Hoop and Eskaminzim were stationed halfway down.

Skewes stopped by Diehl and Romo as his fellow miners trudged toward town.

"No more pumas?" he asked.

"Nary a one," said Diehl.

Romo said nothing. He'd hardly spoken at all the last few hours, obeying Diehl and Hoop's commands wordlessly, replying to questions with nothing more than "yes" or "no."

Skewes nodded. "Good. I'll send up another shift of miners. Millmen and muckers too."

He glanced over his shoulder. Utley was watching them from the corner of the mill.

"Management wants us to make up for lost time," Skewes said. "Do you think those 'guards' you hired yesterday will come back? Still on our side, I mean?"

"Well, I'll be pretty surprised if they *all* show up," said Diehl.

He threw Romo a wry look. Romo just stared back at him stone-faced.

"But I expect a few will want to earn their pay," Diehl went on.

"My boys didn't like it, you know," Skewes said. "Walking past some of the same sons of bitches who'd been beating us and threatening us with guns just the day before."

Diehl shrugged. "Working with sons of bitches is the price you pay for working. If you don't like the ones I've supplied you're welcome to find your own."

"I'll keep that in mind...but for now I guess we'll stick with the SOBs we've got."

Skewes flashed Diehl a smile. Diehl smiled back then looked past him at the top of the hill.

Juana was coming their way. The maid's dark dress and slender build and quick but soundless steps made her seem like a straight black line gliding toward them—something blunt and grim and inexorable.

"Looks like one of us is about to be invited in for tea," Skewes said. "And I'm sure she's not coming for the likes of me. Can't have the parlor mussed up with dirt from the mine. Enjoy the crumpets."

Skewes hustled off to catch up with the other miners.

He was right about Juana. She glanced his way as he left but said nothing until she'd stopped a few feet from Diehl and Romo.

"You are invited for coffee..." she said to Diehl.

Diehl started to smile.

For the first time, he saw Juana smile too.

"With Mr. Cadwaladr," she said.

"Oh. How very kind," said Diehl. "We'd be honored...wouldn't we, Alfonso?"

He looked over at the sullen, silent Romo.

"Gracias, Señora," Romo said to Juana.

She acknowledged him with a nod, her smirk melting, brow furrowing, expression sobering but not souring. It wasn't the same cold scorn with which she regarded Diehl. It didn't quite look like disapproval. More like disappointment.

She turned and walked away, obviously expecting the men to follow her.

"So you work for both Miss Gruffud and Mr. Cadwaladr?" Diehl asked as he and Romo fell into step behind her.

"All the other servants left when the trouble started," she said.

"But you stayed?"

There was a brief pause before Juana answered—a few seconds of silent striding—and Diehl didn't need to see her face to know that the disdain was back.

"Obviously."

"You're very loyal," said Diehl.

"Yes. I am," said Juana. "I wonder if that's something you'd understand."

"You think I'm only loyal to the dollar."

"Not even that. I think you're only loyal to yourself."

"You underestimate me," Diehl said. "I'm *very* loyal to Charles Swain, English poet, January 1801 to September 1874, requiescat in pace."

Juana snorted. "The living need our loyalty more."

"Undoubtedly…but who's as good as Swain?"

Juana snorted again, then gave up on Diehl. No one said anything more as she led them toward Cadwaladr's house. When they reached it, Juana angled away from the front steps, heading instead around the side. Diehl gave the Gruffud home next door a longing look before rounding the corner after her.

The old man was waiting around back at a small, round, linen-topped table on the edge of the cliff. There was one extra folding chair, one extra place setting.

"Good morning, Diehl," Cadwaladr said. "Glad you could join me."

Diehl paused, eyes flicking toward Romo, then walked to the table and took a seat.

"Thank you, sir. Your hospitality is much appreciated," he said. "It's been a long, cold night for my associate, Mr. Romo. Perhaps…"

"Of course, of course," Cadwaladr said. "Juana, give the lad something to eat."

Juana bowed slightly, then led Romo to the back door. The servants' entrance.

Diehl watched them go inside, a pensive look on his face. When the door closed, he turned to the curve-necked silver pot on the table and poured himself a cup of coffee.

"Nice view you have here," he said, nodding at the broad, flat, brown valley stretched out before them and the dark mountains beyond.

"If you enjoy looking at hell," said Cadwaladr. "I'm from Wales, Diehl. The land should be green, by god."

Diehl added a lump of sugar and a dash of cream to his coffee.

"Well, I'm from Ohio...so I agree," he said. "But it's not the land so much as what's under it that really counts, right?"

He raised his coffee cup to the old man as if offering a toast, then took a sip.

Cadwaladr leaned back, his round belly jutting out toward the horizon. The chair beneath him creaked in a way that drew a worried look from Diehl.

"Yes, it's what's under the surface that brought me and Gruffud here," Cadwaladr said. "Noah Gruffud, I mean. Miss Gruffud's father. It didn't make us rich but it gave us this." He flapped a hand at the houses behind them. "I'm grateful to you for your help holding on to it."

"Just doing my job...which might not be done yet. Perhaps we've won the war. Perhaps we've simply survived a couple skirmishes." Diehl took another sip of coffee, then glanced at the sun that was still struggling to clear the mountaintops. "The day is young."

Cadwaladr leaned forward to inspect the basket of Mexican-style breads and cookies on the table. He picked out a bisquet, the egg glaze on top shimmering in the sunlight, then leaned back again. The chair's legs let go another groan but managed not to snap.

"It's the *night* I wanted to discuss with you, actually," Cadwaladr said. He admired the bisquet for a moment, then dropped it onto his plate untasted. "Your social call next door."

"Oh?"

Diehl took another sip of coffee, an innocent look on his face.

"It *was* a social call, wasn't it? Not entirely business?" Cadwaladr said.

He gave Diehl an encouraging smirk.

"Pleasantries were exchanged," Diehl said.

"Ahh. And perhaps intimacies?"

Cadwaladr waggled his bushy gray eyebrows.

"Only if fresh lemonade, agreeable conversation, and the reciting of poetry count as 'intimacies,'" Diehl said.

"Oh ho! More poetry! Love sonnets, perhaps? I'm sure the ladies enjoy those."

Cadwaladr winked.

Diehl put down his coffee.

"Mr. Cadwaladr," he said, "I'd have been dead a long, long time ago if I didn't know a trap when I see one."

Cadwaladr scowled, then almost immediately chuckled at himself.

"I hope you'll forgive an old man for feeling protective of a woman he loves like a daughter," he said.

"Of course."

"Not that she's susceptible to that kind of thing, mind. I've yet to see the man who could trifle with her affections."

"Though there is one here who'd dearly like to win them."

Cadwaladr went back to scowling.

"I'm not talking about myself," Diehl said.

He got up and walked to the edge of the cliff. The drop beyond wasn't as sheer as he'd assumed. It slanted down to the desert floor far below at about an eighty-degree angle. Too steep for a man to climb without ropes, but not the impenetrable rock wall he'd thought it was.

Great. He'd have to think about protecting his rear. Like always.

"Oh. You mean Utley," Cadwaladr said. "Yes, he does a poor job concealing his juvenile fancies, doesn't he? It's just as plain they'll come to naught though."

"Plain to you. Not to him, I think. Tell me—do you think he's genuinely smitten or just ambitious?"

"What do you mean?" the old man growled.

"It's obvious Miss Gruffud has the final say around here. She inherited a controlling interest from her father?"

Cadwaladr squirmed on his rickety little chair. "She did."

"Well, then the man who marries her marries the Gruffud-Cadwaladr Mine, doesn't he?"

"Utley is an employee," Cadwaladr snapped. "He may be deluded about his prospects with Catrin, but in the end, he'll know his place."

Diehl nudged a rock the size of his fist over the edge of the precipice. It alternately slid and rolled down, down, down toward the valley floor.

"Mr. Cadwaladr, did you invite me here this morning to remind me what *my* place is?"

The old man's doughy face flushed.

"Just taking your measure, Diehl. I can see you are a gentleman despite…well…"

Despite your line of work, he'd been about to say. Or something along those lines.

He picked up his bisquet again and finally took a bite.

"Juana makes the most excellent pastries," he said as he chewed. "You really should try some before you return to your duties."

Diehl turned and walked back toward the table, eyes locked on Cadwaladr.

His pride told him to leave. His stomach told him to eat.

Over the years, he'd learned to listen to his stomach.

He sat back down and picked out a cookie.

———

Juana glared out the window at Diehl sitting in the sun eating cookies. Then she went back to dicing tomatoes with renewed gusto.

"It's very kind of you to go to all this trouble," Romo said to her in Spanish.

He was at a little table nearby with a half-eaten concha and a cup of coffee before him.

Juana glanced over at the eggs sizzling on a skillet to her right. They were almost ready.

"It's no trouble," she replied, also in Spanish. There was no warmth in her tone though. She remained a cold, distant woman even as she insisted on cooking him a full breakfast.

She switched to slicing an onion.

"Yesterday I overheard you and Diehl talking as you left the Gruffud house," she said. "It sounded like you were discussing an American university you attended?"

"That's right. Cornell. It's in Ithaca, New York."

"A good school?"

"Yes."

"Expensive?"

Romo didn't reply.

Juana stopped her chopping and swiveled toward him.

He looked embarrassed.

"Yes," he said.

Juana regarded him silently for a moment. Then she turned away and, in a quick flurry of jerky movements, slid the eggs onto a waiting tortilla topped with refried beans, garnished them with tomato, onion, and cilantro, snatched up the plate, and brought it to Romo.

"Por qué estás con estos sicarios?" she said as she slapped the plate down in front of him.

Then why are you with these hired killers?

Romo winced. He struggled for words for a moment, then picked up his fork and gave the maid a tentative smile.

"Un hombre debe comer."

A man must eat.

He took a bite of the huevos rancheros.

"Delicioso, Señora. Gracias."

Juana looked like she was considering taking the eggs back. Instead she stalked off to the counter and began cleaning.

"So your family doesn't have money anymore?" she said.

"Yes. That's part of it."

"And what's the rest?"

Romo slowly chewed another mouthful, then swallowed before answering.

"I don't have a *family* anymore. My father was ruined in the financial panic last year. After that he…"

Romo swallowed again though there was no food in his mouth.

"He and my mother died," he went on, voice flat. "It was… sudden. I had a sister, but she died years ago. There are a few cousins, but we were never close, and they were either wiped out in the Panic or weren't well-off to begin with. They have their own struggles, and I won't add mine to them. So here I am."

Juana turned away from the dirty knives and bowls and skillets. Her air of curt, chilly judgment was gone. In its place was sympathy —and something more. Something that hinted at infinite sadness.

"I'm sorry," she said softly.

Romo shrugged. "Que sea lo que dios quiera."

Let it be what God wants.

Juana's dark eyes glistened. She took in a deep breath and opened her mouth, as if about to begin a long story. But then a movement outside—Diehl getting up from his seat—caught her attention. She blinked and wiped at her cheeks, and a little of her brittle briskness returned.

"Finish your eggs," she told Romo. "Quick. Before your business takes you away."

"Sí, Señora."

Romo dug into the huevos rancheros again.

Juana's thin, pinched lips curved upward just a bit.

"Come back tonight if you can," she said. "I'm making pozole."

———

Hoop glanced back at the top of the hill. He didn't say anything, but Eskaminzim could easily read the sour look on his face.

"Yes…still just the two of us to guard the road," the Apache said. "What do you think they're doing? Getting breakfast?"

Hoop said nothing.

"I think they're getting breakfast," Eskaminzim continued. "I think they're eating and not worrying about us or the road at all. I think they're up there stuffing their ugly faces with eggs and tortillas and beans and meat and bread."

"*I* think," Hoop drawled, "you're hungry."

"Of course, I'm hungry! I want eggs and tortillas and beans and meat and bread! I want to stuff my ugly face with it and not worry about them or the road at all!"

Hoop went back to saying nothing. He was in his green sack coat and Stetson again. His furry buffalo coat and beaver hat adorned a boulder nearby.

"The Mexican gets breakfast before me," Eskaminzim said. "A plate heaping with chorizo and chilaquiles and huevos rancheros, I bet, while I'm down here with nothing to eat but rocks and dirt and a lizard, if I'm lucky." He scowled at the top of the hill. "Did you see that little comemierda last night? I thought he was going to faint. Why does Diehl want him around?"

"Reminds him of himself," Hoop said.

"Diehl used to be a scrawny twelve-year-old Mexican pendejo? I don't remember that."

"You haven't known Diehl as long as I have."

"True. I'm lucky like that," Eskaminzim said. "Well, we don't need them anyway. It's a clear day, and we have your Sharps. No one can get near us."

Hoop squinted at the horizon. "Yeah…but what if *they* have a Sharps?"

"Oh. That *would* be bad. I don't want to be killed from a distance. You can't look a man in the eye that way. Can't spit in his face. Can't call him a maldita polla. Can't slide your knife into his belly and hear him scream as you die." Eskaminzim frowned. "It's boring."

"I want to die boring," said Hoop, still scanning the horizon. "But not today."

Eskaminzim took a big step away from him, then thought about it and took another. He looked over at the rifle Hoop was holding, then grinned down at the Winchester in his own hands.

"I just realized—I have nothing to worry about," he said.

Hoop didn't ask him why.

Eskaminzim explained anyway.

"If someone was out there with a Sharps, and his eyes were good enough to make him dangerous, he'd see that *you* have a Sharps."

Hoop still said nothing.

Eskaminzim had to state the obvious.

"He'd definitely shoot you first."

Hoop focused on a flat brown smudge a couple miles away—the town of Hope Springs—and remained silent.

Eskaminzim began examining the bigger rocks by the side of the road.

"I'm going to go ahead and pick out where to dive when you get shot," he said. "Oh—and try to drop the Sharps where I can get at it. I'll need it to shoot back."

"Your wish might be about to come true," said Hoop.

Eskaminzim peered at him over his shoulder. "What do you mean?"

"Getting killed up close." Hoop jutted his chin at something in the distance. "Here they come."

Eskaminzim spun around to follow his gaze.

Three men were walking up the road. They were too far off still to see much detail, but it was clear they weren't wearing the heavy, dark overalls and caps of the miners. Two were wearing Stetsons.

The one in the middle wore a bowler.

CHAPTER 14

Diehl and Romo's footsteps echoed through the rafters as they stepped into the mill building. The crushers and conveyor belts were still and silent, and despite the morning sunlight streaming in through rows of large windows, every corner was draped in dark shadow.

To Diehl it was just a big, cluttered room with lots of places a man could hide. A very dangerous place on the wrong day. But Romo took it in with excited eyes and a wistful smile.

"What's your professional opinion of the setup here?" Diehl asked him. "Up to snuff?"

"It's not exactly state of the art, but it seems sufficient given the limited size of their operation," Romo said. He reached out to run his fingers along a huge, rusty, cold vat as they passed it. "I hope I get to see it at work."

"Me too."

Something creaked in the darkness to their left.

Diehl's right hand reflexively shot to his holster. Romo's didn't.

Utley stepped onto the mill floor through a side door, a frown on his face. He was dressed for business except that he wasn't wearing his coat, just a tweed vest, and his necktie was loosened and shirt-sleeves rolled up.

"What are you doing in here?" he said.

"Looking for you, actually," said Diehl. "How'd it go with your miners? Smooth shift?"

Utley had stopped about thirty yards away. He made no move to close the distance.

"Seemed to be," he said. "It wasn't a full crew, but I'm expecting more men to come up for the next shift."

"Once they see that the first bunch got home in one piece."

Utley said nothing to that.

"The men who just left," Diehl said. "Know them well?"

"Some more than others. Why?"

"I'm wondering if they're all trustworthy."

"Any that weren't wouldn't work here anymore."

"That makes sense. Just in case though, I'd like you and Alfonso to take a look around the mine. Make sure everything's in order."

Utley glowered at Romo. "I don't need any help checking my own mine."

"I'm sure you don't, Mr. Utley," Romo said. "But I would greatly appreciate a tour."

"Fine. It's settled then," Diehl said before Utley could answer. "You go ahead, Alfonso. Mr. Utley and I will be catch up directly."

Romo paused, looking uncertain, then nodded and headed back toward the door they'd come in through.

Diehl smiled at Utley as Romo's footsteps faded.

Utley glared back.

Diehl reached into his coat pocket and pulled out a light-brown cookie shaped like a pig.

"Marranitos?" he said, offering it to Utley.

Utley just kept glaring.

Diehl lifted the cookie toward his mouth, then changed his mind and slipped it back into his pocket. When he heard the door behind him open then close, he spoke again.

"I wanted a word in private, Utley. To advise you against any further night patrols. It'd be best if you kept indoors after dark."

It seemed to be what Utley expected to hear. He folded his arms across this chest and kept on glaring.

"I don't take orders from you," he said.

"True. So take it as friendly advice instead. My colleagues don't always stop to ask questions when they see someone skulking around in the dark. You're lucky Eskaminzim is…a rather whimsical fellow."

Utley thought it over a moment, stone-faced.

"Fine. I'll limit my activities at night," he said. "*As should you.*"

Diehl smiled again. It was a different smile now though. Smaller, tighter, with no humor or warmth.

"*I* don't take orders from *you*, Utley."

"Take it as friendly advice then."

The two men stared at each other for ten, twenty, thirty seconds. Then Diehl pulled out the marranitos again.

"You sure you don't want a cookie?"

"I haven't changed my mind, Diehl," said Utley.

Diehl bit off the pig cookie's head.

"Well…" he said as he chewed. He swiveled to hold his hand out toward the exit. "Shall we?"

Utley stalked straight toward Diehl, pivoting at the last moment to brush past him.

Diehl took a bite from the pig's belly before following the man out of the mill.

———

When the three men coming up the road were about a quarter mile from Hoop and Eskaminzim—at the edge of the range for the Sharps—the one in the derby lifted a stick and gave it a wave. Tied to the tip was a white handkerchief.

The men were coming under a flag of truce.

"Let's shoot them," Eskaminzim said.

Hoop considered it.

"Nah," he said. "Not yet."

"It's probably a trick."

"I know."

"And white flags are stupid."

Hoop gave that a non-committal grunt.

Eskaminzim threw another glance over his shoulder. There was still no one at the top of the hill.

"And Diehl and the Mexican are still stuffing themselves with fried potatoes and bacon and hotcakes with molasses," said Eskaminzim. He shook his head. "I'd feel better about getting killed before breakfast if they were at least getting killed with us."

The group of approaching men was about four hundred yards off now. They stopped to talk among themselves, and the man in the derby handed something small to one of the others. Then he handed over his stick. There was more conversation, the bowler man jabbing a pointed finger at Hoop and Eskaminzim.

Slowly, with obvious reluctance, the man now holding the flag slipped the little something into a trouser pocket and continued up the hill alone. Hoop and Eskaminzim watched him come silently, rifles at the ready. There was nothing to do now but wait and see what the men wanted.

The go-between gave his white flag the occasional halfhearted wave as he approached. He was a wiry man with graying hair and a droopy hat and a long, poorly groomed Van Dyke beard.

"Morning, fellas!" he called when he was about a hundred yards off. He seemed to be smiling…or trying to smile.

"Gun belt off!" Hoop shouted.

The man stopped to tuck the stick under one arm and awkwardly unbuckle his gun belt. When it was at his feet, he started forward again.

"Spin around! Slow!" Hoop said.

"What?" the man yelled back.

"Stop and turn in a circle!"

The man did as he was told.

"Lift up your coat in the back!" Hoop said.

The man did as he was told again, reaching around to lift the back flap of his gray, fraying sack coat.

Hoop grunted. There was no sign of another pistol tucked into the back of the man's pants.

The man faced them again.

"All right?" he said.

"Hop on one foot!" Eskaminzim told him.

The man began hopping on his right foot.

"The *other* foot!" Eskaminzim snarled.

The man quickly shifted to his left foot.

Hoop glowered at Eskaminzim.

The Apache shrugged. "I wanted to see if he'd do it."

Hoop kept glaring at him a moment, then waved the man forward. "Keep coming!"

The man started forward again.

"With your hands in the air!"

The man's arms shot straight up.

"No need to worry, fellas!" he said. "It's me! Goat!"

"Who the hell is 'Goat'?" Eskaminzim asked Hoop.

"One of the 'guards' Diehl supposedly hired over to our side yesterday."

Eskaminzim peered at the man. "Oh, yeah. I remember drawing a bead on him from the rocks. For a second, anyway." He shook his head. "Too little. Bad target."

His gaze shifted to the men Goat had come up the road with. They hadn't moved from their spot down the hill.

"No long guns on the others," he said. He did a quick scan of the surrounding slopes. "And no one else out there I can see. What do you think this is about?"

"We're about to find out," said Hoop.

Goat stopped twenty feet before them.

"Can I put my hands down now?" he asked.

Hoop asked his own question instead of answering.

"You back to working for the other side?"

"Not at all," Goat said with a grin. "I'm just making an extra dollar before I go back to guarding the road."

"An extra dollar doing what?" Hoop asked.

"Delivering a message." Goat looked at the top of the hill.

"Where's your boss?"

Hoop's eyes narrowed. "Who?"

"The White fella you came with. The one you boys work for."

Hoop's eyes narrowed even more. They were little more than dark slits in his face now.

Eskaminzim pointed at the distant man in the derby waiting and watching. "That payaso with the stupid little hat...is he *your* boss?"

Goat looked over his bony shoulder. "Fortenberry? Nah. He's just some bastard who got me another dollar far as I'm concerned."

Eskaminzim grunted.

Goat missed the point.

"I think *his* boss told him to deliver the message himself," he said. "So he paid me and my pal Whisper—he's another one of the guards *your* boss hired yesterday—to walk up with him. You know. Cuz we work for you now so maybe you wouldn't shoot everybody? Me 'n Whisper just looked at it as a little temporary subcontracting. Can I put my hands down now?"

"This Fortenberry..." Hoop said. "He wanted you to deliver the message to the man who'd hired you yesterday? Wanted it done here? On the road?"

"That's it."

Eskaminzim went back to scanning the arid, rock-strewn terrain around them. Hoop kept his eyes on Goat.

"What's the message?" Hoop said.

"No idea," said Goat. "It's on a piece of paper Fortenberry gave me. In my pocket."

"Give it to me."

Goat shook his head with obvious reluctance. "It's for your boss, remember?"

"He *is* his boss," Eskaminzim said, still watching the slopes.

"Well..." Hoop said to him. "Everybody's got 'em a boss somewhere."

"You're right," said Eskaminzim. He favored Goat with a quick glance. "He is his boss...when he's not around my sister."

Now Goat looked nervous *and* confused.

Hoop held a hand out to him. Goat kept both of his in the air.

"It's not for you," he said. "No offense."

Hoop lowered his hand.

"You supposed to get an answer?" he asked Goat.

"Nope. Just deliver the note...*to your boss*."

"And I suppose this Fortenberry asked you to describe 'the boss,'" Hoop said. "Just in case he wasn't here on the road?"

Goat blinked. "Why, yes. He did want to know what he looked like."

"And you told him."

"I didn't see the harm. I figured he was just...you know...trying to picture the man."

Hoop nodded slowly. "Sure."

"He already seemed to know anyway," Goat went on quickly. "*He* practically described him to *me*."

Hoop nodded again. "Cuz he's seen him before. When our 'boss' and Mr. Schuck had their tea party at the cantina. He just wants to be sure it was him."

"I don't know anything about that," Goat said, a nervous quaver in his voice.

Hoop took a step toward him. "All right...which pocket is it in?"

Goat took a big step back. "Fortenberry wouldn't like it."

"Good," said Eskaminzim. "He can watch us do it anyway."

Hoop took another step forward.

The sound of footsteps pulled all three men's attention to the top of the hill.

Diehl was coming down to join them.

Goat sighed with relief.

"Well, won't be any question about 'the boss' now," said Hoop. He glanced back at the two men waiting in the distance. "Fortenberry's gonna get the look he wanted."

Goat lowered a hand enough to run it over a forehead suddenly shimmering with sweat. "You know, if me and Whisper hadn't come up here with him, one of the other fellas would've. Only difference is we got the dollars. Can't begrudge us that when it's all the same anyhow."

Hoop and Eskaminzim said nothing.

"Right?" Goat prompted feebly.

They went on ignoring him.

Diehl was close enough to talk to now.

"Where you been?" Hoop said.

"Consulting with Cadwaladr and Utley. And taking a look around the mine. I wanted to make sure none of the workers had messed with anything. You know..." Diehl looked past Hoop to Goat. "In case anyone's trying to play both sides."

"No 'trying to' here," Hoop told Diehl. He cocked his head. "How would you know what a mine looks like when it's been messed with?"

"I wouldn't. Which is why I left Alfonso and Utley to it and came down here."

"You sure you weren't up there eating a big breakfast of atole and tamales and molletes and saving none for us?" Eskaminzim asked.

Diehl reached into his coat pocket and pulled out a bolillo roll the size of an unshucked corn cob.

"Here," he said, tossing it to Eskaminzim. "The atole and tamales and molletes wouldn't fit in my pockets."

Eskaminzim grinned and took a huge bite.

Diehl nodded at Goat's raised arms and the white handkerchief hanging limply from his stick. "What's this all about? I assume the Consolidated American Mining Corporation isn't offering its surrender."

Goat straightened his back and raised his chin and generally looked like he was about to salute. "I brought a message for you, sir. From a man, name of Fortenberry, who used to work for Schuck, which means he works for Claypole, which means he works for Consolidated American."

Hoop jerked his head at the distant figures down the hill. "Fortenberry's the one in the derby. Reminds me of a certain gentleman whose acquaintance we made last night."

"It's him," Eskaminzim said. "A man shouldn't wear a hat that dumb if he doesn't want to be recognized."

"So what's the message?" Diehl asked. "Insults to my mother or a party invitation?"

Hoop shrugged. "Don't know. It's in a note."

"For you and you alone," Goat said. He raised his chin higher. "I made sure it stayed private."

"Thank you," said Diehl. "You can hand it over now."

"Yes, sir. I've got it right here."

Goat gave Hoop a triumphant sneer, then lowered his hands and pulled out a crumpled, folded slip of white paper.

"Sorry if I mussed it a bit," he said as he handed it over.

Diehl took the scrap of paper and—holding it so no one could see what was on it but himself—began to read.

Dear Mr. Deal,

Miss Gruffud and Mr. Cadwaladr obviously chose well when procuring the services of a detective agency. I have been impressed by your quick results since arriving on the scene—so much so, in fact, that I'd like to procure your services myself. As you may be aware, a vacancy has opened up in my own operation, and I am in the market for a new manager of security. Mr. Fortenberry, the bearer of this message, is filling the role in a purely interim capacity.

I would like to meet with you face to face to present the many benefits of employment with the Consolidated American Mining Corporation. Since it would be best, for obvious reasons, to keep such a conversation confidential, I propose that it be held at a remote location. There is an abandoned way station of the Arizona and California Stage Company approximately four miles southwest of Hope Springs. I will be there at four o'clock this afternoon. I hope you will join me for a frank yet congenial business discussion that could benefit us both.

Submitted with genuine respect, admiration, and sincerity,
Henry Claypole
Superintendent of Mining Operations, Arizona Territory
The Consolidated American Mining Corporation

Diehl looked up from the note. And he *kept* looking up—up and up and up, his gaze sweeping past Hoop and Eskaminzim to shoot to the sky high above them.

"*You*," Diehl growled, scowling at a cloud. "You're toying with me again, aren't you, you son of a bitch?"

Goat peered upward, didn't see whoever Diehl was talking to (naturally), and furrowed his brow. He opened his mouth, then thought better of whatever was about to come out and shut it again.

"What's it say?" Hoop asked.

"It *was* insults to your mother?" said Eskaminzim. "I've never thought to have them written out before."

Diehl started patting the pockets of his coat and trousers with rough swats. "I don't suppose anyone has a pencil?"

Hoop shook his head.

Eskaminzim laughed. "I left mine in my other pants."

Goat stuffed a hand into one of his pockets.

Hoop and Eskaminzim whirled on him with their rifles.

"Pencil! Pencil!" Goat cried, pop-eyed. "I was gonna write my sister a letter! Guard duty is boring!"

"Show us," Hoop said. "Nice and slow."

Goat did as he was told, pulling his hand from his pocket with painstaking slowness.

Gripped between his forefinger and thumb was a stubby yellow pencil.

"I got p-paper too, if you n-need it," Goat stammered.

"Step to the side of the road and turn around," Diehl told him.

"What?"

"Move over there and look the other way."

Goat's chin started quivering beneath his beard.

"B-but…it *was* a pencil," he said as he turned his back to Diehl, Hoop, and Eskaminzim and trudged toward the rocks. "I was just trying to h-help."

Diehl stepped up behind him and plucked the pencil from his hand.

"And I thank you," he said. "Now hold still."

He spread the note from Claypole across Goat's back and—careful to block it from view—began writing.

"What do you think this means?" Eskaminzim asked Hoop in a low voice.

"I think his second guess was right," said Hoop, nodding at Diehl. "It was a party invitation...and now we see if we're invited too."

———

Fifteen minutes later, Goat walked up to Fortenberry and Whisper.

"They mad at us?" Whisper asked.

Goat put a hand to his ear. It was the hand holding the folded note. His other hand still clutched the makeshift flag.

"What?" Goat said. "Goddamn, Whisper, you need to learn to speak up."

Whisper scowled and jabbed a pointed finger at the three men up the road.

"I asked if they're mad! It looked like they were fixing to shoot you!"

"Oh. Well, the White fella didn't seem that pissed. The other two...it's hard to say." He shook his head. "They're all pretty peculiar."

"Who cares if they're mad?" Fortenberry snapped. "What did the white one say?"

"I care," said Whisper. No one heard him.

"He wrote his own message on the back of yours," Goat told Fortenberry. "Told me not to look at it."

"Oh? Gimme."

Fortenberry snatched the note from Goat's hand and stomped off to the side of the road to read it in privacy.

"Rude," Goat said. "We should've held out for two dollars apiece, Whisper."

Fortenberry unfolded the note and read the reply scrawled across the back.

Dear Mr. Claypole,

Please consider this my RSVP. I appreciate your professional compli-

ments as well as your kind invitation, and I am eager to explore the particu-
lars of your offer—provided we converse <u>outside</u> at your proposed meeting
place, and that we each arrive <u>unarmed</u> and <u>alone</u>. I request that you further
demonstrate your good faith by bringing with you an advance against future
wages. $1,000 cash would be sufficient to convince me to leave my current
employers and put a pause to efforts on their behalf.

O.D.

Fortenberry pushed back the brim of his bowler and scratched
his head. Everything in the message made sense to him except the
four capitalized letters in the first sentence.

"Either of you know what a 'rissveep' is?" he said.

"No idea," said Goat.

"Sounds Dutch," said Whisper.

Fortenberry flipped the paper over and looked again at the lines
Claypole had written referencing him.

...a vacancy has opened up in my own operation, and I am in the market for a
new manager of security. Mr. Fortenberry, the bearer of this message, is filling
the role in a purely interim capacity.

"How about an 'entire-rim capa-city'?"

"Don't know that one either," said Goat.

"Sounds French," said Whisper.

"You're a lot of help," Fortenberry muttered. He refolded the
note and stuffed it away in his shabby suit coat. "Well, boys, time
you decided."

"Time we decided what?" said Whisper.

"Time we decided what?" said Goat (who hadn't heard
Whisper).

"Which side you're really on," said Fortenberry. "I don't think
those hired guns up the way there are ever gonna trust you again.
You could try to keep working for 'em only to have 'em march you
behind a rise and *blam blam.*"

"They wouldn't do that," Goat said weakly.

"'Blam blam'?" said Whisper.

"On the other hand," Fortenberry went on, "vacancies have recently opened up in my own operation, and I am in the market for two new associates such as yourselves."

"What now?" said Goat.

"I think he's offering us jobs," said Whisper.

"I'm offering you jobs," said Fortenberry.

Goat and Whisper looked at each other, glanced back at Diehl and Hoop and Eskaminzim in the distance, then looked at each other again.

"I don't know," said Goat.

"Me neither," said Whisper.

"Four dollars a day," said Fortenberry. "First week in advance when we get back to town."

"Let's go," said Goat.

"All right," said Whisper.

"Good," said Fortenberry.

He walked over to Goat and held out his hand.

"You won't be needing that anymore," he said.

Goat handed him the flag of truce.

Fortenberry untied his handkerchief, broke the stick in two and tossed it away, then led his new associates down the road.

CHAPTER 15

The Western Union Telegraph Company Incorporated
Received at 909 Kohl Building, San Francisco
9:45 a.m., February 13, 1894
From Hope Springs, A.T.
To Kingsley Le May, 1152 Taylor Street, S.F.

Query of 2-12 received. Apologies for slow progress. No need for replacement superintendent. Persuasion efforts ramping up. End to obstruction in sight. Expect results posthaste. You will have what you want. Hope Prince Pudding Paws is feeling better.

Claypole

CHAPTER 16

Diehl rode slowly along the old stage road. He could only go so fast with the balky, grumpy mule tied behind him. He wouldn't have been going much faster without it though. He was in no hurry to get to what lay ahead.

It might be endgame for this job. It might simply be the end for him.

He comforted himself with some Swain.

"'Let tomorrow take care of tomorrow, leave the things of the future to fate,'" he recited. "'What's the use to anticipate sorrow? Life's troubles come never too late.'"

Diehl glared heavenward.

"Much better than your wretched twenty-third psalm," he said.

He ran the verse through in his mind, and his expression softened a bit.

"Yeah though 'I walk through the valley of the shadow of death' is good," he admitted. "Nice use of meter. But the rest is folderol and mixed metaphors."

Diehl's critique got no response.

He focused on the road again. There was a rise up ahead which would give him a better view of the undulating, scrub-pocked terrain all around him. Perhaps his destination was right on the other side. Perhaps his destiny too.

The portentousness of his thoughts made him sigh. He thought about reciting more Swain but decided against it. Swain was portentous too.

When he topped the rise, he saw that the old stage station was directly ahead, about a quarter mile away.

He could ride around it and keep heading south. He could cut east toward El Paso or west toward Yuma. He had a fresh horse and hundreds of dollars left from the money he'd been given for expenses. The mule he could leave to fend for herself. They'd both be happier that way.

He didn't have to stay on this road. He could find another to follow.

Yet he rode on.

The station wasn't much. A crumbling adobe home, a corral to the left, a trough and well to the right, an overturned outhouse behind. A horse was in the corral, and a table and chairs had been arranged just in front of the house.

As Diehl approached, a man appeared in the doorway. He didn't step outside. He stayed in the shadows, barely more than a shadow himself.

"Mr. Diehl!" he said.

"Mr. Claypole!" said Diehl.

He kept riding slowly, placidly toward the corral even as he prepared to roll off his saddle and dive for cover—though there wasn't any cover nearby.

Claypole stepped out into the light. He was a slender, pomaded, mustachioed man in a business suit and a Homburg hat. A gun belt would have looked out of place on him, like canons on the deck of a sleek, one-masted sloop.

A gun belt suited Diehl much better. But he wasn't wearing one either.

Claypole smiled and gestured at the mule. "You were supposed to come alone, Mr. Diehl."

"I didn't think Helen here would count," Diehl said. He

dismounted and tied his horse to a corral rail thirty yards from the house. "Plus I needed her."

He moved toward the basket strapped to the mule's back.

"Gentlemen! Now!" Claypole said.

Two more men burst out of the house behind him.

Diehl froze. He had no gun to pull, no place to hide, no time even for a last spiteful word for the Almighty. If he'd gambled and lost, he was about to find out quickly and definitively.

The men pulled guns as they stalked toward Diehl.

"Hold it right there, mister," one of them said.

"Excuse me?" said Diehl.

He could barely hear the man.

"He said, 'Hold it right there, mister,'" the other man translated.

It was Goat and Whisper.

"Oh. Certainly," said Diehl.

Goat began patting Diehl's coat and trousers while Whisper inspected his horse and mule.

They were searching for weapons. Not shooting him. Not yet.

"Watch out for the mule. She kicks," Diehl said. He offered the men an understanding smile. "I'd noticed you two didn't report back for guard duty today. Better offer?"

"Yup," said Whisper. He took Diehl's advice and kept his distance from the mule's hind legs as he walked around her.

"Nothing personal," said Goat. He bent down to check Diehl's boots for hideout guns or knife handles. "Man's got a right to pursue opportunities."

Diehl shrugged. "Everybody's doing it." He looked over at Claypole, who hadn't moved from his spot just outside the doorway. "*You* were supposed to come alone."

"I did," Claypole said. "These gentlemen arrived hours before I did."

Goat finished his search and stood. He backed off a few feet, gun aimed at Diehl's chest.

"Making sure I didn't get someone here first?" Diehl said to Claypole. "Smart. But as you can see, it's just me. And Helen. Speaking of which—"

He turned to Whisper, who'd begun fumbling with the straps holding the basket to Helen's back.

"Please be careful with that," Diehl said.

"What's in there? Your guns?" Goat asked.

"Gifts, actually."

Goat snorted skeptically.

Whisper flipped back the basket lid and reached inside with both hands. One came out holding a melon-sized chunk of green-tinged rock. The other held a bottle.

"Copper ore liberated from the Gruffud-Cadwaladr Mine. For inspiration," Diehl explained. "And wine liberated from the Cadwaladr larder. For celebration. Once we've successfully concluded our negotiations, of course. It's not champagne, unfortunately, but in Arizona Territory a man takes what he can get."

"Too true," said Claypole. "I like how you negotiate, Mr. Diehl. Shall we proceed?"

He nodded at the table.

Diehl turned to Whisper and held out his hands. "My gifts, if you please?"

Whisper looked past him at Claypole.

"If I was going to bring weapons I think I could've found something more effective than a rock and a California Riesling," Diehl said.

Claypole gave Whisper a nod.

Whisper started to step around the mule.

"Give that gal a wide berth," Diehl reminded him.

Whisper skirted Helen's backside in a long oval and handed Diehl the ore and the bottle. Diehl thanked him, then headed toward the house. As he approached, Claypole took a seat at the table—the one that kept his face to the hills and his back to the doorway. He'd be able to watch the horizon while keeping cover a quick jump away. Diehl, on the other hand, would have his back to the whole wide world, with a table and a chair and possibly an adversary between himself and safety.

He put down the ore to Claypole's right, the wine to his left, and took a seat. Once he was settled, Goat and Whisper moved around the table to take up position behind Claypole, their hands near their guns and their gazes flicking from Diehl to the hills.

Diehl's position had grown even worse. He might as well be facing a firing squad…with another one somewhere behind him, most likely.

He smiled at Claypole.

Claypole smiled back.

"Not much to look at, is it?" Diehl said, nodding down at the chunk of green ore between them. "Misshapen rock with what looks like fungus growing on it. Not a patch on silver or gold. Yet now, thanks to the capricious whims of the marketplace, your employers have decided they need it. This ugly little thing suddenly has great value…as do the ugly little things that could put it in your grasp. Supply and demand is a funny thing."

"Indeed," said Claypole, still smiling. "And your point is…"

"Just sketching out where we stand before we begin in earnest. You represent the demand. I could facilitate, rather than impede, the supply. And I know I've been quite an impediment since arriving here. Imagine that impediment not just removed but placed in the path of those who oppose you."

Claypole chuckled. "I have imagined it. That's why we're here. So…how does Consolidated American bring you into the fold?"

"Every journey begins with a single step, Mr. Claypole. I mentioned yours in my response to your invitation."

Claypole's smile tightened.

Diehl tensed.

If Claypole hadn't brought the money—one thousand dollars cash as a show of good faith—there *was* no good faith. Diehl was dead.

All at once, Claypole, Goat, and Whisper looked up, gazing at something in the distance.

Diehl turned and saw two men on horseback topping the rise in the road a quarter mile back. One of them waved his hat—a stubby black derby—in a wide arc.

Fortenberry. With yet another stray gun hand he'd managed to round up from Schuck's bunch. Sending a signal.

Diehl faced Claypole again. The smile under the man's neatly trimmed mustache had loosened, widened, relaxed.

"You had me followed," Diehl said. "To make sure I came alone."

Claypole nodded. "A sensible precaution, I'm sure you'll agree. And here's another." He gestured vaguely at one of the men behind him. "Mr....umm?"

"Goat," Goat said.

Claypole nodded again. "Of course. Goat here tells me that when you first read my message, you seemed annoyed. Perhaps even agitated. Why?"

"I don't mean to be indiscreet, but there's a sideline I've been pursuing," Diehl said. "One I'll probably have to drop now despite some encouraging progress."

Claypole cocked an eyebrow and waited for more.

Diehl leaned toward him and dropped his voice to a man-to-man stage whisper.

"Progress with Miss Gruffud."

He waggled his eyebrows.

"Ahh. I see," said Claypole though he didn't look surprised in the slightest. He shrugged. "I understand your disappointment, but c'est la guerre."

Diehl leaned back and sighed.

"C'est la *vie*, n'est-ce pas?" he said. "Cherchez la femme."

Claypole widened his eyes, then laughed. "'The capricious whims of the marketplace'? 'Cherchez la femme'? You really aren't the typical hired gun, are you?"

"Yes and no," Diehl said with a shrug. "To be typical again. let's get back to the money."

Claypole held up a finger. "One more precaution."

Diehl heaved another sigh.

"You'll have to forgive me, Mr. Diehl, but I usually keep a considerable distance between myself and these sorts of conversations," Claypole said. "Your handling of my friend Mr. Schuck has forced me to extend myself in ways that make me quite uncomfortable. Why, just being here with you and Goat and...uhh..."

"Whisper," said Whisper.

"This other gentleman," Claypole went on. "It's unprecedented for me. So before I extend myself even further by making a down payment, I think that you should make one too. A show of your sincerity."

"Mr. Claypole, I'd say that my coming here alone and unarmed is quite a show of sincerity already."

"Oh," Claypole said, sounding disappointed. "Then our conversation is over?"

Goat and Whisper straightened up and moved their hands to the butts of their guns. "Then our conversation is over" must have been signal.

Diehl tried to send a different one.

"I didn't say that," he said with a smile. "What sort of 'down payment' were you hoping for?"

"Just a little information," Claypole said. "Tell me...how many men from the detective agency came with you, will they defect with you, and who led those workers up to the Gruffud-Cadwaladr Mine yesterday?"

Diehl glanced at Goat and Whisper. They looked angry. Not so much at Diehl as at what they might have to do to him. They wouldn't enjoy it. But they were steeling themselves for it nonetheless.

"Three men came with me," Diehl told Claypole. "Two will at least hear me out on a change of employers. The third...I don't know. But he's not really a concern. As for the miners, they're led by a man named Jory Skewes. I'm sure there are others with some influence, but without him, they seem to be a rudderless ship."

As Diehl spoke, a huge, almost ecstatic grin spread across Claypole's face.

"Capital!" he said, thumping the table. "Capital!"

He pounded the table once more, his fist smacking down beside the wine bottle in a way that made Diehl flinch.

Claypole didn't notice. He shoved a hand under his coat first on his left side, then his right, searching for something. After some rummaging around, he pulled out a folded piece of paper. He put it on the table and flattened it out for Diehl to read.

I, _____O. DEAL_____, agree to enter into the employment of the Consolidated American Mining Corporation as of _____Feb. 13, 1894_____.
I accept that said employment is exclusive and affirm that I have ended (or
will end immediately upon signing) employment agreements (either written
or verbal) with any and all other individuals and organizations. I understand, furthermore, that failure to abide by the terms of this agreement will
be grounds for immediate termination.

_____

_____Henry S. Claypole_____ (countersigned)

"A contract?" said Diehl.

Claypole nodded happily as he reached into his coat again and fished out a pencil. "You're about to become a Consolidated Amer-ican man, Mr. Diehl. We may as well make it official...and binding."

He handed Diehl the pencil.

"I understand," Diehl said. "Can't have me changing sides at the drop of a hat."

He threw Goat and Whisper a meaningful look.

They weren't glaring at him anymore. Instead they were trying to project professional camaraderie. After all, he was about to become their boss again.

"Precisely," said Claypole. "My superiors don't tolerate such behavior in management personnel."

He looked eagerly at the contract.

Diehl signed it.

Claypole scooped it up and stuffed it away in his coat. Diehl gave him the pencil, and he tucked that away too. Then, from the same inside pocket, he produced a stack of twenty-dollar bills secured with a paper band. He slid it onto the table in front of Diehl.

"Welcome to the Consolidated American family, Mr. Diehl," he said. "It was you who gave me the idea to poach you, actually. If you could hire away some of our men, why couldn't I hire you away?" He sighed happily. "I can already tell we're going to get our money's worth."

Diehl took the cash, pausing to savor the weight of it and run his thumbs over the crisp, slick surface of the bills. The twenties were so new, still so perfect, they felt like they'd been starched and ironed. Like proud, proper, profoundly naïve young gentlemen about to enter a dirty, rough and tumble world. Like Diehl, once.

He put the cash in his coat without counting it.

"You need to get your money's worth at this point, don't you?" he said to Claypole. "I suspect this has already been an unexpectedly expensive acquisition."

Some of the cheerfulness left Claypole's face.

"Yes, well…we were led to believe the path would be smoother. The board…" Something like a grimace puckered up Claypole's mustache. "They aren't happy with how long it's been taking. But with your help, I'm sure we can finally break the impasse and have good news for San Francisco."

"And if the impasse *can't* be broken?"

Claypole's expression darkened even more.

"Then the men we work for will be most displeased," he said. "And when they're displeased, they…express their displeasure."

"I suppose they're not accustomed to be being displeased."

Claypole's smile returned, though rueful now. "They are not."

Diehl nodded, then glanced away to the west. The sun was sinking toward the distant mountaintops, and shadows were beginning to lengthen and deepen.

Diehl stood and stretched a hand across the table.

"Thank you, Mr. Claypole," he said.

"Thank *you*, Mr. Diehl."

The two men shook hands, then Diehl turned and started toward the corral.

"Mr. Diehl, wait!" said Claypole. "We have plans to make! And we forgot to drink a toast!"

Diehl didn't look back. He just kept heading toward the horse and mule tied to the fence rail thirty yards away.

"Can't drink a toast without glasses, can we?" he said.

"I didn't see any glasses in that basket," said Whisper.

No one heard him.

Diehl scanned the horizon again, focused this time on a particular point. The distant rise in the road he'd ridden in on.

A figure on horseback appeared there. A figure moving a bowler hat in a slow, straight-armed arc...then plunking the hat on his head.

A figure with long black hair tied back with a red bandanna and a breechcloth over the top of his buckskin trousers.

"Look!" Whisper said, loud enough for once. "It's that Apache!"

Diehl kept going. He hadn't quite reached the horse and mule.

"Mr. Diehl...what is going on?" Claypole asked.

Diehl picked up his pace.

"The man asked you a question, Diehl," said Goat. "And I'm asking it too."

The tone of the man's voice told Diehl it was time to stop. He turned around.

Goat and Whisper had their guns drawn and pointed at Diehl.

"Put those away," Diehl said. "You don't want anything to happen to me."

"Mr. Diehl, *what is going on?*" Claypole asked again.

"A lot," Diehl said. "And what you should know first and foremost is that those guns need to go back in their holsters. *Now.* Because if they don't, one of my associates is going to shoot that bottle. And that's something none of us would want."

Claypole scowled. "Because it would be such a frightful waste of Riesling?"

Diehl shook his head. "The Riesling's already been wasted. What's in that bottle now is a diluted solution of nitroglycerin. One of my other associates, Mr. Romo, prepared it. He's a mining expert, you know. He thinned out the nitro so it wouldn't vaporize half the county the first time my mule kicked. But he assured me that it's still more than potent enough to vaporize *you* if, say, a slug from a buffalo gun should hit it."

Claypole, Whisper, and Goat gaped, pop-eyed at the bottle.

"Think he's telling the truth?" Goat said.

"I don't know," said Claypole.

"Told you I didn't see no glasses," said Whisper.

Goat frowned at him. "No you didn't."

"Believe it or don't about the nitro," said Diehl. He gestured back at the Apache, who was still watching them from a quarter mile away, Winchester across his lap. "You can see I'm not alone— and that you can't count on Fortenberry and his friend to guard your rear anymore. I knew you'd have me followed, so I arranged to have the followers followed...and dealt with. Now we have a nice little standoff going. Have your men lower their guns, I'll ask you one question, and we can end this and be on our way."

Claypole didn't seem to hear him. He balled up his fists, gaze still locked on the bottle.

"What am I even doing here?" he spat. "I'm a mining superintendent. A manager. I should be in my office, goddammit!"

Diehl cleared his throat. "The guns, Mr. Claypole?"

Claypole turned to Goat and nodded brusquely.

Goat and Whisper lowered—but didn't holster—their guns.

Claypole swiveled to face Diehl again, face twisted with fury. "You signed a contract! You accepted an advance! Bad form, Diehl! Very bad form!"

"Good business, Mr. Claypole," Diehl said. "I've just removed one thousand dollars from your operational reserves. I can't imagine even Consolidated American would send you here with carte blanche when it came to cash. You've got a budget for this project... and I mean to make you break it. As for the contract, it's wholly invalid. Which brings me to my question."

"Invalid?" Claypole said. "What do you mean?"

Diehl ignored the man's question and asked his own.

"Who's your spy?"

It hit Claypole like a slap. He jolted back in his seat, blinking.

"What are you talking about?"

"When I first met these two," Diehl said, nodding at Goat and Whisper, "and the other men your Mr. Schuck had on the road to the mine? One of them said a group of 'agitators' was on its way. That made me suspicious. Then when I received your little note suggesting this meeting, those suspicions were confirmed—and I knew I had to accept your invitation."

"What was wrong with my note?" Claypole asked weakly. He'd slumped in his seat. Despite the cooling of the evening air, beads of sweat had begun spreading on his forehead.

"You addressed me by name, Mr. Claypole. You misspelled it—D-E-A-L instead of D-I-E-H-L. But you knew it, even though I hadn't mentioned it to those men on the road or to the ones I encountered when I had my chat with Mr. Schuck. The only people who've heard my name since I arrived are with the G-C Mine one way or another. Which means you have a spy. And once you tell me the name, this can all be over and you can go back to town and get yourself some real wine. Or something stronger. It looks like you need it."

By the time Diehl finished, Claypole was muttering to himself.

"Ruined. Ruined. Thirteen years with Consolidated American, and now I'm ruined."

"I'm sure it's not as bad as all that, Mr. Claypole," Diehl said. "Just tell me what I want to know, and you can have me killed tomorrow."

Goat shifted his weight and brought up his gun. Not all the way —not so it was pointed at Diehl's chest again. But it wasn't far off from his toes. All a shot to the belly would take was the slightest bend of the wrist.

"He's bluffing," Goat said.

"I don't think so," said Whisper. His gun was still pointed straight down.

"Wine bottle full of nitro," Goat continued. "That's the dumbest thing I ever heard."

"So dumb it just might be true," said Whisper.

Claypole acted as though he hadn't heard either of them.

"Do you know that I campaigned for this?" he said to Diehl.

"*Begged* the chairman of the board to send me and Schuck? And do you know why? Because I was afraid when he got his hands on the G-C Mine that SOB would hand it off to someone else to manage! I was afraid of a demotion, so here I am." He waved a limp hand at the desolate, darkening desert around them. "In hell. I'm no thug. No bully boy. I'm a Republican, for god's sake. I'm an Elk!"

"Now, now," Diehl said soothingly, gaze sliding back and forth from Claypole to Goat and back again. "You'll land on your feet. The important thing is to make sure we all live to fight another day. So…the name, please?"

Claypole pushed back the brim of his Homburg. His forehead glistened in the golden-brown light of sunset.

"It's the only real advantage I have left," he said.

"You'll think of something," said Diehl.

"If I have to wire San Francisco for more money and men…" Claypole shook his head miserably. "Kingsley is going to be furious."

"I'm sure he'll be very understanding," said Diehl even though he had no idea who "Kingsley" was. His eyes darted toward Goat and back again. "The name. *Now.*"

"What if I was to get that money back for you, Mr. Claypole?" Goat asked.

"Don't do it," said Whisper.

"You let me keep part of it? Half maybe?" Goat went on.

"It's not worth it," said Whisper.

"I don't think our chances are that bad," Goat said to Claypole. He squared his shoulders and narrowed his eyes, steeling himself again. "Once there's just the Indian to deal with…"

"Oh, I don't know, I don't know," Claypole moaned. "Maybe you're right. Here we are. Carpe diem, hm?"

A trickle of sweat curved around his brow and caught the corner of his left eye.

"Damn," he said, squeezing the eye closed.

He jammed a hand inside his coat.

"No!" Diehl cried.

But it was already too late.

They didn't hear the distant *pop* of the shot. The slug moved faster than the sound. And when the slug slammed into the bottle, there was a new sound. A deafening one.

An explosion that sent glass and timber and metal and flesh flying and flaming in every direction.

CHAPTER 17

First there was blackness and silence.

Then there was dim light.

Then there was sound. A high-pitched whine like mosquitoes hovering inches from each ear.

Then there was motion. Something thudding nearby.

Diehl opened his eyes and blinked up at orange-tinted clouds. He was stretched out on his back on dry, hard-packed earth. He pushed back his head to see what he'd heard falling to the ground behind him.

He saw, upside down, another cluster of mule turds raining down onto the first. Helen had quite a pile going. It looked like the explosion hadn't perturbed her in the slightest. Diehl's horse seemed skittery but uninjured as well.

Diehl focused on what lay beyond Helen's droppings. Two men had appeared out of the hills, walking toward him on the upside-down ground. Both carried rifles.

"He was reaching for a handkerchief," Diehl croaked.

The men couldn't hear him because they were too far off. Diehl couldn't hear himself because the ringing in his ears was too loud.

A minute later they were closer, and the ringing had started to fade.

"He was reaching for a handkerchief," Diehl said again.

He was still on his back. His face and hands and feet tingled in a way that told him standing wasn't an option yet.

"Told you he wouldn't thank you," Eskaminzim said to Hoop.

The Apache was wearing Fortenberry's bowler at such an extreme angle—half on his head, half over his left ear—it was a wonder it didn't fall off. Scattered around him and Hoop as they were approached were bits of blackened wood, scraps of torn fabric, and hunks of meat and bone. Diehl was tired of looking at it all upside down, so he rolled over. The ringing in his ears rose to a deafening crescendo, and his head swam. He sank his face into his crossed arms, staring down into the dirt.

"Looked to me like he was reaching for a gun," Hoop said.

"He was reaching for a handkerchief," said Diehl.

"You get the money?" Eskaminzim asked.

Diehl jerked his head up despite the ringing and dizziness.

The money.

He snaked a hand inside his coat. He let his head droop back down when he felt the straight, hard edge of the cash still safely tucked in an inside pocket.

"I got it."

"Find out who the spy is?" Eskaminzim asked.

Diehl heard the Apache and Hoop walk past where he lay.

"No," he sighed. "Before he could tell me *he reached for a handkerchief.*"

Eskaminzim laughed.

"Funny-looking handkerchief," he said.

Diehl lifted his head again.

Eskaminzim was squatting a dozen feet away. He picked something up off the ground and showed it to Hoop and Diehl.

A white hand, jagged bone jutting from the wrist. The pale fingers were wrapped tightly around a gleaming silver pistol.

Hoop cocked his head and cleared his throat and waited.

"Thank you," Diehl said. Then he put his head in his arms again. "I didn't think he had it in him. Guess I misjudged him."

"You *guess?*" said Hoop.

Diehl just groaned into the dirt.

Eskaminzim turned the hand this way and that to inspect what it held.

"Anybody want a gun?" he asked. He brought the hand close enough to give the pistol a sniff. "Brand new! And fancy! Looks silver-plated." He squinted at the mother-of-pearl grip. "Got some kinda writing on it too."

"All the more reason to get rid of it," said Hoop. "Can't keep the hat either."

Eskaminzim gave him an exaggerated pout. "Aww. I was starting to like it."

"Can't leave a single thing behind," said Diehl. "The gun goes, the bowler goes, the note from Claypole goes, gotta burn a contract he made me sign. Gather up every scrap."

"I know, I know," Eskaminzim said. He looked at the carnage around them and snorted out a chuckle. "Messy, even for us."

Hoop surveyed the stage station as well.

"Gonna be tough to get all this up to that hole in the hill," he said. "Good thing I brought tarps just in case."

"Do me a favor. Wrap me up in one while you're at it," said Diehl.

Hoop scowled down at him. "You gonna be all right?"

"I don't know," said Diehl. "I can't remember what all right feels like."

Hoop kept scowling at him.

Eskaminzim stood and began collecting more body parts. Soon he had arms and legs stacked up like cordwood.

"I won't deny it," he said cheerfully. "The Mexican knew what he was doing."

"Him I haven't misjudged," said Diehl.

"Yet," said Hoop. "You need help getting up?"

"Who says I'm getting up?" said Diehl.

Eskaminzim dropped his load of debris in a pile by the corral, leaning forward just enough to let the derby fall atop it. Then he turned and headed back for more. Hoop hadn't joined in the clean up yet. He was still looking at Diehl.

"Nice little bundle of money you've built up between what the lady gave you and what you got off Claypole," Hoop said.

"Nice little bundle," said Diehl.

"Might make a man wonder why he'd stick out his neck for more."

"Might."

"Might tempt a man to light out before the job is done."

"Might." Diehl turned his head to peep up at Hoop. "Have I lit out on you before?"

Hoop nodded without hesitation. "Three times."

"Have I ever lit out on you *before the job was done?*"

Hoop gave that more thought. "Depends on what you mean by 'the job.'"

Diehl sighed.

"Look," he said, "I'm hoping this job *is* done. Consolidated American tried to buy the G-C cheap, and we've made it costly. There're other copper mines they can get with a lot less fuss. So they'll move on. This isn't war. It's business."

Eskaminzim passed by with another armload of arms and tossed out a phrase he'd picked up as an Army scout.

"Goldbrickers."

"All right. I'm getting to it," said Diehl.

He began pushing himself slowly off the ground.

"I sure hope you're right about Consolidated American," Hoop said as Diehl got to his hands and knees. "Cuz you and I have seen plenty of business that looked a hell of a lot like war."

He turned and headed with swift, sure strides toward one of the biggest lumps of anatomy they had to contend with.

Diehl rose, swaying, to his feet.

"Don't worry, Sergeant," he said. He took an unsteady step, head still bowed. "When have I ever led you astray?"

He took another wobbly step forward, then managed to lift his head and smile.

That was when Helen kicked him.

CHAPTER 18

The private train left Phoenix at 6:44 a.m. Saturday, February 17. Hooked up behind the engine and tender were five cars. Two for horses, one for supplies, one for men, and one—with frosted glass windows and a gated observation platform—for *a* man. And his dog. The train headed southeast on the Union Pacific line, slicing through the Gila River Indian Reservation and the San Xavier Indian Reservation, and rocky hills, and broad, scrub-pocked flats.

South of Tucson it veered west on a spur line. The line continued on to a crude transfer station—just a wooden platform surrounded by piles of shard and sunbaked mule dung—after twelve miles. But the train stopped short, in the middle of nowhere. More privacy. Less jurisdiction.

Working swiftly but not hurriedly—with efficiency, not haste— men got out and began unloading horses and saddles and rifles. The passenger in the special car stepped outside to watch them. And to walk the dog. Two men hovered near him. Each wore a clean, stylish new suit that bulged at the left breast despite fine tailoring.

One of the newly mounted men steered his gray gelding to the back of the train to join them. He looked impassively at the dog—a sleek dark brown dachshund—as it watered a Joshua tree near the tracks. When he shifted his gaze to the man from the special car, his expression didn't change. Which is to say he still had no expression at all.

"You want us to ride in hard or ride in quiet?" he asked.

"We tried quiet, and it was a waste of time and resources," the other man said. "You're here for hard, Captain. Give it to them, with my compliments."

The man in the saddle didn't acknowledge the order except to wheel his gelding around and gallop off. All he had to do was lift a hand and point forward as he rode past the other men on horseback, and they knew to follow. They left a billowing cloud of dust behind them.

Ahead of them was Hope Springs and the Gruffud-Cadwaladr Mine.

Part Two

Le May, Breck, the Consolidated American Mining Corporation, the Dickinson National Detective Agency, More Lawyers Than the Devil Can Fit in Hell, the Relentless, Pitiless, Bone-Crushing Wheels of Progress, the Inexorable Power of Capital, Destiny, and the Goddamn American Way of Life

CHAPTER 19

Adam "Rusty" McFarlane eased back in his saddle, pushed up the brim of his new white Stetson, and sighed contentedly.

"You know," he said to Hoop, "I do believe this is the best job I ever had."

Hoop said nothing. He was riding eight feet to Rusty's right, gaze moving steadily from east to west and back again. Both men were keeping their mounts to an amble so as not to get too far ahead of the wagons rolling slowly down the road from the mine laden with piles of crushed ore on its way to Bisbee for roasting and smelting.

"Drover, muleskinner, tracklayer, lumberjack—I've done it all," Rusty went on. He'd only been working side-by-side with Hoop a few days, but he was already accustomed to the man's silence. "Damn hard work, damn little pay. And damn few opportunities for either, these days. That's why I gave working for that Schuck a try. Man's gotta eat, am I right?"

If Hoop had an opinion about the need to eat, he kept it to himself.

"Of course, I didn't care for the rough stuff," Rusty said. "Not. Pleasant. At. All. But this is different."

A cluster of dust-covered, grimy-faced miners had begun passing them, streaming by on either side of the road; tired men expending their last bit of energy to hurry home at the end of a long, stifling day underground.

"See you Monday, boys!" Rusty said to them. "Enjoy the Sabbath!"

"It's tonight I'm excited about," one of the miners said. He threw back his head and howled. "Saturday night!"

"Easy for him to be excited," another miner said, jerking his thumb at the first. "No kids."

"That'll change, the rate he's going with Inez Delgado," said a third with a broad wink.

Some of the other miners laughed. Several added "See you, Rusty" or "Night, Rusty" or some variation.

Rusty grinned at Hoop.

"See?" he said. "All I have to do is ride up and down this hill with a gun on my hip, and men are actually pleased to see me."

That finally got a response out of Hoop.

"Mine guards ain't usually so popular," he drawled—though he still didn't stop scanning the horizon.

"Oh?" said Rusty, rather than ask why he just smiled. "Well, this one is."

"Time might come that gun you're carrying isn't just for show."

Rusty's smile wilted a bit.

"I suppose."

"'Mine guard' will stack up different against drover, muleskinner, and the rest then," Hoop said.

Rusty's smile disappeared entirely. He started to reply, then thought better of it. He turned toward another gaggle of weary, dirty men passing on their way to the miners' camp.

"Enjoy your rest, fellas," he said. "But don't forget to cut your wolf loose first!"

The miners laughed and kidded each other and wished Rusty a good night. A few even wished Hoop a good night though they didn't expect a response. And they didn't get one.

Hoop stayed focused on the distant hills and plains, his body as still as it could be in the gently swaying saddle. But his eyes were ever moving, ever wary, never for a second at rest.

———

The cook who worked for both Catrin Gruffud and Gareth Cadwaladr was back at work now too. Juana, their shared maid, still insisted on helping out in the kitchen though. That way she could make sure that Romo always started and ended his day with what she called "comida de verdad." Real food.

This evening she brought him out a bowl of chili verde.

"Shepherd's pie," she said, jerking her head at the kitchen door at the back of Cadwaladr's house. Beyond it the cook, Mrs. Jones, was preparing dinner for her employers and two guests—Richard Utley and Oswin Diehl. Juana made a face and shook her head. "No quieres nada de eso."

You don't want any of that.

Romo didn't have the heart to tell the woman that he liked shepherd's pie more than chili verde. He just took the bowl and said "Gracias."

He ate standing up, and both he and Juana turned to gaze out over the cliff behind the house at the sun sinking toward the Sierrita Mountains. They spoke, as always, in Spanish.

"Delicious," Romo said. "The world lost a wonderful cook when you became a maid."

"Not really," said Juana. "I'm not any good with shepherd's pie or Welsh rarebit or cawl or the other glop Cadwaladr likes. It has to be food I know…and I have to *want* to make it."

"Well, I'm certainly glad you want to cook for me."

Romo ate another spoonful of chili verde, then asked Juana the question he'd been asking every morning and evening when she brought him food.

"Why are you so nice to me?"

It was always spoken as a joke, and Juana—beginning to show a humor and warmth she seemed to hide from the rest of the world— would reply in kind.

"Because Saint Francis tells us to care for sickly animals," she would say. Or "I can't have a fellow Mexican going around looking so feeble. Makes us all look bad." Or "I'm not cooking for you, boy. I'm cooking for me. You're just getting the leftovers."

"Haven't you heard?" she said this time. "I'm in love with you."

Romo froze with the spoon halfway to his mouth. He was afraid to look over at the woman—at least twenty years his senior—but he forced himself to glance her way.

Her thin lips were curled into a wry smile.

Romo tried not to look relieved. He *had* heard the snickering about how he'd supposedly won the maid's heart. Diehl kept offering to translate Swain's love poems into Spanish for him, and Eskaminzim's jokes were so crude Romo had been tempted to hit him. Which was exactly what the Apache wanted, no doubt. Hoop hadn't said anything out loud about it, but his raised eyebrow when Romo came back with a splash of fresh pico de gallo on his shirt spoke volumes.

"And I am in love with you, just as they say," Romo told Juana. He lifted the bowl in his hand a little higher. "What Mexican man could resist chili verde this good?"

The maid nodded approvingly. "The correct answer. I'm glad your American teachers didn't turn you into a gringo."

"They tried. Yet I remain as Mexican as an enchilada. Speaking of which…"

Romo gave Juana a puppy dog look.

"All right, fine," she said, taking the hint. "Enchiladas tomorrow."

Romo grinned. "You really are too good to me."

He took another bite. But he chewed more slowly after a moment, and the amused gleam in his eye faded.

"I do wonder about it though," he said once he'd swallowed. "Why *are* you so nice to me? It can't just be because we're both Mexican."

"Why not?"

Romo gave the woman a deadpan frown. "You know our history, Señora. Mexicans don't like each other that much."

Juana laughed at that in a way that was both appreciative and bitter, amused yet bleak.

"Good point. Maybe if you and I were *in* Mexico I wouldn't be so nice." She mulled it over, then nodded. "Probably not. You're a cientifico. A child of privilege. I bet your father loved President Diaz."

"He did," Romo said, his voice suddenly softer.

"Of course, he did. He could afford to send his son to…what was that university again?"

"Cornell."

"Yes. Cornell. Very expensive, I'm sure. Very cientifico. Very Diaz."

Romo put his spoon down in the bowl. He'd quickly come to regret the honest conversation he'd just started.

"I'm not political," he said.

"How lucky for you. I had a brother who was. He would've said everything is political—especially if you're a peon. You remind me of him…aside from the politics, of course. And the fact that you wear a gun for money. I can't make chili verde and enchiladas for Miguel anymore. I can make it for you. Does that answer your question?"

Romo nodded.

The two stood in awkward silence for a while.

"So *eat it*, dammit," Juana finally said.

Romo snatched up his spoon and shoveled in his biggest bite yet.

"Mmm-mmm," he said as he chewed. "Delicious."

"Don't talk with your mouth full," said Juana.

But her little smile had returned.

———

Cadwaladr's parlor room was identical to Miss Gruffud's. It had the same mahogany desk, the same plush armchairs, the same divan, even the same cut crystal glasses and decanter.

Cadwaladr and Utley were making use of the armchairs. Miss Gruffud was making use of the divan.

Diehl was making use of the decanter.

"A fine whiskey you have here, Mr. Cadwaladr," he said as he poured himself a second drink. "Strong but smooth—a combination any man should aspire to."

He smiled at Miss Gruffud.

Utley rolled his eyes.

The lady returned Diehl's smile, but in a prim, tolerant way. The warmth he'd managed to kindle in her had never returned after Utley and Eskaminzim's interruption. She'd been reserved with him ever since, even when he came calling with a whole bagful of fresh lemons—the local grocer having finally received a new shipment. He'd hoped for another opportunity to sip lemonade, discuss poetry, and...well, whatever else might come up. Instead Juana had taken the bag at the door and sent him away with an icy, "Miss Gruffud isn't available. I think enough employees are smitten with her already without encouraging *you*."

Oh, well. If he couldn't have lemonade with the lady—for now, he wasn't giving up—at least he could have free whiskey.

Diehl lifted his glass to eye level to inspect the amber liquor.

"Just the right color. Coppery. Apropos." He took a sip and looked over at Cadwaladr. "From Wales?"

The old man looked skeptical as if he suspected Diehl was simply buttering him up to justify another trip to the decanter. Which was correct.

"No, but close," Cadwaladr said. "From Kentucky but distilled by the sons of a Welshman."

"Ah. Heirs carrying on for the father. Admirable." Diehl turned again to Miss Gruffud, raised his glass, and repeated the Welsh toast Cadwaladr had used a few minutes before. "Lechyd da."

The lady raised her aperitif—a glass of sherry—and took a demure sip.

Utley threw back a gulp of whiskey and shifted irritably in his chair.

"We'll send nearly a ton of ore down to the depot today," he said. "By the middle of next week, we'll have enough there to ship to Bisbee, and not long after that, the money'll start flowing in

instead of out. Within the month we'll be profitable again...
assuming we eliminate some of our excess expenditures."

He shot a sneer at Diehl—though without meeting his gaze—
just in case there was any doubt which excess expenditures he was
thinking of.

"That's excellent, Richard," Miss Gruffud said. "I don't think
we should be in a rush to cut costs, however. We've only been in
operation again a few days. It's too early to say which expenses are
truly excessive."

"But Catrin, you know my concerns about the liquidity situation," said Cadwaladr. "The need for *cash*..."

He raised his bushy eyebrows but said no more, leaving the rest
unspoken in a "not in front of the children" sort of way.

Diehl drowned a sigh with another drink of whiskey. He'd seen
this same scene many times over the years. The second a job was
done, and some of those it benefited wanted him gone. Who needed
the reminder of unpleasant times and unsavory solutions...espe-
cially when it was costing them money?

"Don't worry," he said. "I expect you'll be able to start trimming
the fat soon enough. If another couple weeks go by with no new
complications, I'll happily trim myself."

"Another couple weeks?" Utley grumbled.

"Of course, there is the matter of the bonus to the A.A. Western
Detective Agency if your issues with Consolidated American are
conclusively resolved," Diehl went on. "My instructions from
Colonel Crowe indicated there would be one. I only know my
portion of it, but of course I assume the lump sum is considerably
more. You might want to consider that—especially in light of your
'liquidity situation'—when deciding when to release me and my
colleagues from our duties here."

The more Diehl talked, the more Utley fumed and Cadwaladr
looked queasy.

Miss Gruffud, on the other hand, widened her smile. It was still
unclear to Diehl if the lady cared for his sense of humor, but his
business sense she obviously appreciated.

"In other words," she said, "it would be more expensive to terminate your employment than continue it."

Diehl nodded. "For the moment, yes. When you can cover our final payment out of petty cash, by all means fire us. In the mean-time...well, we'll try not to get in the way."

"Fair enough," Miss Gruffud said. "That's settled then."

Cadwaladr threw down a gulp of whiskey that emptied his glass.

"It's your decision, Catrin," he said. "Anyway, that's enough business talk. Let us be sociable."

"An excellent suggestion, Gareth," Miss Gruffud said.

Everyone looked at each other for a moment, waiting for the sociability to begin.

No one knew how to begin it.

The strained silence stretched on until the door opened and plump little Mrs. Jones, the cook, came in.

"Dinner is served," she said.

Thank God, Diehl thought.

Utley rose from his chair and took a step toward Miss Gruffud.

Diehl slipped in front of him and offered her his arm.

"If I may?" he said.

It was hard to read the look she gave him. Amused? Exasper-ated? Both? Neither? But she took his proffered arm and stood up.

Utley and Cadwaladr glowered at him as he led the lady away.

From a bluff high above the road, Eskaminzim watched the wagons and miners head down the hill. He could see Hoop and the man called "Rusty" down there on their horses too, guarding the rocks the whites were fighting over.

The copper ore wasn't even pretty, like silver. To Eskaminzim it looked like huge piles of rabbit scat. But he supposed it had some sort of use. It didn't really matter to him. Whites wanted it, so it was worth money.

Once, long ago, money hadn't mattered to Eskaminzim either. But he'd learned. Now money meant horses and bullets and knives.

And food and clothes and livestock for his sisters and cousins and nieces and nephews and uncles and aunts and friends on the Mescalero Reservation. Money meant life.

He was happy to earn it this way—from death—though he was bored at the moment. Anything else the whites might pay him to do would be a thousand times more boring and make even less sense. He tracked and fought and killed, and it wasn't other Apaches he was expected to track and fight and kill anymore. If he had to have a "job," this was the job for him.

One of Eskaminzim's cousins was a farmer, and one of his brothers-in-law—the one who wasn't Hoop—was an apprentice in a blacksmith's shop. He kept waiting for them to go crazy with frustration and run off into the desert screaming, but it hadn't happened yet. He didn't understand it. That's what he would have done.

Years ago, before any kind of raid or fight, the men of Eskaminzim's band would gather by a bonfire and beat drums and sing songs about their warriors. When one would hear his name, he would step forward and walk around the fire as the men sang about his feats in battle. Anyone who wished to fight under his leadership would get up and follow him. It was a good system, and the songs were wonderful. Eskaminzim missed them.

No one would sing about his feats, and at the moment he had nothing to do except watch and wait—and wait and wait and wait —alone from the cliffs. So he began to drum on a boulder and sing the Mescalero-Chiricahua words he would've liked to hear by a fire.

Eskaminzim! Eskaminzim!
He kills Whites! And Mexicans!
And they pay him to do it!
This man is amazing!
He's cunning. And quiet. But hilarious. And good-looking!
We pray in the four directions, and he is unstoppable in
*   them all.*
In the South, he fought Mexicans and Chiricahuas and Warm
*   Springs Apaches.*
So many! So tough!

> *In the North, he fought white thieves and bandits and*
>   *pistoleros.*
> *He once killed one with a can of tomatoes!*
> *In the East, where the sun rises, he knifed a white railroad*
>   *guard who tried to brain him with a blackjack! He was*
>   *fourteen years old!*
> *(He had to escape Pittsburgh! And he did!)*
> *In the West, where the sun sets, he has killed a lot more of*
>   *everybody.*
> *He's not picky! You want to fight? He'll fight!*
> *Eskaminzim! Eskaminzim!*
> *This man is amazing!*

Eskaminzim was about to start over again—this time he'd work in the time he fought off three Navajos with a cactus—when something in the distance caught his eye.

To the southeast, just beyond Hope Springs and the miners' camp, a little yellow puff had blossomed. It quickly bloomed larger and higher and darker.

It was a cloud of dust of a type Eskaminzim knew well.

Horses. Lots. Ridden hard.

Eskaminzim grinned and snatched up his rifle and started hurrying down the hill toward the road. And toward whoever was coming their way.

Eskaminzim was sure he'd soon have lots of new things to sing about.

CHAPTER 20

Every child in the miners' camp was outside in the dying light of day. There weren't many of them, this being Arizona Territory. Women weren't quite as rare there as they'd been a decade before, but a miner with a wife by his side could still feel like he'd struck gold. One with kids had hit the mother lode.

Most of the children were down by the stream. The older girls watched them while doing laundry. The older boys were off in the mesquite trees supposedly gathering firewood but actually sneaking a last smoke with paper and tobacco stolen from their soon-to-return fathers.

Light and the smells of cooking came from the shacks with wives in them. Most of the shacks were dark. Lisette Skewes stepped from hers to gaze past town at the towering mound of yellow-brown earth and rock—not big enough to be a mountain, far too big to be a mere hill—where her man spent most of his time. Six days a week he was deep in its bowels. Which meant six days a week she had to worry if he'd ever come out again. Every day, Monday through Saturday, was a day he could be crushed to a pulp in a cave-in or plummet down a shaft to be lost in the darkness forever.

But now it was the best time of the week. Saturday night. Soon the men would come trudging back, dirty and stinking and exhausted but *alive*. And Lisette would get a whole day to live free of fear. So long as she didn't think about Monday. Or the Consolidated American Mining Corporation.

One of Lisette's neighbors, Mrs. Perez, stepped from *her* shack to gaze north too. Distant specks, like a line of ants, were visible on the road from the mine. Lisette spoke no Spanish, Mrs. Perez no English, yet they looked at each other and said all they needed to with smiles. It was going to be a good night.

Mrs. Perez must have noticed the sound first, for her smile was the first to collapse, her eyes the first to widen.

A rumbling like distant thunder—only it didn't stop as the seconds wore on and other women stepped outside frowning. It grew louder.

Lisette walked to the side of her shack to look south. A low cloud the yellow of desert dust billowed up over the hills and tree-tops. It was obvious now what the thunder really was.

Hoofbeats.

"Guadalupe! Francisco!" Mrs. Perez screamed. "Ven a casa ahora mismo!"

The other mothers started yelling for their children too.

Lisette had none to call in, but she started shouting all the same.

"Get inside! Get inside!"

Yet she stayed outside. Maybe the women were wrong about what was coming. And even if they weren't, she wanted to see it for herself. See *them*. Look at least one of them in the eye and show him all the contempt he deserved.

The creek and its surrounding trees swooped east just south of camp, so Lisette couldn't see the riders until their hoofbeats had risen to a roar. They rounded the bend a hundred yards away, coming at a full gallop as some of the mothers hustled their children indoors. Were there twenty-five of them? Thirty? It was impossible to tell. They just kept coming and coming, the ones in back obscured by the dust from those in front.

They weren't cowboys, that was plain. None wore chaps, only a few had ropes, and though their clothes and hats were those of working men they lacked the frayed, faded fabric and drooping felt that came from endless hours under sun and rain.

The lead rider—an older, mustachioed man with steel-gray hair and a long, bony body—seemed to notice Lisette looking at them. He headed straight for her.

Kids were still scurrying up the from the creek, their homes too far off to reach before the riders swept into camp. Lisette rushed over to cut them off.

"Get in! Get in!" she cried, pointing at her own doorway nearby.

Half a dozen children turned and dashed inside.

Then the riders arrived. They swept through the camp, tearing down clothes lines and trampling vegetable gardens and chickens. The leader kept coming at Lisette, riding toward her so hard and straight it seemed impossible that he wouldn't trample her too. She stood her ground though, eyes locked on his. When at last he reined up, his gelding skidded to a stop mere feet before her.

"What are you doing?" she said. "Who the hell are you?"

"We have a warrant," the man announced loudly. "We've been deputized to serve it."

"What kind of warrant?" Lisette demanded.

The man turned to the other riders who were now milling about nearby.

"Search everywhere," he said. He pointed at Lisette's shack. "Starting there."

Some of the riders began dismounting.

Lisette stepped quickly to the right, positioning herself in front of the door.

"I asked what kind of warrant," she said.

The thin, gray-haired man fixed her with a quick, cool, appraising look.

"Resisting a duly sworn peace officer," he said. Not to her. It was an announcement to his men.

Two of them came stalking toward Lisette.

"Don't you dare!" she said, taking an involuntary step backward.

Then they were on her.

"Resisting a duly sworn peace officer," said one.

He backhanded Lisette across the face. She staggered to the side, tripped over her skirts, and fell.

"Resisting a duly sworn peace officer," said the other man, kicking Lisette in the stomach.

He kept on kicking her while the first man marched inside and, ignoring the children's screams, began destroying everything he could touch.

It was the same all through the camp. Men striding into homes and tearing them apart from the inside, punctuated by wails and cries and the occasional *"Resisting a duly sworn peace officer"* followed by thuds and grunts and whimpers.

Only the gray man and one other rider—this one slightly younger and much heavier—remained mounted.

"Sure is nice to be a duly sworn peace officer again," the tubby one said with a grin.

He was watching one of the shacks at the far end of camp go up in flames, probably because one of the men had accidentally—or not—thrown something large and flammable onto a cooking fire.

The lean, gray man watched the fire spread too. But there was no satisfaction on his face. Just dour determination. The flames, the screams, the once-defiant woman now curled in a bloodied ball in the dirt outside her door—it was just part of the job.

He turned away to focus on the road leading up to the Gruffud-Cadwaladr Mine. When he saw the high-sided ore wagons and the miners streaming down the hill around them, his eyes narrowed.

"That's enough!" he called out. "Moving on!"

"You heard the captain!" the portly man shouted. "Mount up! Mount up!"

A moment later, the old man gave his gelding his spurs, and the thunder of hoofbeats once again followed him up the trail.

———

Eskaminzim came bounding down out of the rocks.

"Here they come!" he called to Hoop.

Hoop was on his horse near one of the wagons. Rusty was to his left, also still mounted. To his right was Jory Skewes. The other workers heading home from the mine, about two dozen total, were clumped in milling, muttering clusters along the road.

They were all looking down at the south end of town and the cloud of dust that was growing again there...this time mixed with black smoke.

"Who are 'they' and what are they doing?" Skewes said.

"We'll find out soon. Can't be any doubt about who sent 'em though," said Hoop. He glanced back at Eskaminzim. "What you think? Around twenty-five or thirty?"

Eskaminzim cocked his head and gave the dust cloud an appraising squint.

"Thirty-two," he said.

Rusty looked over at him to see if he was joking.

The way Eskaminzim smiled back, it was impossible to tell. If the Apache *wasn't* joking, he was strangely pleased to know there were dozens of men riding hard up the hill toward them.

"What are you gonna do?" Skewes asked Hoop.

Rusty didn't say anything, but the way he turned to Hoop, wide-eyed and pale, silently repeated the question.

Yeah...what are *you gonna do?*

Hoop looked around at the ore wagons, the rough, rut-grooved road, the surrounding bluffs and boulders. Then he turned to Skewes again.

"We fall back."

"*What?*" said Skewes.

Hoop nodded at the bottom of the hill. "Three men couldn't hold them off long, and there's no time to get the wagons turned. So we leave the wagons, you and your men scatter, and the fighting men get back up to the mine."

"But—" Skewes began.

"'The fighting men'?" said Rusty. He didn't seem pleased to be a mine guard anymore.

Hoop kept his gaze on Skewes.

"The G-C can afford to lose a few wagons. What it can't lose are its men or the mine itself. Those we have to protect until we know what we're up against. So this ain't the time to throw lives away on a fight we can't win. We fall back. Now. Cuz those riders are gonna be here in less than two minutes."

Skewes grimaced as though chewing on something sour he couldn't force him to swallow. "Running away again. Already..."

A distant—but not *too* distant—sound rose up as he spoke. The rumble of approaching horses.

Skewes turned and spoke to the miners.

"Everyone off the road! Head up! Into the rocks! Quick!"

The miners didn't need time to think it over. They darted off, headed for high ground.

"What about us?" the nearest wagon driver asked.

"Set your brakes and go with 'em," Hoop said. He looked at Rusty, said "Let's go," and turned his horse toward the top of the hill.

"Race you back to the mine?" Eskaminzim said as Hoop trotted past.

"Another time," said Hoop. He stretched out his left hand without stopping his horse.

Eskaminzim darted forward, grabbed Hoop's arm, and swung up behind him. The second he was settled, Hoop kicked his horse up to a gallop.

Rusty paused to look with something like envy at the miners and teamsters scattering into the rocky bluffs. Then he glanced back and saw the men on horseback charging up the road—just indistinct shapes in the distance, but close enough now to confirm that Eskaminzim's count wasn't far off.

He gave his horse a "Yah!" and sped away toward the mine.

———

The lean man slowed when he reached the first mule team.

"Vollmer, Feger, McClintock, Parsons—search these wagons," he said. "*Thoroughly*."

He looked to his left at the gaggle of unarmed men climbing up the slope to escape them. One glared down at him from a cliff and made a rude gesture.

"You know what to do if anyone interferes with the performance of your duties as a sworn peace officer," the tubby rider said.

"Yes, sir, Mr. Kozolooski, sir!" said Vollmer, pulling out his rifle.

He'd mangled Eugene Kozlowski's name, as most of the men did. Yet the heavyset man smiled.

The rider called Feger was already off his horse to approach the first wagon on foot, while McClintock and Parsons pulled out ropes as they rode closer. The lean man and Kozlowski and the rest carried on up the road.

Feger and McClintock and Parsons worked quickly and efficiently. There was no searching. The mules were unhitched and run off, the ropes secured, the wagon upended, the piles of milled ore sent streaming down the hillside.

A rock the size of a loaf of bread bounced out onto the road nearby, gravel clattering down around it. Though his horse skittered and shook its head at the surprise, Vollmer was able to take aim at a man standing about fifty yards above him—maybe the one who'd thrown the rock, maybe not—and with a squeeze of the finger send a slug through his head.

———

Diehl froze with a forkful of shepherd's pie halfway to his mouth. What he'd heard was a tap little different than the clatter of cutlery against porcelain and the thump of crystal set upon wood. Miss Gruffud and Cadwaladr and Utley didn't notice it at all. They kept eating and drinking while Cadwaladr regaled Diehl—or thought he was regaling Diehl—with the story of his long, winding journey to America with Miss Gruffud's father forty years before.

"Of course, like I said, Noah had the head for business, but I was the one with the grit. And the luck," Cadwaladr was saying as one chapter—how they'd acquired their first grubstake before their ship even arrived in New York—wound down. "So it was me who took that four-flushing Irishman aside. Protestant or Catholic, real men agree on what's truly holy. A straight flush beats a full house, and a bet's a bet no matter how much whiskey went into its making."

Though Miss Gruffud must have heard the story a thousand times, she looked at the old man sharply with something like a scowl on her angular face.

Cadwaladr seemed to note her annoyance but carried on anyway.

"Well, McCarty acknowledged the truth of that when he saw the Atlantic Ocean below him and his ankles in my hands above."

Cadwaladr chuckled at the memory. He looked at Diehl expecting him to chuckle too.

Diehl put down his fork and pushed back his chair.

"Is something wrong?" Miss Gruffud asked.

"Duty calls," Diehl said.

"Is that some kind of euphemism?" Utley asked. He was on his third glass of wine.

Diehl ignored him.

"Excellent shepherd's pie," he said to Cadwaladr. "I hope to be back for the pudding and port."

He gave the lady a little bow, then walked quickly out of the dining room, across the foyer, and out the front door. As he trotted down the front steps Romo and Juana came around the side of the house.

"You heard it too?" Diehl said to Romo.

Romo shook his head. "Juana did. She said it was a rifle."

Diehl looked at the tall, gaunt maid with new respect.

She scowled back at him with her same old contempt.

"From the road," she said.

"I think so too," said Diehl. He put a hand to his side. "Dammit."

He wasn't wearing his gun. Formal dress was expected at a dinner party, not a forty-five.

Romo had on his holster, and Diehl glanced over at it, tempted to ask the young Mexican to give it to him.

"Come on," he said instead, hurrying off.

He didn't know what was really going on between Romo and Juana, but he wouldn't humiliate the young man in front of the woman. Not unless he had to.

Romo followed him as he headed around the mill. To Diehl's surprise, Juana did as well. He started to tell her to stay at the house, but the glare she gave him shut his mouth. If she wanted to rush toward gunfire, it would obviously take more than him to stop her.

Diehl heard hoofbeats as they rounded the building, and seconds later two horses came charging up from the road. One carried Hoop and Eskaminzim, the other the mine guard called Rusty. Eskaminzim hopped off before Hoop even brought his mount to a halt. The Apache used the momentum to carry him toward Diehl, Romo, and Juana at a sprint.

"Men coming from the south!" he said. "Lots of them!"

"Who fired?" said Diehl. "Us or them?"

Hoop and Rusty reined up nearby.

"Them," said Hoop.

"I think they shot one of the miners," said Rusty. "I saw someone fall from the bluffs."

"*Damn*," Diehl spat.

He could hear more horses approaching now. Their riders would be on them in less than a minute. He had seconds to come up with a plan.

He made his decision and acted on it immediately, because given a few more seconds to think it over, he knew he'd change his mind.

"Hoop, Eskaminzim, Romo, Rusty—take cover," he said. He looked over at Juana. "You do whatever you want, but I'd prefer if you stayed right here."

"And what are *you* going to do?" the maid asked.

"I'm going to stop them."

Juana arched a thin black eyebrow. "And how do you think you're going to do that?"

"I'll ask nicely," Diehl said.

Juana scoffed. Everyone else managed not to, but they all looked deeply skeptical.

"I'm an unarmed White man in daylight with witnesses," Diehl said. "If they shot a miner, they probably had an excuse. I won't give them one. Remember—this might feel like war, but it's not. It's business. They want this mine intact, and they want the acquisition to look legal. That should keep me alive if I play this right."

Eskaminzim did scoff now, apparently at the notion of Diehl playing it right.

"You sure about this?" asked Hoop.

"Of course not," Diehl said. "But you got a better idea you can tell me in the next three seconds?"

Hoop shook his head.

"*Go,*" said Diehl. "They're almost here."

Hoop and Rusty dropped from their saddles. Eskaminzim jogged off toward the stable, heading for a trough he'd apparently chosen as his breastwork. Romo turned to Juana.

"You don't have to stay," he said in Spanish. "It's not going to be safe here."

"That's why I *have to* stay," she replied. She looked this way and that, then pointed at a pile of gray slag nearby. "Now get behind that and keep your head down."

Diehl, meanwhile, had begun walking swiftly toward the south end of the plateau, where the mesa dipped and narrowed and angled off into the road to town. He was still trying not to change his mind. He felt some relief when he realized he couldn't change his mind anyway.

The riders were almost there, and he was out in the open with nowhere to hide and no way to defend himself.

He had no other options. "Ask nicely" would have to work.

He could see the men coming toward him now. To his surprise, they weren't racing up the hill in a sloppy, strung-out jumble. They were in two neat lines, with a single rider out front—a rider who kept coming and coming, showing no sign that as small an obstacle as Oswin Diehl was going to slow him in the slightest.

Diehl planted his feet and held up his arms and decided what to say.

This is private property. Proceed and you're trespassing.

Legalistic but direct. Firm but not a threat. It might keep him alive…if he got a chance to say it.

The leader was a hundred yards away now, still closing fast.

Diehl could see that he was tall and lean and gray.

At eighty yards, Diehl could see his mustache.

At seventy yards, he could make out his long, lined face.

At sixty yards, Diehl cursed and lowered his arms.

At fifty yards, the man finally started to slow his horse.

At twenty yards, he stopped, his men still lined up neatly behind him.

"We have a warrant," the man said. "We've been deputized to serve it."

He wasn't even looking at Diehl as he spoke. He was gazing past him at the mine entrance and the mill and the stable. One unarmed man didn't concern him. In his mind, he was already past Diehl, doing whatever he'd come to do.

"Don't come another step closer," Diehl said.

The man finally looked at him. His gaze was cold, detached, dismissive. He started to turn to say something to his men. *Ride this dumb son of a bitch down*, probably, or words to that effect.

Then his eyes widened ever so slightly, and he froze.

"That's right. Warrant or not, you need to stop right here," Diehl told him. "Because if you keep going, Captain Breck, there's a man up there with a Sharps rifle who's going to kill you the second he sees your goddamn face."

CHAPTER 21

There were murmurings and stirrings among the mounted men on the road behind Breck.

"Did that son of a bitch just say what I think that son of a bitch said?" growled the squat bullfrog of a man who was so often at Breck's side—Kozlowski.

Breck brought silence and stillness with a single word.

"*Steady*."

Then he spoke again to the man blocking his way.

"Lieutenant…Dial, isn't it?"

"Diehl."

Breck nodded. He seemed to warm just a bit. Not with any friendliness toward Diehl though. He glanced away, transported to a past he savored more than the present.

"Do you mean to tell me one of your old troopers is up there at the mine?" he said.

"That's right. Sergeant Hoop. Corporal Hoop when you and he crossed paths. Remember him?"

Breck thought it over.

"No," he said.

"Well, believe me," said Diehl. "He'll never forget *you*."

Whatever nostalgia was bringing life to Breck's craggy face faded away.

"That doesn't matter, Diehl," he said. "We're going to search this place, and you can't stop us."

"Search it for what?"

For a moment, Breck coolly considered the question. And coolly considered, Diehl knew, riding right over him and taking his chances with Hoop. But at last the older man slipped a bony hand inside his plain brown coat and pulled out a folded piece of paper. He snapped it open, leaned down, and handed it to Diehl.

Diehl read quickly.

To any peace officer of Pima County

Greetings:

WHEREAS, I have the power to deputize citizens to enforce the law and carry out court orders, and WHEREAS, I have done so in the case of Thomas S. Breck et al., operatives of the Dickinson National Detective Agency, and WHEREAS, I have reviewed a sworn affidavit establishing that Henry Claypole of Tucson went missing while negotiating for the purchase of the Gruffud-Cadwaladr Mine in Pima County, and WHEREAS, that affidavit sets forth substantial facts establishing that probable cause does exist for the issuance of a search warrant, THERE-FORE, you are commanded to permit and, if requested, assist in a search of the Gruffud-Cadwaladr Mine and all associated property of its owners and operators.

SIGNED, ENTERED, AND ORDERED this 17th day of February, 1894, to attest to which I subscribe my name.

W.F. Gorman
Justice of the Peace
Pima County, Arizona Territory

Diehl handed the warrant back to Breck.

"All right. You've got the law on your side…for now," Diehl said. "But the fact remains that if you ride past me, warrant or no, your horse's haunches are going to be painted with your brains, Breck. In fact, you're lucky you've gone so gray the last fifteen years." Diehl favored the man in the saddle with a grim smile. "If you hadn't grown old, you'd be dead already."

Breck gave Diehl a long, icy look as he stuffed the warrant away.

"I'm remembering you better now," he said. "You're a buffoon."

Diehl shrugged, unoffended. "Better men than you have said so. Worse men too. Who aren't around to repeat it. What matters is that you're already in range of Sergeant Hoop's Sharps. So why don't you and your boys ride back down this hill and give me a little time to talk to my employers? I'm sure we can come to some—"

"Diehl," Breck cut in, "do you *really* remember me?"

Diehl's face hardened. "I do."

"And would the Captain Breck you recall give one single damn about a Sharps rifle or a Gatling gun or half a company of cavalry where he intends to go? Would he ride away? Or would he do his job—and send in his men with orders to kill any dumb bastard who got in the way?"

"That sounds familiar," Diehl said.

"Good. Then you know I mean it when I say that's precisely what I'm about to do. We have the right to conduct a search and conduct it we will…as we see fit."

Breck leaned back in his saddle and half-turned toward the men lined up two-by-two behind him.

"Three minutes. Then we're going in," he said.

Kozlowski replied with a smugly satisfied, "Yes, sir!" The rest of the men just stared at Diehl. They looked serious, but not scared. When Breck sent them in, Diehl could see, they'd go without hesitating.

Breck turned to face Diehl again.

"The clock is ticking," he said. "Whatever happens next is on your head."

Diehl glared at the man a moment—a moment he knew he didn't have. Then he spun around and started marching back toward the mine. A part of him wanted to run. Another part—the part that had already realized and accepted what he was going to have to do—didn't want to go at all.

———

Romo watched Diehl approach from his spot by the slag heap. It had been hard to tell what was happening from so far away, but there seemed to be some sort of stalemate. Diehl didn't appear panicked, and the men on horseback were keeping their distance. They weren't leaving though, and Eskaminzim and Hoop were still staring down the barrels of their rifles from their hiding places to Romo's right and left.

Romo noticed Rusty peeping back at him around a corner of the mill. Romo hoped he didn't look as nervous as Rusty did.

Diehl smiled and flapped his hands as he drew close, motioning for the men to step out from cover and join him. For some reason the smile made Romo almost as nervous as the mounted men waiting and watching a hundred yards away.

"Change of plan," Diehl said.

Juana joined the five men as they gathered out in the open. Diehl gave her a look that suggested he wasn't so anxious to have her around as a witness anymore, but he quickly shifted his attention to Hoop.

"I need to borrow your rifle for a second," he said.

"What for?" said Hoop. "You never been much good with it."

But he handed over the heavy Sharps anyway.

"Thanks," Diehl said.

He stepped back two paces and pointed the rifle at Hoop's stomach.

"Alfonso, Rusty—cover Eskaminzim," he said.

Romo was too stunned to move. He could barely get his mouth in motion to say, "What?"

Rusty looked just as shocked but managed to unholster his gun and point it at the Apache.

"Drop your rifle, Eskaminzim," Diehl said. "And Rusty—give him a little more room. You're too close."

"R-right," Rusty said, taking a big step back.

Eskaminzim let his Winchester fall to the dirt.

"You're lucky," he said to Rusty. "You *were* too close."

Romo finally got his gun out, but he couldn't bring himself to point it at anyone in particular.

"What's going on?" he asked Diehl.

"He is betraying us," Juana sneered.

"I'm keeping everyone here from getting shot," Diehl snapped back. "Alfonso—relieve Hoop of his sidearm. Quickly. And carefully."

Romo just blinked at Hoop, still frozen in confusion.

"Go ahead," Hoop told him. "It ain't you I blame for this."

He went on talking—to Diehl now—as Romo slowly leaned in to slide his Colt from its holster.

"In the long goddamn history of dumb things you've done, this has got to be the dumbest. What are you trying to do?"

"Like I said," Diehl replied. "Keep you alive."

A voice called out from the road—a voice that made Hoop stiffen and clench his fists and scowl with an instant, murderous rage.

"Thirty seconds, Diehl!" it said.

"*Captain Breck*," said Hoop. "That bastard…here…in Arizona…" He glowered at Diehl. "And you're protecting him."

"He's with the Dickinsons now, apparently, and he's got thirty-some men and a search warrant," said Diehl. "Now's not the time for old business."

Hoop looked like he was going to spit in Diehl's face. "'Old business'? This has got nothing to do with business."

"Who's Captain Breck?" Romo asked. "Someone you knew from the Army?"

"In a way," said Diehl.

Hoop looked over at Eskaminzim.

"It's the Ranger," he said.

"*The* Ranger?" said Eskaminzim.

Hoop nodded.

"Ahhh," said Eskaminzim.

He gazed wistfully down at his rifle, seeming sad that something he suddenly wanted so badly was so near yet out of reach.

The men on horseback started toward them again, approaching at an easy, confident canter.

Diehl turned to Juana. "Go tell Miss Gruffud and Mr. Cadwaladr and Utley that a group of Dickinson detectives are here, and they've been deputized and they have a search warrant and they've already shot one man. We can't interfere with them or provoke them in any way."

The maid just glared back at him, looking disgusted that a man such as him should presume to tell her what to do.

"They would just *love* a chance to gun down Miss Gruffud and the old man, and I don't want them to get it," Diehl said. "Hurry, dammit!"

Juana finally spun around and dashed off.

Diehl turned back to Breck and his men. They were spreading out as they trotted up, some headed for the stables and corrals, some for the mine entrance, some for the mill, and some— including Breck and Kozlowski—still coming straight at Diehl and the others.

"Drop the guns," Breck said to Romo and Rusty.

He didn't ask why those guns were pointed at Hoop and Eskaminzim. He seemed to understand—and it obviously amused him.

"Not hard to figure which one of you is Sergeant Hoop," he said. "One of the few good things about the Tenth Cavalry. Always easy to spot its troopers in a crowd."

Hoop clenched his teeth and said nothing.

Romo and Rusty looked at Diehl. He nodded, then bent down to put the Sharps gently on the ground. Romo and Rusty put their guns down too.

Breck glanced back at Kozlowski.

"You watch 'em, Koz," he said. "Might give you a chance to play with your new Spencer."

The fat man grinned and nodded, then slid from his saddle and pulled a shiny-barreled long gun from its scabbard. He pumped a round into the chamber.

"Pretty, ain't she? Repeating shotgun," he said. "Wanna see how it works?"

He pointed the barrel at Hoop.

"No thanks. We've seen 'em," said Diehl. He looked hard at Breck. "A demonstration will be entirely unnecessary."

Breck jerked his head at Kozlowski.

"That's up to him," he said.

Kozlowski's grin grew wider.

Breck spurred his horse and galloped off toward the mill. Several of his men had already dismounted and headed inside, and the sound of splintering wood and shattering glass blasted out through the opened doors. The men by the stables were conducting their "search" the same way, tearing down fence rails and tossing tack and harnesses and bridles from the hayloft. The men heading into the mine were toting pickaxes they'd found nearby.

"What are they looking for, anyway?" said Rusty.

"Nothing," said Hoop.

"Claypole," said Diehl.

Kozlowski laughed.

"They're both right!" he told Rusty. He shifted his gaze to Hoop. "So you know the captain from the good ol' days in Texas, huh? You remember *me*?"

Hoop narrowed his eyes and studied the man's jowly, jeering face.

"I seem to recall another asshole with a badge who looked a little like you," he said. "Only he wasn't so damn fat."

Kozlowski laughed again. "Yeah, I've put on a few pounds. Slowed down a bit too."

He gestured at the Sharps with his shotgun. It was on the ground about three yards from Hoop's feet.

"Maybe you could even dive for that and get off a shot before I could," he said. "You still got an easy shot at the captain if you wanna try to take it."

Hoop remained absolutely still, eyes locked on the fat man. Eyes filled with hate. Kozlowski's grin started to wilt under the heat of it.

Kozlowski glanced around. The men he'd ridden up with were

all off doing what they could to wreck the mill and the stables and the mine.

His grin bloomed again.

"You know, maybe you did make a try for that rifle," he said to Hoop. "Who's to say you didn't?"

"Us," said Romo.

Kozlowski shrugged. "Who's to say you *all* didn't go for your guns?"

"Goddamned Rangers," Hoop muttered. "Bastards never change."

"Why should we?" Kozlowski said with smirking satisfaction. "If something works…"

He took three steps back, putting more distance between himself and his prisoners—and putting more of them in the shot spread when he pulled the trigger. One squeeze now and he might hit all five at once. Two squeezes and he definitely would.

"I think you're gonna get that demonstration after all, Lieutenant," he said.

"N-now just hold on there, m-mister…" Rusty stammered, putting up his hands.

"Damn you, Diehl," said Hoop.

Diehl opened his mouth to get in the last word.

"I'm—" he said.

That was as far as he got.

CHAPTER 22

"Pull that trigger, gordito," said Juana, "and I pull mine."

Kozlowski jerked his head to the right, eyes wide with surprise.

His five prisoners—Diehl, Hoop, Eskaminzim, Romo, and Rusty —were surprised, as well. They didn't dare turn toward the voice coming from behind them though.

The maid had positioned herself against the southern wall of the mill twenty-five yards away, out of sight of the men rampaging inside and across the courtyard in the stables and the mine. No one could see her—or the rifle in her hands—but Kozlowski.

The fat man lowered his shotgun. A bit.

"You don't wanna do anything stupid, Señora," he said. "One shot and you'll have thirty men over here filling you full of holes."

As he spoke, he slowly, casually moved the barrel of his shotgun toward the mill—and Juana.

"One shot is all I need for you," she said. "And I'm taking it if you don't point that thing at the ground."

Kozlowski gave her a cheeky, boyish grin, like he'd been caught helping himself to an extra slice of pie behind his mother's back. He didn't change the position of his shotgun though. A quick pivot and it would be pointed straight at Juana. Though his smile lingered, the man's eyes turned cold, the mind behind them calculating.

Even if she got off a shot, she'd probably miss. And with a shotgun at this range, you pretty much can't *miss…*

A quick look passed between Hoop and Eskaminzim.

Diehl tried to catch Romo's eye, but the younger man was staring at Kozlowski, transfixed by the standoff. There was no way to send him the message.

Get ready. The men who aren't shot in the first couple seconds might have a chance to reach their guns.

"One," said Juana. "Two."

"Juana, what are you doing?" a woman's voice called out. "Mr. Diehl said not to interfere!"

Miss Gruffud came hurrying along the side of the mill, Cadwaladr and Utley not far behind.

When Koz saw them, he finally pointed his shotgun at the ground. His grin remained though. It was a fun little game they'd just played, but now there were too many spectators.

Juana lowered her rifle too.

"Yes, ma'am," she said. She straightened her back and squared her shoulders and resumed the air of dispassionate efficiency with which she showed guests to the parlor.

When Utley and Cadwaladr saw Diehl, they turned to march toward him angrily, oblivious to the executions they'd barely averted.

"They're tearing everything apart!" Utley barked.

"What's this about a warrant?" said Cadwaladr.

Diehl faced them stiffly, reluctant to turn his back fully on Kozlowski and his shotgun.

"Do you know a justice of the peace named Gorman?" he said.

"Who?" said Utley.

"Never heard of him," said Cadwaladr.

The two of them still hadn't noticed the wary way Diehl and the others were watching Kozlowski. They just threw cursory glares at the man—who was still grinning, enjoying the show—as if he were someone else's impudent servant.

"We *have* heard of him, Gareth," Miss Gruffud told Cadwaladr.

She approached the men more cautiously, with slow but steady steps that indicated she was aware of the danger even as she moved herself closer to it.

"William Gorman," Miss Gruffud went on, explaining to Diehl. "A holdover from Governor Murphy. Quite a friend to the old Tucson Ring and the eastern interests. Our lawyer warned us about him."

"With good reason," said Diehl. "It looks like Gorman has friends in San Francisco too. The warrant's got his signature on it, and it gives these gentlemen from the Dickinson National Detective Agency—" He nodded at Kozlowski, who took a bow. "The right to search the premises."

"I told you we should hire the Dickinsons," Utley said, giving Hoop, Eskaminzim, Romo, and Rusty—and the weapons lying at their feet—a contemptuous glance.

"And I told you we should sell," Cadwaladr growled.

"We couldn't afford the Dickinsons, remember?" Miss Gruffud said to Utley.

She turned toward Cadwaladr, then Kozlowski.

"And I will *never* sell this mine," she said.

Kozlowski laughed.

"That's the spirit," he said. "Make us men fight for it. We like that, don't we, fellas?"

He stroked his shotgun and ogled Miss Gruffud lasciviously.

Utley took an angry step toward him. "Now, listen, you—"

"*Utley*," Diehl snapped. "You have work to do."

Utley stopped and gaped at him. "I do?"

"Extremely important work too," Diehl said. "Grab a pencil and some paper and start keeping track of every bit of damage these men do." He looked over at Miss Gruffud. "For the lawsuit. And if your lawyer's worth his salt, there *will* be a lawsuit."

The lady smiled grimly. "Oh, our lawyer's worth it. Richard, do as Mr. Diehl says."

"Make sure they see you doing it," Diehl added. "Especially their leader. Thin, pale older man. Corpse with a mustache."

"Thomas Stephen Breck is his name. And I'm Eugene Milosz Kozlowski Jr.," the fat man told Utley. "Let me know if you need help spelling any of that, clerk."

Utley scowled at Kozlowski then Diehl then Kozlowski again, as if trying to decide whose face to spit in first. Then he spun around and stalked off.

"Juana, go with him...without the rifle," Diehl said. "He'll need a witness, and we have Miss Gruffud and Mr. Cadwaladr here with us now."

Juana didn't move until Miss Gruffud gave her a nod. She leaned her rifle against the mill wall and hurried off after Utley.

"And now what do *we* do?" Cadwaladr said. "Just stand here while these thugs tear our mine apart?"

"Yes," said Diehl. "The warrant says they can look for Henry Claypole. They'll have to leave when they see he's not here."

Kozlowski chuckled. "It's gonna take a while. Captain Breck can 'look' pretty hard."

"Well, no one's gonna try to stop him," Diehl said. He looked over his shoulder at Hoop, Eskaminzim, Romo, and Rusty. "Are they?"

"No," said Romo.

"Not me!" said Rusty.

Hoop just glowered.

Eskaminzim smiled at Kozlowski.

"I like your toy," the Apache said, nodding down at the man's shotgun. "Perfect for a man who can't shoot straight."

Kozlowski returned the smile.

"I'll show you how straight I shoot, Indian," he said. He gave the barrel of his shotgun another loving stroke. "Sooner or later."

"Knock it off," Diehl told Eskaminzim. "No provocations."

Eskaminzim furrowed his brow. "No prova-what? I don't know that one."

"It means keep your mouth shut and sit tight while these assholes do like they do," Hoop said. "I've heard it before. Too many times."

Kozlowski laughed again. "Uh oh! Dissension in the ranks! Might be a mutiny brewing!"

"There's not," Diehl said. "We're just going to stand here and wait, nice and quiet and cooperative—*all of us*—while Breck executes that warrant."

Kozlowski shrugged. "We'll see."

He locked eyes on Hoop, puckered his lips as if about to blow a kiss, and began whistling "Dixie."

Diehl gritted his teeth.

It was going to be a long wait.

———

It had been nearing dusk when Breck and his men rode up the hill. By the time they started preparing to ride down again—breaking whatever windows and equipment they could as they headed back to their horses—it was almost dark.

"You get harder to see by the second," Kozlowski jeered at Hoop as the other men began to mount up. "Good thing I've got excellent hearing."

Hoop said nothing.

"You won't hear *me* when the time comes, gordo," said Eskaminzim.

Kozlowski turned his shotgun on him. "A threat, huh?"

Diehl slid a step to the left to put himself between them.

"Not at all," he said. "He just meant there'll be nothing to hear because we intend to honor your authority as deputized officers of the court and maintain a respectful distance as you go about your duties."

Kozlowski laughed some more. Diehl wondered—and wished to see—what could make the man *stop* laughing. But he didn't say so or let it show in his eyes.

Kozlowski glanced over at Miss Gruffud and Cadwaladr. They were still standing nearby watching despite the old man's muttered curses as the sounds of destruction continued in the distance.

"Whatever you're paying this bunch, it's too much," Kozlowski said.

"I entirely agree," said Cadwaladr.

"*Gareth*," said Miss Gruffud.

Cadwaladr looked down and muttered another curse.

The sound of approaching hoofbeats snapped his head up again.

Breck rode out of the darkness on his ghostly gray gelding.

"Time to go, Koz. We're done here," he said. "For now."

"Right," said Kozlowski.

He started to walk toward his horse, which had wandered over to one of the troughs a short distance away. But after a few steps, he swerved to snatch up the Sharps rifle on the ground near Hoop.

"That belongs to me," Hoop said.

"I know," Kozlowski said with a smile. "I'm just borrowing it in case you're tempted to do something stupid as we get on our way. I'll leave it over here for you, all right? Night, pretty lady."

He waggled his bushy eyebrows at Miss Gruffud, then jogged off, gut bouncing. A moment later there was a loud splash from the water trough.

"Are you the scoundrel responsible for this outrage?" Cadwaladr asked Breck.

"Yes," Breck said. He shifted his detached, aloof gaze to Diehl and the other men Kozlowski had been guarding. "Any of you picks up a gun before we're gone is dead."

He let his eyes linger on Hoop in a way that seemed more coolly curious than threatening. Then he wheeled his horse around and set off toward the road at a canter.

"Now, wait just a minute," Cadwaladr said. "I would have words with you!"

Breck didn't look back. His men followed him to the road down the hill, one of them—Kozlowski—lifting his hat to Miss Gruffud as he passed.

"Come back here!" Cadwaladr bellowed. "You will hear me out!"

"Let it go, Gareth," said Miss Gruffud. "They're leaving. That's a good thing."

"It would have been better had they been stopped before they got here! Better if our 'guards' had done their jobs and protected this mine instead of standing idly by while it was wrecked!"

"Your mine's not wrecked, Cadwaladr," Diehl said. "It's just mussed up a bit—*because* we 'stood idly by.' But go ahead. Fire us if you want. We'll collect our wages and go. Then you'll have no one to help you with whatever comes next. And believe me…this was just the beginning."

"No one is fired," Miss Gruffud replied calmly. "We'll discuss our next move at my house. Mr. Diehl—you'll find Mr. Utley and have him join us?"

Diehl couldn't tell if the lady was truly unflustered or just a marvelous actress. Either way, it was impressive. He found himself giving her an admiring look he hoped it had grown too dark for anyone to fully see.

"Certainly," he said.

Miss Gruffud nodded, then turned and walked away.

Cadwaladr shot Diehl a scowl before stomping off after her.

"Finally," Rusty said.

He wasn't watching Cadwaladr. His eyes were on the road.

The last of Breck's men had just ridden out of sight.

Rusty squatted down to pick up his pistol, then plopped down in the dirt, his legs splayed out in front of him in a V. He hunched over and heaved a sigh.

"I think maybe I'll become a farmer," he said.

Romo retrieved his gun, then sat down like Rusty.

"I wanted to work for mines." He gazed sourly at his Colt. "But not like this."

"Don't mope. We're still alive," said Diehl.

He paused to search his memory for the perfect piece of Swain.

"'But what though adversity test the courage and vigor of man,'" he recited, "'they get through misfortune the best who keep the heart light as they can.'"

He turned toward Hoop and Eskaminzim with a conciliatory smile. They had some talking to do.

Hoop beat him to the punch. Literally.

The blow snapped Diehl's head back and catapulted him instantly from the murk of nightfall to the absolute blackness of oblivion.

CHAPTER 23

Diehl's eyes popped open.

"Stop him!" he cried.

Two faces loomed into view, blotting out the stars in the swath of dark sky Diehl was staring up at.

"Stop who?" said Rusty.

"You mean Hoop?" said Romo.

"Yes! Stop him!"

Rusty gave Romo a worried glance, then looked back down at Diehl.

"It's a bit too late to stop him, isn't it?" Rusty said.

"What do you mean?" said Diehl. "What has he done?"

"Well, Mr. Diehl…he up and punched you."

"I know that, dammit! Why else would I be lying here in the dirt?"

"You're worried that he's gone after that Dickinson detective? Breck?" said Romo. "To kill him?"

"Yes! Exactly!"

"Hoop's not going after Breck," said Rusty. "After he knocked you cold, he fished his rifle out of the trough, yeah. But then he went off to send Utley to the house like Miss Gruffud asked."

"Oh."

Diehl tried to sit up and take a look around, but a wave of dizziness sent him sinking back to the ground. It was a familiar feeling.

He'd been laid out flat on his back four times in the past week and a half. Maybe he should've stayed a store clerk.

"What about Eskaminzim?" he asked.

"What about him?" said Rusty.

Romo understood the question though.

"I don't think he's going after Breck either," he said. "He did take his rifle over to the road. To watch in case the Dickinsons come back, he said. But he didn't seem to be in a big hurry to shoot anyone."

"He was more interested in you," Rusty added.

"Worried?" Diehl asked.

Rusty shook his head. "Couldn't stop laughing."

Diehl grimaced, then held up his hands.

"All right, help me up," he said.

Romo took his left arm, Rusty his right, and they both pulled.

Diehl rose slowly to his feet, swayed for a moment on wobbly knees, then gave the men a nod.

"Thanks. I'm good now."

They let go with obvious reluctance, standing close to catch him if he went down again.

"Really, I'm fine," Diehl said. He waggled his sore jaw and put a hand to his aching head. "I'm getting used to this."

"Why would Hoop and Eskaminzim want to kill that Captain Breck?" Romo asked.

The question made Diehl's headache worse.

"Later," he said. "Right now I need you to do another inspection of the mine and works, Alfonso."

"Checking for sabotage again?"

"Exactly. And you…" Diehl turned to Rusty. "Watch the road with Eskaminzim."

Rusty didn't looked enthused about going.

"I doubt he thinks he needs any help from me," he said.

"You're not helping him," said Diehl. "You're keeping an eye on him. Understand?"

Rusty nodded—though without seeming any happier about his assignment.

"Yessir," he said.

He trudged off toward the road.

Romo started to leave too. After taking a few steps he turned to face Diehl again.

"You sure you're all right?"

Diehl shrugged. "Good enough."

"What's your plan now? How do we deal with all these Dickinsons?"

"No idea. Ask me again in about forty-five minutes."

Romo frowned, then started away again.

"Alfonso," Diehl said.

Romo glanced back over his shoulder.

"Hoop and Eskaminzim and I have been in worse situations than this," Diehl said.

Romo furrowed his brow. "Is that supposed to be comforting?"

"Umm…yes?"

"Well, it doesn't fill me with faith, Mr. Diehl. It makes me question your sanity. Why would you keep putting yourself in such situations?"

Diehl thought about it. Really, really thought about it. It was a question he'd thought about a lot over the years, actually. One he'd talk through with Romo another day perhaps. Over a bottle of whiskey. If they were lucky.

There was no time for that now though. And no good answer.

He shrugged again.

"Habit?" he said.

Romo shook his head and walked away without another word.

———

Three of the windows in Cadwaladr's house had been broken, Diehl noticed as he approached. Half the windows in Miss

Gruffud's house had. Inside, furniture was overturned and fixtures broken, and loose papers were scattered everywhere.

Juana had paused her cleaning to let Diehl in. He saw her broom leaned against a wall beside her rifle.

"Thank you for what you did," Diehl said as she led him across the foyer. "I doubt I'd be alive now if not for you."

"Yes, you'd be dead," Juana said. "But it wasn't *your* life I was saving. You just happened to be there."

"Well, I'm grateful all the same. It surprised me how comfortable you were with a rifle."

Juana frowned. "Comfortable? No. Just…"

She searched for the right word.

"Competente," she said.

It was Spanish, but Diehl didn't need to ask for a translation.

Juana threw him a quick sidelong glance, then went on in English again.

"It looks like somebody punched you."

"Somebody did."

"One of those matones sent by the other mining company?"

"No."

Diehl expected Juana to smile at that. Maybe even laugh. Instead she just pursed her lips and cocked an eyebrow.

She opened the door to the parlor room and stepped aside to let Diehl past.

Cadwaladr and Utley scowled at him as he walked in. Miss Gruffud didn't, but her expression was grim.

Juana closed the door. She did it softly, yet to Diehl it felt like a cell door slamming behind him.

"More than three thousand dollars in damage and counting, Diehl!" Utley said, shaking a notepad at him. "Some of it to sensitive equipment it'll take days to recalibrate."

A decanter of brandy had somehow escaped the carnage unharmed, and Diehl was tempted to pour himself a glass. His head still ached, and the conversation ahead was going to make it ache more. He resisted the urge though, instead stopping a few steps into the room and standing at attention. It was like the old days when Colonel Crowe would call him in—at Fort Clark then Fort Davis then Fort Apache and finally the Southern Pacific Railroad office in Ogden—so Diehl could try to explain away the latest calamity.

"It's a mess, yes, and I'm sorry about that. But I doubt anything irreplaceable was ruined," Diehl said. "Consolidated American still wants this place. In working order. The visit this evening wasn't about destruction or revenge or whatever happened to Henry Claypole. It was about pressure."

"And no doubt there will be more in the days ahead," said Miss Gruffud. She leaned forward and squinted at Diehl's face. "Did somebody—?"

Voices rose up in the foyer, along with the sound of swiftly approaching footsteps. Diehl stepped back and faced the door, both grateful for the interruption and silently cursing himself.

He was still dressed for dinner—without a gun.

The door opened again, and a woman swept in past Juana. Like Miss Gruffud, she looked like a respectable lady somewhere in the vicinity of her late thirties, forty at the most. She wasn't as tall as Miss Gruffud though, and her hair—parted in the middle and pulled into coiled braids in the back—was brown instead of blond.

"Catrin!" she said, rushing toward Miss Gruffud without even a sidelong glance at Diehl. "Are you all right?"

"Eva!" Miss Gruffud said.

For a moment, the two women clasped hands.

"I'm fine," Miss Gruffud said. "A lot of damage was done, but no one was hurt."

"Maybe not up here," a man snapped from the foyer. "But my wife was beaten, the other miners' families were terrorized, and Max Kogan is *dead*."

Jory Skewes stomped into the room. He was still dressed in his dirty work clothes, and he didn't take off his cap. He looked angry and defiant, as if daring anyone to point out that he hadn't been invited in.

"Who's this Kogan?" Cadwaladr asked him.

"One of our muckers," Utley said, looking aghast. "The Dickinsons killed him?"

Skewes nodded. "Someone threw a rock at them—just one damned rock—so they took a potshot at us. Max was hit in the head."

"What happened to your wife?" Diehl asked.

"Before they hit the ore wagons and came up here, they raided our camp. Lisette tried to talk to that old son of a bitch they've got in charge. That was enough to earn her a thrashing. A bad one."

"I'm sorry, Skewes," Diehl said quietly. But the woman who'd come in with the miner—Eva—talked over him.

"They set fire to one of the miner's homes too. It spread to two of the other houses before it was put out," she said. "When I saw the smoke, then heard those men had come up here..." She gave Miss Gruffud a dewy-eyed look. "I was terrified."

"So you jumped in your buggy and went tearing up to the mine even though the Dickinsons were still around and you could have been killed yourself?" Miss Gruffud said gently. "Eva, you're supposed to be smarter than that."

The woman gave Miss Gruffud a small, tremulous smile, then straightened her back and smoothed down the tweed jacket over her high-necked white blouse. "Yes, well...I now intend to demonstrate just how smart I am. What's this I hear about a warrant?"

"Mr. Diehl saw it," Miss Gruffud said. "He says it was signed by William Gorman."

The woman barked out a scoffing laugh. "Of course. That hack. He's been on the outs ever since Grover Cleveland slipped back into the White House. Why not sell his services to the highest bidder? It's not like he's going to get a judgeship now that the Democrats are running the territory again."

Diehl cleared his throat. "Your friend seems remarkably well-informed," he said to Miss Gruffud.

"Indeed she is, and for good reason," Miss Gruffud said.

She turned to the woman and held a hand out toward Diehl, about to make a formal introduction.

"You must be Diehl," the woman said first. "I'm Eva Nilsen."

Diehl gave her a small bow. "Pleased to make your acquaintance, Miss Nilsen."

"Yes, nice to meet you," she said briskly. "So—you read the warrant? What did it say exactly?"

"Well, there was a lot of whereas this and whereas that, but the gist was that the Dickinsons are deputized and authorized to search G-C property."

Miss Nilsen's eyebrows shot up in surprise. "Then they've made a misstep. The Gruffud-Cadwaladr Mine isn't like the big operations. It doesn't own the miners' homes and charge them rent. So that camp's not covered by the warrant. We'll use that. Now how about the rationale? Any warrant has to state its reason for being. What did this one say?"

Diehl was impressed. This Miss Nilsen really was well-informed. He wondered why he hadn't heard about her before.

"It's Henry Claypole—the Consolidated American representative who went missing last week," he told her. "The Dickinsons are looking for him. Supposedly."

Miss Nilsen's expression turned cagey, and she waved the subject of Claypole away with a flutter of the hand. "Flimsy pretext. Nothing to do with us. It's not our fault if Consolidated employees run off to Juarez with company funds or the like, is it, Mr. Diehl?"

The look the lady gave him—eyebrows arched, mouth tight—told him clearly that the question was rhetorical, no response needed or desired. She wasn't asking. She was telling. *This is our position.*

It was a look and a message Diehl had received many times over the years, particularly during his work with the Southern Pacific Railroad. And—occasionally, due to the nature of his assignments from Colonel Crowe—its attorneys.

Diehl suddenly realized that he *had* heard about Miss Nilsen. Just not by name.

He'd suspected that Miss Gruffud's attorney might be betraying the woman. He *hadn't* suspected—not for a second—that Miss Gruffud's attorney might be a woman herself.

He fought to keep his jaw from dropping. But not hard enough, apparently.

"Miss Nilsen is the second woman to pass the bar in Arizona Territory," Miss Gruffud said with obvious pride. "I consider us lucky to have procured her services."

"Ah," said Diehl. It was the only thing he could come up with in the moment.

"Well, what's she going to do about the Dickinsons? That's what I'd like to know," Skewes said. "What's going to be done about my wife and Max Kogan and the families without homes tonight?"

Cadwaladr spun around to face Skewes, face flushed, mouth open.

"They won't be forgotten, Mr. Skewes," Miss Nilsen said quickly, speaking over Cadwaladr's snapped "Now you see here!"

"These attacks—and Mr. Kogan's *murder*—will force the sheriff to act. He's managed to keep himself out of it up to now, but he can't keep hiding in Tucson with Pima County citizens dying at the hands of outsiders. As for Justice of the Peace Gorman, we can go over his head. He doesn't have much pull in Phoenix anymore—and none in the governor's office. We'll make him regret that warrant. The same with Consolidated American and the Dickinsons. They've gone too far. That's how we'll stop them."

"Hear, hear!" cheered Utley. He lifted his notepad and gave it another waggle. "And we'll sue for damages! They'll pay for what they've done!"

"All right then. Good," said Skewes with a firm nod and a little sidelong glare at Cadwaladr.

"Yes, well...I hope you're right, Eva," the old man muttered.

Miss Nilsen didn't reply. She and Miss Gruffud were both looking at Diehl—and the skeptical expression on his face.

"What do *you* think, Diehl?" Miss Nilsen asked.

"I think you sound like an excellent lawyer, and you should proceed exactly as you've described," he said. "I also think we don't have time for all that. Getting the sheriff to intervene could take days. Getting the governor to step in could take weeks. Consolidated American has good lawyers too. They know the clock is ticking—

and that if they move quickly and aggressively enough, they *will* win. What we saw today is only the beginning of a full frontal assault. And we don't have the strength to fight it off."

Miss Gruffud and Miss Nilsen shared a long look, each obviously hoping the other could point out why Diehl was wrong. Utley and Skewes did the same thing.

None of them spoke.

"So we're helpless!" Cadwaladr thundered, throwing up his hands. "Defenseless! Hopeless!"

"I didn't say that," Diehl said. "There might be a way to fight back on Consolidated American's terms. But we'll have to act fast."

"And do what?" Cadwaladr demanded.

Diehl sighed. "That depends" wouldn't be much of an answer, so he kept it to himself. He didn't want to explain what—and who—it depended on.

He looked past the old man.

"Utley," he said, "where did you last see Hoop?"

———

Hoop had found Utley in the millworks cursing over battered machinery and scattered, torn ledger books. He sent the man to Miss Gruffud's house, as the lady had asked. Then he stood there alone a moment, surrounded by crumpled paper and shattered glass.

He didn't see any of it. His eyes were open, but his gaze unfocused. He was seeing something that had happened years ago and miles away.

The weight of his Sharps brought him back to the moment. It pulled down on his hand, his arm, his shoulder, his back, reminding him that he had things to do. Responsibilities. Duties. Debts. And a wet rifle to take apart and dry and clean and oil.

When he was done with all that, he moved off to watch the road. Eskaminzim and Rusty were already there, standing guard at the top of the hill. Rather than join them, Hoop climbed up into the rocks above, leaning against a boulder and looking down on the distant, flickering lights of town. He wasn't in the mood for questions.

"Hoop?" Diehl said. "Can we talk?"

Hoop had heard him coming, of course. Diehl had taken care to make some noise as he climbed up to join him.

Sneaking up on Hoop in the dark was a very, very bad idea.

Hoop turned around. Diehl was about twenty yards away, in the rocks and scrub slightly below him. Keeping his distance.

"You mean can we talk without me punching you again?" Hoop said. "I don't know. What you got to say?"

"Well…the first thing is…"

Diehl took a deep breath and rubbed his aching jaw.

Hoop just watched him, silent and still.

"I'm sorry," Diehl said. "I didn't trust you not to kill Breck—and get yourself and the rest of us killed in the process. Perhaps I should've had more faith in…your professionalism."

Hoop mulled the apology over a moment. The "perhaps" rankled. The "professionalism," too.

"Brains is all you needed to give me credit for, Diehl," he said. "Maybe once I would've killed Breck no matter what, but that was a long time ago. Now? After all these years?" He looked away again, gazing down the hill at Hope Springs. "I can bide my time."

For a moment there was no sound but the fluttering wings of a nighthawk swooping past in the darkness.

"Uh…anything more you'd like to say?" Diehl asked. He put his fingers to his jaw again.

"Nope," Hoop said. "Not till I hear what more you got to tell me."

"Right. Well…there's something I need you to do. A job I can only trust you to do right."

Hoop let out a grunt that was almost, but not quite, a chuckle. *Thought so*, it said.

"We need help," Diehl went on. "And this 'A.A. Detective Agency' we're part of—it's too small and too far away to give us the kind of help we need. So we're going to have to recruit our own help. Fast."

"More hired guns."

"Exactly. We can use the money I got from Claypole and what's left of what Miss Gruffud gave me."

"How much is that?"

"One thousand two hundred twenty-three dollars and seventy-seven cents."

The specificity got another amused snort out of Hoop. But when he spoke again his tone was grave.

"Enough for a few good men. Or a few more not-so-good ones. The 'fast' part makes the 'good' part hard."

"I know. It's harder still because Hope Springs is played out, talent-wise. The kind of men we're looking for...you'd need to go down to Nogales, maybe. Or over to—"

"Tombstone," Hoop said firmly. "All right, Diehl."

And that was that. It was settled. The part about whether or not Hoop would go, anyway.

"Good," Diehl said. "Don't worry about taking a turn on watch tonight. Just get some sleep. You and Rusty will need to be up early and ride hard. I'll do my best to stall the Dickinsons until—"

"*Rusty?*"

Diehl nodded. "Yes. Rusty. You know why."

A look of disgust came over Hoop's face. It faded quickly into resignation.

"You need Eskaminzim here," Hoop said. "And I'll need a White man to carry the money and do the talking and act like the boss."

"Exactly."

Hoop turned away to gaze again at the small, star-like lights of Hope Springs.

"Anything else?" he said.

"No...unless *you* have something more you'd like to say to *me*."

"Yeah. I suppose I do."

Diehl folded his arms and waited for an apology for the punch.

"You ever have a gun pointed at me again," Hoop said. "I'll do more than hit you, you crazy son of a bitch."

Diehl's head drooped.

"Right," he sighed.

They stood there together a moment—Hoop looking down at town, Diehl staring down at his feet. Then Diehl started picking his way down through the rocks to tell Rusty he was getting a promotion.

CHAPTER 24

Romo wasn't on guard duty alone, but he might as well have been. He hadn't seen Eskaminzim in over an hour. He thought he'd *heard* him a few times, but maybe that really had been a poorwill singing in the dark. Why would Eskaminzim be sneaking around imitating birds? Practice?

Well, maybe. That would actually make more sense to Romo than some of the other things the Apache did.

For a few minutes Romo marched crisply back and forth across the road with his rifle—a Winchester Diehl had given him to replace his rusty old carbine—on his shoulder. It was just an excuse to move, to stay alert, awake. But he'd worried Eskaminzim would see him looking like one of the tin soldiers he'd played with as a boy. So he stopped and just stood there, the mine and millworks behind him, until his chin started to drop toward his chest and his eyes fluttered, opened, fluttered, closed.

The poorwill trilled again. Romo's eyes snapped wide.

He heard movement. The soft shushing of fabric. Footsteps on sod. Behind him.

He turned to see a tall, slender, dark figure moving through the shadows by the mill. He took the rifle from his shoulder.

Before he could aim it, Juana stepped into the moonlight. She walked toward him with a coffee pot in one hand and two mugs in the other.

Romo sighed and smiled at the same time.

"You shouldn't be out in the middle of the night," he told her in Spanish. "It's not safe."

"I'll be less safe if you fall asleep," she said. She held up the coffee pot. "This is fresh and hot."

"You talked me into it."

After she'd poured Romo a cup and handed it over, Juana looked past him into the blackness beyond the top of the hill.

"You can have some too," she said.

"I don't like coffee," a voice replied from somewhere east of the road. "But I'll take some."

Romo and Juana both peered into the dark, but they could see nothing other than the dull gray outlines of boulders and jutting saguaro.

"Just leave it on the ground for me, and I'll come for it later," the voice said from the west side of the road now. "If I have to drink it, I like to drink it cold."

"Fine," Juana said.

She filled the second cup and put it down on a rock nearby.

"We were lucky more people weren't hurt today," she said to Romo as she stood up.

"Was it luck?" Romo said. "Or was it because Mr. Diehl had us back down?"

It was hard to tell in the dim light of the moon, but it looked like Juana didn't scowl as much as usual at the mention of Diehl.

"He was right," she said. "Though not everyone will see it."

"And even some of those who *can* see it won't like it." Romo blew on his steaming coffee, then took a sip. "We're especially lucky you weren't hurt, you know. You shouldn't have been running around with a rifle, Señora."

"I have more business with a rifle than you do, *crío*," Juana snapped.

"Crío" meant "kid." *Boy child.*

Romo wondered if she'd seen him marching back and forth like an idiot. He was grateful for the darkness that concealed the blush he felt reddening his face.

"What do you mean?" he said.

"This place…" Juana jerked her chin at the mill and the mine entrance beyond. "…it's ugly, and it stinks of sulfur and sweat and capitalism. But it's been my home for years now."

If Juana could see the raised eyebrow "and capitalism" got, she didn't show it. She just kept going.

"I didn't think I'd ever have to fight for the mine the way I once fought and bled for my real home. *Our* real home, Alfonso. But I was wrong—and it's time to fight again."

"You fought…for Mexico?"

"Yes. And for its soul. And lost. Twice."

"I don't understand. You were a Juarista?"

"When Juarez was trying to kick out the French, yes. But you can win the war and still lose. When Juarez turned to stealing land from peasants, we tried to fight *him*."

"You mean you and Miguel?"

Juana nodded, looking both sorrowful and pleased that Romo had remembered her brother's name.

"And that's when Miguel died?" Romo asked.

Juana nodded again. "I assume you know your history. How Juarez liked to deal with his enemies?"

"Firing squad?"

Juana's expression turned bitter.

"If I am to die with my back against a wall," she said, "it will be with a rifle in *my* hands too."

For a moment, the maid just stared silently into the darkness. Then she turned to pour more coffee into Romo's cup.

"Now stop asking Señora so many questions about her past," she said. "It's not polite."

"Si, Señora. No more questions," Romo replied dutifully, like a child admonished by an aunt. "But perhaps one day, Juana, you will *choose* to tell me more."

It was risky, using her given name like that, especially after being reminded of the respect he owed an older lady. He was being presumptuous, possibly offensive. But even before the woman replied, Romo could tell he'd chosen the right words. The stiff lines of the woman's silhouette softened, the shoulders relaxing, the head cocking.

"Perhaps, Alfonso," she said, her voice softer again. "Hasta luego."

She left the coffee pot by the cup for Eskaminzim, then walked off into the shadows.

"She *is* skinny, isn't she?" Eskaminzim said.

Romo was so startled he nearly dropped his rifle. The Apache was suddenly five feet behind him.

"And tough. Like a strip of jerky," Eskaminzim continued. "So…are you two…"

He made a gesture with both hands that Romo did his best not to look at. A change of topic was called for.

"I'll tell you if you answer a question for me," Romo said.

Eskaminzim walked over to the coffee Juana had left for him, touched the cup, then sat down without picking it up.

"Questions questions questions. Why are children always so curious? But all right. I've got time while I wait for my coffee to go cold. Ask."

"Why was Diehl so worried that you and Hoop would kill that man Breck?"

Eskaminzim looked disappointed. "Oh. I thought you were going to ask how I got to be so good at fighting. You sure you don't want to ask about that? I have many stories…"

"Maybe another time. Right now I'd like to know about Breck."

Eskaminzim shrugged. "Fine. I'll tell you what I know. But I wasn't there for it myself. It happened before I met Hoop and Diehl."

"So why did Diehl have us pull on our guns on *you*?"

"Because Hoop's married to my sister! And I owe him a favor or two! And I've heard this story from him! And it's nice having an excuse to kill a white hijo de puta! Now be quiet if you want to hear this."

Romo started to answer, then just put his hand over his mouth and nodded.

Eskaminzim grinned. "That's the way. Mouth shut, ears open. You know, maybe I should tell you stories more often."

Romo rolled his eyes.

"Don't do that either," Eskaminzim said. "Now…this would have been back in '76 or '77. Maybe '78…"

THE TEXAS PANHANDLE—1879

Corporal Ira Hoop sat on his big, slow, swayback mare—another half-dead hand-me-down from the Eighth Cavalry—and watched the party of Kiowa braves in the distance. There were a dozen of them strung out on their ponies, the adults in the front armed with rifles, the boys in the back with bows. They ignored Hoop and the other troopers who'd been shadowing them across the yellow plains all day. They were only interested in mule deer, pronghorn, javelina, maybe—if there was a miracle—buffalo. Any game they could take back to Fort Sill and the families the government men there were failing to feed.

The Tenth was escorting hunting parties from Indian Territory through northwest Texas in search of food. Protecting the braves they used to fight from the Texans who hated Indians and black soldiers alike. Shit orders—like everything the War Department sent the Tenth Cavalry. Shit horses and shit equipment and shit food.

The sound of heavy, ponderous hoofbeats grew louder behind Hoop, and he swiveled in the saddle to look back. Sergeant Carney was galloping up from the end of the column. There was a look of rage on his face Hoop had never seen before, even in the thick of battle. There were contusions there too—scab-crusted leftovers from the beating Carney had taken in the town of Pringle two nights before. A beating that had sent the sergeant staggering back to camp with the chevrons and trouser stripes cut from his blood-covered uniform.

"What is it, Sarge?" Hoop said.

Carney just kept going until he reached the officer leading the twenty-man detachment from K Troop. Lieutenant Robert Stowers. One of two black officers in the entire US Army.

There were few men Hoop respected more than Sergeant Carney and Lieutenant. Stowers. Carney because he'd been born a slave with nothing and had gone on to earn forty dollars a month and three stripes in his chevron through skill and brains and stubbornness. Stowers because he'd been born free and won an appointment to West Point and, despite resistance all the way, had entered the Army as an officer and—though many refused to acknowledge it—a gentleman.

Carney reined up beside the lieutenant, saluted, and pointed to the northeast at something beyond the Kiowas. He and Lieutenant. Stowers were too far off for Hoop to hear everything they were saying. But Carney's angry tone reached his ears, as did Stowers' stern "Calm yourself, Sergeant. How can you be so certain?"

Carney made some quieter reply, and both men lifted their field glasses and looked to the northeast. Hoop and the rest of the troopers turned and looked too.

Another group of riders had appeared on the horizon. There were about forty of them, and they were headed for the Kiowas. They spread out to sweep in cavalry-style though none of them wore blue.

"Damn," Hoop spat. "Rangers."

Texans weren't happy about hosting hungry, armed Indians from the Territory. So much so that the governor threatened to send the Rangers after them—with orders to shoot to kill.

The Kiowas scattered. The Rangers started firing.

Stowers and Carney spurred their horses and started toward them.

"Gallop! March!" Stowers called out.

The troopers wheeled to follow. The Kiowas were wheeling now too, arcing toward the southwest as fast as they could go. Trying to put the troopers between them and the Rangers.

"Hold your fire!" Stowers yelled at the Rangers. "This party is under US Army protection! Hold your fire!"

It was doubtful they could hear him. But the sight of twenty blue-clad cavalrymen charging their way seemed to get the intent across. There were indistinct shouts from the scattered Texans—most of them only about two hundred yards away from the troopers now. Slowly, with a reluctance Hoop could feel with each last sporadic pop of gunfire, the Rangers stopped shooting. There were more shouts, and they began regrouping, reforming their line around two men who appeared to be the leaders—one tall and slender, the other stout.

"Halt!" said Stowers.

"Haaaaaallllllllt!" called Carney.

The troopers pulled back on their reins, slowing as they dipped into a shallow wash and stopping a few yards beyond the far bank. The Kiowas were still fleeing to the southwest. Most of them, anyway. Three were stretched out motionless in the dry prairie grass.

Carney kept his eyes on the Rangers.

"That's him, all right," he told Stowers. "I don't even need my field glasses from here. Not with that coat and hat."

He seemed to be staring at the squat Ranger next to the slim one. The man was wearing a long yellow duster that fell away on either side of his belly like curtains. On his head was a brown, flat-crowned hat with the brim turned up in front instead of on the sides.

"He's the one who started it," Carney said. "And led it. And finished it."

"The tall one in charge—was he there?" Stowers asked.

"No, not him. The others it's hard to say. But I bet they was all Rangers."

"Well…" said Stowers.

He let the word hang there alone a moment, the way some officers would when they couldn't tell a noncom what they were really thinking. "There's nothing I can do about that" or "That's your problem" or "I really couldn't care less."

"We now have two urgent matters to discuss with their commander," Stowers said instead. "Have the men dismount for action."

Carney turned away to shout out the orders.

"Dismount to fight! Action front! Jordan, Gore, Williams, Clemont, Kerr—with the horses in that gully!"

The troopers began climbing down from their saddles. One in four gathered the reins of the others' horses. The rest began unslinging their carbines.

Hoop could see restless stirrings along the Texans' line. Any Rangers over the age of thirty had likely fought for the Confederacy, perhaps even as cavalry. They knew what the troopers were doing.

Charging in on horseback was good for effect. Standing firm on the ground with a rifle in your hands was better—much better—for shooting.

Carney and the lieutenant lifted their field glasses again though this time they weren't looking at the Rangers. They were scanning the horizon in every other direction.

Somewhere out there was another detachment from K Troop. Twenty more troopers to even the odds. But they were nowhere in sight.

Stowers and Carney lowered their field glasses.

"All right, then," Stowers said. "With me, Sergeant."

"Yes, sir."

They started toward the Texans at a trot. Young, stiff-backed Stowers in his forage cap alongside burly, hunch-shouldered Carney in his drooping campaign hat. Headed straight for their opposite numbers—the slim man and the thick one —at the center of the Ranger line.

It was obvious when the Texans realized the officer leading the buffalo soldiers was black himself. It was when Stowers and Carney closed to within a hundred yards. The Rangers looked at each other, spitting out words Hoop couldn't hear but didn't need to.

Stowers and Carney didn't stop until they were thirty yards from the Rangers. Close enough for a civilized conversation without shouting. Which was why Hoop could only follow it by the men's gestures.

Stowers offering a salute that wasn't returned.

Stowers pointing back toward the troopers and the Kiowa braves beyond them.

The tall Ranger looking past him impassively.

The portly one leaning back, putting a hand on his bulging belly, maybe... laughing?

Carney jabbing a finger at him, then at another Ranger, then another.

The tall Texan stiffening.

The other Rangers becoming more agitated, their horses dancing anxiously.

The tall one looking at the heavy one and pointing at the troopers' left flank.

The tall one starting his horse forward, cutting past Stowers and Carney.

The other Rangers beginning to follow him.

Stowers yanking his reins to the side, digging in his spurs, cutting off the leader, shouting.

The tall Ranger pulling out a pistol and shooting Lieutenant Robert Stowers through the head.

Hoop was watching Stowers slide from his saddle, dead, even as the man's last word reached the troopers.

"...stop!"

Then the pop of the gunshot.

Some of the troopers gasped. Some blurted "No!" Some cursed.

Hoop called out "Sarge! Don't! Run!"

Carney was grabbing at his black-flapped holster—the one holding his Army-issued Colt revolver. The tall Ranger shot him in the shoulder, then the chest, then once more in the stomach as he toppled from his horse.

Hoop spoke again as the sound of the shots echoed across the plain. One word that came blasting out of him.

"Fire!"

He lifted his carbine and pulled the trigger.

It was a hasty shot, taken in rage, and the bullet passed over the tall man's head. Hoop cocked the rifle's hammer and worked the lever and tried again. But the tall man was already swinging to the ground on the far side of his horse. The tubby one and the rest of the Rangers started doing the same—taking away the easy targets they'd made riding tall against the horizon—as more troopers opened fire.

There were puffs of smoke from the Rangers' line as they began firing back.

It had been one thing to stand there, carbines in hand, sending a message to the Texans. It would be another thing—suicide—to keep standing there now with bullets flying.

Hoop crouched low and began backing toward the gully behind them.

"Fall back to cover!" he said. "Firing at will!"

He went to one knee and tried to put the tall man in his sights again. But most of the Rangers were down in the grass and shrubs now, and it was impossible to find him.

A bullet thudded into the ground six inches from Hoop's right toe.

He turned and scurried the last few steps to the arroyo.

The other troopers dropped into the gully too. None of them had been hit yet, but the Texans had their range now, and more shots were coming in close.

"Thank god!" one of the men with the horses yelled. "Look!"

Hoop glanced back. The trooper was staring off to the south even as he struggled to keep the agitated horses from rearing.

Hoop looked south too. He saw clouds of dust and specks of blue and brown and black, all growing larger.

The other detachment from K Troop was on its way.

"Covering fire!" Hoop ordered. If his men kept the Texans pinned down, the new arrivals could strike the Rangers' right and roll up their whole line.

It didn't happen. Instead of hitting the Rangers, the cavalrymen headed toward Hoop, riding with their heads down and their sidearms holstered. The young lieutenant in charge was yelling as they rode down into the wash.

"Cease fire! Cease fire! What the hell is going on here?"

The lieutenant slid from his saddle but kept his head down and a hand on his reins.

"Well?" He locked eyes on Hoop. "Report, Corporal. Where are Lieutenant Stowers and Sergeant Carney?"

"Dead, sir," Hoop said. "Killed by those Rangers."

"What? My god. Why?"

"The Rangers attacked a Kiowa hunting party. We stopped them. And the sergeant said it was some of the Rangers who beat him in town the other night. When he and the lieutenant approached to talk to their commander, he shot them."

"My god," the lieutenant said again. He turned to get a look at the Rangers' line. There were no puffs of smoke from there now. All firing had stopped.

"Obviously, there's been some kind of misunderstanding," the lieutenant said. "I'll go see if I can straighten it out."

He slid his saber from its scabbard, then stuffed his free hand into a pocket. He pulled out a white handkerchief and began tying it to the end of his sword.

"You're going to surrender?" Hoop said.

The lieutenant looked up, surprised by the disgust Hoop couldn't keep out of his voice.

"I'm going out for a parley under a flag of truce," he said. "However this started, it needs to stop. There's nothing to be gained from more bloodshed."

Hoop's grip on his carbine tightened so much he wouldn't have been surprised had the rifle snapped in two. He could think of something to be gained from more bloodshed.

Justice.

Hoop just glared back at the lieutenant though, saying nothing more. What would be the point? This young shavetail, half a year out of West Point, was too green—and perhaps too white—to see what had happened. There had been no misunderstanding. There had been murder.

Second Lieutenant Oswin Diehl climbed back into his saddle, lifted his sword with its handkerchief high, and sent his horse forward out of the arroyo.

As Diehl rode slowly toward the Texans, Hoop realized he'd forgotten to salute him.

For that he was glad.

———

"There were a couple councils afterward because of what happened," said Eskaminzim. "I don't remember what the whites call them."

Romo muttered a muffled word into his palm.

"You can talk now," Eskaminzim told him. "The story's pretty much over."

Romo took his hand away from his mouth. "You mean trials?"

Even in the dark Romo could see Eskaminzim's offended frown.

"You think I don't know what a trial is? I've been to a dozen. I've been *on* trial twice!"

"Oh. Of course," Romo said. "Sorry."

Eskaminzim swiped a hand and grunted out something along the lines of "Bah." He'd been sitting on the ground as he told the story, the coffee Juana left nearby. Now he finally reached out and poured himself a cup.

"Just right. Good and cold," he said after taking a slurp. "So... Texas had its council, and the Army had *its* council. Inquests? Inquiries? Inquisitions? Something like that. Whatever the name, it was just a lot of whites going yap yap yap...and a few buffalo soldiers talking, though no one wanted to hear them. Lucky for Hoop none of the Texans died, and the other troopers wouldn't say which of them started the shooting after the lieutenant and the sergeant were killed. So the whites agreed it was all the lieutenant and the sergeant's fault for firing at the Rangers as they rode up. That's what the Rangers said happened, and the lieutenant and the sergeant weren't around to give their side. So it was all swept under the bed."

"You mean..."

Romo was about to ask if Eskaminzim meant "swept under the rug," but thought better of it.

"The Ranger captain got away with murdering two American soldiers?" he said instead.

"Two *Black* soldiers. In Texas. You're Mexican. Is that really a surprise to you?"

Romo shook his head. "No. I guess not. But I am surprised Hoop and Diehl were still…associates after that."

Eskaminzim guzzled the rest of his coffee, then slapped down the cup. "They were in the Army together! They had to associate! And Diehl was just a dumb kid in the beginning. He got less dumb with time. Though things didn't really change between him and Hoop until…"

Eskaminzim jabbed a pointed finger at Romo.

"I see what you're doing! You're trying to trick me!"

"What? No!"

"Don't deny it! You want another story! And you want me to forget that you owe me an answer!"

"I do?"

Eskaminzim repeated the rude gestured he'd made a while before. "Are you and the Señora…?"

"Oh. That," said Romo, looking away. "No. She says I remind her of her dead brother. And I'm Mexican. So she's kind to me. That's all."

"Ahh…"

Romo expected Eskaminzim to be angry about the lack of salacious detail, as if he'd gotten the poor end of a bargain. Instead the Apache relaxed and nodded approvingly.

"That's one thing I like about you Mexicans. At least the good Catholics," he said. "You are chaste, like my people. Not so much…"

He made the rude gesture yet again. And yet again Romo did his best not to look at it.

"The whites…" Eskaminzim rolled his eyes. "It seems like all they want to do is—"

He made the gesture even more forcefully.

"Yes, well, umm, hmm, maybe," Romo said, looking up at the stars.

Eskaminzim sprang to his feet and started to jog off into the darkness without a goodbye or good night. Their business was concluded.

"Wait! You didn't tell me everything!" Romo said. "What about that Ranger captain?"

"*More* questions?" Eskaminzim groaned. But he stopped and turned around. "What about him?"

"That's Captain Breck? The Dickinson?"

"Of course it is! I thought you were supposed to be smart."

"Well, what's Hoop going to do?"

Eskaminzim shrugged. "His job. Like always. But if they're both alive when the job's over..."

The Apache grinned, then turned and disappeared into the night.

CHAPTER 25

Diehl got up with Hoop and Rusty when they rose before sunup and shuffled out of the stable half-asleep to saddle their horses. Once he'd said his goodbye—a simple "See you soon" that only Rusty acknowledged with a wave and a hearty "You bet!"—he expected to follow them to the road to tell Eskaminzim and Romo to get some sleep. Instead he found he had unexpected company.

Cadwaladr came striding toward him out of the purple-gray pre-dawn gloom. He was dressed in black boots and jodhpurs and a heavy herringbone Ulster.

"Where are they going?" he asked, nodding at Hoop and Rusty.

Diehl hadn't told his employers he was sending for reinforcements. Just that they needed to slow the Dickinsons down while Miss Nilsen tried to get the law on their side. They were supposed to meet again at her office in town to discuss next steps, but that wasn't until eleven.

"Scouting," Diehl told the old man.

Cadwaladr glowered at him, waiting for more. "Well," he grumbled when he realized he wouldn't get it, "as long as you're up, help me saddle a horse."

"What for?"

Cadwaladr's eyes popped wide. "So I can ride it, of course!"

"Where to? We're not due at Miss Nilsen's for hours."

Cadwaladr obviously wasn't accustomed to such questioning.

"I would remind you that this is Sunday morning," he snapped. "There might not be a parish of the Church of England in this blasted land, but there is an Episcopal church. And that's close enough for me when I've been lying awake all night worried sick and need to take some comfort from the word of God and a few hymns and the company of decent Christians who aren't conniving to steal what I've shed blood, sweat, and tears to earn!"

"Oh...I didn't realize you *were* a 'decent Christian,'" Diehl said. "Far be it from me to come between a man and his god." He swept an arm out toward the stable door. "After you, sir."

Cadwaladr huffed once in annoyance, then marched inside.

As they gathered gear in the tack room, the old man noticed that Diehl was picking out two bridles, two breast collars, two latigos —two of everything.

"You're not coming with me," Cadwaladr said.

"Someone is," said Diehl. "It would be insane to let you go down that road alone after what happened yesterday."

Cadwaladr patted a bulge in the side of his herringbone coat. "I can take care of myself."

"I was going to talk to you about that, actually. Leave the guns to the gunmen. Believe me—you'll be safer that way."

"A man must defend himself!"

"A man must also stay out of trouble. But suit yourself," Diehl said with a shrug. "You are not going alone though."

Cadwaladr gritted his teeth and flushed red.

"I'll take your Indian," he said, snatching up a black English saddle. "You annoy me, and your Mexican looks fourteen years old."

Diehl shrugged. "All right. I suppose there's only so much trouble you can get into during one Sunday service. And the Consolidated people didn't cross the line within town limits yesterday. They won't want to give the local law a reason to butt in. So

Eskaminzim it is. I'll meet you at Miss Nilsen's afterward with Miss Gruffud."

Cadwaladr clearly didn't like that Diehl was giving him permission to do what he planned to do anyway. But he muttered, "Fine," and started toward the door.

"One thing though," said Diehl.

Cadwaladr stopped to look back at him.

"It's been a while since I was in church," Diehl said. "Put in a good word for me."

Cadwaladr spun around and stomped out without saying whether he would or wouldn't.

———

Romo was having a horrible nightmare. A struggle. Shouts. A gun shot.

Eskaminzim was having a wonderful dream. A struggle. Shouts. A gun shot.

Diehl walked into the barn and woke them both with a "Hey" and a kick to the wall.

"Bleah!" Romo blurted out.

Eskaminzim sat up and yawned. "What now?"

"Cadwaladr's insisting on going into town," Diehl told the Apache. "For church, he says. I don't know though. Skewes mentioned he has a weakness for cards. Maybe he's hoping there's a Saturday night game that hasn't broken up yet. Either way, I need you to hurry after him and keep him out of trouble."

"Keep him *out* of trouble? Sounds boring," said Eskaminzim. But he leaped up from the straw and hurried off to get a horse.

Romo pushed himself up slowly. "You need me to do anything?"

"Yeah. First, sleep. For a couple more hours, anyway. Then, watch."

"Watch what?"

Diehl shook his head. "Not what. Who."

And he explained.

When Romo laid back down a minute later, he found it very, very hard to fall asleep again.

———

A couple hours later, Diehl was back in the barn playing stable hand for the second time that morning. For Miss Gruffud now. Someone had to get her boxy covered buggy ready for the ride to town. Diehl woke Romo again—with a much gentler "Hey" this time—to help him pull it out to the courtyard and get a horse in harness. Just as they finished, Miss Gruffud came around the side of the mill in a pale-blue afternoon dress with lace around the collar. Diehl swept off his Stetson and bowed.

"'Leave thy ivory palaces! Your chariot awaits for you,'" he said.

"I've heard that one. Your Mr. Swain wrote it?" Miss Gruffud asked, looking impressed.

"No, actually. C.H. Spurgeon."

"The famous Baptist preacher? I didn't take you for a religious man, Mr. Diehl."

Diehl cleared his throat. "I appreciate a good turn of phrase. If I may?"

He held out a hand. The lady's gaze flicked back toward the mill —and the office Utley had been living in—before accepting it. Diehl helped her up into the seat, then walked around to the other side of the buggy.

"We should be back in a couple hours," he told Romo. "It's up to you to keep an eye on things."

Diehl's gaze flicked back toward the mill too.

"I understand," Romo said.

Diehl climbed into the seat beside Miss Gruffud and turned to her expecting to take the reins. She already had them in hand—and gave them a snap. The horse trotted off toward the road to town.

Diehl was going to be a passenger, not the driver. Miss Gruffud watched his reaction out of the corner of her eye.

He made a show of leaning back and relaxing.

"'Twas on a Sunday morning, before the bells did peal, a note came through my window with 'Cupid' on its seal,'" he said. "'And soon I heard a whisper, as soft as seraphs sing. 'Twas on a Sunday morning, before the bells did ring.'"

"Now *that* sounds like Swain," Miss Gruffud said.

Diehl nodded. "It seemed apropos. Sunday morning, church bells, etc." He heaved a theatrical sigh. "No love notes or gentle whispers though. So far."

"I certainly wouldn't expect any from the Dickinsons."

Diehl sat up straight again. "Well, that takes all the poetry out of the moment. And here I was hoping we could have a little break from business the way we did the other night."

"I've come to think that was a mistake, actually. I'm not sure it was appropriate to take a 'break from business' with so much hanging in the balance. It certainly wouldn't be now, after what happened yesterday."

Diehl shrugged. "In my experience, you should take your breaks where you can get them. Who knows when—or if—the chance will come again?"

"'Eat, drink, and be merry, for tomorrow we die'?" Miss Gruffud shook her head. "That might work for a man like yourself. It wouldn't work for me."

"A man like yourself" got a little grimace from Diehl.

"Oh. I understand," he said. "A lady in your position...with your responsibilities...you can't go getting entangled with every underling who takes an interest."

Miss Gruffud stiffened and gave the reins another snap even though the horse was making good time down the hill.

"That is a crude, self-centered, and unflattering way to put it, Mr. Diehl," she said.

"Miss Gruffud...you are entirely correct. I apologize. And of course you're right about my timing, as well. I was being... frivolous."

Miss Gruffud eyed the man beside her, searching for signs of insincerity.

Diehl just gave her a gentle smile.

After a moment, she smiled back.

"Apology accepted," she said. "You know—I've been told that I could do with some frivolity. Perhaps when all this is over you could help with that."

Diehl put his hands to his heart. "Miss Gruffud, if it's frivolity you need, I'm your man."

Then he turned away and set himself to the very serious business of watching the rocks for sharpshooters.

———

They saw no one as they made their way down the hill. Not even Eskaminzim, though he was lurking somewhere in the brush. Eskaminzim could keep Cadwaladr safe on the open road, but on the streets of a remote Arizona Territory town, an Apache would need a bodyguard himself. Miss Gruffud eyed Diehl when they rolled into Hope Springs, as if half-expecting him to take the reins from her now that they were in sight of other men. He didn't. He was too busy watching those other men. Looking for faces he'd seen the day before.

Miss Nilsen's law office was a single room above Hope Springs's only funeral parlor. It was cool and drafty inside because the windows were cracked open, apparently in the hope that a breeze could clear out the various smells—some sharply chemical, some pungently organic—that radiated up through the floorboards. It didn't work. Diehl hoped it wasn't an omen.

Cadwaladr was already in Miss Nilsen's office when they arrived, occupying one of the scuffed, probably secondhand armchairs. Miss Nilsen rose from behind her desk—also scuffed, also probably secondhand, but with folders and lawbooks and inkwell all positioned atop it with meticulous geometrical precision. Her practice didn't seem to be flourishing, but it wasn't for lack of neatness.

She beamed at Miss Gruffud, but Cadwaladr spoke before she could welcome them in.

"Eva was just updating me on her progress…and I use the word 'progress' loosely indeed."

"Gareth, really," Miss Gruffud said, exasperated with him already.

The old man swiped a hand at her. "Oh, I'm not saying it's Eva's fault. But the gist of it is we're begging for help from far away while getting none right here where it's needed."

"Ah," Miss Gruffud sighed. She turned to Miss Nilsen. "You spoke to Constable Kelner."

Miss Nilsen nodded. "The miners' camp is outside city limits, of course. And the Dickinsons told Kelner that Mrs. Skewes and Mr. Kogan, the miner who was killed, assaulted *them*...a group of lawfully deputized citizens carrying out an order of the court. As I expected, that's more than enough excuse for a town constable to stay out of it. Especially if he desperately *wants* to stay out of it."

"So she sent telegrams to the sheriff and the governor's office and the US marshal's office and a few newspapers, then started shuffling papers around for a lawsuit," Cadwaladr said. "And in the meantime, there's no one standing between us and Consolidated American's *army*."

The old man glowered at Diehl just in case there was any doubt about whose fault he thought that was.

"At the moment, anyone standing between you and that 'army' is going to end up like Mrs. Skewes or Mr. Kogan," Diehl said. "Until the odds shift in our favor, we need to be anticipating, out-maneuvering, and harassing. Not confronting. Now, with that in mind..."

Diehl cocked his head, then froze.

"With what in mind?" Cadwaladr asked.

Diehl put a finger to his lips.

He was listening to something. A second later, the others heard it too.

The sound of footsteps on the exterior staircase leading up to Miss Nilsen's office. Small, clattering footsteps at first. Then heavier ones. Lots of them.

Diehl began backing away from the door.

"Get behind me," he said to Miss Gruffud.

"You told us the Dickinsons would tread lightly in town," she said—while following his command.

"Yeah, well…I've been known to be wrong every once in a great while."

The footsteps grew louder, closer.

Diehl looked over at Miss Nilsen. "You might want to get under your desk."

She sat up straight in her wheeled banker's chair.

"I will not," she said.

"I understand," Diehl said. "I've been hoping to die with dignity too."

The footsteps reached the landing outside the door.

Diehl's right hand hovered half an inch from his forty-five.

The knob turned, the door creaked open.

A dachshund came skittering in. It looked up at Diehl and barked.

"Now, now. Don't be rude," a voice from outside said. "We're the ones intruding, Prince Pudding Paws."

The dog barked again.

A man stepped into the room holding its leash. He was tall and thickset and bearded, with dark eyes and a fleshy, oval face. He wore a black suit, the coat long, the necktie tucked under a starched white collar in a way that had gone out of style years before. The clothes were immaculate and snugly tailored though. Here was a man who could afford fine new clothes—and to ignore fashion, if he chose.

Three men followed him inside. The first two—both burly, thirtyish, hard-eyed—were as well-tailored as him though more *a la mode*.

The third man was Captain Breck.

"Allow me to introduce myself," the man holding the leash said. "I am Kingsley Le May, and I am the majority stockholder and chairman of the board of the Consolidated American Mining Corporation."

He gave Miss Gruffud a little bow and a smile.

"Although it's probably more accurate to say I *am* Consolidated American," he went on. "And I think it's time we talked, don't you?"

CHAPTER 26

Hoop couldn't keep his horse at a gallop *all* the time. Not without baking it to death under the bright, late morning sun. So he had to limit himself to a trot for long stretches. Which worked out well for the horse. Not so much for him.

The horse wouldn't die of heat stroke. But Hoop had to listen to Rusty.

"I've managed to avoid Tombstone so far," the gangly, red-haired man was saying as they rode past what might have been the millionth towering saguaro cactus of the day. "Doesn't sound like there's much to it unless you're looking for silver, the clap, or a stray bullet. Then again *copper*, the clap, and a stray bullet is about all Hope Springs has to offer, and somehow I wound up there. So don't think I'm saying I'm picky."

Hoop made his usual reply. Which was none.

As was his way—though Hoop still couldn't understand how—Rusty took this as encouragement to keep going.

"Of course, Tombstone's still a good place to go if you're looking for gunmen too. Maybe it's not the magnet for hard cases it was fifteen years ago, but I bet we'll find more than enough men willing to sign on with us. Twelve hundred bucks can buy you a lot of bastard in Arizona Territory!"

Rusty laughed at his own joke. It was, he'd learned, the only way his jokes would get any reaction at all while he was alone in the desert with Hoop.

Hoop swung his gaze Rusty's way—then kept on swinging it past the man as he swiveled to scan the horizon behind them.

He was looking for dust or silhouettes against the pale-blue sky. Signs that they'd been spotted and followed as they slipped around town on their way to recruit reinforcements for the G-C Mine.

Hoop saw nothing but desert.

He faced east again. Toward Tombstone—and the sixty bleak, barren miles they still had to ride through to get there.

"Not that I'm saying all hired guns are bastards, you understand," Rusty went on. "Present company excluded—including myself! I bear no ill will for any man. Well, except the one who robbed me in Rio Rico. And the one who stole my horse in Yuma. And the two who beat the tar out of me in Gila Bend. And maybe Grover Cleveland. And my brother, Paul." Rusty leaned out and spat at a cactus. "Miserable, backstabbing son of a bitch."

Hoop considered speeding up to a gallop again. Surely the horse could take it for a while.

"That's one of the things that puzzles me about your Mr. Diehl," Rusty said. "Here he is in the hardest of hard businesses, but not only is he not a bastard—that I've seen anyhow—he's got what you could call a softness about him. You know…with all that flowery talk he spouts off when the mood strikes him? Now I know you got call to be mad at him after how he did you and the Apache yesterday, having me and the kid draw on you and all. But even then, he was just trying to keep a bad situation from getting even worse, if you don't mind my saying so."

Hoop finally turned to look directly at the man riding beside him. He hadn't made up his mind yet what he was going to say—maybe "I *do* mind" or "You don't know what the hell you're talking about" or possibly just "Shut up"—when he caught a distant glint of light out of the corner of his eye. Sunlight gleaming on oil-polished metal. Then suddenly it was gone, obscured by a tiny puff of smoke that dissipated quickly in the breeze blowing over the desert.

Hoop knew then what he *had* to say.

"Get down!"

And he threw himself from his saddle.

Before he even landed he knew it was too late. He heard the nearby *thud* a split second before crashing to the dry, brown-yellow desert bed. He absorbed the shock of hitting the ground, blinked once in pain, then pushed himself up to look for Rusty.

The man's horse was charging away with a limp, bloodied body splayed out on its back. Rusty had collapsed backward with his arms stretched out, boots still in the stirrups, lifeless eyes staring up at the sun. He was galloping out of sight when the second shot came—this one for Hoop.

———

Eskaminzim passed the time watching the road out of Hope Springs by sharpening his knife against a rock. When he grew bored with that—which didn't take long, and his knife was already sharp anyway—he checked and rechecked his Winchester. Which was fine. Of course. He'd cleaned it the day before. That done, and done again, he practiced standing on his head for a while.

Eskaminzim knew that left him vulnerable—moccasin-booted feet sticking up over the big cluster of yucca he was hiding behind— but there was no one around to see. The whites in town were either in church or in bed sleeping off hangovers or perhaps in church with hangovers. Nobody had been on the road to and from the mine except for Cadwaladr, who'd ridden in hours before, and Diehl and the lady, who'd passed by in the buggy twenty minutes ago.

Eskaminzim could tell Diehl had been looking for him in the rocky bluffs above town, and he'd been tempted to jump out and show himself. Show his ass, to be specific. Maybe give it a slap to get the lady's attention. She seemed like the kind of woman who'd never seen a man's ass before, so it would be educational. He decided against it though. He hadn't noticed any sign of the old Ranger and the rest of the Dickinson men, but why make a target of himself (and his beautiful ass) until he needed to? He could find another way to embarrass Diehl later.

After a minute on his head, Eskaminzim noticed that one of the upside-down twigs he was staring at—shed from a palo verde tree nearby—was the perfect size for a game of toe-toss-stick. He snatched up the twig as he rolled to his feet, then used it to draw a line in the dirt.

He'd been an excellent toe-toss-stick player as a boy. This was going to bring back happy memories.

He took two steps back, then bent down to balance the stick on his right toe.

That's why the first shot zipped past a foot above his head to blast through the yucca behind him. The second shot was even closer, throwing up a spray of rock and dust inches from Eskaminzim's side even though he'd thrown himself out flat on the ground now.

Eskaminzim began wriggling furiously away. The shots had come from above and behind him. He'd been watching the road when he should have been watching the bluffs. Now someone was trying to kill him, and they had the high ground.

He risked a grab at his Winchester as he crawled past the boulder he'd propped it against. Another shot hit the stock, jerking the rifle from his hands. It spun away and landed with clatter out of reach.

Eskaminzim kept going. He'd be at a huge disadvantage without the Winchester. But if he didn't find better cover immediately, he'd be dead.

Three more shots rang out in quick succession, one thunking into the palo verde tree, the other two ricocheting off a big rock above and to the right of Eskaminzim. They couldn't have come from the same gun in the same place.

There were at least three someones trying to kill Eskaminzim. Possibly more. All from high ground, with rifles, when all Eskaminzim had was a knife. And a twig, he realized. He was still clutching the stick.

He tossed the twig aside. His game would have to wait. First things first.

Eskaminzim had to figure out how to survive.

————

Romo was back at the top of the hill again, guarding the entrance to the mine grounds. Though what he was supposed to do if the Dickinsons came back, Diehl hadn't said. Romo ran through the scenario in his mind and could only come up with two options: run away from them or get shot trying to stop them. Romo hoped he wouldn't learn which option he'd choose.

Diehl had been more clear about what to do if Romo saw Utley or Juana leave the grounds.

"Follow them," he'd said. "Discreetly."

Romo didn't want to see how that would go either. Following someone seemed easy enough, but he wasn't sure he was capable of doing it "discreetly" on a long, winding road in broad daylight. What was he supposed to do if they saw him? Pretend he was out picking flowers?

And Diehl hadn't explained *why* he was supposed to follow Utley or Juana. It was obvious they disliked the men from the A.A. Western Detective Agency—Diehl, in particular—but the same could have been said—at first—of most of the mine workers. Who liked hired guns? Romo probably wouldn't have liked them if he hadn't been one of them.

He walked over to his favorite rock—he'd gotten to know all of the big ones at the top of the hill quite well given how much time he'd been spending there—and sat on it. As he gazed down at the road and the creek and the town, he pulled out the concha Juana had brought him for breakfast. If she'd stayed maybe he'd have asked her what to do if the Dickinsons came. If he could work up the nerve. It would be pretty humiliating—a man asking a woman what to think, what to do. A man's supposed to just know, right? But he had the feeling she'd give him a good answer. The way she'd held her rifle on that fat Dickinson made Romo think she'd been more than a revolutionary. She must have been a good one.

A soft, distant *pop* pulled him up off the rock. As he stood there staring south, toward the bottom of the hill, he heard another *pop*, then three more. *Pop-pop-pop*. It was coming from down near town.

Eskaminzim was around there somewhere, watching out for Cadwaladr. And Diehl and Miss Gruffud had gone that direction not long ago too, heading into Hope Springs to meet with the lady lawyer.

Maybe they never made it. Maybe they'd been ambushed.

Another *pop-pop-pop* gave Romo a start.

Maybe Diehl and Miss Gruffud were being murdered that very moment.

Romo looked over his shoulder to see if Juana had heard the gunfire and come to investigate…and tell him what to do. He might have even listened to Utley if the man gave him a command with enough confidence.

But no one was coming. Romo was on his own.

The gunfire continued sporadically, a shot then a pause then two shots then a pause, like corn just starting to get hot enough to pop. Surely whoever was being shot *at* couldn't stay unhit for long.

Romo made up his mind. He had a horse saddled at the corral —ready in case he needed to try out his discretion following someone at a moment's notice—and he ran to it and jammed his rifle in the scabbard and hauled himself up into the saddle. Juana ran into the courtyard as he dug in his heels, scowl on her face and rifle in her hands. But the horse was galloping and Romo was hanging on tight and somehow stopping seemed impossible.

Juana shouted to him as he charged down the road, but he couldn't make it out. He was focused on the bottom of the hill.

He could already see shapes down there. Brown and black blobs moving along the bluffs.

Hats and coats. On men—five, he saw as he rode closer—firing rifles at scrub-covered rocks below them. He couldn't see what they were shooting at, but he could guess. The fact that he *couldn't* see whoever it was gave him a clue. And the fact that there was no sign of the buggy Diehl and Miss Gruffud had taken to town.

Eskaminzim must have been trapped down there somewhere. And it was up to Romo to *un*-trap him. But how? He wasn't a good enough shot to pick off the men on the bluffs. Certainly not before they turned and picked off *him*. The best he could do was create a distraction and hope Eskaminzim would slip away in the time he could buy him.

He pulled out his rifle and tried to take aim without even realizing that when the moment had come for a decision—for action— he hadn't needed anyone to tell him what to do after all.

He'd underestimated how hard it is to fire a rifle on a galloping horse though. He'd seen it in plenty of magazine illustrations. Rider perfectly still, rifle barrel perfectly straight. Yet here he was with his right arm flapping up and down so violently he was afraid he'd either drop his new Winchester or shoot his horse.

He started pulling back on the reins. But even that was difficult now that he only held them in his left hand, and another forty yards went by beneath him before he finally got the horse to stop.

The sound of gunfire continued as he swung out of the saddle. Not distant pops now. Sharp bangs and ricochets.

He stepped away from his horse and brought up his rifle. He was close enough now for the shapes below to have definition. They weren't just blobs of dull color now. They were people. Men. Like him.

Romo picked one and put his finger on the trigger and got ready to squeeze.

That's when the blast came from behind to spin him, screaming in pain and surprise, into the dirt.

CHAPTER 27

Kingsley Le May followed Prince Pudding Paws as the dog tugged him across Miss Nilsen's office to a bookshelf topped with a bust of Lincoln.

The dachshund lifted a stubby leg and unleashed a stream of urine onto the lowest row of law books.

Miss Gruffud gasped.

"If you please, sir!" Miss Nilsen protested.

"I'm sorry," said Le May, making no move to stop the dog. "But nature must take its course."

"In the alley out back, perhaps!" Miss Nilsen said.

Le May shrugged. "Some things are irresistible. Why pretend otherwise?"

His two burly guards, positioned now on either side of the door, smirked.

Breck just glanced down at the dog impassively, then locked eyes on Diehl.

When the dachshund was done peeing, he looked up at Le May and wagged his tail.

"Aww...now who could say no to that?" Le May said.

He pulled a little piece of dried meat from his coat pocket and squatted down to give it to Prince Pudding Paws.

"Those any good?" Diehl asked Breck, pointing at the dog treat.

Breck said nothing.

"How many did you get yesterday for killing a man and beating a woman?" Diehl said.

Still, Breck remained silent.

"Quiet, Diehl," Cadwaladr said. He shifted his bulk in the armchair he occupied and beetled his brow at Le May. "What is the meaning of this? Have you come here to threaten us?"

Le May patted Prince Pudding Paws on the head, then stood and smiled. "Quite the opposite. I've come to *remove* a threat…and deliver great rewards. A fair price for your mine, peace and harmony for your community, and peace of mind for you."

Prince Pudding Paws yipped at him.

Le May looked down and shushed him.

"Don't be greedy," he told the dog.

"You need not bother, Mr. Le May," Miss Gruffud said. She was still standing before Miss Nilsen's desk—Le May and his men—and dachshund—had barged in before she'd had a chance to sit in the small office's remaining armchair. Now she took a step forward, back straight, head high. "Once, weeks ago, I was willing to at least consider your company's offers, insulting though they were. But after all that's happened…" She shook her head. "Consolidated American will *never* own the Gruffud-Cadwaladr Mine."

Le May snorted, amused. "That's very emotional of you, Miss Gruffud. Very un-businesslike. But you're right. Consolidated American will never own any 'Gruffud-Cadwaladr Mine.' When it belongs to us, we're going to call it 'The Copper King.' That's got the kind of ring to it stockholders like. I had the sign made a month ago. Our man Claypole put it in storage someplace."

Le May looked squarely at Diehl for the first time.

"We'll find it eventually," he said.

"Mr. Le May," Miss Nilsen said, "let me remind you that you are intruding in a private—"

"Thirty thousand dollars cash and a thousand shares in Consolidated American," Le May said, swiveling to face Miss Gruffud again. "Final offer. I wish we could do better, but with the price of silver where it is, not to mention the stock market…" He shrugged again, spreading his hands this time in a "What can one do?" way. "I still think it's generous under the circumstances."

Miss Gruffud opened her mouth to answer.

"We'll need time to think it over," Miss Nilsen cut in.

"I understand. You'd like a few days to go over the numbers. Weigh the different factors. *Wait for help*," Le May said. He pulled a silver pocket watch from his vest and popped it open. "You have one minute."

"I don't need one second," Miss Gruffud said. "The answer remains no."

Cadwaladr leaned forward in his chair and dropped his voice to a whisper—though everyone in the room could hear him all the same.

"Let's at least consider it, Catrin. Thirty thousand dollars is a lot of money."

"It's not even half what that mine is worth," Miss Nilsen said.

Cadwaladr threw the lawyer a scowling glance, then focused on Miss Gruffud again. "We can come out of this ahead or we can get more people hurt and end up with nothing."

Le May kept his eyes on his watch while Prince Pudding Paws sniffed some of the law books he hadn't soaked. The guards by the door stared straight ahead like twin statues.

Diehl watched Breck.

Breck watched Diehl.

"I will not sell to this man," said Miss Gruffud.

Le May's expression changed as he looked up from his watch. A moment before, he'd seemed cool, confident. But his cheeks started to flush now as his face hardened and his air of slick, smug composure dropped away.

"Really?" he said.

"Really," said Miss Gruffud.

"Really?" Le May repeated a little louder.

"Really," Miss Gruffud said again.

Le May stuffed his watch away and balled his fists.

"*Really?*" he said.

Prince Pudding Paws flattened his ears and slinked off as far as his leash would let him.

Miss Gruffud exchanged a nervous glance with Miss Nilsen before replying.

"*Really*," she said.

Le May's face went beet red.

"*Really?*"

"Yes, really, Mr. Le May!" Miss Nilsen said. "I don't know why you keep expecting a different answer. We will not give in to extortion."

"*Extortion?*"

Prince Pudding Paws pulled so hard on his leash it popped from Le May's hand. The dog escaped to a corner, whimpering.

"I will thank you not to use that ugly word in public!" Le May thundered at Miss Nilsen. "I have lawyers too, you know! In fact…"

He took a step toward Miss Gruffud that sent her stumbling back into Miss Nilsen's desk.

"You seem to think you're saying no to *me*," Le May said. "And you are. Which is foolish enough! But when you say no to this offer, you're not just putting yourself in my way." He jerked his head—a head now trembling with uncontrolled rage—at Breck. "You're putting yourself in *his* way! And he, I will remind you, is more than a him. He is the Dickinson National Detective Agency, just as I am the Consolidated American Mining Corporation. And when you try to defy me, him, them, *us*, you're not just pitting yourself against our money and our will and our skill and our lawyers. More lawyers than the devil can fit in hell, missy! You are placing yourself squarely before the relentless, pitiless, bone-crushing wheels of progress—wheels that have mashed the very life juices out of a million individuals with more strength and resolve than you. You're trying to defy the inexorable power of capital. You're trying to defy *destiny*. You're trying to defy the goddamn American way of life! And it will not be defied or denied or defiled by some deluded fool of a woman in a shitty little office in a shitty little town in this squalid shithole of a territory! It will not, and *I* will not! Do you understand?"

By the time Le May was done, his shouts were so loud they were shaking the glass in the windowpanes, and someone had begun thumping on the ceiling downstairs.

"Keep it down!" a man's muffled voice said through the floorboards. "We got people trying to grieve down here!"

Miss Gruffud, Miss Nilsen, and Cadwaladr gaped at the panting, wild-eyed Le May in aghast astonishment.

Diehl looked at Breck and the guards. They seemed unfazed. Apparently such tantrums were nothing new to them.

The soft sound of trickling liquid drew everyone's attention to the corner.

Prince Pudding Paws was cowering there, ears down, tail tucked under his little black rump.

"Now look what you made him do," Le May said as another yellow puddle grew on the office floor. "It's all right, Puddin'. Daddy's not mad at *you*."

The dachshund just shivered and kept peeing.

"I would thank you to leave," Miss Nilsen said. She stepped out around her desk to stand shoulder-to-shoulder with Miss Gruffud. "Now."

Le May stood his ground and sneered at her.

"I'll go when I've concluded my business," he said. He shifted his gaze to Miss Gruffud. "So...have you seen the light?"

"All I've seen," the lady replied softly, "is an unhinged display by a petulant bully."

"'Unhinged'? I've been talking sense to you, woman!"

Miss Nilsen looked past Le May to Diehl.

Aren't you going to do *something?* the look said.

Diehl had no idea how to throw out a deranged tycoon and his huge bodyguards and his personal Dickinson detective and his dachshund. Somehow it had never come up before.

He cleared his throat.

"Mr. Le May? I think this conversation is—"

"Oh, shut up," Le May said. His tone was calm and his voice

steady though. He took a deep breath and smoothed back his hair with both hands. "I heard. The lady's answer is 'no.' Which means we'll have to continue our search for Mr. Claypole. Captain Breck's men are out scouring the countryside for him this very moment. Who knows what they'll run across? *Who* they'll run across? Of course, they'll return to the mine anytime they like, thanks to that warrant. I expect you and the captain will be seeing a lot of each other, Miss Gruffud."

"We'll see what the governor has to say about that," Miss Nilsen said.

Le May cocked an eyebrow at her. "Will you? And will he hear *you*?"

"What does that mean?" Miss Nilsen asked.

"What does what mean? I didn't say anything." Le May turned to the more barrel-chested of his two brawny guards. "Did you hear me say anything, Francis? Anything at all in this horrid little pissoir of an office?"

"I never hear nothing," the man said.

Le May looked at the other guard. "Casper?"

"I never hear nothing neither."

"Well…there you have it," Le May said to Miss Nilsen. He glanced over at Breck. "Time we were on our way?"

Breck gave him a single, silent nod.

"Right," Le May said. He moved toward the corner and picked up Prince Pudding Paws's leash. "If you come to your senses and change your mind, you'll find the prince and I at…oh, whatever this little Podunk's best hotel is called. The Hope Springs Arms or what-have-you. You've been muleheaded and insolent, but you'll find we can be forgiving…if we get what we want. Good day."

Le May started to walk off, tugging Prince Pudding Paws with him. Francis opened the door for him but Casper slipped out into the sunshine first, eyes already darting this way and that, right hand hovering near the bulge in his coat over his left shoulder. Le May followed him outside, then scooped up Prince Pudding Paws and started down the stairs. Francis lumbered out after them, leaving Breck the final, solitary interloper.

"You're awfully quiet this morning," Diehl said to him. "Nothing to say for yourself?"

Breck regarded him coolly a moment before replying.

"I'm saying it."

There might have been a little smile on his thin lips as he turned to go, but it was hard to know for sure. He closed the door after himself, but before he'd even reached the bottom of the stairs, Diehl was yanking it open again.

"God *damn* it," Diehl spat as he stepped out onto the landing and gazed off toward the north.

He was hearing gunfire there. Lots of it. Right where Eskaminzim was supposed to be watching for Cadwaladr on the road from town.

CHAPTER 28

Hoop rose to his knees to check on Rusty—a mistake he instantly regretted. As he watched Rusty's horse carry the man's limp, lifeless body toward the horizon, a bullet passed so close to him it blew through his coat, tearing out the left pocket and tugging him forward toward the dirt again. He went with the momentum, throwing up his hands and rolling down into a gully so shallow it was little more than a foot-deep dip in the desert bed.

He stopped himself there, face up, arms and legs straight, and hoped he was out of sight.

Someone was hunting him with a buffalo gun—while his own was still on the horse that had gone galloping off with Rusty's. He still had his pistol—he could feel it there in its holster despite his tumbling—but it would be useless at long range.

His only chance was also the reason he might die. The men trying to kill him were professionals. They'd want to be sure they'd finished the job.

Hoop would make them come close to do it.

Only one of them was any good at a distance, Hoop figured. But he was very, very good. A breeze had blown in not long before, whipping up wisps of dust—and complicating any long-range shooting. Yet Rusty had been hit square in the back from hundreds of yards away. If there'd been two shooters that good, they'd have fired at the same time so as to end the business all at once. Instead, the sharpshooter had to pick a target to take down first. And he'd gone for the white one. The one in charge, presumably. Which was the only reason Hoop was lying there alive in what might yet be his grave.

If they were smart, they'd take their time. Watch for a while, then send in a few men when they saw no movement. Keep the sharpshooter back so he could pick off their prey if it got flushed out.

Hoop had to hope they weren't that smart. That they'd be sloppy. That they'd rush. But why should they, with him pinned down and no one to help him?

He squirmed just a bit, only enough to get a little more comfortable. Something was digging into his side near his right hip. A lump he took for a rock at first. Then he remembered—and knew what he had to do.

Carefully, keeping his hands flat against his body, Hoop reached into his right coat pocket and drew out the wad of cash Diehl had given him to hire more guns for the mine. One thousand two hundred and twenty-three dollars. He separated about a third of the bills—there was no time for a careful count—and stuffed them away again. The rest he lifted up just high enough for them to flutter in the wind. He fanned them out like a hand of cards, then let them go.

Most of them immediately fell back onto Hoop's chest. But half a dozen bills, caught in the breeze, lifted off into the sky. A moment later more followed upward, and the rest began spreading out low to the ground, quivering and tumbling like wind-blown leaves.

Hoop slipped the little leather guard loop from the hammer of his Colt Army revolver, then slid the gun from its holster and waited.

Any sound from the men there to kill him would help. Footsteps, whispers. They'd tell Hoop where his enemies were—and that they weren't being cautious enough.

What he heard first were hoofbeats. Then a whinny, then voices, then a laugh. And Hoop's question was answered.

These men were not smart. Whether they were *fast* though, remained to be seen.

"—before it's spread from here to Texas!" one of them was saying as they drew closer.

From the southwest. At Hoop's seven o'clock.

"Every man for himself!" whooped another.

From due west. At nine o'clock.

"Slow down, ya jackasses! We gotta make sure that black bastard's dead first!" said a third.

Also due west, nine o'clock. Behind the other one. Riding straight toward Hoop.

The hoofbeats were pounding so hard now Hoop could feel them. The men were close. There were three for sure, but it felt like more.

Hoop had five bullets in his Colt—the hammer resting on an empty chamber so he wouldn't shoot off his foot the first time his horse stumbled. He'd have to make every shot count.

The hoofbeats started to slow. In a moment, the men would dismount and it would be too late to catch them tall in the saddle, reins in their hands. Perfect targets.

It was time to act.

Hoop sat up and found the first man he'd heard—bearded, thirtyish, in a long yellow duster—exactly where he expected. Slightly to his right, about forty feet away. Hoop shot him in the chest, then pivoted to the next man without waiting to see what happened to the first. The look of surprise Hoop saw was obliterated by the smashing impact of the next shot, and the man flopped backward out of his saddle.

The third man should have been behind the second, directly in the line of fire. But he'd veered to the right when the shooting started, ducking low and grabbing at his pistol. Hoop drew a bead as he galloped past and put a bullet through his side.

There was a *bang* behind Hoop, and a sharp pain stabbed into his left arm just below the shoulder. He cried out in anguish and shock but managed to keep his eyes open and his gun in his grip. He swiveled back to the right to find a fourth rider—close enough for Hoop to see his handlebar mustache and upraised Remington—bearing down on him.

Hoop shot at the man. And missed.

The man shot at him. And missed.

Hoop shot again, firing off the last round in his gun. And didn't miss.

The mustachioed man dropped his gun and reins, clutched his stomach, screamed out an obscenity, slumped, and fell. He landed in the dirt not ten feet from Hoop's little trench, his horse carrying on without him.

As the hoofbeats of all the now-riderless horses faded and slowed, Hoop became aware of another sound. Wheezing. Moaning. Muttering. Movement.

He turned toward the sound and saw that the first man he'd shot, the one with the beard and the duster, was struggling to get up. He looked vaguely familiar. All the riders had, of course. Hoop had watched them ride up to the mine with Breck the night before.

This one had a pistol in his right hand but couldn't seem to raise it.

"Gonna kill you," the Dickinson groaned. "Gonna kill you."

A raspy gurgling was coming from the wet hole in the middle of his blue bib shirt. He'd be dead in ten minutes. But that was still plenty of time to take Hoop with him if he worked up the strength to lift his gun.

Hoop tried to move his left arm and had to stifle a scream. The bleeding wasn't too bad—the bullet had ripped through muscle without hitting an artery or shattering bone—but the hand wasn't going to be much use to him for now. Reloading his Colt was out of the question.

"Gonna kill you, you son of a bitch," the bearded man said.

Hoop forced himself to take a deep breath, then another. He needed to gather his strength even as each second left him with less blood.

No rest for the weary. Or was it "no rest for the wicked"? He'd heard it both ways.

Oh, well. It didn't matter. Either one fit.

He slowly pushed himself to his feet and started looking for a rock the right size. Just a little bigger than his fist. When he found one, he picked up, then turned and started toward the man with the beard.

Once Hoop was done with him, he'd move on to the others. He wasn't going to make the same mistake they had.

"Gonna kill you," the Dickinson said again.

Hoop almost told him that he talked too much, but what would be the point?

A few seconds later, Hoop cured him of the habit.

———

There were four men shooting at Eskaminzim, he knew now. They'd fired enough rounds for him to become quite well acquainted with their weapons.

The two with Winchesters were above him slightly to the left. The one with the twenty-two caliber carbine—a Colt Lightning, probably—was above him to the right. And above and straight ahead, behind a boulder the shape and color of a peach, was the idiot who kept popping away at him with a Webley Bull Dog. A snub-nosed handgun! From fifty yards! It was insulting. If that was the one who killed him, Eskaminzim would never forgive himself.

He knew exactly how he'd escape if he got the opportunity. Wriggle here, slide there, climb here, dive there, crawl here, duck there, run run run here. He could see it all in his head even as he lay flat on his belly with bullets zinging past overhead.

The problem was getting through the wriggle. He'd be exposed for three or four seconds before he got to the slide. An easy target. Even the pendejo with the Bull Dog would have a good chance at him.

What he needed was a distraction. Maybe Diehl would come running out of town to investigate the gunfire, and Eskaminzim could slip away while the Dickinsons concentrated on trying to kill *him* for a while. That would be perfect! But Eskaminzim couldn't count on it.

All he could count on, if he didn't get out of there soon, was a really disappointing death. Pinned down, outflanked, and shot without even taking one of the Dickinsons with him. He could see that clearly in his head too.

A boom from the northwest jerked his head up. It was more gunfire, but different this time. Further off. Closer to the mine. From a shotgun.

The fire from the hillside above Eskaminzim stopped. The Dickinsons were listening too. Wondering what the shotgun blast meant. Maybe—hopefully—craning their necks to peer up the road. Distracted in just the way that might give Eskaminzim a chance.

He had no choice: He started wriggling. One second, two seconds, three seconds, four. Then he was sliding—alive—and climbing and diving and crawling and ducking and running running running.

He'd made it. He was around the southern side of the hill, safely out of sight of the Dickinsons. They started shooting at his old hiding place again, oblivious to his absence. Now he could zigzag back up through the rocks and come in from behind and knife them one by one. He'd save the Bull Dog man for last.

"Hey!" someone shouted behind him. "Y'all shootin' at an Indian?"

Eskaminzim glanced back.

A small crowd had gathered at the north end of town, drawn by the sound of gunfire and the promise of entertainment. A gray-haired man in a white frock coat and a plantation hat pointed toward Eskaminzim.

"He ain't in them rocks anymore! He's over there!" he yelled.

"Dammit!" one of the Dickinsons spat.

Another called out "Thanks, mister!"

Eskaminzim often took pride in the fact that his native language had no obscenities. Other times—such as now—he wished he had some to fall back on. They really did come in handy occasionally.

"Vete a la mierda!" Eskaminzim shouted, and just in case his meaning wasn't clear—as he doubted the old man in the plantation hat spoke Spanish—he lifted an arm and gestured in a way he'd first learned from vaqueros as a boy.

Then he was concentrating on the tasks at hand—running, dipping, dodging, darting—as he made his escape around the hill.

———

"Dios mío," Romo sobbed.

He was on his back in the road staring up at wispy white clouds. The stinging pain in his right shoulder was excruciating. He squeezed his eyes shut and rolled onto his left side. That helped a little.

He reached his left hand back and felt the shredded, wet fabric of his shirt, wincing as his fingertips brushed the torn flesh beneath.

He'd been shot from behind. His rifle lay a few feet away, out of reach. He still had his pistol holstered to his side though. He wondered if he could draw it without screaming.

He moved his right hand toward the gun's grip.

"Don't do it, amigo," a man said.

Romo heard a metallic *click-clack-click*.

"I've got four rounds left in this shotgun," the man continued. "My first shot just clipped you, but I could put the rest up your ass in three seconds flat."

Romo let both hands drop down into the dirt.

"That's the idea," the man said. "Now you just stay there nice and still, and I'll let you keep breathing."

Romo nodded, face contorted with pain. He tried to stay still, but it was hard not to squirm. He clenched his fists and gritted his teeth and kept his eyes squeezed tight to hold back his tears. For a moment, the agony blotted out everything—even the sound of the men stepping out onto the road to surround him. One of them reached down to take Romo's pistol, kneeing his shoulder in the process.

Romo screamed.

"Hurts, don't it?" the man said. He sounded close.

Romo opened his eyes.

The pot-bellied Dickinson, Kozlowski, was squatting nearby, shotgun balanced on his knees.

"Well, get ready, José. It's about to get worse," he said. "You've been invited to a little shindig—and to get there you're gonna have to ride."

"I...I can't," Romo said. "I don't even know if I can stand."

"It's ride or die, José."

Kozlowski smiled. Not because he was joking.

He was smiling because he wasn't.

"I'll try," Romo said.

"I suppose that's all I can ask of you," said Kozlowski. "If you can't handle it...well, that's just how it was meant to be."

He stood and spoke to someone behind Romo.

"Get him on his horse."

"Yes, sir."

Kozlowski looked back down at Romo and cocked his head.

"Oh, and Vollmer? Gag this little priss first, will you?" he said. "I do hate to hear a man scream."

———

The gunfire stopped as Diehl sprinted toward the north end of Hope Springs. By the time he reached the foothills that started just beyond town limits, a strange new sound was rising up instead.

Booing.

Twenty or so townspeople—mostly men, but with a few women and children mixed in—were watching as four Dickinsons picked their way down a rocky incline not far away.

"What's happening?" Diehl asked. "Why are you booing?"

A gray-haired man in a white plantation hat glanced back at him.

"Those fools had an Indian buck trapped over there, and they let him get away," he said.

He turned toward the Dickinsons again and went back to booing.

Diehl scanned the rocky bluffs to the left and the trees and brush and flatlands to the right. As he expected, he saw no sign of Eskaminzim.

What he did see was a cloud of dust in the distance. It looked to be over the road, but it didn't stretch due south toward Hope Springs or north toward the mine. It seemed to head southeast. Around town.

And away from witnesses.

CHAPTER 29

Three hundred forty-seven dollars. That's what Hoop had left in his coat pocket after he used the rest to lure the Dickinsons in close. He was able to pluck another thirty-one off cacti as he shuffled around the desert trying to calm and catch the least spooked of the horses. His own mount was long gone—along with his beloved Sharps.

Not that the rifle would do him any good at the moment with his left arm in the shape it was. The bleeding wasn't too bad, but he'd applied a tourniquet just in case. Now the forearm throbbed, the hand tingled, the whole thing hung useless.

The piebald mare he was slowly, soothingly pursuing had belonged to one of the dead men. Once he had it by the reins, he led it back to the bodies, which he proceeded to search for more money. Hoop didn't like doing that—usually such a thing would be beneath his dignity—but he needed cash. What kind of army could you hire for three hundred seventy-eight dollars?

It was four hundred and twenty-two dollars by the time he was done going through the Dickinsons' pockets. Burying them was out of the question, but that probably didn't matter. Half a dozen turkey vultures were already circling up above, patiently waiting for Hoop to move on. What they didn't rip and eat and scatter the wolves and coyotes would fight over that night. Within twelve hours there would be nothing left of the men but gnawed bones and boot leather garnished with a sprinkling of unused bullets.

So it had been for many of the hired guns Hoop had encountered over the years. No funeral, no grave, no marker to say "He killed for money. He died for money. Rest in peace." Maybe it would be the same for Hoop one day. But not today.

Or would it? He was about to haul himself up onto the mare when he noticed movement on the horizon. Maybe more horses returning? Maybe his own? Hoop squinted at the distant shapes, hoping.

His hope didn't last long. Horses were approaching, yes. Four of them. With men on their backs.

Hoop saw straight black hair and flat-brimmed hats and ponchos.

Pima Indians. Their reservation—Gila Bend—was miles to the north. Who were they to be this far south? Cattle thieves? Renegades?

Hoop flexed his left hand and bent his left elbow…and had to swallow a yelp of pain. There was a Winchester in the saddle scabbard on the mare's right side, but it didn't matter. Hoop lacked the strength to hold it, let alone use it. And his holstered Colt was still empty.

The Pima language was related to Shoshone and Comanche, so Hoop knew a few words that might be understood. He'd have to talk his way out of this. Which was usually Diehl's job. Hoop had never had much interest in persuasion. He'd have to get good at it fast.

He stood by the mare and waited to see if the men riding toward him would give him the chance to try.

The pain from the buckshot in his back was so bad Romo could hardly believe the Dickinson detective could make it worse. But Eugene Kozlowski seemed to be an expert at inflicting pain. He'd started with slaps and hair pulling and punches to the gut, but soon he got creative. With Romo's ears. With his nose. With his genitals. With his wounds.

But for all the variety in the torture, the questions never changed.

"What happened to Henry Claypole?" And "Where's the body?"

Romo's answers didn't change either. Because they were the truth.

"I don't know! No one told me anything! I don't know!"

And Kozlowski would go back to work.

The one thing Romo did know—that Diehl had asked him to booby-trap a wine bottle with nitro a few days before—he'd managed to keep to himself so far. Kozlowski hadn't asked the right question. If he did, Romo didn't trust himself not to answer.

It was just Kozlowski and Romo in the stockcar—part of Le May's special train, still parked on the spur line miles from town. Where there was no one to hear Romo's screams except for the man causing them and more men outside who didn't care.

After a while—Romo couldn't tell whether it was an hour or a day—one of the side doors slid open, letting in a hot blast of sun that blinded him. He squeezed his eyes shut and twisted in the wooden chair he was handcuffed to.

"Hey there, Captain," Kozlowski said cheerfully. "Come to join the fun? I saved you a spot."

Romo felt a finger poke him in the side just below the ribcage

"Here. Right over his left kidney," Kozlowski said. "Haven't touched it."

"Thanks," a man said. "We'll see if that's necessary."

Romo heard the side door slam closed again. He opened his eyes and found Breck standing before him, his long, lean form striped by the bifurcated light streaming in between the slats.

"You're Roma, right?" the old man said.

Romo just looked at him, steeling himself for the blows to come.

"Come on—speak up, José," Kozlowski said. "I've been going easy on your mouth too, but that doesn't have to last."

Romo took a deep breath. Or started to. His lungs were only

half-full when the pain from his bruised ribs forced him to blow the breath out again.

"*Romo.* Alfonso Romo." He threw Kozlowski a glare. "Not José."

"You'll always be José to me," Kozlowski said.

He drew back a hand to give Romo another slap.

"Koz," Breck said.

Kozlowski froze.

Breck shook his head.

Kozlowski grinned and patted Romo on the head instead.

"Alfonso," Breck said, "do you know what we're after?"

Romo nodded.

"And you won't give it to us?" Breck said.

"I don't know it!"

Kozlowski rapped the top of Romo's skull with a knuckle. "Speak respectfully to the captain."

Romo's head drooped. A sob welled up in him, but he managed to turn it into words.

"I don't know."

"Alfonso," Breck said. "*Alfonso.*"

Romo looked up into the man's gaunt face.

"What did your friends tell you about me?" Breck said. "Diehl and the Black?"

"Nothing."

Breck cocked his head, looking skeptical. "Really? They didn't bother explaining how they knew me? Why the Black would want to kill me?"

"No. That's just it. There's a lot they don't tell me. But Eskaminzim—the Apache they work with—he told me a story. About you shooting two soldiers? A cavalry officer and a sergeant? I don't even know if it's true."

Breck straightened up again.

Kozlowski grinned.

"Oh, it's true," Kozlowski said.

"Did your Apache tell you *why* I shot those soldiers?" Breck asked Romo.

"No. I just assumed it was because they were black."

The old man gave his head another slow shake.

"I killed them," he said, "because I had a job to do, and they got in my way."

"*And* they were black," Kozlowski added, smiling at Breck.

Breck almost looked like he might smile back—if he knew how to smile.

"Yes, all right. And they were Black," he conceded. "And I'll remind you, *José*, that you are a filthy Mexican bean-eater. Which means—"

Breck stepped in and slammed a fist into Romo's side, hitting the spot Kozlowski had pointed out a moment before.

Romo howled and slumped and retched.

"I don't give a shit whether you live or die," Breck said once he was sure Romo could hear him again. "That's what made me a good Ranger...until my devotion to the work started to make certain weak-kneed people uncomfortable. So now I work for the Dickinson National Detective Agency and, through them, the Consolidated American Mining Corporation. And believe me, José —they give less of a shit about people like you than I do. So if you want to get out of this boxcar alive, you're going to tell me what I want to know. Do you understand?"

Romo was still hunched over, panting.

Breck reached down and softly ran his fingertips over the bloody holes in Romo's shoulder.

Romo stiffened and gasped.

"*Do you understand?*" Breck repeated.

"Yes," Romo said. He slowly pulled himself up to look Breck in the eye. "But *you* have to understand. I truly don't know what happened to Henry Claypole."

"And no idea about a body?" Breck said. "That's what really matters. Evidence."

"Leverage, you mean," Romo could have said. "A tool to get at Diehl and Hoop and Eskaminzim. And, through them, Miss Gruffud and Mr. Cadwaladr and the mine."

Romo was an engineer. He understood the application of force

—and how to increase it in one place by bearing down somewhere else.

He shook his head. "I'm not lying, Mr. Breck. No one told me what happened to Claypole."

Breck stared back at him for a long, silent moment. Then he sighed.

"You know what?" the old man said. "I believe you, Alfonso."

Romo sighed too. Or started to. The deep intake of breath sent more pain stabbing through his shoulder. He winced, then started to relax.

Breck turned to Kozlowski.

"Keep at him," he said.

"*What?*" said Romo.

Breck gave him a shrug. "In case I'm wrong."

He turned and headed for the side door. Kozlowski waited, smiling and flexing his fingers, while Breck went out. Then he got back to work.

———

"I can't believe they haven't shot you already," someone said.

Diehl jerked in shock but managed not to cry out or upset any of the loose, gravelly soil at the top of the ridge he was stretched out on.

He looked over his shoulder and saw Eskaminzim crawling up to join him.

"This is the most obvious place to watch their camp from," the Apache said. "That's why I came here to look for you."

Diehl returned his gaze to the train and tracks down below. The Dickinsons had set up neat rows of tents and a roped-off paddock for their remuda nearby.

"Yeah, well," Diehl grumbled, "maybe you shouldn't be lecturing anyone about avoiding traps today, hmm?"

"At least I got out of mine."

Eskaminzim wriggled up the last few feet on his belly. Just as he got settled, the side door to one of the boxcars slid open, and Breck dropped down to the tracks. It was hard to see into the car, and the door wasn't open long before Breck slammed it shut again, but for just a moment two shapes could be seen inside.

Men. One seated, one standing. The first slight, the second stout.

Romo and Kozlowski. Diehl didn't need the door open to know why they were together in the boxcar. He could see it clearly in his mind.

"Dammit," he said.

"Good thing you didn't tell the Mexican what happened to Claypole," said Eskaminzim. He looked over at Diehl. "You *didn't* tell him…right?"

"No. I didn't. But that doesn't matter now. What matters is getting Romo out of there."

Eskaminzim narrowed his eyes. "You know, Diehl—as your hair turns gray your heart turns soft. Maybe your head too…though that's not so new. Even if we stay around here till dark without getting killed, there's no way we could get him out of that camp alive." He looked past Diehl, his gaze turning dreamy. "Although it might be fun to try."

"We're not doing it like that. We've got to think of something else."

"Too bad Hoop's not here. Maybe when he gets back with those new men…"

Eskaminzim and Diehl looked at each other again.

"*If* he gets back with those new men," Eskaminzim said.

Diehl nodded grimly. "We have to assume Breck knew about him and Rusty. But there's nothing we can do about that for now… except make sure the Dickinsons don't learn anything else we don't want them to know."

"And you know how to do that?"

Diehl nodded again.

"So you know who betrayed us?" Eskaminzim said.

"Yes. I think so," Diehl said.

"Tell me." Eskaminzim reached down and touched the handle of his knife. "And then I *will* have some fun."

CHAPTER 30

"Los mataré!" Juana said as she paced back and forth across the carpet in Miss Gruffud's parlor room. "Las derribaré como perros!"

"What in god's name is she raving about?" Cadwaladr asked the others.

"I don't know," said Miss Gruffud.

Utley just shook his head and took a skittish step away from the maid, looking alarmed by her fury—and the rifle she clutched in her hands.

"Something about dogs," said Miss Nilsen. The dour expression on her face indicated that she knew more than that though—that she understood. "I will kill them! I will shoot them down like dogs!" And that a part of her felt the same way.

"Get a hold of yourself, woman!" Cadwaladr snapped at Juana. "And for god's sake, speak English. Or better yet, just get out if you can't compose yourself. I honestly don't know why you're still in here with us anyway."

Juana stopped pacing and glared at Cadwaladr. He was in an armchair about a dozen feet from her, and she looked tempted to close the distance swinging her rifle like a baseball bat.

"She's here because we have few friends or allies left, Gareth," Miss Gruffud said. "And Juana has been loyal to us through thick and thin. We need her—and she is good enough to stay."

Juana acknowledged the lady's words with a little nod, and some of her usual icy serenity seemed to return. A hint of rage still smoldered in her eyes though.

"I apologize for my display of emotion," she said to Cadwaladr. "And I will remember to speak in English from here on."

Cadwaladr's only reply to her was a grunt. He saved his words for Miss Gruffud and Miss Nilsen, who were perched side by side on a divan like two birds on the same branch.

"Actually, I don't think there's much to discuss," he said. "Our only choice now is to—"

"Shhh!" said Juana. "Someone is coming!"

She kept her rifle at hip level but pointed the barrel toward the room's open door.

"I don't hear anything," said Cadwaladr.

"Me neith—" Utley began. He pulled a small revolver from his coat pocket with a trembling hand. "Horses."

Everyone in the room went silent as the slow clopping of hooves grew louder. A moment later, it stopped.

There were footsteps on the porch. Then a knock at the front door.

Utley took aim with his little pistol.

The door swung open, and a man leaned inside.

"Yoo-hoo!" Diehl called out. "Anybody home?"

Juana reached over and pushed Utley's arm down.

"Thanks for not shooting," Diehl said. "Mind if we join you?"

Eskaminzim leaned in beside him.

"Mr. Diehl! Of course! Come in! What a relief!" Miss Gruffud said, stepping up behind Juana and Utley. "The way you went charging off after our encounter with Le May…and all that gunfire…"

"Do you know what's happened to Alfonso?" Juana asked as Diehl and Eskaminzim walked across the foyer. "His horse is gone, and I found fresh blood on the road."

She and Utley and Miss Gruffud stepped back to let Diehl and Eskaminzim into the parlor. Diehl greeted Cadwaladr and Miss Nilsen with curt nods before answering Juana's question.

"Romo's alive. But things are complicated."

"What does that mean?" Juana said.

"I'll explain in a moment. First…" Diehl turned to the others. "Is there any news for me? Anything you've learned since the meeting in town?"

"Yes. The telegraph line is down," Miss Nilsen said. "Le May's comment about us not hearing from the governor or vice versa concerned me, so I checked. Hope Springs has been cut off for hours, and there's no telling when it'll be fixed."

"We're on our own," Utley said.

Diehl nodded, unsurprised. "Mr. Le May has turned out to be quite single-minded."

"You underestimated him," Cadwaladr said.

"I misjudged him. Most men you can understand and predict with some good old 'Cui bono.' 'Who benefits?' But some others are…"

Diehl spun his hands, searching for the right word.

"Crazy sons of bitches?" Eskaminzim suggested.

Cadwaladr and Utley gasped, offended on behalf of the ladies.

The ladies smiled.

"Exactly," said Diehl. "I didn't anticipate that Le May would turn out to be…one of those. Having now met him and heard him out, and knowing that he has someone as ruthless and coldblooded as Captain Breck here to do his bidding, I've reassessed our position."

"And?" said Miss Nilsen.

Diehl shrugged. "It's even worse than I thought, and we could all be killed any second."

Miss Nilsen took this in with a calm nod.

Cadwaladr, meanwhile, threw his hands in the air and cried out, "My god!"

"Gareth," Miss Gruffud said.

"Don't defend him, Catrin!" the old man railed. He pointed a quivering finger at Diehl and Eskaminzim. "We hand over our money and our lives to some piddly detective agency no one's heard of, and this is all that's left to show for it in our hour of need? A savage and an incompetent come to tell us we're about to die?"

Eskaminzim put a finger to his own chest. "'Savage'?" he said. He looked over at Diehl. "At least that's better than 'incompetent.'"

"Gareth, this isn't helpful!" said Miss Gruffud.

"Thank you, miss," Diehl said, stepping between his employers. "But Mr. Cadwaladr's right about me." He threw Eskaminzim a quick, irritated glance. "To some extent. I made a mistake, and it's cost us."

"What mistake?" said Miss Nilsen.

"Does this have something to do with what happened to Alfonso?" Juana asked.

Diehl nodded. "I think so."

Juana glowered and tightened her grip on her rifle.

Diehl eyed her warily, then turned to answer Miss Nilsen.

"When my associates and I arrived, it didn't come as a surprise to the men Claypole had hired to harass the workers. Quite the opposite: They seemed to be expecting someone like us. Later, I received a communication from Claypole. Delivered to me with my name on it."

"What kind of 'communication'?" Miss Gruffud asked.

"I can't recall," Diehl told her, "and I've since misplaced it. Permanently."

He looked over at Miss Nilsen again, arching an eyebrow.

The attorney nodded approvingly.

"Please go on," she said.

Diehl gave her a slight bow, then continued.

"I hadn't used my name in town or with any of the men we hired away from Claypole. Not at that point. So only a few people knew it. Which told me the G-C Mine had a spy. Someone who'd been communicating with Claypole about what went on here. I suspected two people. Employees with personal agendas of their own."

Diehl looked first at Utley, then at Juana. Judging by the expressions on their faces, they were both about to call him a crazy son of a bitch.

"But it was *you*," Diehl said.

He turned to face Cadwaladr.

The old man's bushy gray brows shot high above his widened eyes.

"I beg your pardon!" he blurted out.

"You won't get it," Diehl said. "You sold us out. All of us."

"Preposterous!" Cadwaladr roared. He turned to Miss Gruffud. "Pathetic is what it is! He's trying to avoid responsibility for this fiasco by shifting the blame to *me*."

"This *is* a shocking accusation, Mr. Diehl," the lady said. Yet she didn't look that shocked.

Miss Nilsen leaned close to whisper in her ear, and the two women locked eyes for a moment. The lawyer didn't look that shocked either.

Miss Gruffud turned to Diehl and Cadwaladr again.

"If you don't mind, Gareth, I think we should hear Mr. Diehl out," Miss Gruffud said.

"Well, I *do* mind, as a matter of fact! I can't believe you'd let this jackanapes go on insulting me!"

"'Jackanapes'? That's a new one," Eskaminzim said to Diehl.

"Not to me," Diehl whispered back.

The Apache nodded slowly, clearly filing away "jackanapes" for future reference.

"Do continue, Mr. Diehl," Miss Nilsen said.

Cadwaladr kept on objecting—"Et tu, Eva?" he snapped at the attorney—but Diehl did as he was told.

"Cadwaladr insisted on going into Hope Springs this morning, against my advice, and the only guard he'd let me send along was Eskaminzim. A man he knew couldn't safely set foot in town, let alone walk into a church with him. Eskaminzim would have to wait and watch from the outskirts…where the Dickinsons soon tried to kill him *after* Le May crashed our meeting in Miss Nilsen's office. A meeting Le May knew about how…? They also captured Romo when he came down from the mine to help—"

"What?" Juana cried.

Yet still Diehl kept going.

"—and God only knows what's happened to Hoop and the man we sent with him. The Dickinsons knew *everything* we were doing this morning. Where each and every one of us were. And I think they knew because Cadwaladr here went to town and maybe even went to church…and then went out the back door and went to Le May and had his own conversation with the man. Just like he'd had his own conversations with Claypole. Because he's wanted to sell out all along. But you, Miss Gruffud…you own the controlling interest in the mine."

Everyone in the room turned to stare at Cadwaladr. Miss Nilsen and Juana looked livid. They were convinced. Utley seemed confused, unsure. Eskaminzim appeared amused, but mostly because he already knew about Cadwaladr. When Diehl told him who'd betrayed them, his first response had been to debate where he was going to knife the man first. Cutting out his tongue seemed apropos, but a quick, simple gutting could be quite satisfying too.

Miss Gruffud, as was so often the case for Diehl, was harder to read. Her eyes were narrowed, her lips clamped tight, her back and long neck straight. Was she furious with Cadwaladr? Or just annoyed that an employee would dare impugn his honor?

One word—one syllable—gave Diehl his answer.

"Why?" Miss Gruffud asked the old man.

"Catrin," he said.

That was all he could manage just then. He put his face in his hands and wept.

"It's his gambling," Juana said to Miss Gruffud, voice trembling with barely checked anger. "It must be. You know how he gets with brandy in his stomach and cards in his hands."

Cadwaladr didn't look up to deny it.

"You could've told me, Gareth," Miss Gruffud said. "I could have helped."

"No, you couldn't," Cadwaladr sobbed into his hands. "You *wouldn't*. The mine…that's all that matters to you."

"That's not true," Miss Nilsen said. "*You* matter to her."

"I could've bought you out," Miss Gruffud said.

The old man finally lifted his puffy, tear-streaked face. "You don't have the cash, Catrin! Not enough to pay what my forty-nine percent is worth and give me what I need!"

"So your answer is to go behind her back to the scoundrels trying to force her to sell?" Miss Nilsen said, head shaking with disgust. "Help them beat and *murder* men working for you?"

"Oh, don't be so self-righteous!" Cadwaladr shot back. "How many men have died working in that mine? Ten? A dozen?"

"Thirteen," Utley said quietly.

Cadwaladr ignored him.

"For years we've been sending men down into that damn hole to risk their lives clawing out money for us," he went on, wiping the tears from his face with soft, fat-fingered hands. "And if some of them don't come out again, that's just the price of doing business, isn't it? Well, I made the same calculation for myself."

"It's *not* the same," Utley said. "We don't send miners into a shaft then blow it up. These men—" He waved a hand at Diehl and Eskaminzim. "You stabbed them in the back."

"Why, Utley…I didn't know you cared," Diehl started to say.

Miss Nilsen jumped in first.

"You stabbed us all in the back, Gareth."

Cadwaladr scowled back at her, his remorse already turning to defiance.

"Enough!" Juana said. She stalked forward to put herself directly in front of Cadwaladr's chair. "What are we going to do with him?"

The way she glared at the man made it obvious she knew what *she'd* like to do. Something Eskaminzim would probably approve of.

"That depends on whether he stops helping himself and starts helping us," Diehl said. He stepped beside Juana so that both of them were glowering down at the old man now. "Cadwaladr—look at me. Look at Juana. Look at Eskaminzim."

The Apache drew his knife and admired the way the light played off the polished steel.

"Hell, look at anybody here," Diehl continued. "We are all very, *very* unhappy with you."

Cadwaladr leaned to the side, trying to see around Diehl and Juana and look Miss Gruffud in the eye.

"Catrin…"

Diehl shot a hand out toward the old man—and snapped his fingers three inches from his bulbous nose.

"Don't be rude. I'm talking to you," Diehl said. "You can help us save someone you betrayed. Someone whose life was just another chip on the table to you. You'd like to redeem yourself that way, wouldn't you?" Diehl leaned closer and dropped his voice. "You'd like to have a few less people craving your death?"

"Catrin, *please*," Cadwaladr said, eyes still on Miss Gruffud.

"You should be listening to this, Gareth," she told him coolly.

Eskaminzim stepped over to block the old man's view, his knife now balanced on one finger. He let it drop, caught it by the handle, flipped the blade upright again, and gave Cadwaladr a smile.

Cadwaladr sank back into his armchair trembling.

"Wh-what can I do?" he said.

"You can tell me everything you learned this morning about the one individual who might be able to save Alfonso Romo's life," Diehl said.

"Who? Le May?"

Diehl shook his head.

"Breck?"

Diehl shook his head again.

"One of Le May's bodyguards?"

Diehl kept shaking his head.

"Dammit, I don't understand then!" Cadwaladr cried.

So Diehl told him—and Cadwaladr still didn't understand. Neither did Juana, Utley, or Miss Gruffud. But Miss Nilsen seemed to get it right away.

"Are we really that desperate?" she said.

She held up a hand before Diehl could answer.

"I withdraw the question," she said. "Of course we are."

"'Oh, Distress is a ship in which many must sail, but—Providence with us—we'll weather the gale,'" Diehl said. "Charles Swain."

Utley rolled his eyes. "Moronic doggerel."

Diehl ignored the review and turned back to Cadwaladr.

"You don't have to know why I'm asking, old man," he said. "Just start talking."

CHAPTER 31

Breck took three men with him when he left the train for town. Just in case Diehl or the Indian were out there somewhere. He didn't think they'd be dumb enough to take a shot at him when their Mexican friend was the Dickinsons' prisoner, but still—better to play it safe. Breck had learned not to count on anyone to be smart or sane. You stayed alive by preparing for dumb and crazy.

He wanted the extra men with him when he rode past the miners' camp too. He took them in close, trotting by just forty yards from the burned-out shacks at the edge of the encampment. The scruffy, tired-looking men and women picking through the charred debris glared at the Dickinsons hatefully, but Breck didn't speed up or put any extra distance between them. The miners needed to know he could return any time he chose, do anything he wanted. He didn't even kick his gray gelding up to a gallop when their leader, the stocky little miner called Skewes, hurried out to call him a filthy son of a bitch, a bullying bastard, a boot-licking dog of his San Francisco master, etc. It was a great opportunity, actually. Nothing would underscore the miners' helplessness quite so nicely as ignoring their empty, impotent indignation.

The townspeople in Hope Springs stared at the Dickinsons too.

Some with resentment, some with admiration. Neither meant anything to Breck. They were irrelevant. Only the job and surviving long enough to finish it mattered.

He left the other Dickinsons in front of the hotel.

"Wait here. Watch," he told them. "Come get me if you spot that bigmouth fool working for the mine. Diehl."

"Yes, sir," the men said.

Breck went inside. The clerk behind the front desk looked up at him, then quickly dropped his gaze again. He knew who Breck was and that he had permission to go upstairs whenever he wanted even though he wasn't a guest. There was no need to talk to Breck. And no desire, nor any point. Breck had already made it clear that any "Good afternoon" or "Can I help you?" would be met with nothing but silence and a steady stride as he went about his business.

Le May's bodyguard Casper didn't bother with a greeting either. When he saw that someone was heading down the hallway toward him, he opened the door he was stationed before and said one word: "Breck."

"Send him in," said Le May.

Casper took a step back and held a hand out toward the doorway. When Breck walked past him into the room, he closed the door again.

Le May was sitting on the bed, back against the wall, papers on his lap and a silver pistol by his side. His other bodyguard, Francis, was standing in a corner like a piece of furniture.

Prince Pudding Paws was lying on the bed near Le May's feet. He got up, toddled the few steps to the edge, and gave Breck a single bark. Then he wagged his tail with self-satisfaction, apparently considering this a job well done.

"So," Le May said, "getting anything from our guest on the train?"

"No."

"Too bad. I was hoping we could wrap this up with some quick blackmail or maybe murder charges. Now we'll have to do something else to move things along."

Breck walked to the window and looked out at the rooftop across the street. A man with a rifle—the Dickinson he'd placed there, after paying the butcher below ten dollars for the privilege—gazed back at him.

"Whatever our next move is, we need to get to it," Breck said. He scanned the dusty street. "We can't keep cutting the wires forever. And even if we could, the sheriff or a US marshal or even the damn Army would show up sooner or later. We don't have long to act without interference."

"Agreed! So who can we kill?"

Breck turned to face Le May again. The man was smiling but didn't seem to be joking.

"I mean, Diehl and his Indian, of course…if we get another chance," Le May went on. He picked up the pistol beside him and squinted down its glossy barrel as if contemplating shooting off a toe. "But they're slippery."

Breck took a step to the side—he'd learned long ago not to hover at windows with your back turned—but said nothing.

Le May went on musing.

"How about the lawyer? Presumptuous, meddlesome bitch. She'd deserve it. Plus lawyers always have enemies. Lots of directions for pointing fingers to go. Everyone would know it was us, but proving it wouldn't be easy so long as you do it right."

He imitated two gunshots, like a child. *P-chew p-chew.*

Still without saying a word, Breck looked from Le May to the bulky bodyguard in the corner and back again.

"Oh, don't worry about Casper. We can say anything in front of him," Le May said. He put down the gun and leaned forward to stroke Prince Pudding Paws' long, lean body. "And the prince here is most discreet. Aren't you, baby? Oh, the things you could tell. But you don't, do you? Because you are a very good boy."

The dachshund flattened his ears and looked up at Le May with a mixture of love and fear.

"The black and the Indian and the Mexican. Even Diehl. A nobody. That's one thing," said Breck. "But a White lady? An attorney? That's something else."

Le May switched from strokes to playful pats on Prince Pudding Paws' rump.

"What's the use of acting without interference if you act as though someone will interfere?" he said. "We will do as we choose."

"Of course. I'd just prefer us to choose wisely."

Le May's little pats turned into a hard swat, and Prince Pudding Paws yelped and crawled to the edge of the bed.

"*Casper*," Le May snapped. "Don't let him hurt himself."

The bodyguard hurried over and scooped up Prince Pudding Paws before he could jump away from Le May. The dog squirmed and whined in the man's big hands.

"Are you questioning my orders, Breck?" Le May asked, teeth gritted, as Casper kneeled to place the dachshund on the floor.

"Yes. Questioning. Not refusing. *Are* they orders, by the way? I thought we were still reviewing options."

Prince Pudding Paws scampered to the door and began scratching at it, tail tucked under tight.

"All right. Fine. Options," Le May said. "Give me another, then."

"Miss Gruffud's house up at the mine. You don't need that, do you?"

Le May's eyes lit up.

"No, I do not!" he said, smiling. "What are you thinking? Dynamite? At night? While she's asleep?"

Prince Pudding Paws kept scratching at the door.

"Casper," Le May said.

"Yes, sir."

The bodyguard swiped a leash off the bureau and went to attach it to the dog's collar.

Le May let his dachshund relieve himself anywhere, on anything —even on any*one*—so long as it wasn't in his own rooms.

"If properly arranged, a fire would be more subtle," Breck said.

"'Subtle,'" Le May sneered.

The word seemed to fill him with disgust. But he had enough respect for subtlety to wait for Casper to open and close the door before finishing his thought.

"Suit yourself, Breck. Fire. But a few casualties would be nice. Menials and whatnot, whoever you can manage. Maybe even the Gruffud woman, if she's unlucky. We can make the old man accept it. He's a worm."

Breck didn't object—didn't respond in any way at all—yet Le May acted as though he had.

"Don't pussyfoot! You said yourself time is running out!" Le May snapped, jabbing a finger at him. He flipped the hand over and spread out all five fingers. "I want the deed to that mine in my palm by Wednesday or, by god, I'll have this whole damn town burned down!"

Breck just stared back at the man coldly a moment. Then he gave him what he seemed to want.

"Yes, sir, Mr. Le May," he said.

Le May grunted with satisfaction and dropped his hand to the bed. He picked up a sheaf of papers and began fingering through them, pausing every few pages to squint at something he read.

The meeting was over.

Without another word, Breck headed to the hallway. Once he was down the stairs and out in the street, he'd turn right and walk to the hardware store three doors down. Not to buy anything. So he'd know where they kept the paraffin. The kerosene.

After dark he'd send a couple of the men in to collect as much as they needed.

———

Prince Pudding Paws scuttled into the alley behind the hotel, straining at the leash in Casper's outstretched hand. The dachshund was panting excitedly, overjoyed to escape from Le May's room. And Le May. Out here there was no one to loom and love and then scold and strike. No one to caress him and then—without warning —lash out. Instead there were all the beautiful things in life. Garbage. Decay. Musk. Urine. So much to see, so much to smell. So much to pee and poop on. The alley was paradise.

It wasn't paradise to Casper, but he and Prince Pudding Paws

agreed on this much: It was nicer than hanging around with
Kingsley Le May. The man paid Casper handsomely and didn't ask
him to do much except follow him everywhere looking imposing
and take the dog out a few times a day and occasionally break someone's ribs or smash someone's knees or crack someone's skull,
depending on Le May's mood. A fine enough job, on the whole.
The best Casper ever had, actually. But Le May was a creep.

It wasn't about good or bad, right or wrong, decent or evil.
Casper was neutral on all that. It was just an uneasy feeling Le May
gave him. An *ick* he was always glad to escape.

Prince Pudding Paws snuffled to the back wall of the building
across the alley—a photography studio—and nosed open a paper
bag on the ground. There was something edible (at least by dog
standards) inside, and the dachshund began wolfing down whatever
it was.

Casper let him. In fact, all he said to the dog was "Slow down.
There's no hurry."

Prince Pudding Paws didn't seem to hear him. He was too busy
burying his face in food.

Casper looked to the left, hoping to catch a glimpse of a woman
walking past the entrance to the alleyway as long as he was stuck
standing there. And he did see a woman—though not the pretty
young chippy or señorita he'd been hoping for. This one was tall
and gaunt and dressed in black, as if in mourning. Her back was to
him, and she held a large brown leather valise in her left hand.

Not your usual alley-dweller. The strangeness of it reminded
Casper to look in the other direction, as well—something he
would've done immediately if he'd been stepping out with Le May.

To his right was a more familiar sight for such places: a
hunched-over man leaning against a brick wall. He didn't seem to
have puke on his shoes, but it looked like just a matter of time.
Casper made a mental note not to let Prince Pudding Paws sniff
around that part of the alley anymore. The dog eating who-knew-
what out of a bag was fine by him. Watching him eat a drunk's
lunch…no thanks.

The rustle of fabric drew his gaze back to the lady.

She was walking toward him. And she *was* dressed for mourning, he could see now. There was a black veil over her face.

"Excuse me, sir," the woman said, reaching a bony hand into her now-opened valise, "if you wouldn't mind...?"

"Yeah?"

The woman pulled out a forty-five and pointed it at Casper's chest.

"Give him the dog," she said, indicating with a jerk of the chin that he should look behind him.

He did. The "drunk" was coming toward him too, a handkerchief mask pulled up over his nose.

The man held out a trembling hand for the leash.

"Well, this is new," Casper said. "Dogs worth a lot all of a sudden?"

The masked man didn't reply. He just stopped a few feet away, hand still out, eyes wide with fear.

Casper gave him the leash—then jammed his now free right hand under his coat, reaching for the snub-nosed, hammerless thirty-two holstered there.

There was another shush of movement under crepe, and a cold, hard pressure just below his left ear froze Casper in place.

"Take that hand out," the woman said, "or this alley will be sprayed with more than piss."

She pushed her gun even harder against the base of Casper's skull.

He slowly slid his hand out and held it up where she could see it.

The woman tossed her valise to her partner. He caught it and turned toward Prince Pudding Paws, who hadn't even glanced back to see what was going on behind him. Whatever was in the paper bag was obviously delicious.

"Good dog. Nice dog. Good dog," the man said as he moved closer.

He crouched and put the valise down beside the dachshund.

"You're crazy," Casper said. "Do you know whose dog that is?"

"Of course, we do, idiot," said the woman. She had a strong accent, and "idiot" came out with a hint of an "uh" at the end, like the Spanish "idiota." "We have two messages for him. First, if he wants his little friend back, he must see that no further harm comes to Alfonso Romo, and he must keep his thugs away from the mine. If we spot so much as a single Dickinson taking one step toward the G-C, he'll never see his darling prince again. We will send instructions for an exchange of prisoners."

The masked man scooped up both the paper bag and the dachshund and quickly transferred both into the valise. Prince Pudding Paws growled for a couple seconds but never stopped chewing.

"All right. I'll tell him," Casper said. "Was that all still the first message? There was a lot to remember."

"Yes. That was the first message," the woman said. "Here is the second."

She clubbed him over the top of the head with the barrel of her revolver. The *thunk* of steel on bone made the masked man wince.

Casper yowled and dropped to the ground.

"Stay down until we're gone or I will have a third message for you," the woman said. "This one I'll send with the trigger."

Casper just groaned and pressed his hands to his skull. He was lying on his stomach, and blood began to pool around his head.

The masked man stared in horror.

"*Go*," the woman snapped at him.

He closed the valise, got to his feet, and hurried off down the alley.

The woman backed slowly after him, gun pointed at Casper.

Casper kept moaning and bleeding but nothing more.

Near the end of the alley, the man pulled down his mask and waited for the woman. When she reached him, she handed him her forty-five and took off her veil. The man tucked the gun into his pants and covered it with his coat.

The two looked at each other, then linked arms.

Utley and Juana stepped out onto the sidewalk, turned, and headed for the buggy waiting for them—Miss Gruffud at the reins, Miss Nilsen beside her—around the next corner. They picked up their pace when a muffled barking started coming from the valise in Utley's left hand, but no one they passed seemed to notice.

CHAPTER 32

It wasn't hard to find Hoop and Rusty's trail. The four riders who'd been following them—that made it easy. Then the black pinpricks spinning against the amber sky to the east made it easier still.

There was a reason the turkey vultures were circling rather than feasting. A pack of coyotes had moved in on the bodies, forcing the birds to end their first course and take to the air to await whatever might be left for dessert. The coyotes slunk off into the brush as Diehl and Eskaminzim rode up. They watched warily as the men examined the half-eaten remains and the shell casings and hoof-prints scattered around them.

"This is Rusty," Diehl said.

He looked over at a glistening-moist glob a few yards to his right.

"That too," he said.

"No Hoop," said Eskaminzim.

He led his horse away from the bodies, eyes still on the ground.

"More horses. Four or five," he said. He looked up and nodded to the north. "They came from that direction and went back that way too. With Hoop."

"More Dickinsons?"

"Could be. But from the north not the west?"

"Then who could it be?"

Eskaminzim swung back up onto his horse. "Let's go see."

Diehl looked eastward. Bands of pink and purple stretched across the horizon. The day was nearing its end.

"Dammit," Diehl said. "We don't have much time. Even if Juana and Utley manage to get the dog, we don't know for certain how Le May's going to react. Maybe he'll give us a chance to get Romo back. Maybe he'll just send Breck in to kill everyone."

"Maybe maybe maybe," Eskaminzim said. He pointed straight ahead. "They took Hoop that way."

He gave his horse his heels and rode off.

"*Dammit*," Diehl said again.

He looked to the west—toward the mine and the clients and the job.

He looked to the north—toward Eskaminzim and, beyond him somewhere, Hoop and who-knew-who.

Diehl didn't even know which direction he was going to choose as he climbed atop his horse again. Only when he was settled in the saddle, both boots in the stirrups, was it clear to him.

He went north.

They rode fast while they could. They had less than an hour of light left to track by, and it was growing darker by the minute. Already it was too late to get back to the mine without a long, slow night ride. Yet they kept following the trail as long as they could see it.

They slowed from gallop to canter to trot as the gloom grew thicker around them and the stars came out overhead. And then, just as they pulled their horses back to a walk and the last gray light of day faded away, a figure appeared in the distance. One man on horseback leading a pack mule, heading south. Just a silhouette. But that was all Eskaminzim and Diehl needed to see, for they knew it well—even if it seemed more slumped than usual.

Diehl cupped his hands around his mouth.

"Hoooooooooooooooooooooooooooop!"

The man on the horse turned and looked. His only response was to stop his horse and mule and wait for Diehl and Eskaminzim to ride up.

Diehl found himself grinning with relief as they approached, but he forced the smile off his face when they got close. Hoop would have hit him with some caustic comment about it. "Why you so cheerful? Cuz I almost got killed?" or something like that.

Seeing Hoop up close would've wiped the smile off anyway. Even in the dark Diehl could see that his left arm was in a sling. He hadn't straightened his back, and his head drooped a little to one side as if he might fall asleep any second.

"Are you all right?" Diehl asked him.

"I look all right to you?" Hoop said. "You got a funny idea of 'all right' if I do."

Diehl stifled a sigh. Sometimes trying to avoid caustic comments wasn't worth the trouble.

"You don't look all right to me. You look like shit," said Eskaminzim. He pointed at the sling. "Just the one wound or were you even more careless than that?"

"Just the one, other than cuts and bruises. Rusty got the worst of it."

"We saw," said Diehl.

"What happened after?" said Eskaminzim. "It looked like you rode off with someone."

Hoop nodded. "Pima tribal police. Off the Gila Bend Reservation looking for cattle thieves. They found me instead. Took me back and patched me up good as they could. Didn't want me to leave cuz I've lost a little blood. But you know…"

He shrugged, then winced.

"Work," he managed to say.

"Think you can you make it back to the mine?" Diehl asked.

Hoop scowled at him. "Would I be on this horse if I didn't? I'd be half a mile closer if I hadn't stopped to jaw with you two."

"All right. Good. We'll carry on," said Diehl. He looked over at the pack mule tethered to Hoop's saddle. It was carrying two large canvas-wrapped bundles, one on each side. "I'm sure you could gallop all night and all the next day, but she's gonna slow you down. What's the cargo?"

"I went looking for more hired guns. Well..." Hoop said. He nodded back at the mule. "This here's the closest I could get."

Diehl opened one bundle while Eskaminzim opened the other.

Spread out before them on Miss Gruffud's dining room table were twenty-three rifles, four revolvers, a bow, five arrows, and a slingshot.

"We're supposed to fight off Le May and his army with this?" Utley said.

He picked up one of the rifles—a Springfield 1870 with a cracked stock and a barrel covered with scuffs and chinks.

He held it out to show Miss Gruffud and Miss Nilsen. Juana was off in the parlor guarding their two prisoners: Gareth Cadwaladr and Prince Pudding Paws. The dog had been spending his time in captivity, laying claim to the room with one spritz of piss after another. Cadwaladr was passing the time getting drunk.

"I don't know anything about guns, and even I can tell this is garbage," Utley said.

"It ain't garbage," Hoop said. "It *is* what you can rent on a reservation at a moment's notice with four hundred twenty-two dollars in your pocket."

"*Rent?*" said Miss Nilsen.

Hoop already looked uncomfortable thanks to his arm and all the talking. Now he looked not just pained and impatient but embarrassed.

"We're supposed to return them...if we can," he said. "I wasn't in the best position to negotiate."

"I'm sure you did the best you could, Mr. Hoop," said Miss Gruffud. "But aren't the quality of the guns and the terms under which you procured them rather beside the point? You could have brought back fifty howitzers, and it wouldn't make any difference. What would we do with them?"

"Fight!" said Eskaminzim.

"Us?" Utley scoffed. "Against all those Dickinsons?"

"Why not?" said Diehl. "You and Juana—you've already stood up to them. Just keep standing. And you're not the only ones with a stake in this."

Diehl smiled in a way that he hoped was reassuring rather than deluded.

"Who knows, Utley?" he said. "There might be more 'us' than you think."

———

They made their preparations throughout the night, switching Utley to guard duty so Juana could help. There wasn't much guarding to do at that point anyway. Cadwaladr was sprawled across an armchair snoring. Prince Pudding Paws was asleep on the floor nearby, belly up and tongue out.

At dawn Miss Nilsen roused Cadwaladr and gave him the instructions for Le May. Miss Gruffud said her farewell to him with extra instructions of her own.

"Don't come back, Gareth. If Eva and I survive this, we'll figure out some way to buy your share of the mine and your house for all they're worth. You'll get what you wanted. But I never want to see you again."

"Catrin, I—" the old man began.

"You heard her," said Miss Nilsen. She was standing shoulder to shoulder with Miss Gruffud. "Go."

Cadwaladr blinked at the two of them blearily a moment, stammering incoherently.

"I...it was a...you wouldn't...I never meant to..."

Hoop had been hovering by the parlor door with Diehl, and he took two heavy steps forward that woke the dog and sent him skittering toward a corner. Hoop looked bad—weary and hurt and still dirty from the trail—and it was clear he knew who to blame for it.

Cadwaladr threw up his hands as if to ward off a blow.

"I'm going I'm going I'm going!" he cried.

They had a buggy waiting for him out front, a packed carpetbag on the seat. Miss Gruffud managed to hold back her own tears until he was out of sight. Then she turned to Miss Nilsen and wept.

Diehl glanced at Hoop and jerked his head toward the stables. The two began walking that way—slowly, since Hoop was still sore from his leap out of the saddle the day before.

"It's going to be a rough day, Hoop," Diehl said.

Hoop looked over at him sharply. "You think I don't know that?"

"No. But yesterday was a rough day for you too. You were shot, for god's sake. There's probably going to be a lot more blood shed today, and you don't have a drop to spare."

"You telling me something?" Hoop growled.

"No, I'm not *telling* you. Not giving you orders and certainly not pulling a gun on you. I'm just letting you know what I think. And I think you'd be better off sitting this one out."

Hoop stopped and pivoted—still slowly and awkwardly—to turn a scowl on Diehl.

"After all these years together, you really think you can talk me into 'sitting this one out'? With everything on the line? And Breck out there? That's how much you still don't know me?"

Diehl took a deep breath. "I'm just asking you to consider hanging back. You can still be helpful without putting yourself in the line of fire when you're too banged up to do much firing back."

Hoop snorted.

"Any other dumb-ass thing you want me to 'consider' before all this gets started?" he said.

Diehl shrugged. "Just try not to get shot again, all right?"

Hoop mulled it over.

"No promises," he said.

He turned and went back to walking slowly, stiffly, but steadily toward the stables.

———

Cadwaladr stood before Le May literally hat in hand.

"They say they want to do the exchange on neutral ground," the old man said. "Someplace outside town and completely unconnected to the mine. So everyone avoids questions of legality." He nodded at Breck, who was standing beside the bed Le May lounged upon. "And he and his men can't charge in shooting and claim it was another search gone wrong."

"And you assure me Prince Pudding Paws is all right?" Le May asked.

Cadwaladr nodded so eagerly his jowls flapped. "Oh, yes! The little fellow slept curled in my lap last night! When last I saw him he was wagging his tail at me."

Cadwaladr looked a bit like a dog himself standing there in Le May's hotel room. One desperate for a pat on the head.

Le May dismissed him with a wave of the hand instead.

"Thank you—you may go. Your willingness to help won't be forgotten."

"Uh...perhaps there could some show of appreciation now? And we could discuss terms for my part of the mine. I know you need a controlling interest, but—"

"When I have Prince Pudding Paws back!" Le May snapped. "Good day!"

The old man cringed and went slinking out. Casper—sporting a bowler to cover the bandages wrapped around his head—opened and closed the door for him.

Le May stalked over to the room's four-post bed.

"The second I have Prince Pudding Paws back, I want them crushed," he said. "All of them. Everyone up on that hill. Everyone who's defied me. Everyone who dared to lay their grubby hands on my sweet prince!"

He snatched up something bulky weighing down the middle of a pillow like a heavy head. When he spun to face Breck the gun in his hand gleamed even in the room's dull light.

"And when it's time for that bitch Gruffud to die," he said, "I want to be the one who pulls the trigger."

Breck thought it over. It was beyond unwise. It was insane. Yet he replied with words that came easily to him after years of practice.

"Yes, sir."

He'd been told what to do. The why was immaterial. Most of the how—his domain since it determined his odds for success and survival—was still up to him. So there was no need to quibble with a little niggling detail like who would shoot who.

He put on his hat and went to make the arrangements.

The old man had said they'd make the exchange at a spot west of town and the train. An abandoned stagecoach way station. So step one would be checking for a trap.

Step two would be setting one.

CHAPTER 33

Kozlowski jerked the blindfold off Romo, then took a big step back.

Romo cried out as the bright noon sun seared eyes that hadn't seen anything for the past half hour and had spent the many hours before that in the darkness of a closed box car. He hunched and slapped his hands over his face.

"Don't move, José," Kozlowski said. "We're about to say adios, you and me. You wouldn't want to spoil it, would you?"

Romo slowly lowered his hands and straightened his back. Both movements hurt. *Every* movement hurt. Not moving hurt too. There wasn't a spot on his body that hadn't taken abuse.

But his eyes—that's what hurt the worst. That pain was fading though. When the light no longer stung him through his closed eyelids, he tried to look around again. He winced and blinked, tears streaming down his cheeks. But after a moment he managed to keep his eyes open.

There wasn't much to see. Just the usual for this place. Yellow, sandy soil dappled with tufts of brittlebush and yucca. Scattered rocks and saguaro. Bluffs in the distance. And what might have once been a road—it was little more than a dusty gap in the scrub now—

that shot straight ahead, disappearing over gently rolling hills only to reappear here and there all the way to the horizon.

Romo stole quick peeks to either side. About thirty yards to the left was a dilapidated well. Directly to his right were the broken, bleached, skeletal remains of a corral fence.

"Well, well—I'll give the dumb bastard this," Kozlowski said. "He's punctual."

Romo looked straight ahead again. Two hazy smudges were cresting one of the hills along the road. They disappeared into a gully, then returned atop another with more shape.

A man on horseback, leading another riderless horse. Romo couldn't make out the man's features yet, but he knew who it was.

Diehl.

It was a windy day, and Diehl disappeared into a swirling cloud of dust. Romo heard him before he saw him again—the steady *clop-clop* of the horses rising up over the nearest knoll. Then Diehl was there, approaching slowly, no sign of his usual sardonic smile. His left hand held something bulky propped upon his saddle horn. A large, brown leather valise.

As he drew closer and got a better look at Romo—and all his bruises and contusions and open wounds—he scowled.

He stopped thirty yards away.

"You all right, Alfonso?" he said.

Romo tried to answer, but all he got out was a croak.

He cleared his throat—which hurt—and tried again.

"I'm alive...I think."

Diehl nodded grimly. "I'm sorry I got you into this, kid. But now I'm gonna get you out."

"Thanks. But just so you know..."

Diehl cocked his head. "Yeah?"

"I quit," Romo said.

Diehl nodded again, a little wisp of a smile curling one corner of his mouth. "Can't say as I blame you."

He looked past Romo—at Kozlowski—and the little wisp disappeared.

"Turn around," he said, circling his right hand in the air.

Romo heard a shuffle of movement behind him.

"I'm unarmed, just like you wanted," Kozlowski said. "You gonna get down off that horse and show me you're the same?"

"If you insist."

Slowly and smoothly, careful to keep the valise level, Diehl dismounted. When he had both feet on the ground, he swiveled first to his right, then his left. He wore no coat—the night chill was long gone—so there was nothing to lift to show the back of his trousers. It was clear he didn't have any weapons tucked there. He wasn't wearing his gun belt, and no rifle butt protruded from the scabbard tucked under the left fender of his saddle.

"And I'm supposed to believe the mutt's in that bag, am I?" Kozlowski said.

"Yes, as a matter of fact," said Diehl. "You can open it and check for yourself as soon as you like…then explain to Le May how you let Prince Pudding Paws jump out and get away. You can even show him the bite on your hand if you want."

Diehl lifted the valise to his ear.

"Still growling. He likes it in there about as much as Romo liked wherever you kept *him*," he said. He lowered the valise. "Can we get this over with?"

The wind kicked up again, sending a stinging fog of dust sweeping over them. When it had passed, Romo felt a hand shove him from behind, and he stumbled forward on wobbly legs.

"Vaya con dios, José," Kozlowski said. He pushed Romo again. "Don't forget to write."

Romo began trudging ahead.

Diehl dropped the reins he'd still been holding in his right hand and started toward Romo.

"Can I ask you a question, Kozlowski?" he said.

"Shoot," Kozlowski said with a laugh. "Or maybe I'd better say 'What would you like to know?'"

"You've been with Breck a long time. Would he do this for you? What I'm doing now?"

"What? Stick out his neck? Trade away an advantage? Oh, hell no! He's about as sentimental as a Mexican wolf."

"And yet you've kept working with him all these years. A man with no loyalty."

"I didn't say he's not loyal. He says the Pledge of Allegiance every day…to the almighty dollar and getting the job done."

"That your pledge too?"

Kozlowski laughed again. "Guess I'm not very sentimental either. You done trying to fill the awkward silence with talk?"

Romo and Diehl were only a few yards from each other now.

"Not quite," Diehl said.

He stopped, put the valise gently on the ground, and slid it forward. Then he straightened up and began backing toward the horses, gesturing for Romo to keep coming.

"The kid and I are gonna ride out of here now," Diehl said.

"Sure. Of course, you are. That was the deal," Kozlowski said. "No one'll stop you."

"That's right. Not you with that shotgun you've got buried under a tarp by the corral."

Romo's eyes widened.

"And not the three men hiding in the station house behind you," Diehl went on.

Kozlowski chuckled.

"Oh, really?" he said. "And what's to stop us, Diehl? The dynamite you planted in the house last night? We found the detonator hidden at the end of the fence. The cord's been cut for two hours now."

Romo began looking around frantically for cover, expecting Kozlowski to put another load of buckshot into his back any second. The corral fence was nothing but slanting slats of rotting wood—not enough to protect them for long. And the well was too far off. He'd never make it.

Diehl shook his head and waved from him to keep walking.

"You were supposed to find that cord," Diehl told Kozlowski. "So you'd feel smug enough about *your* trap to let me put a whole new load of dynamite right under your belly. A load of dynamite a sharpshooter's got a bead on right now."

Diehl and Romo finally reached the horses. Without taking his eyes off Kozlowski, Diehl reached back and grabbed the lead horse's reins. Then he jerked his head, indicating that Romo should get himself mounted—something Romo wasn't sure he had the strength to do. He walked to the second horse to try.

"Go ahead. Take a look," Diehl said to Kozlowski. "There's six sticks in that bag. Enough to blow even your fat ass all the way to the moon."

"It's horseshit, Koz," said a voice Romo didn't recognize. "He's trying to buffalo us."

Romo looked back toward Kozlowski for the first time.

Three other Dickinsons were lined up behind the man in front of a run-down, scorched building. They hadn't drawn their guns, but two of them had their hands hovering over their holsters. The third was holding a Winchester rifle.

Kozlowski was staring at the valise, a smile on his broad, puffy, stubble-covered face.

"This *is* an interesting situation," he said. He started strolling toward the bag, rubbing his sweaty jowls thoughtfully. "What to do, what to do?"

Diehl put his left hand on his horse's withers, preparing to slip boot into stirrup. Romo did the same despite the pain shooting through his shoulders.

If there really were six sticks of dynamite in that valise—and Romo had no idea if there were or weren't—a well-placed shot would indeed set them off…and the resulting explosion might just blow him to the moon too. Of course, Romo had no idea if there was really any "sharpshooter" either. Maybe it wasn't explosions he had to worry about. Maybe it was getting shot in the back.

"*Koz*," one of the Dickinsons said, clearly anxious for the order to shoot.

"Ahh!" Kozlowski said, smile widening with delight as some inspiration came to him. It was a look Romo had learned to dread in the last twenty-four hours.

Kozlowski bolted toward the valise, moving with surprising speed for a man his size. When he reached the bag, he scooped it up —and immediately threw it at Diehl.

Diehl instinctively caught it in both arms.

"Can we start shooting now?" one of the Dickinsons asked.

"Do it!" said Kozlowski, swerving toward the corral fence.

"Oh, shit," said Diehl, staring down at the valise cradled to this chest.

The Dickinson with the Winchester brought it up to fire. Before Romo could stagger away from his horse and at least present a moving target—albeit one not moving very fast—there was a *pop* from somewhere behind him, and the Dickinson with the rifle staggered back against the building with a hole in his chest. As he sank to the ground, leaving a bloody smear on the rough, blackened adobe, the Dickinsons with him ducked for cover and began firing wildly with their revolvers.

The horses twirled and jerked their heads in fear.

"Shit shit shit…this going even worse than last time," Diehl said as he hurried after them, the valise tucked under his left arm.

"Last time?" said Romo, voice squeaking.

Diehl was too busy to explain. He managed to jam his right hand into his rifle scabbard and yank it out again with a forty-five before more gunfire sent the horses galloping away.

Kozlowski was kneeling near a far corner of the fence now, pulling something out of the ground and whirling around in a cloud of dust.

With a *click-clack-click* he pumped a round into the chamber of his repeating shotgun.

"Ha!" he said.

"Ha *ha!*" said Diehl.

He hurled the valise at Kozlowski. It landed four feet in front of him.

"Shoot it, Juana! *Shoot it!*" Diehl shouted.

"Juana?" said Romo, turning to look at the hills in the distance.

With a "Get down!" Diehl tackled him, sending them sprawling toward the fence.

There was another *pop*, and the valise went zipping across the sod. It stopped directly in front of Kozlowski.

There were two holes in it now, one on either side of the handles.

The bullet had hit the bag but passed through without touching the dynamite.

"Ha ha *ha!*" said Kozlowski.

"Shoot, Juana! Shoot!" Diehl yelled.

But before Juana could try again, Kozlowski picked up the bag and whipped it back toward Diehl.

"Don't shoot, Juana! Don't shoot!" Diehl yelled.

The valise sailed over his head, hit a crooked fence post, and bounced off.

It landed on Romo's back.

———

Breck lifted his head as the first distant cracks of gunfire sounded in the west. It was what they'd been waiting for—him and the two dozen Dickinson men he had left. They couldn't ride for the mine until part one was done.

Kozlowski with Prince Pudding Paws. Diehl and the Mexican dead.

Now they wouldn't have to worry about the damn dog. They could just finish the job.

"There it is!" Le May said. "Let's go!"

He was in a rented, open-topped surrey parked beside the train. Francis was in the driver's seat, Casper in back beside their employer.

"Well, what are you waiting for?" Le May barked at the Dickinsons all around him holding their mounts by their bridles. "Move, dammit!"

They looked at Breck.

He turned to his gray gelding and started to lift his foot toward the stirrup. When he was in the saddle, tall and straight, he'd say "Mount up!" Then once again he'd lead men off to fight and kill, as he'd been doing for thirty-three years. When he'd begun, he'd told himself it was for a great cause. Texas, the Confederacy, freedom.

Now it was something else. He did it because he was good at it—
better than anything else he'd ever tried. So this was his calling. This
was his job. And it was time to go to work.

A woman's voice stopped him.

"Thomas Breck, Kingsley Le May, and all of you with them!
You are under arrest!"

"What the hell?" said Le May.

The Dickinson men murmured and milled, and the engineer
and fireman from the humming locomotive behind them—ordered
by Le May to fire up for a triumphant run to Tucson once the local
rabble was dealt with—leaned out of the cab looking alarmed.

Breck turned toward the voice. It seemed to have come from the
rocky bluffs overlooking the train tracks about a hundred and fifty
yards away.

"Who are you to arrest anybody?" Breck called out.

"Eva Nilsen, attorney-at-law!" the woman called back.

Le May scoffed. "The lady lawyer. Pathetic!"

He rose up out of his seat and cupped a hand to his mouth.

"A law license doesn't make you a deputy, woman! Go home and
learn how to cook!"

Some of the Dickinsons laughed. Breck didn't.

"This is a citizen's arrest!" Nilsen said. "Section thirteen of the
Compiled Laws of the Territory of Arizona gives a private person
the right to arrest individuals suspected of kidnapping, aggravated
assault, and murder! I charge you with all three and order you to
put down your weapons and prepare to be taken into custody!"

Breck scanned the rocks as the woman spoke, trying to spot the
one she was hiding behind. The men he'd sent to take care of the
black cavalryman, Hoop, hadn't returned yet. It wasn't likely, but
maybe the man was still alive—and up there with the lady. And he
knew the Apache had escaped their trap, but Breck assumed he'd be
watching Diehl or the mine. If one or the other was here now, that
could make rooting the woman out tricky. Probably costly. But it
could—and would—be done.

He had to blot out two distractions as he looked: more gunshots
in the far distance and, much closer at hand, Le May's giggles.

"Would you listen to the little fool?" Le May said. "She cites territorial code and expects a posse of Dickinsons to surrender to her!"

"Not just to me, Mr. Le May!" Miss Nilsen said.

Breck spotted her at last. She'd stepped out from behind a round tower of rock that pointed up at the sky like a huge orange-yellow finger. A figure emerged on the other side of it too.

The Apache. With a rifle in his hands. But without his black friend with the old, old grudge.

Breck allowed himself a rare indulgence—a small smile—at that. The Apache was dangerous, but soon dealt with.

Breck was about to give the order to scatter, swarm, attack when another figure appeared on the bluffs, then another and another and another. More men with rifles. At least twenty in all, most emerging from rocky cover they could quickly drop behind again.

Breck recognized one of them as the stocky little man who'd yelled at him as he'd ridden by the workers' camp the day before. Skewes. The dark-skinned woman Breck's men had beaten— Skewes's wife—was a few feet to his right, a carbine in her hands.

Another woman stepped out to stand beside Miss Nilsen, this one tall and fair and blond. Miss Gruffud herself, dirtying her dainty hands with a Winchester.

So she and the miners were willing to fight. Or at least make a show of it. And they had weapons and the better tactical position.

It wouldn't matter. Breck had the professionals. All he had to do was delay as they maneuvered out of the open so the first volley wouldn't do much damage. Then he could send men up the ridges on the flanks and trap the miners in their own hidey-holes in the rocks. It might take a while to pick them all off, but he was sure the Dickinsons could do it. They'd have better rifles and sharper skills and the cold, relentless resolve of men going about their chosen business.

Miss Gruffud had done him a favor, actually. Spared him the ride up to the mine. His only worry now was that one of the Dickinsons would kill her before Le May could.

"Let's talk this through, Miss Nilsen!" Breck said. "There's no need for anyone to get hurt!"

Before his words were finished echoing off the cliffs, he'd speak low to the nearest Dickinson.

"Pass the word," he'd say. "The men are to move behind their horses and get ready to break for cover."

But Le May spoke first.

"What are you talking about? There's *every* need for them *all* to get hurt," he said to Breck. "And here the fools are right in front of us. Let's get this over with!" He looked at the Dickinsons around his surrey and flapped his hands at the hills, shooing them away. "Have at it!"

Some of the Dickinsons started to mount their horses. Some looked to Breck.

"You have three seconds to surrender!" Miss Nilsen called from the rocks. "Three!"

"Unbelievable!" Le May exclaimed. "Would you listen to that presumptuous bitch?"

"Hold there!" Breck snapped at the men climbing up onto their horses. "No order's been given!"

"Two!"

"No order's been given?" Le May said, face flushing with rage. "Who do you think gives the orders? You do what I say, and I said have at it!"

"At the right time, Le May," Breck said. "Don't be a fool."

Le May's face went from hot pink to rhubarb red.

"They!" he roared.

He simultaneously stamped a foot and jabbed a trembling finger at the bluffs.

"*Took!*"

"Stay calm now," Breck said.

"*My!*"

"You're scaring the horses, Mr. Le May," Casper said weakly.

"*Dog!*"

"One!" Miss Nilsen shouted. "What is your answer?"

Le May jammed a hand into a pocket of his black frock coat.

"She wants my answer? She shall have it!"

Many men would long remember what happened next. They could say they were there the day Kingsley Le May pulled out his hammerless double-action revolver—custom made in silver by the Hopkins & Allen firearms company of Norwich, Connecticut—and pointed it at Eva Nilsen one hundred and fifty yards away. They couldn't see the grip—mother-of-pearl—or the inscription on it *"May your aim be ever true—CAMC Board of Trustees—Christmas 1892,"* or the five thirty-two caliber bullets, also special-made, also silver, in the gleaming cylinder. But they would never forget Captain Thomas S. Breck's reaction to it—a grimace and what was for him an uncharacteristically strong epithet—or what Le May did with it.

He pulled the trigger.

A silver bullet was blasted into the Arizona sky. It shot over the bluffs and into the arid wastelands beyond, never to be seen again.

The Dickinsons' horses winced and whinnied, and a chilling sound—both ferocious and joyful—echoed down from the cliffs.

An Apache's war cry.

There was a puff of smoke from the rocks, and Francis the bodyguard dropped the reins he'd been holding and toppled from Le May's surrey, crimson blossoming across his broad chest. The harnessed horse surged forward, sending Le May flipping backward out of the buggy while more tufts of gray smoke sprouted here and there from the ridges.

Glass shattered and wood splintered along the train, a man cried out and spun to the ground clutching his side, and the rest of the Dickinsons grabbed for their rifles or drew their sidearms and began firing.

What would come to be known as the Battle of Hope Springs had just begun.

CHAPTER 34

Juana took aim as Diehl snatched the valise off Romo's back and tossed it in a high arc toward the other end of the corral fence. She had to wait for it to nearly complete its fall toward Kozlowski before firing. She was there to cover Diehl and Romo, not blow them up.

She got off the shot—and the top of a fence post near Kozlowski exploded into splinters.

There was a *bang* from behind her to the left, and a puff of dust went up less than three feet from where Romo and Utley lay.

Diehl glared back angrily at the hilltop Juana was stretched out on.

She threw her own glare at the rocks behind her even as she reloaded her Springfield 1873 model carbine. Utley was crouched there with his battered old Henry rifle raised.

"Oops," he said.

"Leave the shooting to me for now," she said. "Just keep watching my back, sí?"

"Right," Utley grumbled.

More shots came from the abandoned stage station, and a slug went buzzing between them like an angry bee.

"And get down before you get your head shot off." Juana

squinted down the barrel of her rifle again, waiting for the target she knew was coming. "Dios nos salve de los aficionados."

God save us from amateurs.

Kozlowski had disappeared somewhere at the far end of the fence. Juana kept her gunsight trained on the slats there. Any second now...

The valise sailed up into the air. Juana fired, and it instantly spun back down to where it had started.

"I hit it again! And nothing!" Juana spat, flipping open the carbine's breech block and jamming in a fresh cartridge, fingers moving so quickly and nimbly they were a blur. "Maldita sea, Utley —are you sure the dynamite you put in there was good?"

"I don't know. I would've thought so."

The valise—tattered sides flapping now—flew up again before Juana had a chance to steady her aim. She fired, but it was a clean miss this time.

The bag landed a few feet to Diehl and Romo's right.

It was a perfect throw. The valise was in the clear line of fire for the two Dickinsons who now crouched inside the half-collapsed station house. If Diehl or Romo tried to pick it up and throw it back, they'd be an easy target. But if they *didn't* try to throw it back—

"Shoot it!" Kozlowski shouted from his hiding place by the fence. "Shoot it fast, you idiots!"

Juana had already begun reloading, and when she squeezed off a shot, the second the breech block was closed. There was no time for precision. She was just aiming at the house, hoping to keep the men inside pinned down—and Romo and Diehl alive.

Adobe shattered, and the Dickinsons ducked down into the rubble.

As Juana reloaded again, she heard gunfire to the east. Utley heard it too.

"I guess they didn't surrender," he said, voice trembling.

Juana took aim more carefully now, watching the house for a head she could blast apart like a ripe casaba. A paid killer she could send straight to hell, like in the old days in Mexico. With her brother.

".Bueno," she said.

———

"This ain't good!" the engineer cried as he ducked low in the locomotive cab and the Dickinsons and their horses scattered under a hail of gunfire.

"Oh, thank you, Jim! Thank you for letting me know!" his fireman shot back as he scurried, knees bent and back hunched, into the tender. "I would've thought everything was just fine otherwise!"

"Well, what should we do?"

The fireman hunkered down next to the coal with his hands over his head. A slug slammed into the side of the tender with a hard, metallic *tong* that made both men jump.

"I'm not running away if that's what you're asking," the fireman said.

"Why the hell not?"

The fireman zigzagged a pointed finger in the air. "Because out there's where the damn bullets are, Jim!"

A slug hit the locomotive's bell, making it ring, then another smashed into the ash pan directly under the cab.

The engineer crawled into the tender and squeezed in beside the fireman. Together they stared miserably at the hellish orange glow of the burning coals in the firebox, flinching in tandem at the loudest gunshots, ricochets, and screams.

"A cushy job, you said. Nothing to do but run a millionaire to nowhere and pick daisies for a few days, you said," said the engineer.

A slug shattered the headlamp, then two more pinged off the roof of the cab.

"Shut up, Jim," said the fireman.

———

Up on the bluffs, Eskaminzim watched Breck scramble to where Le May lay flat on his back beside the tracks. Breck hauled him to his feet and pushed him toward the train, probably telling him to get to cover on the other side or crawl underneath like some of the Dickinsons were doing.

The Apache smiled with satisfaction then swung the barrel of his Winchester left, tracking Casper the bodyguard as he climbed into the front seat of Le May's runaway surrey. He was groping for the reins Francis had dropped there. Even from a distance, the big man's broad back made an easy target.

Eskaminzim put a bullet in it.

A few feet to his left, Miss Nilsen and Miss Gruffud stood pressed against the big finger of upraised rock, eyes wide as the Dickinsons below sent more bullets up into the bluffs. Miss Gruffud leaned out to send one back at them, then returned to Miss Nilsen's side as she awkwardly worked the lever on her Winchester.

Down below somewhere one of the miners cried out. His rifle clattered as it bounced down the cliff.

"I was hoping it wouldn't come to this," Miss Gruffud said.

"I wasn't," said Eskaminzim.

He thought it was silly to hope your enemies wouldn't fight. Wouldn't give you a chance to settle what lay between you.

He risked a quick peek to look for whoever had been hit. It was one of the miners Eskaminzim had helped train—though there's not much you can teach about marksmanship in a couple hours in the dead of night. The man was sitting in the rocks with a bloody hand clutched to his shoulder, breathing heavily. About twenty yards further off another one lay crumpled, his rifle by his side. Dead. Yet the rest of the miners and their women stayed in place and kept shooting.

They wanted to settle this too.

Eskaminzim shrank back against the big rock and began firing slowly and methodically, aiming at the puffs of smoke around the train. Every Dickinson shooting back at them was to be his target now. Within a minute there were fewer puffs, and a minute later fewer still.

The Dickinsons' horses had fled in all directions. After the initial moments of chaos, the Dickinsons themselves fled in one. They went east to the train. Or, in some cases, beyond it.

Most of the men were taking up position under or beside the cars. But half a dozen of them kept going, sprinting into the flat expanse on the other side of the tracks.

Le May had retreated to the eastern side of the train too. When he saw the Dickinsons carrying on into the desert, he screamed after them, enraged.

"Stop! Get back here, you cowards! I'm paying you to fight! Stop!"

Some of the fleeing men looked back at him. None of them stopped.

"Traitors!" Le May shrieked, raising his silver thirty-two.

He fired twice. And missed twice.

Breck looked back from his spot perched on the coupling between the lead boxcar and the tender.

"Stop that!" he snapped. "If you want to shoot off that toy of yours, at least aim it at the people shooting at *us*."

Le May spun to face him, gun still raised.

Breck looked at the short, glinting barrel now pointed at his groin.

"Please," he added coolly. "*Sir*."

Further down the train, a man grunted, staggered back, then collapsed on his back. Underneath the nearest car, another man let out a shrill cry.

"I'm hit!" he said. "Oh, god…god, would you look at that? I'm dead, boys. Oh, I'm dead!"

"Shut up down there!" Le May said.

A part of Breck wanted to tell him to leave the dying man alone. He'd gotten his money's worth out of him.

Instead Breck turned away and squeezed off another shot at the cliffs though he knew it was probably useless. When the shooting started, he'd immediately run to help Le May rather than pause to pull out his rifle, and his gray gelding had galloped off with the rest of the horses. Now he was firing at men behind rocks more than a hundred yards off with a forty-one caliber Colt, and his eyes weren't what they used to be. But useless or not, he wouldn't quit.

Le May stepped up to the coupling he was on, his gun still held out before him. But it was pointed at the bluffs now. He squeezed off a shot that didn't seem to be aimed at anyone in particular. Just *them*. Out there. The Enemy.

A slug *thwocked* into the boxcar a foot over the crown of Breck's hat. Breck stared up at the hole it made, then looked to his right and saw gun smoke lower on the ridges. Closer.

Some of the miners were moving to flank them now that they were pinned down.

Breck sent a shot at them, then hopped down beside Le May and fired again.

One way or another, this was almost over.

Diehl darted toward the valise sitting on its side ten feet from him and Romo. A shot from the station house plowed into the dirt directly in front of him, sending him scurrying back to the fence.

As he crouched beside Romo again, another blast threw up dust inches from the bag.

"*Juana*...keep them down," Diehl muttered between gritted teeth.

As if at his signal there was a shot from the ridge, and a shower of shattered adobe sent the Dickinsons ducking into the rubble again. They wouldn't stay down long though. Juana could only reload her old Springfield carbine so fast.

Diehl got set to make another dash for the bag. A *click-clack-click* from the other end of the fence froze him in place.

Kozlowski was ready with his shotgun. Diehl and Romo only had seconds before they were blown away, one way or another.

Diehl held out his Colt to Romo. "Can you cover me?"

Romo stretched out an unsteady hand. "I can try."

"Just say 'Yes,' dammit. Otherwise I'm not gonna have the nerve for this."

"Yes, dammit," Romo said weakly.

Diehl slapped the gun into his hand.

One of the Dickinsons in the house got off another bad shot at the valise, and once again Juana responded from the ridge.

The moment had arrived. The last chance Diehl and Romo would get to keep themselves in one piece.

"Do it do it do it!" Diehl said, yelling at himself as much Romo.

Romo hauled himself up firing wildly. Diehl sprinted away from the fence.

He made it this time. Five strides and he was there with the valise within reach.

He bent down, scooped it up, and started to fling it away.

Kozlowski stepped into the open and immediately fired his shotgun.

The shot was wide—but not wide enough. Diehl felt a dozen stabs of fiery pain sear up and down his left leg. He cried out and started to crumple as the leg gave way beneath him. He was falling with the bag still in his hand.

There was no fighting it so he curled into it instead, turning the fall into a spin that gave him one last bit of momentum. As he came around to face the house again, both knees so bent they were already practically in the dirt, he let go of the valise.

It arced toward the house just as the two men inside leaned out again, guns at the ready. They saw it coming but couldn't get a bead on it in time.

Juana could. There was a *pop* from the ridge, followed a split second later by a deafening *boom* from the house.

Diehl was already face-down on the ground, so the spray of adobe and wood and Dickinson peppered his backsides. After a few stunned seconds, he lifted his head to see if Romo was all right.

He couldn't tell. There was too much smoke and dust aswirl in the air.

"Alfonso?" he said, his own voice muffled by the dull buzz in his ears from the explosion. A sharp, metallic sound cut through the hum.

Click-clack-click.

Kozlowski was still out there. Romo heard him too.

"Hijo de puta," he said.

Son of a bitch.

The haze cleared enough for Diehl to see Romo lift the Colt and point it toward the sound of the shotgun. He squeezed the trigger three times, but there was only one shot. He was out of bullets.

Yet one shot was all Romo needed. There was a clatter and a thud, and a moment later when the thick clouds of smoke thinned to wisps, they could see the body lying at the other end of the fence, its big round mound of a belly pointed up at the sun.

Romo lowered the gun and began to weep with relief. Diehl started crawling toward him but didn't get far. He rolled over and looked at his left leg and could think of only one thing say.

"*Ow!*"

———

Breck was reloading his pistol when the sound of the blast reached the train. He leaned around the back of the tender and saw a thin, distant gray-yellow plume whirl up to the west—where Kozlowski was supposed to be dealing with Diehl.

"Prince Pudding Paws?" Le May said, crowding in behind Breck. "Prince Pudding Paws!"

Another shot slammed into the car to their left, sending splinters spewing onto their shirtfronts. Breck moved back behind the tender, pulling Le May with him.

The miners almost had them flanked now. Another couple minutes and even the train wouldn't give them cover.

A slug pinged along the undercarriage of the car, and a man gasped and then was suddenly quiet.

"That better not have been the prince, Breck!" Le May fumed, wagging a finger westward.

He didn't seem to notice the sound of the man's death nearby or the other bullets that zipped past just a few feet over their heads.

"We've lost this fight," Breck told him. "We've got to either surrender or retreat."

Le May took the words like a slap, eyes going round, jaw dropping.

"What? No! Neither! Never!"

"Surrender or retreat, Mr. Le May. The only other option is for all of us to get shot."

Le May just clamped his mouth closed and glared.

"Why not live to fight another day?" Breck said. "You'll still have the Dickinsons and all your lawyers behind you. You'll make that bitch pay."

A shot clanged into the bell hanging over the boiler, making both men flinch.

"You've got about sixty seconds before the decision's made for you," Breck said as they straightened up again.

"*Fine*," Le May said.

He spun around and stalked to the engine cab. He climbed up a step, looking this way and that for the engineer and fireman.

They were still huddled in the tender by the coal with their hands pressed over their ears.

"Stop cowering. It's time to go," Le May said.

"Go?" said the fireman, uncovering his ears.

"Yes! Go! Leave! Now!"

The engineer started climbing cautiously to his feet.

"Yes, sir! Sounds like a good idea to me!" he said as the fireman rose up beside him.

"I don't care if it does or doesn't," Le May said. "Get us out of here. I'll be in my private car."

Le May dropped back down to the ground and turned to go.

"Uhh...aren't there still men under the train, sir?" the fireman asked.

"Just do your jobs," Le May murmured, barely listening. He was glaring at Breck again. "This is all your fault," he snarled as he swept past toward the back of the train. He was still holding the silver thirty-two that had fired the first shot.

Breck pivoted to watch him go, locking eyes with one of his men —another former Ranger named Kuskie—who'd been looking at Le May with obvious disgust from the far end of the first boxcar.

"We're leaving!" Breck announced. "Anyone under the train needs to get out now!"

Men started crawling out into the sunlight. Two emerged pulling a third by the feet. He screamed as his bloody torso was tugged over the track. The engine huffed and the whistle blew, blotting out the shrieks for a few seconds.

Kuskie and Breck hustled over to help get the injured man out from between the wheels, then kneeled down to check beneath the cars.

"Jesus," Kuskie said.

Four men still lay there, motionless.

"Nothing we can do for them," Breck said. "Come on."

He stood and headed for the first passenger car. Several Dickinsons were on the nearest set of steps struggling to get the gut-shot man up, so Breck and Kuskie had to hurry to the back of the car. Just as they reached the stairs, the train lurched into motion. They jumped up and rushed into the compartment, as anxious to avoid the snapping, squelching sounds coming from beneath the train as to get to cover.

There were ten Dickinsons inside the passenger car. Breck had arrived with thirty.

The dying man was groaning on the floor near the front door. Most of the others were at the broken windows on the west side of the compartment, trading shots with the miners again as the train rolled backward up the tracks. The pace of the gunfire had slowed considerably though, and after a moment it stopped entirely.

A new sound went up from the hills as the train picked up speed. Cheers.

"Bastards," Kuskie spat.

"They won't have long to gloat. Le May will make sure of that," Breck said.

He thought about Gene Kozlowski—and the black cavalryman and his fool lieutenant and their pet Apache. He assumed he'd never see Kozlowski again. The others he assumed he *would* see. He'd be looking forward to it.

"*Breck.*"

He turned toward the voice. Le May stood in the car's rear doorway.

"Come to my car. Now," he said. "We need to talk."

"Yes, sir."

Le May stepped back and closed the door.

"See?" Breck said to Kuskie. "He won't let it drop. This job's not over yet."

It was supposed to be reassuring, but Kuskie didn't look pleased. In fact he glowered at the door Le May had disappeared through with something like hatred on his face.

Breck didn't notice. He'd been called, so he went, heading from the passenger compartment with its rows of simple wood seats to the opulent Pullman car once at the back—now the front—of the train. As he stepped into the carpeted interior, he found Le May standing stiffly just a few feet before the door, blocking his path past the private water closet and curtained sleeping berth to the office-slash-drawing room beyond.

A sharp noise cut through the whistling of the wind and the chugging of the engine. A familiar noise that froze Breck a step past the doorway. A noise he shouldn't have been hearing.

The barking of a small dog.

Le May stepped to the side, gesturing for Breck to continue into the compartment.

"Lock the door behind you," Le May said, voice flat, mechanical.

Beyond him, Breck could see now, was a man standing with a gun in each hand. To his left was an armchair turned to face the other direction. Prince Pudding Paws peered around the side, his ears hanging like black curtains draped to either side of his narrow, doleful face.

"You heard your boss," said Hoop. "It's time we had a word in private."

CHAPTER 35

The gun in Hoop's right hand was a common Colt forty-five. But the other hand—crimped awkwardly to accommodate the sling bending his left arm—held Le May's shiny silver thirty-two. Both guns were pointed at Breck.

Breck did as he was told, closing and locking the door to the compartment. When he was done, he turned to Le May, who was flattening his back against the dark oak paneling as if trying to turn himself into wallpaper.

"How did this happen?" Breck said.

"I don't know!" Le May shot back. "He was already here when I came in! If Francis and Casper had been with me this wouldn't have happened."

"Ah," Breck said, nodding. He looked at Hoop in a way that was almost admiring. "So you made sure they *weren't* with him."

"Well, not me personally. I'm in no shape for sharpshooting," Hoop said with a quick glance down at his sling. "No shape to be making citizen's arrests either. Which is why I decided to make myself useful elsewhere. Just in case you tried to drag this out by running off. Diehl's plans are...*original*, I give him that. But they have their loopholes—and I'm usually the one has to plug 'em."

Hoop began backing away from the corridor into the main room, guns still trained on Breck. Three armchairs were grouped in the middle of the compartment—one with Prince Pudding Paws sitting attentively on the cushion, one beside it, and another alone facing the first two. Between them was a squat brown end table with a crystal decanter and tumbler upon it.

Once Hoop was past the chairs, he gestured at the one next to the dog.

"That one's for you, Captain," he told Breck. He tilted his Colt down at the other empty armchair—the one separated from the others. "And this is for you, Le May. Come have a seat."

Le May shot Breck a look that was both incensed and imploring —half a blaming *how did you get me into this* and half a pleading *how will you get me out of this?*

Breck looked at him impassively and stretched out one of his long arms.

"After you, Mr. Le May," he said.

The angry half took over all of Le May's face. But he managed to peel himself off the wall and go to the chair Hoop had indicated. Hoop was standing directly behind it now. He covered both men as they seated themselves.

"You look like you could use a drink, Le May," he said. "Help yourself."

"I don't want a drink," Le May said.

Hoop pressed the muzzle of his Colt against the back of the man's head.

Le May was suddenly so stiff in his chair Prince Pudding Paws cowered on his.

"I said pour yourself a drink," Hoop said.

"All right, sh-sure, I'm d-doing it!"

Le May stretched shaking hands out to the decanter and slopped an inch of the amber liquid within into the tumbler.

"A big one," Hoop said.

Le May poured in another inch.

"*More*," Hoop said.

Le May tilted the decanter again and let another five inches of liquid—brandy by the woody, smoky smell of it—glug into the glass.

"Hook, isn't it?" said Breck.

"*Hoop*."

Breck gave an apologetic, tilted-headed nod. "Hoop. Right. Look. We're leaving. Your side won. It's over. All you can do now is get yourself in a lot of extra, unnecessary trouble."

"You and I both know this ain't over," Hoop said. "Drink, Le May."

Le May raised the tumbler but kept it hovering, the brandy rippling and sloshing, four inches from his lips.

"You brought back Prince Pudding Paws," he said. "I'll pay you for that. A nice, big reward. A thousand dollars. Two thousand dollars. Three thousand dollars!"

Hoop poked the back of the man's head again with the forty-five.

"Drink," he said. "All of it. Quick."

Le May finished lifting the tumbler and began guzzling, coughing, and guzzling some more. Brandy streamed through his beard to turn his starched white collar and shirt front soppy brown.

"What do you think you're doing?" Breck asked as Le May drank.

"Testing something I heard once," Hoop said. "And giving you more of a chance than you gave Lieutenant Stowers and Sergeant Carney all those years ago."

Le May slammed the tumbler down on the table and sat back gasping.

"There. I—"

Le May's words were interrupted by a tremendous belch.

"I did it, damn you," he finished.

Prince Pudding Paws shuffled, slinking, to the edge of his chair. The men's noise and agitation was making him nervous, and it looked like he wanted to find something to hide behind.

"It's all right," Hoop said to him soothingly. "Stay, boy. Stay."

Prince Pudding Paws settled down on the cushion and gave his tail a halfhearted wag.

"I see why you're fond of him, Le May. Really is a good little dog," Hoop said. He looked at Breck, and his voice grew cold. "Does whatever he's told."

"I had a job to do," Breck said. "You should understand that."

Hoop nodded. "Sure. And you should understand this." He pressed the forty-five hard against Le May's head again—hard this time. "Don't move a muscle, you understand?"

"R-right," Le May whimpered.

Keeping his eyes on Breck, Hoop stepped around Le May's chair. The muzzle of the Colt slid from the back of Le May's head to a spot over his ear as Hoop bent toward the table. Slowly, wincing, Hoop stretched out his left hand—and put down the silver thirty-two. He left it there between the tumbler and the decanter, mere inches from Le May's knees but feet out of reach for Breck.

Hoop returned to his position behind Le May's chair, the forty-five at the back of the man's head again.

"All right. Here's the deal I'm giving you, Le May," he said. "There's one bullet in that fancy gun of yours. You can take a chance and try to kill me...and I'll blow your head off. Or you can use it to shoot somebody else in this room. Anyone of your choosing. Man, dog—you pick who gets the bullet. Just take the gun and point it and pull the trigger, and I'll let you go...assuming it ain't yourself you choose to shoot. Which I do assume, but I could be wrong. The choice is up to you."

"You're insane," Le May said. He put a hand to his forehead, his face sweaty and flushed. He looked like he was about ten seconds from vomiting.

"Not at all," Hoop said. "Like I said, I'm just testing out something I was told. Diehl said it to me years ago. In a cantina in Juarez. Said it was a common expression though I never heard of it. 'In vino veritas.' You know that one, Captain?"

Breck was eyeing the thirty-two. The train was speeding backward across the arid flats at what must have been forty miles an hour now. A sudden lunge, when the train shimmied and threw Hoop off balance perhaps, and maybe he could get to the gun...

Hoop shook his head. "Captain, don't. You know a little thing like Mr. Le May's head wouldn't stop a bullet from a Peacemaker at this range. I could shoot the both of you with one pull of the trigger."

Le May's eyes went wide and wild.

"Breck, don't be a fool," he said.

"And answer my question," Hoop added. "'In vino veritas'?"

Breck gripped the arms of his chair like he was trying to crush them in his pale fists. Yet he remained utterly expressionless.

"In wine is truth...or something like that," he said.

Hoop nodded. "That's it. The truth was in tequila when Diehl said it. Today it's in brandy."

"What truth?" Le May said.

"Let's find out," said Hoop. "Choose."

Le May swiped the perspiration from his face and rubbed it across the front of his coat. "I can't! This is sick!"

Hoop brushed the back of his neck with the Colt. "Choose or it's chosen for you."

"All right, all right! Don't shoot! I'm doing it!"

Le May leaned forward and slowly picked up the silver gun with slick, fumbling fingers. His eyes rolled to the right, judging where Hoop was and how far he'd have to swing back his hand to aim at him.

Too far. It was hopeless.

His gaze moved to Prince Pudding Paws. The dog noticed the attention and began to whimper.

Le May's eyes watered. Then he looked over at Breck, and something behind them hardened.

Breck saw it.

"You worthless son of a bitch," he said.

Le May shot him through the heart.

Instantly, before Le May was even done slumping back in his chair in horror and relief, Hoop leaned into the gun smoke and brought the barrel of his Colt down on the top of the man's head. It was harder than a tap but not a full-strength blow—just enough to tear open Le May's scalp and send him sinking, groaning to the floor.

Hoop paused to savor the sight of Breck's lifeless body. But though he was tempted to say something to it, he didn't. So many words were wasted on people when they were alive to hear them. Why bother when they were dead?

Hoop cocked his head and listened instead. A thirty-two was loud up close, but was it loud enough to cut through the rattling and squeaking of the cars and the rumble of the steel wheels on the tracks and the moaning and raving of wounded and dying men?

Apparently not. There was no knock on the compartment door. No "Is everything all right, Captain?" No "What's going on in there?" The train might get to Tucson before anyone knew that Breck had been shot. By Le May's gun. By Le May.

Hoop reached out and smashed the decanter with a swipe of his forty-five. Brandy splattered over the table and the floor—and the unconscious man curled up like a baby at the foot of his plush armchair.

After that, there were only two things left for Hoop to do— disappear, and make sure the only proof he'd been there at all disappeared with him.

Hoop turned to Prince Pudding Paws.

The dog had retreated into one of the corners. When he saw Hoop looking at him, he wagged his stubby tail uncertainly.

A moment later they were outside on the platform at the rear of the car. The dachshund squirmed for a moment in the crook of Hoop's right arm, but only to make himself a little more comfortable. He'd gotten used to being ferried around by Hoop that morning. Now though, he didn't know it, his ride was about to get a lot more bumpy.

Hoop moved down onto the step from the platform. The ground was just another foot-and-a-half below, but it was whipping past fast. Hoop would have to jump. He'd have to hope the engineer and the fireman weren't looking his way as he hit the ground and the train sped by. He'd have to hope he didn't stir up too much dust and catch a Dickinson's eye. He'd have to hope he didn't snap an ankle and fall back under the wheels. He'd have to hope for luck. Lots of it.

A bend in the tracks was coming up. The train would swoop northeast. To the southwest, on the side of the tracks Hoop was facing, a stretch of thick sage and brittlebush was approaching. Not a lot of cover, but as much Hoop was going to get.

He looked down at Prince Pudding Paws and—seeing the large, dark, round eyes staring back up at him—broke his own rule about unnecessary words.

"Just so you know, I was sure he wouldn't shoot you," he said over the whistling of the wind. "But if we're both dead in the next sixty seconds, I apologize. Just doing my job."

The dog cocked his head.

Hoop jumped.

CHAPTER 36

Hoop hit the ground running.

After two wobbly steps he was already falling.

He clutched the dog tight as he started to sprawl.

He stumbled, moving far too fast, feet leaving the ground, through a patch of sage.

He sailed over a rock, more sage, a grasping green hand of prickly pear.

His shoulder hit another rock, a big one, and his feet flipped over his head.

His back destroyed a stand of buckhorn.

His head hit and slid through dirt.

A shoulder landed, then his neck, then another shoulder, then his back.

His left ass cheek bounced off a barrel cactus.

He yelped.

The dog popped out of his arm.

He tumbled and rolled, yelping some more.

He came to a stop flat on his back, left boot propped on another barrel cactus.

He groaned.

He stared up at the sky.

He listened to the train go by.

He waited to hear it stop.

It didn't.

He lay there and made an inventory of his pains.

It was a long list.

He wondered if anything was broken.

He wondered if anything was ruptured.

He wondered if anything was sliced open.

He wondered if anything would grow infected.

He wondered if he would survive.

He didn't wonder if it was worth it.

He did wonder if Eskaminzim was still alive.

And he wondered if Diehl was still alive.

His eyes widened.

He was wondering if the dog was still alive.

A long, dark shape loomed up over him.

It began to lick his face.

CHAPTER 37

They left eight days later, after the town constable showed up with his questions and the county sheriff showed up with his questions and the deputy US marshal showed up with his questions and the reporters showed up with their questions and the coroner's jury was done with its questions. There was a scandal, yes, but it was for the Dickinson National Detective Agency and the Consolidated American Mining Corporation and Kingsley Le May's lawyers to deal with now. There would be no charges for the supporters of the Gruffud-Cadwaladr Mine—honest, hard-working citizens whose backs had been pushed to the wall by outsider ruffians. The governor of Arizona Territory wanted the mess swept up fast and the mine back in business under its original, rightful, *local* ownership. Kingsley Le May wasn't one of his constituents or even a member of his party, and the newspapers were having a field day with him— "FROM ROBBER BARON TO DUKE OF DEATH!!!" The man's monomania, greed, and instability had led to nearly two dozen deaths—at least one, most people believed, by his own hand. The murder charges against him would stand.

Eskaminzim was cheerful but fidgety on his horse, eager after more than a week of waiting and talk to move on to something, *anything* else. But preferably something dangerous enough to be interesting.

Hoop and Diehl, on the other hand, were stiff and still in their saddles, every movement and jostle aggravating some only half-healed contusion.

And Romo—he wasn't on a horse at all. Because he wasn't leaving. He stepped away from the others gathered to say goodbye near the mine's corrals—Juana, Miss Gruffud, Miss Nilsen, Utley, Skewes —and held a hand out to Hoop.

Hoop couldn't bend down to take Romo's hand. Not with pain shooting up his spine and Prince Pudding Paws tucked under his coat. The dachshund was the fugitive of the bunch. He couldn't show his furry face in Arizona Territory lest it lends credence to Kingsley Le May's wild stories about what happened on the train. But he and Romo managed to shake.

Romo took leave of Eskaminzim with a nod, then walked over to Diehl—being careful as he did so to give a wide berth to Helen the mule, who was hitched to Diehl's saddle.

"It's not too late to change your mind," Diehl said as the two men clasped hands. "You and I could get back to looking for that abandoned mine down in Sonora."

Romo smiled. "I'll stick with this mine right here, thank you."

"Yeah, but assistant to the mine manager? When you could be half-owner, half-operator with me?"

Romo stepped back and shrugged. "Assistant to the mine manager sounds just fine. It fits me better than…"

He searched for the right word. A couple seemed to occur to him that he was afraid would be offensive.

"Whatever I am," Diehl said for him. "You're probably right."

"Vaya con dios, Mr. Diehl," said Romo.

"So long, Alfonso." Diehl looked over at Juana. "Last chance for you too. The offer stands."

The maid didn't just glare at him with contempt anymore. There was a small measure of respect now. But it was *very* small.

"I don't fight for money," she said. "I've put my rifle away, and I hope I never take it out again."

Diehl nodded, expression turning rueful. He'd tried putting his rifle away, as well. More than once. And here he was.

"I really should be offended," Miss Gruffud said. "Look at you —trying to hire away two of my most cherished employees right in front of me."

She was smiling though. It was a smile Diehl had seen more and more over the last week, as the stress and trauma of the battle with Consolidated faded. A little more time, a little more verse, a little more frivolity, and perhaps Miss Gruffud would have succumbed to Diehl's charms. Or at least reassured him that they still existed. But he was feeling the pull of other challenges, other possibilities... somewhere.

"Oh, I knew they wouldn't come with me," Diehl told the lady. "They'd be crazy to leave you."

After that Miss Gruffud was smiling *and* blushing.

Diehl returned her smile and reached up to tug the brim of his hat.

"Goodbye, Miss Gruffud, Miss Nilsen, Skewes, Utley."

"Thank you," said Miss Gruffud. "All of you."

"We'll never forget what you did for us," said Miss Nilsen.

"Never," added Skewes.

Utley just put on a smile of his own though his was different from Miss Gruffud's and Diehl's. It looked like a smile of relief to finally see Diehl leave.

Diehl dug in his heels and steered his horse and Helen—who brayed once in complaint before deigning to comply—toward the road. Eskaminzim went with them. Hoop paused for a final nod to the little group watching them go, then caught up with the others.

Nothing was said between them for the first few minutes even though there was much to discuss. Starting with where they were going. Maybe it was straight to the Gila Bend Reservation to return the rifles—and the unused bow, arrows, and slingshot—to the Pima Indians they'd been rented from. Maybe it would be over to Las

Cruces to wire Col. Crowe for instructions. Maybe it would be up to the colonel's office in Utah to collect their bonuses and hand-deliver the last bit of evidence in need of hiding, the one watching the road slide by from Hoop's coat like an Apache baby staring out at the world from a cradleboard. Maybe it would be over to the Mescalero Reservation to check on Hoop's wife and the rest of Eskaminzim's family. Maybe it would be back to Mexico for more prospecting. Hell, maybe it was finally time to go home to Ohio.

Some options were for all of them, some for Hoop and Eskaminzim, some for Diehl alone. They'd all been discussed. Yet the only decision the three of them had come to had been "Time to go."

They passed the test excavation they'd visited twice in the dead of night—the deep, black pit now containing what remained of several men like themselves. None of them looked at it.

As they neared the bottom of the hill, Hoop drew parallel to Diehl and matched his paint's pace. He looked over at the man riding beside him and said nothing, but his long, steady gaze asked a question.

So…?

"'Many hope that the heart may outgrow the folly that leads it astray; till tomorrow arrives but to show the heart just as weak as today,'" Diehl recited. "'Repentance still losing its aim, forgotten in profitless tears, while experience but finds us the same in everything else but in years.'"

"Swain!" Eskaminzim yelled back at him.

"Yup. Swain," said Diehl.

"And what the hell does it mean?" asked Hoop.

"Why, that's for each man to decide for himself, isn't it? That's the beauty of poetry."

"Bullshit," Hoop muttered.

Diehl smiled. "Maybe."

"Anyone ever tell you Swain's poetry stinks?" said Hoop.

"I have!" said Eskaminzim.

Hoop waggled a thumb back at him. "Other than him?"

"Sure. Lots of people. In fact, his poetry *does* kind of stink,"

Diehl said. He mulled it over a moment, then shrugged. "But it's easy to remember."

Eskaminzim laughed. Hoop scoffed. Diehl kept smiling.

When they reached the bottom of the hill, they turned west together.

A Look At Book Two: No Hallowed Ground

In a relentless chase across Missouri, four brave souls confront a hidden cabal of Confederate conspirators in a battle for the nation's future.

When the A.A. Western Detective Agency needs to hunt men down, it turns to its toughest operatives: former cavalrymen Oswin Diehl and Ira Hoop and their Mescalero Apache scout Eskaminzim. So when the Double-A is asked to catch bank robbers fleeing across Missouri toward the Indian Territories, it sends the three to head the gang off. Along for the hard ride is Hoop's wife and Eskaminzim's sister, Onawa, who's tired of waiting around to learn who won't be coming home from the A.A.'s latest assignment.

But when the four reach Missouri, they learn that there's much more at stake than the holdings of a single bank. The "gang" they're after is actually a company of former Confederate Cherokees—and they're backed by a powerful cabal of conspirators bent on avenging the South's defeat in the Civil War.

What starts out as a chase to track down bandits turns into a battle for the future of the country…one our outnumbered heroes can't possibly hope to win.

AVAILABLE OCTOBER 2023

ACKNOWLEDGMENTS

Writing a novel is mostly a matter of sitting by yourself for hours and hours and hours and thinking, planning, writing, revising, and (just when you think you might be done) revising some more. It takes a ton of self-motivation and self-confidence. But that doesn't mean you can do it all by yourself.

First, there's the stuff you don't know — the stuff even the most detailed books and articles don't make entirely clear. Stuff, say, about copper mining in Arizona in the 1890s. I didn't need to know a lot, but I did need to know *enough*. And getting there wasn't easy. Fortunately, Carrie Gustavson, former director of the Bisbee Mining & Historical Museum, and Doug Graeme of Queen Mine Tours were willing to walk me through it. Any mistakes related to mining operations are purely my own doing (and hopefully too obscure for anyone other than Carrie and Doug to notice).

Even the most go-it-alone writer also needs feedback. Does this character make sense? Is that plot twist too obvious? Is this joke just plain dumb? Sometimes you need someone else to tell you. Jason Rekulak, Josh Getzler, Alice Henderson, and Patrick Monahan were my someones for *Hired Guns*. If you thought the jokes were *still* just plain dumb...well, that's on me, too.

And writers don't just run on coffee (though I know it deserves its own acknowledgment in my case). They also need encouragement and opportunities. For this project, those were provided by Eric Beetner, Paul Bishop, Richard Prosch, James Reasoner, Patience Bramlett, Rachel Del Grosso, Wolfpack Publishing, and last but far from least the super-talented artist Emmit Scott, whose enthusiasm and vision for Diehl, Eskaminzim, and Hoop convinced me to stick with them until *Hired Guns* was done. If I were wearing a Stetson as I type this, I'd tip it to all y'all. Instead I'll just raise my coffee mug.

Finally, no writer writes without inspiration. No matter how original we might think our work is, we're building with tools and material we borrowed from other creative people. I hope *Hired Guns* feels fresh and unique, but it didn't come out of nowhere. It wouldn't be quite what it is (whatever that might be) without Larry McMurtry, Charles Portis, Robert B. Parker, Frank O'Rourke, Richard Brooks, Burt Kennedy, Marcello Giombini, Bruno Nicolai, Luis Bacalov, Ennio Morricone, and Sergio Leone. Fellas — I'm raising my mug to you, too.

Oh, and there's one more person I need to thank. Years ago, I set out to write a Western action-adventure novel of the kind I wanted to read. But that would've been a heck of a lot of work to put in just so *I* could read it. So thank *you* for giving *Hired Guns* a try. I hope you'll be back for more.

About the Author

Steve Hockensmith's first novel, the western mystery hybrid *Holmes on the Range*, was a finalist for the Edgar, Shamus, Anthony and Dilys awards. He went on to write several sequels—with more on the way—as well as the tarot-themed mystery *The White Magic Five* and *Dime* and the *New York Times* bestseller *Pride and Prejudice and Zombies: Dawn of the Dreadfuls*. He also teamed up with educator "Science Bob" Pflugfelder to write the middle-grade mystery *Nick and Tesla's High-Voltage Danger Lab* and its five sequels.

A prolific writer of short stories, Hockensmith has been appearing regularly in *Alfred Hitchcock* and *Ellery Queen Mystery Magazine* for more than 20 years. You can learn more about him and his writing at stevehockensmith.com.

Printed in the USA
CPSIA information can be obtained
at www.ICGtesting.com
LVHW030305210824
788785LV00011B/222